"Savannah Russe artfully blends humor, mystery, intrigue, and fabulous sex appeal, while letting us know that there is more than one way to tell a good vamp's story."

—Victoria Laurie, author of *A Vision of Murder*

Rebound

Fitz didn't let go of my hand, so I gently eased it away but left it close to his. We were playing a subtle game. I just wanted to be distracted from Darius, to feel attractive. I was feeling a bit guilty about the fact that I was supposed to be working, or at least I thought I was supposed to be working. I didn't know what I was working at, but trying to get picked up by a good-looking guy was probably not what the boss had in mind.

Just being next to a healthy young male was doing me worlds of good. I could feel the heat from his body. I tried not to stare at his neck, which was strong and muscular. I had bitten only one other human—and that was Darius—in nearly two hundred years, but I couldn't help thinking about it. The urge to bite is nearly irresistible for a vampire. It's like Tantric sex, only even more intense and pleasurable—an amazing fusing of souls.

All in all, I was really savoring the moment, starting to get pretty hot and bothered, when a girl climbed right up on the bar and started dancing. She was clearly stoned out of her mind. But then the girl stopped dancing and started to choke. She seemed to be clawing at invisible hands around her neck, trying to breathe or scream. She fell down hard, her face rapidly turning blue. . . .

Past Redemption

THE DARKWING CHRONICLES
BOOK TWO

Savannah Russe

A SIGNET ECLIPSE BOOK

SIGNET ECLIPSE
Published by New American Library, a division of
Penguin Group (USA) Inc., 375 Hudson Street,
New York, New York 10014, USA
Penguin Group (Canada), 90 Eglinton Avenue East, Suite 700, Toronto,
Ontario M4P 2Y3, Canada (a division of Pearson Penguin Canada Inc.)
Penguin Books Ltd., 80 Strand, London WC2R 0RL, England
Penguin Ireland, 25 St. Stephen's Green, Dublin 2,
Ireland (a division of Penguin Books Ltd.)
Penguin Group (Australia), 250 Camberwell Road, Camberwell, Victoria 3124,
Australia (a division of Pearson Australia Group Pty. Ltd.)
Penguin Books India Pvt. Ltd., 11 Community Centre, Panchsheel Park,
New Delhi - 110 017, India
Penguin Group (NZ), cnr Airborne and Rosedale Roads, Albany,
Auckland 1310, New Zealand (a division of Pearson New Zealand Ltd.)
Penguin Books (South Africa) (Pty.) Ltd., 24 Sturdee Avenue,
Rosebank, Johannesburg 2196, South Africa

Penguin Books Ltd., Registered Offices:
80 Strand, London WC2R 0RL, England

First published by Signet Eclipse, an imprint of New American Library,
a division of Penguin Group (USA) Inc.

First Printing, April 2006
10 9 8 7 6 5 4 3 2 1

Printed in the United States of America

To all the girlfriends, who have shared the good times and gotten me through the tough ones—Priscilla Adams, Rosanna Chiofalo, Susan Collini, Cindy Dente Mauriello, Faythe Roberts, Ann Schwartz, Carol Terrell.

Introduction

They say, "Lucky at cards, unlucky in love." Well, I must be one helluva poker player. I accidentally killed the first big love of my life, and when another great guy finally came along (after two hundred years!), I bit him. It was a love bite, of course, but for a vampire, a love bite is more than a hickey. Once he got over the shock . . . well, you want to talk about a really bad breakup.

What I have left is my career. And that's okay, because I'm not just a vampire. I'm a spy.

Chapter 1

The Fall

Even before I finished getting dressed, I had a bad feeling about the evening ahead. The miserable February weather added to my misgivings. The sleet that had started an hour earlier sounded like roofing nails being thrown against the windowpane. Wind was howling around the corner of my Upper West Side building like a wolf racing after its prey. My whole apartment seemed unusually frigid and empty, hollow within just like me. As a vampire, I chill easily, and now with a cold and tremulous hand, I pulled on my boots, grabbed the black leather motorcycle jacket that matched my leather pants, and headed for the door.

I didn't want to go out, but I had been summoned by my boss, whom I know only as J. If I had my way, I'd still be in my flannel jammies, the ones with cowboys on them from Jackson Hole Traders, my feet toasty in UGGs, and a mug of herbal tea in my hand while I sniffed and moped around my living room thinking about my ex-boyfriend, Darius. Things hadn't worked out as I hoped. He was gone but not forgotten. To crank up my misery to its max, I'd be playing the golden-oldies CDs that make me cry, like Foreigner's "I Want to Know What Love Is" and anything by October Project.

But J called and told me it was time I got back to work. Being a spy employed by an ultrasecret American intelligence agency is sort of like being in the military. The higher-ups issue orders. I follow them—even when my instincts tell me they're dead wrong. *Ours not to reason why, Ours but to do and die.* Tonight I couldn't guess what arcane plot or secret plan lay behind J's directions not to come to the office, but instead to head over to an Irish bar in Hell's Kitchen. I'd been to that bar before. If you like pub fare, they serve some killer potato skins with cheddar, bacon, and chives. I'd be better off with food that appealed to carnivores like me, something nearly raw and bloody. It might supply me with a needed infusion of energy and even optimism. But depression over the breakup and the death of my romantic dreams had killed my appetite. However, considering the urges of my dark side to dine on human blood, a lack of hunger is not entirely a bad thing.

A strange uneasiness about tonight hit me from the minute J told me to get dressed and show up ASAP at the bar that was called Kevin St. James. As I listened to his instructions, an icy hand clutched my heart. I should trust my instincts. They've kept me alive for nearly five hundred years. I should have told J I was sick. I should have stayed home where it was safe. But I didn't. I followed orders.

When I arrived downstairs in the apartment-house lobby, the doorman hailed a taxi for me, then opened the back door of the cab as I dashed through the sleet and got in. I pulled the door shut, and with my pale white fingers pushed a damp strand of hair away from my face and tucked it behind my ear. "Eighth Avenue, between Forty-sixth and Forty-seventh," I said. "West side of the avenue, a pub, Kevin St. James."

The driver grunted an okay at me and took off fast, jolting me against the back of the seat. He had an air freshener hanging from his rearview mirror. It was supposed to give the cab a faux leather smell. It smelled more like faux barf. My stomach did a twist and roll. Just what I needed. Anxiety and excitement had already made me queasy. Obviously J had another assignment for me and the other vampires of Team Darkwing, and I wasn't mentally prepared. I had been wallowing in self-pity. All because of Darius, damn him. Some action might be just what I needed to distract myself.

The city streets were wet and getting slick; the cabbie was going too fast and the taxi skidded every time he stopped for red lights. Neon yellows and blues reflected off the icy pavement, and the world seemed to be breaking up into a kaleidoscope of crazy colors. I felt unsettled and apprehensive. As the taxi raced through the streets, I sensed the future speeding toward me, and I had the distinct premonition that something on the magnitude of a freight train was coming, and I couldn't stop it. I was just going to have to ride it wherever it took me.

I pushed open the pub door into a blast of warm air smelling of beer. Loud music bounced off the brick walls. I didn't even get two steps into the place when I heard a voice from south of the Mason-Dixon line shriek, "Daphne! Sugar! Over here!" My colleague and good friend Benny Polycarp, a native of Branson, Missouri, stood next to a table and was waving frantically at me. I elbowed my way through the crowd to her side and was immediately crushed in a hug.

"Oh, it's so good to see you," Benny said as she put her lips right next to my ear which is about the only way I could have heard her over the din of a Matchbox Twenty song. She smelled like hairspray and shampoo, and she looked twenty-five, although she's been undead for over seventy years.

"Good to see you too," I said back at her and looked over her shoulder at the two guys sitting at the table.

"Hello, Cormac," I said flatly, sounding like Jerry Seinfeld greeting Newman. The slightly built, pouting young man barely gave me a nod. Cormac always looked sulky; sometimes I felt he was a great black hole that drained the energy right out of me with his negativity. Other times he just pissed me off. But we'd known each other for the better part of two centuries, and I'd often seen him at his worst and only rarely at his best. Then I gave a genuine smile to the Buddha in a baseball cap sitting next to Cormac. "And hey to you, Bubba Lee. How are you?" I yelled over the music.

"Jest fine now, little lady," he yelled back and winked at me. Bubba's face was ruddy from alcohol, so I guessed he had already downed more than a few beers. "What can I get you?" Bubba asked as he pulled his bulk out of the seat. Bubba's not fat anywhere except his belly. He's big and solid, like a redwood tree.

"Guinness," I said.

"You got it," Bubba answered and started making his way to the bar.

I rarely drink, but this was an Irish pub, and they had Guinness on tap. It would be a sacrilege not to take advantage of that amenity. Besides, who gets drunk on one Guinness? I figured I could keep my wits sharp and my mind clear.

I peeled off my jacket and dropped into the seat next to Benny. "What's going on?" I asked. "You get a call?"

"Yeah, J phoned me. I don't know what's going on though. Cormac and Bubba were already here when I walked in. They don't know anything more than I do. We've been sitting around, that's about it."

From across the table, Cormac nodded in agreement. "I had a date. You know, it *is* Friday night," he whined. "And for what? Nobody knows why we're here. I had plans. I mean this really sucks." He slumped farther in his chair and returned to moodily picking the label off a bottle of Killian's Red.

"Do you think J's going to join us?" I said to Benny.

"Uh-uh, I don't think so. I mean we can't discuss anything in this place—even if it wasn't top secret. We can barely hear each other. He must have something in mind, but who knows? But the hell with that, girlfriend, how are you?"

I shrugged my shoulders. "You know, up and down. Bad days. Good days."

"Have you heard from Darius?" she asked, her big eyes warm with concern.

"No, not a word. I found out he got out of the hospital and nothing else."

"Oh honey, he just needs some time to think. He'll call you when he gets himself together. I just know it," Benny said, squeezing my arm in sympathy.

"Yeah, sure he will," I said sarcastically. "He *hates* me, Benny. I bit him, and you know . . . now he's . . . now he's . . . "

"A vampire," she said. "*And* immortal. And superhuman. Hate you? He should thank you girlfriend! He's just an asshole!" Then she shrugged, saying, "*All* men are assholes, my friend. And you're too pretty to be shut up in that apartment grieving. Let's forget about Darius. And let's forget about our uptight boss and whatever he's planning for us, and have a good time tonight." She surveyed the room, her eyes sparkling with delight. "Look at this. I love this place! Big bar, fireplace, great music. It's Friday night in New York, we're single, we're out on the town, and here's Bubba with your drink."

The big man put a tall dark pint with foam cascading down the side in front of me. I nodded my thanks, and he gave me a nod and a wink.

"And I brought this here concoction for you, Miss Benny," Bubba said as he gently set a cocktail on the table before her. "I was gonna get you one of them there cosmopolitans, but Jennifer, the bartender, told me they was 'strictly passé' and to try a green fairy or Absolut Apeach. I can't get ahold of the idea of drinking anything called a fairy, so I chose Apeach on the rocks for the prettiest lady in the room." His weathered face was creased by laugh lines, and his eyes looked kind as he smiled at her.

"Well, thank you, sugar," she crooned at him in her deep Southern accent and made his day.

Kevin St. James can be a quaint Irish pub some nights, with mostly firemen at the bar and Kevin, the mad tattooed owner, telling stories and everybody laughing a lot. Other times, like tonight, it's a zoo—packed wall to wall with a mostly young crowd making noise, drinking a lot, and looking to hook up. Upstairs in the second-floor lounge an Irish group called Beyond the Pale was slated to play songs from its newest CD, *Queen of Skye,* according to a notice chalked on a blackboard. Starting time of the first set was 10 p.m. Meanwhile pop music was blasting over a sound system.

I picked up my Guinness and sucked in some of the foam. Cormac sat picking at his beer-bottle label while he threw a pity party for himself. Benny and Bubba put their heads close together and were talking a mile a minute: They seemed to be arguing about recipes for the best cornbread. I caught the part about using a cast-iron skillet for a baking pan. Nobody in the pub was paying us any attention: We were four undead, blood-drinking, down-and-dangerous vampires in the big city, but we looked like everyone else, and actually a lot less strange than many New Yorkers.

Sitting there and starting to unwind thanks to the Guinness, I decided to just open up my senses to what was going on around me. I figured I should be watching this place, observing it. After all, why did J want us here? At first glance I didn't see anything out of the ordinary. Right in the middle of the room some hotties in little tiny T-shirts that exposed their belly buttons were acting silly and looking messed up. I figured they were drunk or high—or both. Nothing unusual about that. Nobody looked like a suicide bomber planning to blow up city buses or the subways, and that's what I figured Team Darkwing would be dealing with next. I focused my mind and took in one person at a time, slowly, carefully. I practice Zen meditation regularly with an occasional session of Tai Chi; my philosophy is to take wisdom where you find it. Now I told myself, *Be like the motionless cat crouching in the grass, eyeing an unsuspecting bird.*

Crowded up against the bar, I saw a dozen young guys in expensive suits whom I figured for lawyers or bankers. Negative energy stirred in their vicinity, but I didn't know why. My wariness heightened.

At two tables right under the fancy crest that says KEVIN SAINT JAMES NYC sat a party of tourists with fanny packs. Radiating a well-fed Midwestern wholesomeness, they seemed kind of dazed and thrilled at the same time. My gaze shifted to a table of four striking men and women who were nursing beers and projecting an air of desperation. I guessed that they were out-of-work actors. I moved my attention to the next table where two edgy, thirtysomething women wearing nearly identical glasses periodically glanced toward the door. I pegged them for editors, calling it a day after working ridiculously long hours at their jobs in the publishing industry, which still clusters its offices in midtown Manhattan.

Toward the rear of the bar, as far away from the door and as close to the TV as possible, sat a couple of regular-looking guys. I thought they might be off-duty firemen. Chatting with them were two older guys I pegged for plainclothes cops. One was a short guy with basset-hound eyes who dressed down in an old army jacket. The other was a muscular black man in a sports coat, whose eyes darted back and forth and suddenly looked right at me. I shifted my own gaze to a middle distance above his head. When I looked again, the black cop and his partner had taken up positions against the brick wall where they leaned back, not drinking, unsmiling, watching the crowd. Were they narcs? Now there was a tip that something wasn't entirely kosher in here tonight. I wondered what, and again figured J had his reasons for sending us here.

Finishing up my observation of the room, I studied the rest of the crowd, small groups of suburban boys and girls dressed in designer labels. As they drifted together and then moved apart in a modern mating dance, their laughter came in staccato bursts, too fast and too loud. Most of them were probably making this pub their first stop in a long night that would end in Soho. I clearly felt an aura of discordant energy emanating from them, and it was something besides frustrated sexuality and raging hormones. What it was, I wasn't sure—except that it wasn't anything good.

Then the sea of people momentarily parted in the back of the room where a twelve-foot projection TV screen was showing a soccer game. I was in the midst of taking a drink of Guinness and started choking when I saw who stood not fifty feet away from me. There, large as fucking life, was Darius. The blood drained out of my face, my mind went numb, and I sat still as death.

Benny heard me cough and started to ask "Are you okay . . . ?" when she saw my face, turned her head to where I was staring, and yelped as she also spotted Darius before the people shifted again and he disappeared from view.

Without thinking I was on my feet and rushing into the mob packed around the bar, trying to get to the back of the long room as fast as I could, trying to get to Darius. It wasn't rational, but I needed to see him, to get him to talk with me, to occupy the same space on this planet as he did. Four guys in soccer shirts holding beers blocked my way. "Excuse me, I need to get through," I said as I wedged between them. "Excuse me, sorry, I need to get by." Like thick syrup they moved slowly apart, and I squeezed the rest of the way past them until I could see Darius's blond hair and the brown leather of his bomber jacket. I ducked past a tall guy's elbow and found myself a few feet from Darius, nearly close enough to reach out and touch him.

"Darius," I said loudly enough for him to hear me over the music. My heart was racing. He looked thinner than he had been when we met; his skin was paper-white and his cheekbones more angular with the skin stretched tight over the bones. But he stood tall, commanding, filled with his usual self-assurance. And he was gorgeous, damned breathtakingly gorgeous.

He turned toward me, and a blaze of emotion flashed between us like a lightning bolt in a summer storm. Relief washed through me. Then a door slammed shut in his face, turning his features to stone. His eyes got hard. His mouth became angry. "Darius . . ." I began to say and took a step toward him just as an Angelina Jolie lookalike in a black sequined tube top and tight jeans came up behind him and put her hand through the crook of his arm. She spun him around, pulling him toward her, laughing as she leaned close and whispered something in his ear. Then she lifted her gaze and stared directly at me with a cruel triumphant smile. Her eyes glittered with hatred.

My reaction to her was visceral; I literally saw red. Adrenaline shot through me, and my senses clanged like a fire alarm. I stopped in my tracks. What I felt was a mixture of jealousy, fury, and imminent threat, as if I had encountered an enemy who wanted me dead. Meanwhile Darius was focusing on this woman as if she were the only person in the room, and I didn't exist. He turned his back toward me, and I stood there stunned as they walked away together arm in arm. He never glanced back.

Pure anguish ripped through my stomach and blasted up into my throat, bringing with it pain and tears. But the next thing I felt was rage, pure and cold and shiny as liquid silver flowing through my veins. My body seemed to grow bigger and stronger. A flame of energy started to travel across the surface of my skin, and I felt the urge to change into bat form. I wanted to fly at Darius, catch up to him, and tell him off but good. *That son of a bitch. Who does he think he is? It didn't take him long to find someone else. He told me he had been looking for me all his life. That I was his destiny. Seven weeks later it's as if I never existed. Son of a bitch! Was he handing me a line, or what?*

Benny's voice came from close by. "Daphy, are you all

right?" She must have been right behind me as I hurried across the room, covering my back. She put her hand on my arm. I was trembling with emotion, madder than I'd ever been. "Let's find the ladies' room," she said, steering me toward the bathroom. It was empty, and she pushed me into the small space and closed the door behind us. It was none too clean, and we were squeezed in there close enough to be Siamese twins. "Breathe," she ordered.

"In here? Are you nuts?" I growled and reached for the doorknob. "Just let me out. I want to kill the son of a bitch."

"Hold on a minute, sugar. Get a grip. It's been a shock, that's all. And maybe that was his sister."

I gave her a you've-got-to-be-kidding-me look. "Yeah, right," I said.

"Okay, so it wasn't his sister. But you don't know if he's on a date or what the story is. Whatever—just let it go for now. You're too good for him anyway. Daphy, let's face it. You're caviar. He's a fish sandwich at Long John Silver's. You're Bloomingdale's. He's the greeter at Wal-Mart. You're . . ."

I looked at Benny as if she had two heads before I realized she was babbling nonsense, trying to get me to cool off. She knew I was on the verge of losing it, and when a vampire loses it, the results can be dangerous. It sure would blow my cover if I became a giant bat in front of two hundred people or so. Hiding who we are is rule number one for all vampires. Exposure is usually followed by the pursuit of a vampire hunter, a desperate flight and escape, or death at the end of a stake.

"Do you think he's bitten her?" I said, blurting out what was on my mind first and foremost.

"No! She didn't have a fang print on her," Benny shot back, then folded her arms and smiled. "And honey, that little tramp sure was showing so much skin I would have spotted a hickey at a hundred yards."

I burst out laughing. I couldn't help it. The whole thing

was just so insane. I had turned Darius into a vampire when he got shot on our last mission—in order to save his life. What did I get for it? Gratitude? No, I got shit on, that's what I got. And so why was I carrying a torch for him? Okay, I had loved him. I still loved him. *Get over it!* I told myself. "So do you think J set this up?" I said to Benny.

"Nah. He wouldn't have had all of us down here for that. It's true he doesn't like Darius and chances are he's jealous of him too, but I think running into Darius here was coincidence, that's all."

I didn't say anything for a minute, then looked my best friend in the eye and said with a hard edge to my voice, "Benny, I don't believe in coincidences. Especially not this one."

She stuck to her guns. "I don't know about that, Daphy, but I just don't think J had anything to do with it."

Somebody pounded on the bathroom door. "Let's get out of here, Benny. I'm okay, really." I pulled the door open, and there were at least four girls waiting outside.

"They were probably doing a line of coke," one of them whispered to her friend, a tiny blonde in lace-trimmed jeans and a designer denim jacket with rhinestone buttons that had to have cost a thousand bucks.

Then the small girl giggled. "We have something a lot better than coke," she said and opened her hand to reveal a glass ampoule.

"Don't let anybody see that," her friend whispered back and stepped in front of her.

I looked at Benny, who shrugged her shoulders and shook her head. "Maybe it's a popper," she said in a low voice.

"I don't think so," I said. "Must be something new." Then I forgot about the girls and their happy dust, whatever it was, as I got back to the table. Still standing, I reached down, grabbed my pint of Guinness, and chugged it. Both Cormac and Bubba were looking at me wide-eyed. Like I said, I usually don't drink.

"You want another?" Bubba asked.

"I'll get it myself, thanks," I answered. A half-baked plan was forming in my brain. I had seen this really cute guy—a man, not a kid—sitting at the bar as Benny and I came back from the bathroom. When we walked past, he smiled at me in a way that told me he was interested. Armed with some liquid courage, I figured I'd go chat him up.

"Guinness," I said to the woman tending bar as I stood between a heavily made-up, middle-aged drinker on one bar chair and the cutie I had spotted earlier on another.

The bartender drew the Guinness and let it stand to get a head while the guy on my right, as I predicted, started talking to me. "Guinness? Not a lady's drink. You Irish?" he asked.

I turned a megawatt smile in his direction. "No, but thanks for the compliment. I just prefer a drink that has some bite to it—and is bold enough to get my attention."

"Not a Harp drinker then?" he said mischievously, naming one of Ireland's lighter beers.

"Harp's for sissies," I answered back and leaned my hip against the bar, which put me close enough to the guy to feel his body heat. The steady drinker behind me graciously shifted her chair to give me more room to maneuver.

"Let me introduce myself," he said. "I *am* Irish, second generation. St. Julien Fitzmaurice." He gave me his hand to shake. It was warm, strong, and firm. "My friends call me Fitz."

"Nice to meet you, Fitz. I'm Daphne Urban. Mostly Italian with some Romany thrown in way back, I think," I said.

Just then the guy sitting on the other side of Fitz left his seat, and with practiced precision Fitz stood up and took it before anyone else could grab it, motioning me to sit down in his old seat. "Join me while you drink your Guinness?" he asked.

"Sure," I said and sat down facing him.

"You work in New York or just visiting?" he asked.

"I live uptown. Work here too. And you?"

"I live out on the Island. Work in the city."

The chemistry between us was nice, not shooting sparks yet, but humming along and heating up. The Guinness I had already drunk made me feel fuzzy at the edges and the room cozier. My second one slipped down with ease, giving me a little buzz. I took a closer look at Fitz, who was wearing a Brooks Brothers blue shirt and an Irish tweed jacket. He didn't look at all like Darius. Fitz's hair was dark, almost black, cut neatly. His face was long and aquiline, and I judged his age to be around thirty. That's okay. I only look twenty-seven or twenty-eight even if I was born in the sixteenth century. He smelled good too, citrus and spice. When he had stood up to change seats, I saw that he was pretty big, maybe six-two or six-three. He was flat-bellied but not skinny. He had a tan in January. He looked even better close up, and the only thing I couldn't figure was why some guy this yummy was here alone. I hoped there wasn't some major kink hidden behind his friendly face. But then, who was I to talk about kinks? Fitz didn't know it, but he was flirting with a vampire.

Neither of us was saying anything and as if reading my thoughts, Fitz said, "Sorry if I'm a little quiet. I had a bad breakup with my steady girlfriend, my fiancée actually. She's now going with the guy I thought was my best friend. I don't feel like going home to an empty house, so I've been hanging out here after work. It's usually pretty quiet during the week. The weekends—that's something else. What about you? Married? Single? Committed?"

"Free. And me too. Bad breakup. You wouldn't believe how bad. My friends dragged me out here tonight." I took a long swallow of the Guinness. It was bitter. "You know, at some point, you just have to put the past behind you and move on," I said, giving a sanitized version of the truth.

"Agreed," he said and tapped his drink against mine in a toast. "But easier said than done, Daphne, m'girl. For me, it's the betrayal that's hard to swallow. For months they had been seeing each other behind my back while she was still buying stuff for our house and going to dinner at my family's. I didn't have a clue. Want to hear the whole story?" he asked as he sloshed what looked like whiskey on the rocks around in his glass.

"If you feel like telling it, I'd be glad to listen," I said leaning toward him a little and holding his eyes, as gray as the Irish Sea, with mine.

"Well one night, no reason in particular, I decided to get my golf clubs out of the trunk of my car. Her bag of clubs was in there too. I was supposed to tee off early the next morning with a foursome of other guys, and I figured if she had any new golf balls, I'd borrow them, so I unzipped the side pocket of her golf bag. There was this note folded up in there. To this day I don't know why I picked it up, but it was like my hand was guided right to it. I unfolded the paper. It was a love letter. I figured Jessica, that's her name, Jessica, was writing it to me. My birthday was coming up. I thought it was really sweet. I stood there and started reading. The note was corny but nice, about how I was the sunshine of her life and all. Then I got to the line *I feel so guilty about Fitz, but what you and I have makes my feelings for him seem like an innocent Hershey's Kiss compared to a whole box of rich, sensual Godiva chocolates. He's just a little boy, but you're a real man. Oh Billy when can we be together forever?* Right then my whole world stopped. *Billy?* I don't remember much after that except charging into the house like an enraged bull. I threw the letter down in front of her, and she confessed everything. She apologized and said something like feeling relieved that she didn't have to go on living a lie. Then she used her cell phone to call *Billy*—my best friend since Andover—and they rode off into the sunset in his Alfa Romeo. She didn't even come back for her clothes. One of her girlfriends came over with a U-Haul, and my ring was returned by the FedEx guy. I was really dumb, right?"

"No, it sounds like you're a nice guy and she's a lying bitch, if you don't mind me saying so," I said feeling like a hypocrite over the "lying" part since it's one of the things I do best. I reached over to the hand he had on the bar and gave it a little squeeze. My hand was icy cold. His was warm and alive. He gently took my fingers. "You feel as if you're freezing," he said.

"Thin blood," I answered truthfully. "I'm not a winter person."

"Typical Italian," he said and gave me a gentle smile. "I confess that I love the snow. I ski every chance I get." He didn't let go of my hand, so I gently eased it away but left it close to his. We were playing a subtle game of interested, but not easy; available, but not a slut. Look, it's not like I stopped caring for Darius. I just wanted to be distracted, to feel attractive and desirable after being thrown away like a used Kleenex. I was feeling a tiny bit guilty about the fact that I was supposed to be working, or at least, I thought I was supposed to be working. I didn't know what I was working at, but trying to get picked up by a good-looking guy was probably not what J had in mind.

Fitz went on talking. "Your turn. I spilled my guts to you. I'm ready to listen if you want to spill yours."

"Not really." I looked into his face again with mine as blank as a poker player's. "I don't want to talk about it. Not yet anyway. The wound's too raw."

"How new?" Fitz asked.

"Right before Christmas. Isn't that the way it always goes? Holidays are the worst time to be alone."

"You've got that right." Fitz gave a brittle laugh and downed the rest of his drink. "Jennifer," he called to the bartender. "Another, please."

"Sure thing. Jameson coming up," she said in a way that disclosed he'd been there more than once or twice and she liked him. A lot.

Just being next to a healthy young male was doing me worlds of good. I could smell the subtle masculine scent of his body. I tried not to stare at his neck, which was strong and muscular. I have bitten only one other human—and that was Darius—in nearly two hundred years, but I can't help thinking about it. The urge to bite is nearly irresistible for a vampire. It's like Tantric sex, only even more intense and pleasurable. And it fills one up with life in an amazing fusing of souls. I pushed the thoughts away. The bite is frequently fatal for the human involved. If it's not, it can eventually make the human a vampire too—which is usually unwelcome. Becoming a monster pursued by vampire hunters armed with stakes and silver bullets, being forever an outsider despised and feared by most people, and being always hungry to feed on blood make for a tough alternate lifestyle. There are benefits, of course . . . like eternal youth, near immortality, and superhuman strength.

Fitz interrupted my musings. "So what is it that you like to do in your spare time, pretty Miss Daphne Urban?"

"Oh, I'm into art. I love music. Going out at night. And shopping. I'm shopping-addicted. And you?"

"Sailing. Horses. Skiing. Golf. Pretty much an outdoors kind of guy, but I can do museums and concerts. I'm civilized. My family has a summer home in the Hamptons and another on the Cape. We're all into sailing. Do you summer in the city or do you have a country place?"

Boy is this one a bad fit, unless he's into midnight cruises and nighttime skiing, I thought to myself. It really didn't matter. I was looking for a diversion, not a relationship. And the physical thing between us was building, from a hum to a zing. I brushed his hand with my fingers and the electricity raced up my arm. Nice! "Hmmm, I sort of have a country place. It's a villa south of Florence in a little hamlet called Gigliola, near the town of Montespertoli. I don't get over there much, but it's home I guess." I wasn't at all interested in doing much more talking. I was thinking about inviting him back to my apartment.

Fitz looked at me with a deeper intensity as if he could read my thoughts. "Florence, huh? I'm planning to go over to Ireland in March, and maybe I could fly down to Italy. I always wanted to go." Then he got to his real point. "Would you mind if I e-mailed you to get some help with planning the trip, if I do?" He was smiling at me now, and we were beginning to drown in each other's eyes.

"Sure," I said, my voice getting lower and turning into an invitation, "I'd be glad to help you . . . any way you need me to."

He didn't take his eyes off me as he reached inside his jacket and pulled a small notepad out of the inner pocket. He flipped it open, retrieved a Montblanc pen from the same pocket, and handed it to me. "Would you write down your e-mail address? I'd really like to e-mail you, if that's okay."

"I'd like that," I said and meant it. While I wrote, he downed his Jameson fast, without a cough, like a man who knows how to drink and probably does it too much. *Well, he said he was Irish*, I thought as I jotted down the information. Irish men drink when they're happy and drink even more when they're sad. And I felt that behind Fitz's easy smile was a man desperately wounded by love, his heart broken like my own. I also felt he had finished off a number of Jamesons before I walked over and would pay for it tomorrow. As the proverb goes, *Is milis dá ól é ach is searbh dá íoc é.* It is sweet to drink but bitter to pay for.

I handed the pad and pen back to him. "Thanks, Daphne," he said and put them back in his pocket. Then Fitz picked up my fingers again. "This room is warm, but your hands are so incredibly cold," he said and cupped them in both his own, trying to warm them. "Maybe you need vitamins?"

I could have told him that the only thing which would heat them up was drinking blood, but I wisely remained silent on the issue.

Gently holding my fingers, he went on saying, "Your skin reminds me of an Easter lily." His voice was filled with wonder—and whiskey. "It's so white and smooth, truly beautiful." My knee had somehow butted up against Fitz's knee, and we both were clearly enjoying the contact. All in all, I was really savoring the moment, starting to get pretty hot and bothered, and trying to figure out how to broach the "why don't you come up to my place" invitation, when one of the young hotties climbed right up on the bar and started dancing. It was the little chick with the rhinestone denim jacket I had seen outside the bathroom. She was clearly stoned out of her mind.

Springsteen's "All the Way Home" blared over the sound system, and the little chickie was playing Coyote Ugly while her boyfriend pleaded, "Mackenzie, come on, get down." She ignored him while she did a shimmy out of her jacket and kept time to the music. Out of the corner of my eye I saw a big bruiser pushing his way toward the bar, probably the resident bouncer, but before he got her, the girl stopped dancing and started to choke. She seemed to be clawing at invisible hands around her neck, trying to breathe or scream, but no sound was coming out and no air was going in. She fell down hard practically in front of me, with a look of absolute horror on her face, which was quickly turning deep blue. Somebody started screaming "Call nine-one-one!" and I saw Jennifer the bartender grab the phone and punch in numbers. The weird thing was that the girl's heart was beating so loudly I could hear it. I have exceptional hearing, but somebody had cut off the sound system and in the hushed silence I knew the whole room could hear the racing beats of her heart. They sounded like someone quickly tapping a small bongo drum. *Tap tap tap tap tap tap.* It went faster and faster, louder and louder. Then it just stopped. Silence. People stood still in shock. Suddenly the girl was convulsing on the bar, and the black guy I had tagged as a cop was pushing aside the crowd.

Fitz had already jumped up off his chair, and now he stepped back to let the black guy in the suit jacket reach the girl first. He tried to pry her hands away from her throat. It looked to me as if she was strangling herself, but I don't think you can really do that. The short guy in the army jacket whom I also thought was a cop had his cell phone at his ear. I heard him saying, "We've got another one. Kevin St. James. Seven-forty-one Eighth Avenue." He was stationed by the door. I figured he was watching who left, and when I looked around for Fitz, I didn't see him. *That's strange,* I thought, but then my attention was drawn back to the bar with the girl now lying completely still on top of it. I could feel, as well as see, she was dead. The black guy was doing CPR, but I could have told him she wasn't coming back. Her face and even her arms and legs were blue. She had once been pretty, but now her features were distorted into a look of terror, her tongue protruded from her slack mouth, her eyes bulged from her skull and were wide open as if staring at something unutterably horrific.

I saw the club's bouncer talking to her boyfriend. "Did she take anything? Any shit, drugs, you know?"

The preppie kid looked scared to death. He nodded his head yes.

"Do you know what she took? Come on man, do you know what she took? I need to tell the EMS when they get here. Maybe there's still a chance to help her."

"Su-su-su-susto," the boy stuttered. "She took this new stuff they call susto."

Chapter 2

The world is full of strange vicissitudes,
And here was one exceedingly unpleasant.

—*Don Juan,* canto IV, verse 51, by Lord Byron

Right away Jennifer, the bartender, came over to me, her face as pale as mine. "Can you stick around until the EMS arrives?" she asked me in a voice that was high and tight from emotion. "You got a good look at the weird stuff that had just happened. And everybody else who was sitting at the bar has taken off."

She shook her head and blinked back tears. "This isn't the first time some kid OD'd," she added. "Watching a kid going out on Ecstasy is really bad. But I've never seen anything like this. It just gives me the creeps." She shivered then, shaking from head to toe. As she stood there, the music started up again over the sound system, and people faded away, going back to whatever they had been doing before the girl died. The excitement was over. The novelty gone. Like a sentry, the pub's bouncer stood in front of the body and crossed his arms.

Jennifer's eyes seemed unfocused, seeing inward, not outward. She was talking, but mostly to herself. "I hope they send a squad car. But I doubt one will come. It's Friday night in Manhattan, and every precinct in the city has calls up the wazoo." She looked over at the girl's body, which somebody had covered with a coat. "This was just an OD," she said sadly.

I nodded at her. New York cops on a Friday night were swamped with calls reporting stuff such as a rape in progress, shots being fired, or people outright killing each other. In all likelihood, nobody forced anything down this girl's throat. She had taken a drug and OD'd. As far as the NYPD was concerned, this call was an "aided"—someone in need of medical help—not a crime. But without saying it outright, both Jennifer and I knew this OD was something else entirely, macabre and scary as hell.

A waitress at the far end of the bar needed a drink order, so Jennifer gave me a quick thanks for sticking around and got busy pulling beers. I barely had time to say, "Sure, no problem," when I heard the sirens of the ambulance, and shortly afterwards two EMTs came crashing through the pub's door with a gurney.

One of the EMTs, a short, heavy-set Latina wearing a blue jacket, brusquely asked me if I knew what had happened while they positioned the gurney next to the bar. I told her about the audible sound of the girl's heart and how she had seemed to be strangling. The EMT could see the girl was the color of a Blue Man in full makeup performing in Vegas so I didn't mention that part. After taking the girl's vitals, the EMTs didn't even bother with CPR and went out a lot more slowly than they had come in. The whey-faced boyfriend had already left, and I motioned to Jennifer that I was heading back to my table.

I felt as if a dozen people were staring at me as I walked across the room; my three teammates sure were. I sat down and told them I had to wait around a little. They nodded, and nobody even suggested leaving without me. I was keyed up and jittery. I crossed my legs. I had the bad habit of bouncing my knee and jiggling my foot around when I was nervous, like a little kid. I made a mental note to keep still.

Bubba reached one of his big hands across the table and gently touched my arm. "We all need to talk about what happened. But not here. Later?" I nodded. He looked around at

Cormac and Benny. They nodded too. "As soon as we get out of here," he promised.

Just then, a waitress arrived with drinks for everybody at the table, including another Guinness for me. "Jennifer sent these over," she said. The girl's death had sobered me up fast. A third Guinness wasn't going to make me drunk tonight, and I needed something to take the edge off. I took a swallow and felt it slide down my throat. The taste was bitter and unkind.

"Thanks," I said to her, then looked at my team members. "Should we call J? Do you think this had something to do with why we were sent here?"

"Yeah, I think we should," Bubba said, and added that he'd walk outside and call on his cellular phone.

The rest of us got quiet then. Death is unsettling even to a vampire. This sudden, violent dying seemed to send us all into the dark places of our minds, perhaps thinking about our own ultimate fates. We are undead, but we can be killed. And then what? Nothingness? I suppose I'd prefer oblivion to being a spirit wandering for eternity. Truth is, I didn't know squat about life after death, but I have seen what I believed were ghosts and deep down I had the suspicion that nobody dies, and vampires least of all.

"She was the girl we saw outside the bathroom, right Daphy?" Benny said, breaking into my black musings.

"Yes, that's the one."

"If the cops show up, are you going to tell them what we overheard?" she asked.

I shrugged. "Might as well. I think the cops need to know about it. And we're just innocent bystanders this time."

I felt an icy wind that made me shiver and looked over at the door. Bubba's big frame filled it, the cold air clinging to him as he lumbered back to the table. "J says we should head down to the office as soon as we're done here. He'll be there."

Benny laughed a little. "Well he surely can't keep bankers'

hours if he's working with us. I wonder if he gets a bonus for the night shift."

I came close to smiling, but not quite.

Benny looked around at the others. "Y'all want to play a game of Hangman while we're waiting? Make the time pass faster?"

Cormac rolled his eyes. "You've got to be kidding."

"You have such a bad attitude, Cormac O'Reilly," Benny snapped. "I'm just trying to be sociable. And I like word games. I find them calming, and, honey, right now I need something to get my mind off of that poor child turning the color of a blue-raspberry Slurpee. I can still hear her heart thumping away like it was going to jump right out of her chest. I'll be dreaming about it, I just know I will."

"I'll play a round with you," Bubba said, opening up a paper napkin to write on and getting out a pen. "And so will Cormac. Won't you, Cormac?" the big man said, giving O'Reilly a look that would freeze Cleveland. "You in, Daphne?" he asked.

I shook my head no. "Sorry. I want to look around the room. Maybe I'll stand a while. Did any of you see where the guy sitting next to me at the bar went?"

"Sure did," Bubba said. "He hurried out the front door like the devil was right behind him."

"Wonder why he ran off?" Benny added.

"Damn good question," I said. "Damn good question."

I stood, picked up my glass of Guinness, and walked away, leaving them to their game. I found a spot where I could lean against the wall and see most of the room. As I sipped my drink, I did another survey of the pub, just as I had been doing earlier when I spotted Darius. I concentrated my energy and heightened my sensual awareness—what I smelled, saw, heard, and felt. Soon I had homed in on two young men. One was maybe five feet from me; the other one was half a room away, but what made me watch them was that they were glancing at each other every now and then.

The guy near me was dressed in Ralph Lauren from shirt to shoes and fashionably in need of a shave. The other wore glasses and looked a little nerdy. Nothing about them seemed out of the ordinary; they appeared to be a couple of college boys out on a Friday night hoping to hook up. But I sensed a tension in each of these two. I smelled the unmistakable acid odor of fear on the one nearest me. The muscle in his jaw was tight as if he was clenching his teeth. The movement was very subtle but there. Without seeming to stare I sipped my Guinness and gave each of them another look. I was trying to latch on to something to help me remember these two nondescript guys who could have been anybody.

The one near me I mentally nicknamed "Green Day." He had heavy eyebrows and dark circles under his eyes that reminded me of the Goth-like eyeliner used by Green Day's guitarist Billie Joe Armstrong. Then I smiled to myself. Oh yeah, the guy with glasses was definitely "Buddy Holly," the long-dead, not undead, rocker whose plane went down in Iowa in 1959 with the Big Bopper and Richie Valens. That crash happened nearly fifty years ago, a lifetime for many people. My throat tightened up a little with sadness when I realized half a century was just yesterday for me. The passing of time, the constant changes, and the loss of all that is familiar are huge issues for me.

Now, having tagged the two men with names, I wouldn't forget them. Something told me I needed to remember them, and I've learned to listen to my "inner voice." Just then Green Day looked in my direction. He had sweat on his upper lip. His eyes with the darkness around them darted away from mine, and he nervously readjusted his watch band and tugged down on the cuff of his sweater. He looked over at me again, and his body jerked slightly, but he recovered himself in a nanosecond. Then he grabbed his coat from the back of a chair and nearly ran for the door. He didn't look back as he pushed out into the night, and the cold wind touched my face again.

The black guy I figured for an undercover cop walked over and casually stood next to me, leaning back against the wall just as I was. He didn't say anything for a minute or so. I wondered if he were playing head games with me. Then he looked at me. Why he didn't like me before we'd even exchanged a single word, I didn't know, but I could see suspicion and distrust in his eyes. Occasionally a human is especially intuitive and picks up on something dangerous about me. It's not a conscious thing; it comes from a primitive place in the gut, not the head. Immediately I felt wary, but I also decided to be my usual smart-ass self.

"You a cop?" I said.

"I think a better question is what the hell you are," he said, without missing a beat.

"Screw you," I said as I pushed myself off the wall and started to walk away.

"Hold it!" he yelled at me and grabbed my arm.

I looked at his hand on my arm, turned slowly, and said, "What do you think you are doing?" in a voice so laden with frost that my every word was brittle. Out of the corner of my eye I saw Bubba stand up, ready to come over.

The black guy saw him too and let go of my arm as if he had been bitten by a snake. He got his words out as rapidly as he could, "I was out of line. I apologize. Can I talk with you for a minute? About what happened to that girl. It's important."

"It depends on who you are," I said.

He hesitated a split second then said quietly enough that no one else could overhear, "Detective Johnson. Moses Johnson. NYPD." He moved back against the wall, carving out a place in the crowd where we could talk. "And your name is?"

"Not until I see some ID."

"I can't show you any. I'm off duty," he responded in a voice so low only I could hear him.

"Yeah, sure you are. I say you're undercover, and your wallet's in your boot along with a flashlight."

"How do you know that?" he asked, clearly taken aback.

"Let's just say from experience."

He reached out his hand, took mine, and palmed me his business card. "My number's on there, so is the precinct's. Call it."

I didn't look at the card, but slipped it into my pocket. "Okay, I'm Daphne Urban. And I work for the government, for the National Park Service." That didn't exactly get me in the brotherhood of police officers, but I figured it might buy me a modicum of respect. It was a long shot, and Johnson gave me a long look. "National Park Service. Yeah, right," he said under his breath, then asked in a louder voice, "Can you tell me what you saw?" Clearly the interview had started.

"Sure. This young girl got up on the bar. She looked drunk or high to me, you know, her face was flushed and her movements were unsteady. She started yelling something like 'Wahooo!' and began dancing. Her boyfriend came over and tried to coax her down. She started getting unsteady on her feet, pulled off her jacket, and suddenly grabbed her throat. She seemed to be choking and unable to breathe. Before I realized what was going on she collapsed. I jumped up. I think my chair fell over. Somebody yelled to call nine-one-one. The girl started going into convulsions, then you pushed past me and started CPR. She had turned blue from head to toe. That was about it."

"Did you know her?" Johnson asked, his brown eyes boring into mine with an almost fanatical intensity. I was hyped and antsy. This man was clearly driven.

"No," I said, my voice even.

"Had you ever seen her before?" he asked, slowing down his voice and looking at me in a way that might have unnerved a suspect. I wasn't guilty. I wasn't a suspect. And I wasn't unnerved. I was, however, getting pissed.

"Before what? Before tonight? No."

"Before she got up on the bar, earlier tonight," he persisted.

"Yes. Maybe a half-hour before she died, she was waiting outside the bathroom. I saw her when I walked out. She was with another girl."

"Do you remember what the other girl looked like?"

I looked around the room. I didn't see her. I brought my eyes back to those of Detective Moses. His dislike of me was still apparent in them. "Yeah, I remember," I said. "She weighed maybe a hundred and five pounds, five feet two, her hair was dark except for the parts that were dyed pink and blue. She had on a white T-shirt that said, KISS THE BOYS AND MAKE THEM CRY. That enough?" I had spoken my piece in a snotty tone of voice. Detective Johnson chose to ignore it.

"Yes. Good, thanks," he said and went on. "Did you see anything else? Overhear anything?"

"Yeah, outside the bathroom, the girl who died had something in her hand, a glass ampoule I think, and she said something to her girlfriend about getting high. I assume that's why they were going into the john."

"And were *you* getting high in the bathroom?" Moses Johnson said, and he didn't say it nicely. He had deep lines next to his mouth. His lips were well shaped, and his nose was fine and straight with flaring nostrils. His head was shaved, and his left ear was pierced with a diamond stud that glowed white against his chocolate-colored skin—dark bitter chocolate like the intonation of his voice. He would have been a handsome man except for the anger he wore like armor. His dislike of me seemed to grow by the second.

"No, I was not," I said, keeping my voice flat and unemotional.

"But you weren't in there alone?" he said and leaned forward. Either he had been watching Benny and me or, more likely, he had already talked to the dark-haired girl.

"No. I had been in there talking with a girlfriend of mine. Is there a law against that?" I said getting more of an attitude by the minute.

He ignored my comment and asked another question. "So what happened to your boyfriend?"

For a minute I felt confused, thinking he meant Darius. I must have looked blank. "Huh?" I said.

"The guy you were with at the bar. He left in a hurry. Why?"

"I don't know. I was just talking with him for a couple of minutes. I never saw him before."

"Can you give me his name?" he asked and pulled a little notepad out of his jacket pocket, keeping it mostly hidden in one hand. He had a small ballpoint pen in the other.

"No. Not really. He just told me to call him Fitz." That was a white lie. I don't know why I told it, but I didn't feel like giving Detective Johnson any more information than I had to. He didn't like me. I didn't like him. And besides, lying is second nature to me.

"Do you know how I can contact him?" He was clicking the ballpoint open and closed in a really annoying way.

"I have no idea," I answered, breaking the word *idea* into three distinct syllables and saying them carefully one at a time. I was contemplating just cutting this conversation off. I felt I had done my civic duty.

"Did you come here with friends?"

"Yes, friends from work. We all work for the federal government, Detective Johnson," I said.

"Can I have their names?"

"Not from me." I added sweetly, "If you want them, feel free to go ask them yourself. Now, are you done with me? I want to leave."

He put away the pen, then let out a deep breath and shook his head. The heat of his anger seemed to have cooled when he looked at me again. "Look, I won't bullshit you. You know as well as I do that what you saw wasn't just a routine drug overdose. I really do appreciate you talking to me. Please call me if you think of something else. Thank you for your help."

"You're welcome, Detective. But I would like to ask *you* something."

"What is it?" he said, taken aback.

"Do you know what killed that girl?"

He paused for a second, then said with an even darker bitterness in his voice, "No. No, I don't."

I walked over to the bar and told Jennifer I was out of there. I gave her my name and phone number before I left. Our eyes met before I turned away, and we exchanged the unspoken understanding that we had seen something both inexplicable and unforgettable. "Come back again," she said while she wiped down the bar. "This is a really nice place. Don't judge it by what happened tonight."

"Sure," I said and started to walk away, then stopped and turned toward her again. "Does Fitz, you know, the guy who was sitting next to me, come in here often?"

"Almost every weekday. Around six-thirty. He stays maybe an hour," she said and gave me a knowing grin.

"Well, maybe I will see you again," I said and grinned back.

"You go girl," she said, laughing, as she set up a row of glasses on the bar.

When I reached the other Darkwings at the table, I said, "Let's get going," and a minute later we were out the door and gathered together on the sidewalk. The sleet had stopped, the temperature had plummeted, and the cold clutched at me with skeletal fingers while the night descended over me like a shroud.

"We'll need two cabs," Cormac said, his voice a nasally whine. "I am not crowding into one. Don't we have an expense account? I think we need to ask for one. I mean we were *summoned* to a meeting at midnight."

"When the boy's right, he's right," Bubba seconded. "Two cabs it is." He strode out into Eighth Avenue, his fingers in his mouth to whistle. Cab number one caromed across four lanes of downtown traffic and slid to a stop. Bubba opened the door, and Cormac started for it. "Now, Mr. O'Reilly, where I come from, ladies go first," Bubba reprimanded him. Cormac retreated, pulling his long black Goth overcoat tighter around his slight body.

Benny and I ducked through the open back door, and I couldn't resist a parting shot. Looking down at Cormac's short boots, which sported a Cuban heel and pointed toe, I said with so much cloying sweetness you needed a glass of water to wash it down, "And Cormac, where did you get those darling Beatles boots? Have they been in your closet since 1963?"

"Bitch!" he shrieked and put his hands on his hips. "I'll have you know I got these directly from Liverpool! Last week! Italian leather! They cost me ninety-nine quid. At least I don't wear shitkickers like *some* people," he said and glanced pointedly at Bubba.

"Y'all can't hurt my feelings," I heard Bubba say as I closed the taxi door. "My boots don't make me walk all pinched up like you."

Cormac gave one of his signature movements with his head: He closed his eyes, lifted his chin with a jerk, and flung his long hair back off his forehead. "Philistines," I heard him say as our taxi driver asked, "Where to?"

I told him to take us to Twenty-third and Fifth Avenue. He pulled into traffic and I sank wearily back against the seat. "Oh man, I'm glad to be out of there," I said, resting the back of my head against the seat cushions. "What a crappy night. I don't even want to think about most of it."

"Right back to you on that one, girlfriend," Benny said.

"And you know, now that we have a minute to ourselves, there's something I'm dying to ask you."

I figured it was about Darius and me, or Darius and that half-naked *putana* he was with, so I lazily swiveled my head in her direction and said, "Go ahead."

"Who do you think Bubba is?"

"What do you mean? You should know better than anyone. He's the cousin of your last boyfriend, Larry Lee. He was recruited to Team Darkwing because you went and blabbed to Larry about us being spies, then Larry went and called him, or something. Instead of a skeleton in the Lee family closet, evidently they had a vampire. You know, Benny, loose lips sink ships."

"Oh, shut up, Daphy. How did I know pillow talk would get out of hand? But I don't mean who Bubba is *now*, I mean who he *was*, before he was Bubba Lee from Belfry, Kentucky, cause I'm just not buying this good-ol'-boy act."

"Act? You're sure it's an act? I mean the man wears a John Deere cap and construction boots. And he's got a beer belly, and Benny, that sure as hell is *real*."

"Oh, Daphy, you just haven't been paying attention. Sure he looks like a redneck and would fit right in at NASCAR races, but he gave me some shellacking at Hangman. Then we played Super Ghost, that word game that's so hard it makes me want to cry, and he wiped the floor with me and Cormac. Cormac was so miffed he refused to play again."

"Well, if Bubba does have a good vocabulary, he certainly takes pains to avoid using it in everyday conversation. Okay, so that's all very interesting. What else do you find suspicious?"

"His ring. I asked to see it. It's from West Point, class of 1854."

"Well, Benny, did you ask him straight out? I've taken on other identities, too, you know," I said as a door in my mind opened up, and a memory emerged. Suddenly it was long ago and far away—very late on a January night in London nearly two hundred years in the past. I was walking through magnificent gilded doors into a crowded English reception room. In front of my face, I held an elaborate mask of black feathers on an ebony stick, and I was dressed in costume—a vividly scarlet gown that was clearly Elizabethan. A ruff encircled my neck and a tight, stiff bodice pushed up, and nearly completely exposed, my small bosom. The style was so much more flattering than the hideous high-waisted neoclassical "nightgowns" then in fashion. I wore tiny golden slippers on my feet, and I had a string of diamonds holding a small gold dagger woven into my upswept black hair. "Lady Webster," the butler intoned. Men stared, and one young man in particular stared intently.

Across the room this man, wearing the rich crimson-and-gold brocade tunic of a Turkish prince, stopped his conversation with a group of admirers and stared directly at me. A silk turban in the same hues was wrapped around his head, and there was a vitality in him that seemed to catch the candlelight and create a glowing aura, encasing him in light from head to toe. A thin mustache rakishly outlined his sensual upper lip. His eyes stayed riveted on me as I moved down a short flight of stairs. I felt the cool smoothness of the marble banister beneath my hand, but the room faded away, time slowed down, the distance between this man and me vanished. I stopped and lowered my mask. He and I stood there motionless. A bolt of sexual energy leaped from him to me and linked us as firmly as iron shackles. I have said before that none of us willingly chooses the person we love. It is fated; it is writ somewhere in a great book and we cannot resist or avoid what is meant to be. And this man was meant to be mine.

I had to come to this ball to find George Gordon Noel Byron, Sixth Baron Byron, one of London's most scandalous celebrities. I knew without a doubt this was he. I had created my elaborate disguise and made my grand entrance simply because I had read a poem Byron had lately written called "The First Kiss of Love." The lines seemed to speak directly to my soul, so as a lark or a silly girl's prank, I had tracked him down and wrangled an invitation to this elegant masked party filled with gentry so different from the exotic dark lady I so obviously was. I had hoped merely to see in flesh and blood the man whose words had pierced me like an arrow. Now the arrow hit again, but this time it entered my heart, and I was suddenly lost, so terribly achingly lost.

"Daphy? Where are you? Hel-looo!" Benny's voice broke into my consciousness, the door to the past slammed shut, and my memory vanished.

"What? Oh, sorry, I thought of something, that's all. You were saying you asked Bubba about his identity?"

"Well, yes, I did. I came right out and said, 'Mr. Bubba Lee, I have my doubts about you. Whatever were you doing at West Point?' "

"So what did he say?"

"He gave me a nonanswer. He told me something like, 'Learning that some men like to fight more than they like to love.' So then I asked him if he had been a fighter or a lover."

"Benny, you brazen hussy," I said and gave her a pinch.

"Ow! Daphy! That hurts." She squealed as she rubbed her arm. "I tell you, under that disgusting green John Deere hat is a brilliant mind and the soul of a Southern gentleman. There's a mystery there, Miss Daphne Urban, and I intend to solve it."

At that point the taxi pulled up in front of the Flatiron Building, whose triangular shape resembles the prow of an ocean liner ungainly run aground between Broadway and Fifth Avenue. Benny and I climbed out of the yellow cab and stood on the sidewalk just as Bubba and Cormac arrived in the second taxi. The earlier sleet had covered the black streets with a thin coating of crusty white, and a bitter chill penetrated my leather jacket and embraced me. I felt an icy hand touch my soul. We were about to find out what mission lay ahead for Team Darkwing. I looked up into Manhattan's inky sky, where no stars shone, and then, like a dark cloud crossing in front of the moon, the thought flew through my mind that perhaps not all four of us vampires would still be walking on this earth when this assignment ended.

A night watchman was waiting at the door of 175 Fifth Avenue to let us into the lobby of the locked and darkened building. We piled noisily into an elevator and got off on the third floor: ABC Publishing. Of course, the name was just a front for the headquarters of the Darkwings, a group of vampire spies operating in a deep black operation—in other words, we don't exist as far as any legitimate agency is concerned. Congress doesn't know about us. Probably one or two people at the Pentagon do. Who else knew? Were we part of the CIA? I honestly couldn't answer either question. Officially I had been hired by the Department of the Interior to work for the National Park Service. I was an exhibit specialist, GS Eleven, working on a theater-restoration project. Unofficially I was part of the U.S. government's most secret effort to stop terrorism. Shortly before Christmas I had gone undercover to get close to a major international arms dealer named Bonaventure. It turned out he was selling a nuclear device to terrorists, and in a race against time, Team Darkwing stopped a dirty bomb from going off in New York City. No matter what else happened I was damn proud of that.

And I have long realized that on the journey through life we come into contact with certain people and experience a handful of moments that completely change the direction of the road we walk. Being recruited by an ultrasecret national-security agency and meeting my boss, a career military man known only as J, had forever altered my life's path. Thanks to my ex-boyfriend, Darius della Chiesa, a former Navy SEAL, I had found out that J had been a Ranger in the Army's Special Forces. Maybe he still was. He acted as if there were a poker up his ass at all times. But the man probably had testosterone in his fingernails he was so virile, and I confess I was not totally immune to his appeal. It was purely a physical reaction; J and I were worlds apart in every way. Okay, so I did kiss him. Twice. I had never even held a conversation with him about anything that didn't involve work.

J, in neatly pressed khaki pants and a khaki shirt with epaulets, was half-sitting on the edge of the big conference table when the four of us burst through the frosted-glass door of Room 3001. A dim light bathed everything in a gray gloom; vampires practically need sunglasses with any illumination greater than a sixty-watt bulb. J stood up and greeted us: "Have a seat, gentlemen. And ladies." Four yellow pads and four cheap government-issue ballpoint pens sat on the table in front of four chairs. We all sat down. I lined up the pad so it was perfectly perpendicular to my chair and uncapped the pen.

"Let me cut right to the chase," J began. A tall, muscular man, he towered over us. His hands were clasped behind him, and he looked hard at each of us with an expression as serious as cancer. "We have a situation that needs Team Darkwing's attention."

"Does it have anything to do with what happened at Kevin St. James tonight?" I broke in.

"Agent Urban, please wait to ask your questions after the briefing. It might save us all some time," he barked, clearly annoyed at the interruption.

I nodded and tried not to take his words personally. J was a bit short on people skills.

"There is an epidemic of a new drug in this city. It's highly addictive. It's expensive. And it is occasionally fatal. More than occasionally. Maybe one in every few hundred users dies in the same manner as the girl you saw collapse tonight. Taking this drug is like playing Russian roulette. Hit the loaded chamber and bang you're dead.

"So far, the media hasn't picked up on these deaths, but

it's only a matter of time before they do. We'd like to stop the distribution of the substance before the press catches on. So far the dealers have targeted only the wealthiest enclaves of the city: Wall Street, the Upper East Side, the Soho art galleries, and some classy Midtown clubs. The users are rich college kids, twentysomething stockbrokers, debutantes, celebrities, playboys, models. I think you get the picture. You saw what it does. We don't know how it does it. We don't have any of this substance to analyze—yet. And the distribution of the drug is very exclusive. It's not on the street. From what we've learned, you have to be *somebody* to get it. The buyer makes an appointment with the dealer to purchase an ampoule, and the ampoules are rationed, five to a customer. We think that's to keep it from being resold."

"Agent Urban, can't it wait?" he said to me, since I was waving my hand in the air like an overeager grade-school pupil.

"Well, I have questions, and I just don't think you're going to answer them," I insisted.

"Okay, ask one. Just one," he conceded.

"Why is this our case? Why isn't it the DEA's case? Or Customs? Or even the NYPD, and by the way, I think it already *is* their case. We deal in national-security issues. This is a drug problem. Yeah, it looked like a different kind of drug, but how does this threaten our government or the safety of the city? I just don't get it." I spoke in rapid fire. My teammates were all nodding their agreement.

"That's more than one question," J sighed, giving me a tired look. He seemed to be struggling with his answer, he rubbed the short hair of his buzz cut, and seconds passed before he spoke. "Look team, there are two, maybe three reasons why this is your case. Number one, we have reason to believe the other agencies you mentioned may have been co-opted. Or at least some members of them have. The amount of money involved in this drug ring is not in the millions; it's in the billions. Quite frankly, you are the new Untouchables. You can't be bought. You can't be intimidated. You can't be scared off. Hell, except under specific circumstances, you can't be killed. Besides that, nobody even knows you exist.

"In the second place, this *is* a national-security issue. For all we know the people behind this epidemic could be terrorists. If this stuff goes citywide or even national, thousands of people are going to die in a way that's sure to scare the pants off Joe Q. Public. Right now it's a Manhattan problem. It hasn't even reached the boroughs. The time to stop it is now."

Bubba spoke up in his booming bass voice. "J, meaning no disrespect, but something doesn't sit jest right with me about this. Are you telling us that this drug has only turned up in Manhattan? If that's the case, maybe it can only be made in small batches and it's never going to spread. Look me in the eye and tell me again this is only a Manhattan problem."

J's face got dark and I could see the anger brewing. He didn't like being questioned and he didn't like being challenged. He again took some time before admitting, "We think it's being used elsewhere."

"Where?" we all said practically in unison.

J took a piece of paper out of his breast pocket and unfolded it. "None of these are confirmed, you understand," he said and began reading. "Palm Beach. The Hamptons. Miami. Beverly Hills. Bel Air. Shaker Heights. Essex Fells. Atlantic City. Carmel-by-the-Sea. Pacific Palisades. Houston. Dallas. Taos. Las Vegas . . ."

"Okay, buddy. Millionaire's row. We get the picture," Bubba said. "So we do have a problem. And it's not a small one."

I tried not to say anything, but the question I really wanted to ask burst out of me. "J, did my mother give us this case?"

"I could say 'Just ask her,'" he shot back, anger breaking

through into his voice, but then he pulled it back and said unemotionally, "Yes, my superior officer, who happens to be Marozia Urban, your mother, is adamant that Team Darkwing be involved with this. I assume she has a good reason. She always does. So leave it at that."

"For now," I said with a hard edge as I stared at my yellow pad, tapping the point of the pen against the paper. I knew that if my mother was behind these orders, then there was a lot more going on here than we were being told.

"To get back to your assignment," J continued. "You have two immediate tasks that go hand in hand: Identify a dealer and get a sample of the drug. The toxicology reports on the users who've OD'd haven't given us anything. Evidently the drug breaks down very quickly once it's inhaled. And yes, it is inhaled, not swallowed. We believe it is a brown powder. It looks like very fine dirt, or so we've been told.

"Ultimately we need to find out where this drug is originating and who exactly is behind its import. We need to find the kingpin, and bring him down."

"In other words," Benny broke in, "this drug is not being manufactured here?"

"We don't think so. We think it's coming from South America."

"You think or you know?" I said.

"We have 'reason to believe,' Miss Urban, but no proof. I don't want you to have preconceptions; let's just deal with facts. Agreed?"

"Right," I said, but still felt we were not being told even remotely close to what was already known. "Specifically how are we to proceed on this?"

"That information is in these envelopes." He took four brown nine-by-twelve envelopes and handed them out. Each one had one of our names on it. "Basically each of you is going to hang out in one of the places we suspect the drug users frequent. The names of the bartenders, the bouncers, and the waitstaff are in your envelope along with some other material you might find helpful. Start on this tomorrow. Hell, try to *finish* it tomorrow. You can call me at any time. If we get new information, I'll call the team in for another meeting. Now does anyone have any questions? Agent O'Reilly?"

"Is it okay if we take a date? I mean, we have to blend in and all. So do you have a problem if I take somebody? It will be Saturday night. . . ." He was barely keeping the whine out of his voice.

"Mr. O'Reilly, do whatever works. That's the bottom line. We don't have rules. We want results. Got it?"

"Yessir," Cormac answered and said under his breath, "Thank you, God, I have something to do besides listen to Gregorian chants all night." Two months ago Cormac had been given an undercover job as the night clerk at the Opus Dei headquarters at Lexington and Thirty-fourth Street. He didn't know why. We didn't know why. And he complained about it every chance he got.

"Anything else?"

"Well, yes," I piped up again. "What's the drug called?"

"Susto. The street name is susto."

Chapter 3

The Hour of the Wolf

The four of us left the building riding on an adrenaline high. We had a mission. We had a purpose. How many people do? I knew what it was like to drift aimlessly through life. I had wandered hither and yon with no direction for centuries. The years passed by with a meaningless sameness. If the days of my previous existence had had a dominant color, it would have been a pale gray, foggy, misty, and indistinct. Before Team Darkwing, I didn't matter. Now I believed I did.

I looked around at this team, we vampires four—as unlikely a bunch of superheroes as ever walked the Earth. I had never analyzed the connection between us, and now I took another look at my old "friend" Cormac. Of medium height, muscular but very thin, Cormac was dressed in his trademark black, a color that most vampires avoid as being too stereotypical. But Cormac was part of New York's theatrical community, dramatic, or should I say melodramatic, to the core. He had danced in *A Chorus Line,* he had auditioned for *The Sopranos,* and tonight he wore his "uniform"—a tight knit shirt to show off his toned dancer's body, black jeans, black boots, long black overcoat. His hair was shoulder-length and wavy, and he usually pulled it back into a ponytail. His nose was straight, his lips full, his eyes the color of root beer. He was extraordinarily good-looking, and would have been more so if he ever smiled. He rarely did. He was petulant and bitter, a state that turned down the corners of his mouth and brought his fine dark eyebrows together in a perpetual frown. He was a talented dancer, but his big break eluded him. Why? Because as time passed and he didn't age, he had to move on to another place, take a different name, and could never accept a role that would make him too known, too public. Wanting to shine, wanting to show the world he could dance better than Mikhail Baryshnikov, which he truly could, he felt aggrieved at the vampire's curse of having to keep secrets and hide who we truly were.

Sometimes behaving as campy and vampy as a transvestite queen, Cormac hid his real personality under a gay persona. He had never found a soulmate, but he had been in a constant search for love since he and I first met in Regency London. Was he gay? Was he bi? After observing him for over two hundred years, I'd say he was indiscriminate, taking love and pleasure in whatever form he found it. Mostly, I guessed, he was just lonely.

As for Kentucky's favorite son, Bubba Lee was the new kid on the block, having been recruited to join us at the end of our previous mission just weeks ago. This drug assignment was his maiden voyage, but he fit in with the team as if he had always been there. I felt I could count on him. I genuinely liked him. He was big and solid, a stone wall of man. Like Benny, I wondered what his identity had been before his vampire days and whether he'd tell us. Among vampires it was considered a great breach of protocol to ask.

Next was Benny, a man-magnet as voluptuous as Marilyn Monroe, but with none of MM's neuroses. A native of Branson, Missouri, Benny, with her big blue eyes and rosy cheeks, projected a wholesome, cornfed Midwestern look. She was bouncy, bubbly, and never met a stranger. She looked about as dangerous as Heidi. She often pretended to be a ditzy blonde, but I knew her mind could cut to the heart of a situation as fast as a laser. I had seen her fight like an Amazon. How did she feel about being a vampire? Relentlessly optimistic, positively merry, and always upbeat, I would have to say she absolutely, positively loved it.

I was the fourth of this vampire quartet. Physically I was tall and almost too thin. My hair was dark, my skin like cream, my eyes the gray-blue of eastern European skies. After my transformation into a vampire, courtesy of a Gypsy king, I had become a wanderer, a seeker, a troubled soul, feeling as if I had lost my goodness to my dark side, that bestial part of me that took over each time I destroyed innocence with my bite. Despite my mother's pleas, I had left Renaissance Italy to travel the world, always drawn to a hero who had the heart of a poet, wanting to align myself with a positive force, and yet fearing I would become the instrument of that hero's fall into darkness. Indeed that fate had happened with alarming regularity as I entered into dangerous liaisons with men whose names you might recognize, but whose identities, outside of Lord Byron's, I prefer not to reveal.

No matter where I went or what name I took (Daphne Urban and Daphne Castagna are both variations on my real birth name), I had always been the outsider, the stranger, the one who doesn't belong. Misunderstood and persecuted, I had spent most of my nearly five hundred years on this planet utterly and irrevocably doomed to be solitary. I realized that here I had been given the chance—perhaps my only chance—to change. I was a member of Team Darkwing, and I was no longer alone.

As we four left the building, we stood on the sidewalk and looked at each other. It was well into the hour of the wolf, that time between dark and dawn where humans sleep and nonhumans prowl. The wide avenue was quiet except for a stray cab. An icy coating on everything reflected the street lights and shop windows.

"So now where?" Benny spoke up, perky as always. She pulled some mittens from her coat pocket and put them on as she stamped circulation into her little feet, which were clad in red Jimmy Choo high-heeled boots and couldn't possibly be warm.

"Nightcap?" Cormac said. A reed-thin wraith in his long black coat, he stood a few feet distant from the three of us . . . with us, but true to his melancholy, misanthropic nature, wary of too much bonhomie.

"Sure," Bubba agreed loudly and stretched his heavy arms over the shoulders of both Benny and me. He drew us in close to him and whispered. "There's a fellow across the street watching us. Let's just walk a coupl'a blocks and see what's what." He linked arms with the two of us. Cormac gave us a questioning look. "Straight ahead, Cormac, my man," Bubba boomed and we all began walking south on Broadway. "Look for neon lights spelling out BAR, one of the prettiest little words in the English language. Well, after BEER that is," he added and laughed out loud.

We headed toward the corner of Twenty-first Street talking loudly about nonsense. We started naming all the beer brands we could think of. For each one Bubba gave a review.

"Miller Light," Benny called out.

"Piss in a bottle," Bubba intoned.

"Coors Light," I offered.

"Weak piss in a bottle," Bubba sagely offered.

"Harp," I said next.

"You can taste the green of Ireland in every glass. Too bad it doesn't taste like beer," Bubba the sage continued.

All the while, though, I was wondering if we were really being followed. A sharp pain pierced my chest as I thought of Darius. He had followed me so many times before we had fallen in love, shadowing me through New York's streets. He had watched me before I knew who or what he was. He had lain in wait for me, and he had wanted me. Oh yes, most of all he had desired me. But his resentment of me was so strong now that I couldn't imagine that desire rekindling. But if I let myself remember how his hard body had felt against mine, if I remembered the smell of his flesh as I snuggled against his bare arms, tasting the saltiness of his skin, feeling his lips soft against my eyelids as he kissed them, if I remembered the sound of his voice saying my name, saying I was beautiful, I might be tempted to dissolve into tears. Yeah, I'm some big bad vampire all right. I blinked hard and shook my head to chase the thoughts away.

The four of us were actually having a pretty good time acting silly when we stopped for a red light at Twentieth Street. There was no traffic, but we halted while Bubba whispered, "Cross when the light changes." It did, and he let go of us as we dashed across the street. He bent down as if to tie his work boots. But in a flash he sprung up, whirled around, and ran back up the sidewalk. Half a block away, in a dark shadowy pocket between the street lights, a man stopped in his tracks and started to run across the empty avenue. Bubba overtook him easily, grabbing him in a choke hold with one massive arm, pinning the man's arms to his body with the other. He brought his captive back to the sidewalk where Benny, Cormac, and I were already waiting.

We all stared at the person Bubba held imprisoned in his arms. Short of stature, with copper-colored skin and high cheekbones, he appeared to be an Indian from Central or South America. He raised his head and looked directly into my eyes with black fathomless ones of his own. I felt a frisson of energy before he looked away. He wore a crudely woven gray-and-white poncho above dark pants and sneakers. His hair was dark and coarse, shaggy, and over his ears. Wrinkles bit deeply into the skin around his mouth. He wasn't young, but how old he was I couldn't guess. He did not struggle in Bubba's arms, and there had been no trace of fear in his eyes when he looked at me.

"Who are you?" Bubba was asking. "Why are you following us?" I could see Bubba had loosened his hold on the Indian but didn't release him.

"I am Don Manuel," the small man said with dignity. "I follow you because I think something about you. Something. You have big magic. And maybe you can help me."

"So why did you run?" Bubba asked.

Don Manuel smiled then, showing very white teeth. "Too big magic. I think maybe I wait for some other time to talk to one of you. Not four."

Bubba looked at us over the man's shoulder, shrugged, and let the man go. Don Manuel just stood there. I could sense a subtle disturbance in the air around him. He reached under his poncho and brought out something he held in his closed hand. He turned to Bubba. "Here," he said picking up Bubba's hand and placing the object in it. "This you look for. I talk to you later," Don Manuel said and stepped back toward the shadows of a doorway.

"Hey!" Cormac yelled. "Where'd he go?"

Where Don Manuel had once stood was nothing but emptiness. All that moved was the wind, which picked up a scrap of paper off the pavement and whirled it crazily up into the air.

"What the hell just happened?" Cormac said.

"He was a shaman," I said. "Probably a shape-shifter. What he did is a magician's trick. You know, like an illusion from Penn and Teller's act."

"How do you know that, Daphy?" Benny asked.

"I've seen it before. Or something like it. In Africa. What did he give you, Bubba?"

Bubba opened his big paw. "It looks like a piece of tree bark."

We conferred on what to do and decided that Bubba should keep the tree bark until he could get it to J to be analyzed. Bubba offered to write up a report on the incident. That was fine by me. I could just imagine J's reaction to the part about

Don Manuel vanishing into thin air. J had a tough time believing in vampires, and he works with us. As far as he's concerned, if he can't see it, smell it, touch it, or kill it, it doesn't exist. Well, as Hamlet noted, "There are more things in heaven and earth, Horatio, than are dreamt of in your philosophy."

Suddenly I had had enough for one night and wanted to go home. The air had gotten even more frigid, and I felt almost transparently pale with no blood in my veins to keep me warm. My leather jacket was more fashionable than functional. My teeth were chattering so much I sounded like a squirrel, and my fingers were stiffening inside my thin leather gloves. As my adrenaline subsided, depression descended on me like a miasma of gloom. In truth I needed a meal of human blood to boost my energy, and I had some home in my fridge, thanks to my standing order with an expensive, but very discreet, blood bank.

Cormac was also ready to leave. Bubba and Benny decided they still wanted a beer or two or three. Cormac and I hailed cabs, separate ones of course. I was going to the Upper West Side where for some years I had lived in a spacious apartment in an old building on West End Avenue in the Nineties. Cormac occupied a studio apartment about as big as a broom closet in Greenwich Village. Once in the cab, I closed my eyes and contemplated a long soak in a hot tub that might get the cold out of my bones. The taxi raced nearly nonstop uptown. Traffic was light, and the balding, middle-aged cabbie (the ID said he was Stewart Weiss from Brooklyn) had all the lights timed right, and they blinked from red to green so perfectly he didn't even slow down at the intersections. I got out at my block, and handed the cabbie some bills through his open window. He flipped on his OFF DUTY light as he pulled out. I must have been his last fare for the night. It was almost three a.m. I took a deep breath as I started toward the glass double doors of the apartment house.

Then a bloodcurdling cry stopped me in my tracks.

* * *

The sound wasn't human. It was an animal's cry filled with desperation and pain. I reacted; I didn't think. I whirled around trying to figure out from where the sound had originated. The horrible cry, a howl really, shattered the night again. It came from above me, but where? A building slated for demolition stood boarded up and empty a few hundred feet down the block. I believed the sound came from its upper floors, maybe from the roof. I ran in that direction, hearing the tormented, anguished cry for the third time. I stood on the pavement looking up. I knew what I had to do.

Ignoring the cold, I pulled off my clothes as fast as a quick-change artist, stashing them behind some trash cans and old boxes piled next to the building's wall. Even as I did this, my transformation had begun. A tingling like an electric charge raced over my skin, the air began to rush around me, a blaze of light spun into a whirlwind as my magnificent bat wings sprung from my back, my limbs lengthened, my nails became claws, my incisors grew long and sharp, and a sleek black pelt that shimmered with bands of light covered my body. My true nature had become manifest. The vampire that I was—a monster, a seductress, a creature of the darkness and void—poised for a breath before taking flight.

Up I rose toward the top of the building, twenty stories above, soaring effortlessly on wings that glowed in the night and left a luminescent trail of St. Elmo's fire in my wake. The sight of my huge bat form would trigger an ancient dread in any who beheld it, but my face retained its human features—except for my eyes. They had become round, and their whites had dissolved into a glittering gold that encircled pools of ebony. These great pupils, which let me see clearly in the darkest night, were disturbing in their depths. Any human so bold as to look into them was given a glimpse of the mysterious nether regions of the undead and the infinite . . . and was pulled irresistibly, should I choose it, into my embrace.

I bounded over the parapet surrounding the building's roof and landed on the patio of a once-grand penthouse, its windows now firmly boarded with plywood. I could sense an animal nearby, a creature filled with pain and fear. I swiveled my head slowly, allowing my sense of smell to lead me to the source. A padlocked shed stood at the far end of the patio, and I began to glide to it when I saw a door open in the shadows to my right. Three figures came rushing out of it, and in an instant the leader slammed his body into mine, driving me backwards and knocking me down. My attacker was huge, probably close to seven feet tall, and heavy with muscles; I felt his weight crushing down on me; I smelled his sour scent. His face was obscured by a ski mask, and his upraised hand held a huge wooden stake. As time seemed to slow down, I watched the stake descend toward my heart. Was this the end of it all? I summoned every ounce of my strength and punched him hard in the face with one fist while I blocked the downward thrust of the deadly stake with my forearm. The impact sent pain shooting into my shoulder, but the razor-sharp point stopped inches from my chest. I stayed alive.

Breathing fast, I rolled free and jumped to my feet. A wave of complete bewilderment washed over me. These were vampire hunters. How had they had found me? But I had no time to wonder where they came from or how long they had been following me. I kicked the first attacker hard, sending him sliding across the roof just when a second black-clad assailant dove at me, tackling my knees in an attempt to drag me down. A smaller ski-masked figure, the last to emerge from the door, ran into the moonlight, which illuminated an archery quiver filled with long sharp stakes slung across the vampire hunter's back. Meanwhile I sank my claws deep into the shoulder of the man attempting to pull me down, puncturing his thick leather coat and penetrating his flesh. He yelled and released my legs. He tried to thrash loose from my grasp. I saw his buddy, the one I had kicked aside, getting to his knees, and the smaller hunter, whose size and more graceful movements seemed feminine, was circling in order to come at me from behind.

Time to get out of Dodge, I thought. Using the mighty strength of my wings, I rose about ten feet into the air, hauling the man in my claws with me as he struggled and began to scream, "Let go! Put me down!"

"You want to get down?" I sneered at him. "Well, sure!" Then I dropped him, narrowly missing his little stake-wielding buddy, who danced backwards to get out of the way. The vampire hunter landed hard, but I give him credit. He staggered to his feet, obviously dazed but seemingly without any broken bones.

I was debating whether to retreat or swoop down for round two with my original assailant when a large dark shadow came up over the edge of the roof. I froze, hovering immobile in the air above the recent battleground. A vampire, one larger than I and lighter in color, gracefully came to rest on the patio as I had recently done and looked straight up at me. My heart stopped when I saw who it was. Darius.

He never got a chance to fight. His arrival was more than enough for the three vampire hunters. They ran off, disappearing through the doorway from which they had emerged moments earlier.

My first thought was what was Darius doing here? But the mental question was interrupted by the sounds from the padlocked shed. In the quiet after the fight, I could hear an animal moaning, its breathing shallow and labored. I didn't have much time if I wanted to save it. I flew down in front of the wooden shack. I hooked my claws into the heavy wooden door and attempted to rip it from its hinges. The wood held firm and I was about to give another mighty heave when Darius came up next to me. He said nothing, but sunk his claws into the door next to mine and together we easily tore rough lumber apart, leaving the lock and hinges hanging uselessly on the door frame.

Inside the shed a large dog lay on its side barely breathing, emaciated and exhausted from trying to claw out of its prison. Darius crouched down and ran his hands gently over the dog's body. The animal looked at me with eyes that were liquid, bright, and aware. My heart beat hard. I heard the dog's thoughts in my mind as clearly as if words were spoken, conveying a heartbreaking sadness and a plea for help.

Darius looked up at me with his bat eyes. "She doesn't seem to be injured, except where she's ripped open her paws trying to get through the door, but she's badly dehydrated and nearly starved. Her body temperature seems down a little, and had she been any other breed the cold would have killed her."

"What is she? She looks like a wolf," I asked feeling as if I were living in a dream.

Darius answered quickly. "She's a malamute. Maybe part wolf though. Let's get her someplace warm fast. How about your apartment?"

My apartment? My mind reeled; the world tilted on its axis. The whole episode was surreal. A few hours ago I had seen Darius with another woman. Before that I hadn't spoken with him in two months. Suddenly I was grappling with the fact that Darius was here, and that he was in bat form. Intellectually I knew that my biting Darius after he had been shot by terrorists had made him into a vampire. Now I was confronted with the reality of what I had done. Darius was monumental in size, his muscles rippled under a silvery pelt, and his long flowing hair did a wild dance in the wind. When he was close enough I observed that his eyes were silver where mine were gold. In all other respects, Darius's face remained unchanged. A jagged scar ran down the side of one cheek injecting an element of violence into his good looks. My body reacted to him with a powerful surge of physical attraction even as I comprehended that he wasn't the *man* I had loved any more. He was no longer human. He was a vampire. And as I stood in the moonlight on a Manhattan rooftop, my anger at him for rejecting me collided with my raw desire for him and my utter confusion as to why he was here.

With his thoughts seemingly far from mine, Darius effortlessly lifted the big dog into his arms and said, "Let's get your clothes first." Together we silently floated down along the front of the building, first checking that the street was empty of pedestrians or passing cars. All was quiet. It was the dead of night. I hit the ground and let myself revert back to human shape. In the few seconds I stood naked in the icy air, I saw Darius watching me. He shifted his eyes away and laid the dog down next to me. I squatted beside her and put my hand on her flank. "I'll be right back," Darius said and flew some yards away where a large cement planter held a potted evergreen. He moved behind it and emerged in the blink of an eye, dressed, and human-looking once more. He strode back to me, again lifted the dog, and I led the way into my building.

Once upstairs, Darius brought the dog into my kitchen. Not liking bright lights or the harsh gleam of white appliances, I had the cabinets and facings for the refrigerator and dishwasher made from weathered gray barn wood. Bright splashes of blues, reds, and yellows were added by Italian pitchers and platters from Caltagirone in Sicily and by a large pink chalkware pig won at a carnival long ago. The floor was slate, and the countertops granite. I could afford this luxury since I not only enjoyed a huge inheritance which was stashed in a Swiss bank account, but I had—and there's no nice way to say this—stolen a million dollars on my last assignment. I'm not a perfect creature, I have made a habit of lying, and I believe the Gypsy in my genes gives me a bent toward thievery.

While Darius waited with the dog in his arms, I grabbed an old quilt from a closet and spread it on the floor. Darius gently put the animal on it. "Offer her some water first," he directed. "Not a lot. We don't want her to get bloat. Just a cup at first."

I glanced over at Darius as I poured a small amount of liquid into a bowl. He was focused on the dog, deliberately avoiding my eyes. The tension between us was palpable no matter how hard Darius was trying to pretend it didn't exist. I set the water down, and the dog lifted her head and drank.

"What about food?" I asked.

"You have some meat?" Darius asked.

I nodded yes. I always had raw steaks on hand and opened the refrigerator to take them out.

"Any rice?" he added.

"A container left over from Chinese carry-out," I said and pulled that out too.

"Good. If you can run some hot water over the rice and put it in a bowl, I'll cut up the meat," he stated flatly. He chopped up a handful of porterhouse and mixed it with the rice. Once he put the mixture down on the floor, the dog struggled to sit, but settled for lying on her belly, the food bowl between her front paws. She gobbled its contents and looked up hopefully. "That's enough for now, poor girl," Darius told her, and she put her head down on her paws. She sighed, rolled onto her side, closed her eyes and fell asleep.

Finally Darius looked up at me, his expressionless face telling me nothing about his feelings. He continued talking about the dog. "I would say to call a vet tomorrow and take her in. I don't think she's injured. Just hungry and exhausted. But get her checked out."

"Darius—" I began, thinking to ask him why he had shown up on the roof, why he was here in my apartment, and so many other whys, but I quickly stopped short. Instead I said, "The dog is wearing a collar, and she has tags." I had discovered this when I had patted the dog earlier. Now, Darius reached down and slowly, without awakening her, lifted the tags so he could read them.

"What do they say?" I asked, moving so close to him I could feel the heat of his body.

"One's a rabies tag, so you'll be able to trace her owner through the registration number. The other is her name." Darius looked at the wall, not at me, as he spoke.

"Oh!" I said, and for some reason I felt so sad. "What is it?"

"Jada."

"Not Jade?"

"No, Jada. It's a family name, a famous breeding line of Canadian malamutes."

"Well, I am going to call her Jade," I decided. "Jade," I said gently, and the dog thumped her tail in her sleep.

Darius stood up, careful not to touch me, and we quietly backed out of the kitchen into my living room. There my overlong sofa was green, plush, and inviting. The wall sconces diffused peach-colored light, bathing everything in a cozy glow. And realizing that I had been cold for hours, I loved best of all that the room was warm.

"Well, I guess I'll be going," Darius said, and started for the door.

My eyes widened and the words I hadn't said before practically exploded from my mouth. "*You guess you'll be going?* Are you out of your mind? I haven't talked to you in nearly two months. You can't just drop out of the sky, fall back into my life, and then say, 'I guess I'll be going.'"

"What do you *want* me to say?" he replied as he stood there with his hands at his sides, his body rigid with tension, his face hard, and his voice laced with bitterness.

I felt anger and hurt welling up in me, but I pulled the emotions back. Screaming at Darius wouldn't get me anywhere. I had to take control, try a different tack. "Darius," I said, keeping my voice steady and low, "I don't *want* you to say anything, but I do have some questions, and I would very much like to talk with you."

He looked at me with eyes that were filled with pain. "All

the words in the world can't change what happened to me, Daphne."

"That's true. But maybe they can change how you feel about it," I said as an edge crept unbidden into my voice.

His face was defined by lines and angles, and any softness in it was gone. I could see the muscle working in his jaw. "I don't know," he said, turning his eyes back to me. "Maybe I can never accept this change. I am no longer a man. I don't know what I am. A monster. A creature I hate."

Overcome by compassion, I crossed to him and took his hand. He didn't pull away. "You are still Darius della Chiesa. You need to believe that," I said as our eyes locked. A sexual charge jumped between us. The connection was still there. Darius reached out his hand and encircled the back of my neck, pulling my face to his and touching his forehead to mine.

"I feel as if I'm in hell, Daphne," he whispered. "I feel trapped in a nightmare I can't escape." I reached my hands up and cupped his face. His lips touched mine, softly, gently. Relief and desire poured over me.

Then Darius pulled back. There was still anguish in his eyes, but he gave me a half smile. "It's good to see you, Daphne," he said.

"Let's sit down"—I suggested as a surge of heat started at my toes. I tried to ignore my hormones—"and just talk."

"Daphne," he said. "I don't know if I can *just talk* to you. Maybe I should go."

That was the last thing I wanted to happen. "Look, Darius. I'd appreciate it if you'd stay a while. And besides," I said in a harder voice, "you owe me some answers."

He raised an eyebrow at that. "Answers? About what?" he said.

"Well let's start with how the hell you showed up on the roof in the middle of the night while I'm fighting with three vampire hunters," I said, my voice rising.

He looked at me, his old rakish grin stealing back. "That one's easy. I was following you."

"You were? For how long?" Incredulity washed over me.

He picked up my hand and shocked me by kissing my fingers. "From the time you left Kevin St. James."

"No shit," I said, dumbfounded, my eyes widening. "I didn't spot you."

"You never do," he said, teasing me the way he used to.

"You mean you've followed me before? I mean recently." He stalled for a second, not answering. "Darius, come on, you have to tell me."

"Yes."

"But when, why? We were broken up but it was your choice, not mine. If you wanted to see me, why didn't you just call me?"

"It wasn't that simple, Daphne. I wanted to see you, but I didn't *want* to want to see you, if you get what I'm saying."

"No, I don't get it," I said, feeling pissed. "That's so stupid. We could have been together all these weeks. You made me suffer for nothing. I mean that's just—"

"Shhh," he said and put a finger on my lips. "Yes, it was stupid. I was stupid. You're right." Serious and sad at the same time, he looked away as he spoke. "But Daphne, I was, and probably still sort of am, deeply angry at what you had done—first the bite, then my transformation into a vampire."

I interrupted and started to explain, "But Darius, you were dying. It was the only thing I could do to save your life. . . ."

"Yes, I know that. And I understand why you did it." He folded both my hands in his and peered intently into my face. "But Daphne, I was a soldier. I always accepted that I could die in battle. I was willing, if it came to that, to make the ultimate sacrifice and give my life for my country. I was proud of who and what I was. You took that away from me. I can't be proud of myself now. I can't even show the world who I am. Do you see? You made me what you wanted me to be, but you took away everything I had worked so hard to become."

I snatched my hands away from his. His words hurt. He was right on one level and so very wrong on another. My voice was defensive, and I was feeling aggrieved as I spat out, "So shoot me, Darius. Keep beating me up because you had to change. Get with it. Life is about change. Nothing is permanent. Maybe I made you a vampire—but that was your fate. Dozens of other things could have changed you, but the card you got dealt was me. Now deal with it. Stop blaming me."

Thunderclouds crossed his face. He stood up and I could see how angry he was. It was the kind of moment when a guy often walks out, slamming the door. But Darius didn't go, I give him that. He stared at the far wall, not at me, while he talked. "Daphne, what you say is true, but try to understand my feelings in all this." He turned toward me, his eyes burning with intensity. "I'm trying to adjust. I'm trying to find my way. Suddenly I'm so strong, I can fight like an animal. I am as powerful as ten ordinary men. I am amazed by what I can do. But I'm in a black place. A valley without light. I don't know where I'm going. Maybe I have turned my rage 'at my fate' at you. But *you* turned my world upside down. First you showed me, a vampire hunter, that I could love the very thing I had hated for so long. And then you transformed me from the man I was into an undead creature that I didn't, and I still don't, understand. Got it?"

"I got it," I said and walked over to him, taking both of his hands in mine. "I'm truly sorry for any pain I caused you. That wasn't my intention." Tears filled my eyes.

"Oh hell, Daphne, I know that. I'm the one who should apologize—for being an asshole about everything," he said, and pulled me tightly against him, body to body. He kissed me forcefully, pushing his tongue into my mouth. I kissed him back. My arms went up around his neck and I held on for dear life. The thrill of his kiss traveled in a shivery arrow down my body to set me on fire with a burning urge for him. He and I together had always been lightning in a bottle. That chemistry had not changed.

Then abruptly Darius stopped kissing me. His fingers tightened on my waist before he took a step back, letting out a breath. "Maybe we should take it slow," he said.

"Taking it slow may kill me," I murmured.

"What did you say?" he said.

"Never mind," I answered. "We agreed to 'just talk.' So that's cool," I said, but I didn't feel cool. I felt hot and frustrated. My brain said it might be emotional suicide to climb back into bed with Darius. He had a lot of "issues," as they say. But my body wasn't cooperating. His kiss made my knees weak. I didn't want to be rational. I wanted to be down and dirty, lost in mindless pleasure. Maybe I'd regret it later. Not maybe. I was sure I'd regret it later, but I was already leaning toward him and he wasn't pulling back.

"You smell of pine forests and soap," I said and brushed my lips across his cheek, and licked his ear.

"You smell like a woman, Daphne," he sighed. "Sweet and musky." His arms tightened around me. "Your heart's pounding," he said. "I can feel it. I haven't kissed you in weeks," he murmured. "I dream about kissing you."

"Then just do it," I said softly. I was seducing him, and I knew it.

"I want to, Daphne," he said. "I want to make love to you. Can you forgive me for being so stupid about everything?"

My fingers were already unzipping his jacket. Then I was unbuttoning his shirt and sliding it off his shoulders. "Come to bed, Darius," I said. "Come with me."

I looked at him, and there was hurt in his eyes where I wanted to see love.

The mattress sighed as we lay upon it, the sheets whispered beneath us. Darius's hands were cool against my flesh as he stripped off my clothes. He stopped and kissed the places on my legs where the vampire hunter had smashed into them and bruises were already beginning to be purple. Then he laid his cheek next to my heart, and I touched his cool hair. He raised himself over me, and with no urgency, but with a tremble, slid his stiff member inside me.

His name escaped my lips like a sigh. His pace was achingly slow. He stared into my eyes the whole while. I was nearly crazy with lust, my breath coming fast, but Darius was not to be hurried. He was gentle, stroking me, savoring each touch. The warm wet of me enveloped him as he took my hands, palm to palm, in his, interlacing his fingers with mine. In this joining, there was only pleasure, the joy of being together again, of losing ourselves within each other. In a moment of golden beauty, we climaxed together.

Later, locked in an embrace, I let my fingers trail across his back, feeling how strong it was. Darius turned his face toward me. He planted kisses on my hair. And wrapped together, we fell asleep, me believing that we could work things out and that this sweet coming together was a new beginning, not an end.

We woke many hours later to the sound of barking. The blinds and blackout curtains of my apartment were shut fast against even a sliver of morning light. Darius could not leave until dusk. I could not venture into the day. And Jade clearly wanted to go out.

"Oh shit," I said. "What am I going to do?"

"Call somebody. A non-vampire somebody," Darius suggested as he sleepily threw on his jeans and walked barefoot into the kitchen. "I'll make coffee."

"Right." I phoned the super who lived in the basement apartment of the building. "Jerry, I need a giant favor," I said. "I need you to walk my dog. What? Yeah, I have a dog. What? Yeah I'll make it worth your while. A hundred? Only if you get up here in five minutes. After that it's fifty." Bless his heart, Jerry didn't ask why I wasn't taking the dog out myself. Money talks. I also grabbed the Yellow Pages and found a dog-walking service. Next I called a vet who had night appointments.

Darius padded back in with a mug of coffee for me, Jade following him with a grin on her doggy face. She was a beautiful dog, with a long thick coat of white fur on her feet and belly, gray and black on her back and head. Even half-starved she weighed over eighty pounds I guessed. Her eyes were yellow and strangely wise.

I put on a long T-shirt and an old pair of jeans. The door buzzer rang. I yelled out, "Just a minute!" to Jerry. To Darius I said, "I need your belt." He looked at me quizzically. "I don't have a leash." He handed over the belt and I threaded it through Jade's collar.

I walked Jade over to the door and opened it. "Go with the nice man," I told her as I handed the buckle end of the belt to Jerry. Jade's tail wagged vigorously, and she did a little dance.

"Holy shit, she's big," Jerry said. He looked at the belt end in his hand. "Miss Urban, I'm going to have to walk bent over, if this is all you have," he complained.

"Hold on a minute," I said. I went into the bedroom and pulled a twenty from my wallet, came back, and handed it to him. "Buy her a leash while you're out. And give her a good walk. I don't want to see you for a half hour. And, Jerry," I virtually snarled. "She better look happy when she gets back."

"Right, Miss Urban. Come on, good doggy," he said and started for the elevator. Before he and Jade got on, he glanced back over his shoulder with a cunning look on his pockmarked face. "A half hour will cost one twenty-five."

"Get the hell out of here, Jerry!" I said and closed the door.

Once Jade left, I thought about making love again with Darius. The desire was there, and I could see it in his eyes.

But I wasn't going to make the first move. I sat on the sofa sipping my coffee. Last night I had just about thrown myself at Darius. He had been more than willing to catch me, sure, yet I still had my pride. Part of me wanted him groveling at my feet begging my forgiveness again for being an asshole; part of me wanted him so overcome by lust he was coming at me like a caveman. Instead Darius did neither. He seemed moody, introverted, and distant. Even when we sat on the sofa with our second cups of coffee and our feet touching, I felt his emotional withdrawal. And there were still questions I hadn't asked, and I still needed answers. I decided to plunge in with them.

"Darius," I said. "Do you know anything about the vampire hunters last night?"

"Like what?" he said, avoiding my eyes.

"Like who they were?"

"I didn't recognize them. I don't have any reason to believe they were from my agency, if that's what you mean."

"Well, who could they be? How did they find me? Do you have any ideas?"

His eyes shifted away, and I had the feeling he was going to lie to me. "Yeah, I have some ideas, Daphne. It's why I shouldn't be around you. I think they followed me and found you."

"Are you sure?" I said, although the same thought had already occurred to me.

"No. I'm not sure." His voice was louder.

"Darius, one of them nearly killed me! Tell me what you know. Have they been following you?"

"It's possible I was followed although I've never spotted them. I've had this gut feeling a few times that I was being watched, but nothing specific." He paused, then his voice took on an edge. "And you know, Daphne, they could have been following you. J hasn't exactly kept the Darkwings a big secret. Many people in the intelligence community have heard rumors about him using vampires. The hunters could have found out about the Darkwings and staked out your office. Who knows? I'm just guessing, that's all. But they're professionals, Daphne. And they're extremely dangerous. I should know, I was one."

"I'm dangerous too," I said with a voice as hard as steel. "And I'm also careful. I don't believe they followed me as a Darkwing. Don't try to shift this onto J. Now the question is—why are they after you?"

"I don't know," Darius said, and I didn't believe him.

"Darius, when are you going to level with me? I'm being dragged into this and I don't know why. What are you into?" He was pushing my buttons. I was getting agitated fast. I was feeling pissed off and more than a little worried. "Look, I have a right to know, Darius. It now involves me."

"And that's exactly why I should stay away from you," he said with angry conviction.

I felt like going ballistic, but I didn't. I took a deep breath. Fighting wasn't going to solve anything. Instead I told myself that women and men have their own ways of looking at things. I chose my words deliberately, trying to defuse the emotions that were escalating into the red zone. "Darius, I care about you. And I do know you care about me. We have emotions for each other that won't be denied, even if we try to pretend we can. It would be painful to not see each other, and at this point it might not make any difference since the vampire hunters have already identified me. And we're both vampires now. If there's a problem, don't you think it might be more effective to tackle it together?" I asked rationally.

Darius sighed. "I've always taken risks without worrying about how those risks were going to affect somebody who cared about me. Other SEALs in my unit had wives and families. I never felt I should if I couldn't promise that I wouldn't come home in a box one day. I'm only going to hurt you, Daphne, one way or another. You're better off without me."

"That's one way to look at it, Darius. I know you think you're right, but you're also being selfish. Love may be worth risking the pain of loss. The alternative is not loving at all."

Darius didn't answer right away. His eyes betrayed his torment, and he looked at me with naked longing. "Maybe you're right, Daphne, but you almost got killed," was all he said when he finally spoke, then his eyes looked away from mine. A wall went back up between us. "I think I'll take a shower," he said and started toward the bathroom. "Let's talk about this later, okay?"

"Okay," I conceded. "But, Darius, there is something else I need to ask you," I called after him.

"What?" he answered as he walked.

"Who was that girl I saw you with at the pub?"

He paused and looked back over his shoulder, his face registering some surprise. "You mean Julie? She's just somebody working with me on a project, that's all." He shrugged and shut the bathroom door, closing me out emotionally once more.

The buzzer rang and Jerry returned Jade along with a brand-new leash. He had actually kept her out a good forty-five minutes, so I gave him his $125 and thanked him. The dog-walking service promised to pick her up around three in the afternoon, so I knew I'd have to set my alarm. She and I marched into the kitchen and I made her up another bowl of rice and steak. If she suffered any lingering ill effects from her imprisonment, she didn't show it. I knelt down next to her. "Jade," I said to her. Her tail banged joyfully against the floor. "Jade. I don't know who owned you or why you were left to die, but nothing and no one will ever hurt you again. You are mine now. That okay with you?" She licked my face and I knew without a doubt she understood every word.

CHAPTER 4

We loved, sir—used to meet:
How sad and bad and mad it was—
But then, how it was sweet!

—"Confessions" by Robert Browning

Darius and I passed the rest of the day in sleep, he on the couch and me in my coffin with the ritual handful of Transylvanian soil under my satin mattress cover. Vampires aren't required to sleep in coffins, although it is traditional. I always have done so. It appeals to my rather macabre sense of humor, for one thing. It reminds me, as if I needed reminding, of my undead status—this coffin is a final resting place I will never need since I shall either live forever or blow away as a handful of dust.

My sleeping atop the soil of Transylvania is more pragmatic. The soil is a connection with my ancestors, but also a source of energy. Within the Earth itself lies a primeval force. Whether a person lies on rock or sand, grass, dry dirt, or buoyant ocean surface, she will feel a joining with the most ancient of powers. All living things need that connection, and yet humans, especially, are always breaking the link. Foolish creatures, aren't we, humans and vampires both? And I, a woman as well as a vampire, am one of the most foolish creatures of all, blinded to reality by my girlish longings and silly dreams.

When the winter evening fell at last and Jade was already back from her walk with her new dog-walking service, I arose from my satin-lined crypt to find Darius awake and dressed, sitting at the kitchen counter. I liked seeing him there, and I smiled. "What are you doing?" I asked sleepily. I wore a bright orange Collective Soul tour T-shirt; my legs and feet were bare. I yawned and pushed my tangled hair off my face.

"I've got to get going," he said, keeping his eyes down. "I was writing you a note." He ripped a sheet off the notepad I leave on the counter and crumpled it up in his fist.

"A note?" I asked, snapping awake.

"I was just explaining, you know," he said lamely.

"Explaining what?" My voice was thin and high.

"That I should stay away from you until I figure things out, get my head straight, you know."

"I don't understand," I said, feeling utterly confused. "Didn't you say last night that staying apart had been, I think your word was *stupid.* Why can't we work this out together?"

I held my breath as the silence lengthened between us. I didn't know what he was going to say, but I expected more of the "I have to find myself" argument. I never expected to hear the words he finally said. "Because I love you, Daphne." He reached out and took my hands in his. "I love you, Daphne, and it's eating me up inside. We're both vampires now, but that doesn't solve the real problem. I don't know who I am anymore, true, but the real difficulty is I've already started something that might put you in danger. I never expected us to have a second chance. I was so *stupid,* yes stupid, not to acknowledge my feelings for you, and now maybe I've already screwed things up beyond repair. I can't be with you and figure it out. I need time, Daphne. And time, I understand, is something we both have plenty of."

Hurt and anger gathered inside of me like a hurricane beginning to spin on the black, cold ocean. The words exploded from me. "Time? *Now* is what we have, Darius. Only now. The past is gone. The future doesn't exist—and may never exist. We only have now." I jerked my hands away from his and folded them up under my armpits.

"Daphne, I'm sorry but—"

I interrupted Darius as the words continued to spew out of me. "You're 'sorry but—' You know what, Darius? You couldn't commit to a relationship when we first met either. You always had an excuse. You haven't really changed, Darius. You are still the same inside of you as you were before I bit you."

"How do *you* know what's inside of *me!* Don't tell me how I am!" His voice became louder until he was yelling. "I'm different now. I'm not human anymore. I don't even know if I'm a man anymore!" His rage was nearly palpable.

In the kitchen I could hear Jade begin to growl. She had heard my raised voice and was on the alert. She came to the doorway. Her hackles were up. Her body was tense. Her eyes bored right into mine. "It's okay," I said to her. She lay down and watched Darius. And in that moment, I had an idea. Something that Darius had said became terribly clear and I knew what I had to do.

"You are a man, Darius," I said calmly. "I'll prove it to you," I said and went over to him, putting my arms around him and pressing my lips to his. He groaned then, and embraced me. "Ohmygod, I want you, Daphne. I don't deserve you, but I can't stop wanting you," he said and picked me up in his arms.

He carried me to the couch, laid me down, and pulled off my T-shirt. He stopped and looked at me. "Do you want me to do this?" he asked.

In reply I sat up and grabbed the belt of his pants and pulled him closer to me. I unbuckled his belt, unbuttoned his trousers, and unzipped his fly. He was hard and ready. I took his penis into my hand and he moaned, putting his hands into my hair as I took him into my mouth. He started saying my name over and over. I sucked deeply, running my tongue along his shaft. I could feel him trembling as his shaft became rigid as steel. He groaned again, and whispered, "Oh my God, Daphy, oh my God. Oh harder, please suck me harder." I did, but not wanting him to come yet and needing him inside me, I suddenly stopped and leaned back.

Darius climbed over me. Poised above me, his weight on his arms on either side of my head, he moved his hips forward and in one violent movement entered me so quickly I nearly screamed. He pumped into me as I sought his lips with my mouth. The sensation was exquisite as he alternated between long slow strokes and fast short thrusts. We kissed long and deep as we both rose toward climax, a wave leaping higher until it crashed down on us both. Darius broke the kiss and arched his back, letting out a deep, primitive moan, spilling his hot seed within me. Staying inside me, he pulled me to him and rolled onto his side, holding me in his arms. I burrowed my face next to his neck, and the temptation rose up in me to bite him. I fought the dark urges, feeling shameful that I could not control them. Darius's voice broke into my thoughts: "Bite me, Daphne, bite me."

He wanted this. My inhibitions disappeared. I couldn't resist and so I pierced his skin with my little sharp teeth and drank in the salty hot blood of him. Never had I experienced anything like this; never had I known a love between vampires before. I seemed to be filled with pearly light, a euphoria that took away my senses, and I thought no more. The world dissolved and was replaced by a phantasmagoria of brightly colored dreams, while Darius's hard-muscled arms held me tight and his sighs echoed in my ears. I climaxed again and again until, fearing I was drinking too much, I lifted my mouth. A trickle of blood ran down his throat from the puncture wounds I left. I touched his blood with my fingertips in wonder. I was enraptured, nearly mad with my lust for him.

And it was not yet over. Darius tenderly pushed my long black hair from off my long white neck. My heart began to race as I realized what he was about to do. I had not been bitten for over four hundred years. Fear and excitement mixed in my breast, but I had no time to react for Darius's teeth suddenly entered my skin, almost cruelly keeping me pinned, like a wolf holding a rabbit in his jaws. "Ohhh," I cried out, and then I was lost. I had become both his prey and his lover. I became incandescent, I felt the rattling closeness of death and soared beyond it. My body shook and I screamed with pleasure. Whatever else I was—a vampire princess, a spy, a woman—turned meaningless, for what I became in that hideous drinking was his creature. Panic briefly overtook me but then I felt a strange peace and surrendered utterly to him.

When it was over, after we lay there for a while clinging to each other, I finally opened my eyes and found myself looking into the wide-open ones of Darius. What I saw there was anguish and horror.

"What have I done?" he said, and he turned his face away. I thought he was going to cry.

"We both did it, Darius," I answered. "It's okay."

He closed his eyes, and his body trembled. "I know what we did, Daphne, and it scares me. When I say I don't know who I am, this is part of it. I have done things with you I never imagined I would or could do. I am afraid of it happening again, Daphne. I'm afraid I will lose myself . . . to madness, I think. Drinking your blood took me somewhere I . . . I just don't understand." He released me then and covered his face with his hands for a moment.

Then he shook himself. "I have to get going," he said with a flat voice and stood up, dressing quickly. He took his jacket from the chair where he had tossed it. "I have to get to work."

"I don't think you should leave right now," I said. "You're upset, Darius."

He looked stricken. "It was a mistake, Daphne—" he started to say.

"A mistake! It most definitely was not a mistake," I blurted out. "We did this together. I wanted it."

"You're not listening to me," he shot back. "You just don't hear what I'm saying. This is not all about you! Yes *you* wanted it. You wanted me to be a vampire too. I'm a blood-drinking monster now. Like *you*. Haven't you done enough!" He went to the door. I sat up and watched him, trying to sort out my feelings. Jade came over and lay at my feet, deliberately, I feel, putting her big body between me and him.

Darius opened the door and then looked back at me. "Oh yeah, check your message machine. Your dear saintly mother called before you got up," he said sarcastically and left.

"Screw you and the horse you rode in on!" I yelled after him. Jade barked. I think she was saying the same thing.

I made him a monster?! I huffed. *I made him a vampire, a member of a long and noble race. He was nothing but a vampire hunter before I bit him. If that's not a monster, what is?* I thought. *Well, if he thinks I'm going to sit around here waiting for him to find himself, he's got another think coming.* Suddenly I had the chills. I felt absolutely miserable. Maybe I was coming down with the flu. I grabbed a tissue and blew my nose. Wrapping myself in a blanket along with my righteous anger, I clomped over to the phone. Sure enough the message light was blinking urgently. There were two calls:

The first was from Benny. "Daphy, honey? Did you open your envelope? Where are you being sent tonight? I've been assigned to the most darling place, the Silverleaf Tavern on East Thirty-eighth Street. It's just so about wine. It's so chic!

Oh I hope we're together. I'm dying to talk to you. Call me! Byeeeee."

The second was my mother, Marozia Urban, or Mar-Mar as her friends call her. "Daphne, sweetheart? It's your mother." *As if I didn't know!* "I'm going to drop by, hmmmm, no later than six o'clock I think. I need to talk to you before you go out. See you and remember, power to the people!"

Oh shit, I thought. Actually I thought, *Oh shit and make it a double.* My mother never just "drops in." She always has a reason. She could just be bringing me a new type of tofu burger, but her motives are usually far more devious. No doubt she wanted to either find out something from me . . . or about me.

Crap! I said to myself as the realization hit me. She must know that Darius was here. But how would she know that . . . unless my building were under surveillance? *Daphne! Hellllo!* I said to myself. *How well do you know your mother? Of course your building is under surveillance.*

My mother, whose ultimate goal I truly believe is to save the world, has always been a do-gooder, but a do-gooder with an immense amount of pull. In Renaissance Europe she had been the power behind more than one throne as well as the lover of a pope, who, I later discovered, had been my father. Well, he had sort of been a pope. Urban VII, or Giambattista Castagna, died only twelve days after he was elected and before he actually took office. The official story is that he died of malaria. My mother always said he was murdered. That would be no shocker. A vampire as head of the Catholic Church would have been their biggest scandal yet, and they've had some whoppers. Mar-Mar, of course, insists he was murdered because of his politics. With my mother, politics is the motive behind every dark deed, yet she relishes being in the middle of political intrigue.

To be honest I don't know much about her past, before she had me, that is. She won't talk about it, and has rarely said anything about my father. Whatever happened then, during the mid-sixteenth century when I was born, remains a closed book. I do know her relationship with the Church has been both a dangerous and stormy one, and the Vatican has remained her greatest enemy.

On a more intimate note, she cannot stop meddling in my love life. She has always insisted that I should only date vampires, preferably ones from notable families. *Who else can a vampire trust except one of our own? Who else can understand us, except one of our own?* That's what she's always said. She has a point, but she keeps fixing me up with the worst losers in the world. Usually they are five-hundred-year-old guys who still live at home with their mothers. She just doesn't seem to get it about the need for "chemistry" and having something in common besides vampire status. *You'll learn to love each other,* she says.

From the first, she hasn't liked Darius. After all, he was a vampire hunter. Even though he's now a vampire, she doesn't feel he's one of us, and she doesn't want me seeing him. I needed to prepare myself for being royally reamed out for being back in Darius's arms even for one night. Honest to God, it really was none of Mar Mar's business. But you trying telling her that. I certainly have.

Just then a more urgent thought broke into my musings about my mother. *The envelope from J. Crap!* Before Benny called, I had forgotten all about it. Sex and Darius had been a dangerous distraction. Getting careless could get me killed. I needed to focus on my job. I retrieved the envelope from my bedroom (my coffin is not in there, by the way; my coffin is in a secret room behind the bookcases in the entry hall). I ripped it open. My instructions were to return to Kevin St. James. A wave of disappointment washed over me. Why should Benny be sent to a sophisticated wine restaurant while I had to go back to an Irish pub? Life wasn't fair. Just as I was thinking that thought, another, from the devilish side of my brain, broke in. *You can see Fitz again.*

According to Jennifer, the bartender, Fitz came in nearly every weekday around six thirty. There was no guarantee he'd be there on a Saturday night, but maybe he would. Did I want to see Fitz again after what had happened last night with Darius? No. But after the way things had ended with Darius tonight, the answer became a resounding *Yes!* I guess if I analyzed my feelings, the urge to see Fitz was either to show Darius that other men wanted me, or to get my ego stroked, or to forget that I was losing hope that Darius and I would ever work things out. Put an X next to "all of the above." That Fitz was tall, dark, and handsome—a real John F. Kennedy, Jr., lookalike—didn't hurt. No, that didn't hurt at all.

Realizing I'd better hurry and get dressed, it struck me that I had to talk to Benny about going with me for some retail therapy. If I was going out every night, I needed some serious new clothes. I had spotted a few designers who were so hot this season they were on fire. One specialized in really cute tops—that was Charlotte Tarantola, whose company was called Brain Surgery. The other designer was Cynthia Steffe. And ohmygod, her stuff was so *me.* Neiman Marcus had this scrumptious Cynthia Steffe jacket with brown fur at the seams, the fabric was shot through with green metallic thread, and it was snugly fitted with a single button front. It was love at first sight, and I had already ordered it online. But I needed *more.* Nothing made me feel better faster than shopping.

Deciding I'd call Benny from my cell phone later, I rushed into the shower, washed my hair, came out, and started pulling outfits out of my closet. I needed some real *payback* clothes for tonight. I intended to look hot and sexy as hell. I settled on a pair of tight jeans but rejected the raspberry cami I really wanted to wear. With fang marks on my throat, I had to go with a black turtleneck, but at least this one was clingy and sheer with cutouts that showed my shoulders and a deep cutout that bared my back. I had gotten it the last time I went to Houston to the Galleria. And yes, it's true, I flew all the way to Texas from New York just to shop. My name is Daphne and I'm a shopaholic.

Shopping and clothes aside, I also have a soft spot for animals of all kinds. On my last assignment I had rescued a white rat named Gunther. We had become roommates of sorts. His cage sat near the windows in my bedroom, and he was now standing up on his hind legs, clutching the bars with his little pink hands like a prisoner. He was fairly hopping up and down as he chattered at Jade, who had just come sauntering into the bedroom. He was one pissed-off rat, that was for sure.

"Hey," I said. "I don't blame you for being upset. But you two have got to get along." Jade walked over to the cage and pushed it with her snout. I just watched, ready to intervene if I had to.

"Woof," she said softly. "Woof." Gunther looked down at her with almost human concern in his worried eyes. "Woof," she said again and returned his stare. A moment passed where neither of them moved. Then her tail wagged softly. She spun around and settled herself down on the rug. Gunther got back down on all fours and walked calmly over to his exercise wheel. A message had been exchanged between them, and the peaceable kingdom reigned.

I went back to getting dressed, putting on ankle-high Manolo boots in leopard print with a four-inch heel. They made my legs look as if they reached all the way to Montreal. Dangling earrings, each featuring four teardrop pearls, and a rigid gold circle necklace with a lavalier holding a huge natural pearl—it looked somewhat like an upside-down ice-cream cone— finished off my outfit. I stared at myself in the full-length mirror on my closet door. All was perfection. *Darius, eat your heart out, and Fitz, you poor, poor boy. You don't stand a chance.*

My preening was rudely interrupted by the front door's buzzer. Mar-Mar had arrived.

* * *

Just as night took a firm grip on the city, Mar-Mar Urban, once beloved by popes and kings, her arms filled with shopping bags, used her butt to push open the door of my apartment. Dressed in a deep green velvet tunic over jeans, Lucchese cowboy boots on her feet, and a hand-knitted Peruvian cap on her dark hair, my mother looked younger than I do. Despite this youthful appearance, she has probably celebrated the big one-oh-oh-oh. She has never told me her birth date, withholding that information as she had hidden so many other things from me. Mar-Mar is deceptive in appearance, Machiavellian in manner, and genuine only in her emotions. However, I also know she has never let her emotions interfere with achieving her goals.

"*Caro mia,* my heart!" she called to me as she deposited the bags on a nearby chair. She reached up with mittened hands to push my hair out of my eyes. I leaned down and kissed her cheek. She smelled of crisp night air.

Mar-Mar dispensed with her mittens and began pulling items from the shopping bags, depositing them on my dining-room table. "I went shopping in the East Village last night. I bought you some things I couldn't resist." One of the items she couldn't resist was an intensely pink candle with a pearly opalescence. Its wax was sprinkled with something glittery, and the long, thin candle had an eerie glow about it. "This is a witch's spell-casting candle," Mar-Mar explained. "It comes with an incantation and this little jar of 'pigeon blood.' "

"Pigeon blood?" I made a face.

"Oh, don't look like that. I'm sure it's only red ink," she scolded. "The instructions for the spell are right here. If you do everything just right, it will attract true love, or so the card-reader told me," she said guilelessly and gave me a sly look. "I had my cards read, too. They predicted a long life," Mar-Mar added with a giggle.

"I also found a wonderful new yoga DVD. I know you're into that," she added.

"Thanks, Ma," I said warily, suspecting that she hadn't stopped in just to give me presents.

Then she pulled out a copy of that day's *New York Times,* folded so the last pages of the first section faced outward. An article was marked off in ink. She handed it to me. Then she dove back into the bags and extracted sections from two other New York papers, the *Daily News* and *New York Post.* These editions had been published earlier in the week. Both also had stories highlighted with a pen. She handed them to me too. At a glance I could see the headlines: *Mysterious Death Probed* in the *Times, Beast Stalks; Druggies Hide* from the *Daily News,* and *Horror Haunts Hoodlums* from the *Post.*

"You need to read these," Mar-Mar said, her voice suddenly grim. "I don't know for sure"—she said. *Yeah, right,* I thought as she continued—"but I think your Darius has decided to become a vampire vigilante."

I looked down at the newspapers and scanned the articles quickly, my heart pounding all the while. Maybe this was what Darius had meant about already "starting something." Even so, I wasn't going to voice my suspicions to Mar-Mar. "None of these stories talk about anybody dying from blood loss," I countered. "Nobody had fang marks on his throat."

"Well, dear, Darius was a professional assassin. You know that. He's not going to be sloppy about his work. He's not biting anybody, at least in these articles he's not. The drug dealer discussed in the *Times* article appears to have died from fright. But his companions were found in a state of shock, babbling about a giant bat. Similar sightings are mentioned in both the other articles. It sounds like a vampire who doesn't know the rules—or doesn't care about them—to me."

"There is no reason to suspect that Darius has anything to do with this," I answered defensively.

"Oh yes there is, Daphne Urban, and you know it." Her hands were on her hips and her voice was strident. "You know full well that vampires take great care to keep a low profile. We had enough of torch-carrying mobs trying to hunt us down in the Middle Ages. Today, to the world at large, we're just a myth—officially. We are aware that the Church has vampire hunters dispatched around the globe. But their numbers are small. If ordinary citizens insist we're real, they're not taken seriously." She paused and said in a voice like a hammer driving in nails, "It's essential that does not change. For all our sakes. And Daphne, for Darius's own sake, these public appearances can't continue to occur."

It was hard to hear what she was saying and hard to look at her. My heart grew heavy as lead. "Yes, Ma, you're right. But I really don't know if it's Darius."

"Well, find out. Talk with him."

"I don't know that I will see him," I said sadly.

"Oh for heaven's sake, Daphne, stop being a drama queen. The man is obsessed with you. I have no reason to believe you will not see him again. Daphne, you need to stop him, or . . ."

"Or what," I said with apprehension clear in my voice.

"Or he'll be eliminated," she said as flatly as if she had told me she had roaches in her kitchen and needed to call the exterminator.

"You wouldn't!" I exploded. "How could you do that to me!"

"I wouldn't. Some others in our community would. They don't give a rat's ass about you. I do," she said, each word cutting me as sharply as a razor blade. The real Mar-Mar, the one I know and most others don't, the woman who was not a bit cute, cuddly, or giggly, was speaking now. Mar-Mar behind the mask was a ruthless "off with their heads" Red Queen who was capable of wielding more power than I could ever imagine. She went on with the life-and-death decree she was handing me. "That's why I'm telling you. Talk to him, and stop him. Before it's too late."

My heart was beating wildly. Would Darius listen to me? I didn't think so. Would he feel threatened enough to stop whatever it was he had started? I doubted if he could be intimidated or scared off. The situation was bad. No matter how I looked at it, it spelled trouble for everybody. "If it's him, I'll stop him," I said, not believing a word of what I was saying, but trying to buy time while I figured out what to do.

"I hope so, Daphne. I don't want to see you hurt, you know that. But I don't want vampire hunters from all over the world descending on Manhattan to declare open season on us. You do understand the gravity of this, don't you?"

"Yes, Ma. I do," I affirmed, and to the very marrow of my bones, I did.

"And there's an item of spy business I need to bring to your attention. . . ." she began as she wandered around my apartment, idly looking at my mail and openly scrutinizing my cell-phone bill before I gently took it from her hands. Then she came to the kitchen door and stopped in her tracks. "Oh. That's the dog you brought in here last night," she said as Jade stood in front of her, staring straight into her eyes.

"That's Jade," I said. "How did you know about her? Are you keeping tabs on me, Mar-Mar?" Even as the words left my mouth, a suspicion formed in my brain. "Mar-Mar, have you bugged my apartment?"

"Daphne! What an idea! I wouldn't invade your privacy like that," she protested.

My eyes narrowed. "Swear to it."

Mar-Mar stamped her foot. "I swear I haven't planted any listening devices in your apartment."

I just looked at her. She had been as careful as Bill Clinton choosing his words to answer questions about Monica Lewinsky. All she had sworn to was that she personally hadn't planted any bugs.

Changing the subject, Mar-Mar asked, "Do you think you can take care of a dog?" She was looking at Jade, who stared back unmoving.

"Certainly I can," I said peevishly. "Why do you even ask?"

"Maybe I meant, do you think you can take care of this dog. This dog is . . ."

"What?"

"I'm not sure," she confessed.

"She's a dog, Ma. That's all. A good dog. And I'm keeping her."

Neither Mar-Mar nor Jade had moved a muscle. Neither had given an inch. There was no fear or hostility visible in either of them. They just seemed to be taking each other's measure. "Okay then. Just don't be too trusting. I think she's a positive force. But there's something about her. Something more than a dog."

"She may be part wolf."

"That might be what I sense. The wildness." Mar-Mar gave a little nod at Jade but made no move to step closer to her. Jade blinked and turned around, put her back toward Mar-Mar and lay down, curling her plumed tail around her nose. Clearly, she and Mar-Mar were two alpha females, and they had settled on a truce instead of a battle for domination, at least for now.

Mar-Mar turned back toward me. "As I was saying, one thing I need to tell you about the drug assignment, the one given to the team last night—"

"What about it?" I asked as I picked up my small leather backpack and put my cell phone inside.

"If you see me in a club, on the street, or, well, anywhere you wouldn't expect to see me, you don't know me."

My eyebrows raised in surprise. "You're working the case too?" I asked.

"To some extent. I feel it's urgent to get as much information as we can as fast as we can. I've assigned myself to the East Village, around Second Avenue and St. Mark's Place. That was, after all, my old home ground," she said with lightness back in her voice.

"Well, you are an expert on drugs," I said sarcastically. She knows I hate her pot-smoking habit.

"Marijuana never killed anyone, dear," she said sweetly. "But yes, I did learn a lot about drugs as a child of the sixties."

"Child? You were nine hundred and fifty years old."

"Now, Daphne, don't be flip. It doesn't become you. I raised you to be a lady. You know I felt so in synch with that era. I was a hippie in my very soul. Young people in that decade truly wanted to change the world. All the sixties fashions are coming back. I can only hope that the social consciousness and idealism return as well."

I stole a look at the clock. I really needed to get out of there so I finished stuffing things into my backpack as I talked. It occurred to me to carry extra cash in case I got a chance to make a drug buy. I went over to the buffet, opened a drawer, and pulled twenty hundreds out from under the tablecloths I never used. Mar-Mar's eyes were boring into my back watching my every move while I kept the conversation going. "I've heard that it was the CIA who introduced hard drugs, heroin in particular, into the movement back in the late sixties. To try to destroy it. Young people were getting too radical. Too revolutionary. Is that true?"

"Whatever the truth was then," she said, sidestepping my question, "the CIA isn't bringing this drug in now. And Daphne, we need to get this drug off the streets as fast as possible."

I turned around and faced her. Maybe I could get some honest answers about this assignment. "Why? I mean why besides the obvious reason, that it's killing people."

"Because we have reason to suspect that the drug presents a danger to the government, perhaps even to the president himself."

"You're kidding me," I said. "How? Is he snorting the stuff?"

"Of course not!" she said and ended the conversation without enlightening me further. I removed a brown leather coat from the closet and put it on. I added a Russian fur hat and a cashmere scarf to keep me warm in the exceptionally cold weather.

"I've got to get going, Ma," I said.

"Well, let's walk out together," she said and linked her arm into mine. "I love you, sweetheart," she added softly.

"Love you too, Ma," I said out loud, and to myself I added, *but I wonder what you haven't told me.*

Emerging into the street I parted from Mar-Mar, who told me to be careful, then walked determinedly down the block toward the subway, looking like a waif in the blustery wind of the evening. As I ventured into the street to hail a cab, I heard an owl's call, its low and mournful tones going *hoot, hoot, hoot.* My blood froze. I did not see the bird itself, but I saw the shadow of its wings dip across the street light. Owls aren't frequent visitors to Manhattan, and to Native Americans an owl's call is a foretelling of death. Was my imagination playing tricks on me? *No,* I thought again, I saw the shadow, I clearly heard the sound. *Could it be the shape-shifter warning me of danger?* I wondered. After the attack by vampire hunters, I had to remain wary and vigilant.

A beat-up old cab pulled over, and the door creaked on its hinges as I pulled it open. The interior was tatty and worn, and as I slid into the shadowy interior it was like entering a tomb. A bulletproof plastic shield separated the back seat from the front, an indication that this taxi picked up fares from rougher neighborhoods than mine. I told the cabbie the address of Kevin St. James through the barrier. He didn't look back at me, but grunted his okay. A sweatshirt hood pulled up over his head obscured his face and I could not see him in the rearview mirror.

Suddenly I was suffused with uneasiness as the cab headed toward Midtown. The radio played the disturbing atonal music of a Far Eastern country like Java. The sound grated on my nerves, and I felt I was being borne along in a hearse toward a gloomy interment of my hopes for love. Feeling foolish at my macabre musings—*it must be my mood,* I thought—I forced myself to focus on the job ahead. I needed to don a deceptive face and play the spy, pledging my body and my soul to a cause greater than my own quest for happiness. Yet, despite my efforts to be matter-of-fact and practical, I sensed that evil stalked New York's streets tonight, and I could feel its approach with every block closer to my destination.

I made myself turn my thoughts to approaching Fitz again, if he showed up on this Saturday night. I was suspicious about his disappearance after the girl's death in the bar last night, but I could not see what his connection to the drug might be. He wasn't a pusher, was he? I really didn't think so. I did think that Green Day and Buddy Holly were more likely candidates for that, and I intended to watch for them tonight. Could I score the drug on my own? From what J said about the security measures these pushers seemed to employ, it would take some maneuvering and a lot of luck. I needed to spot a user, chat him up, and get him to introduce me to a source. It was easier to keep my mind on the assignment for the evening than to contemplate the situation with Darius. I took the Scarlett O'Hara approach and figured I'd think about Darius tomorrow as the taxi pulled up in front of Kevin St. James.

I opened the cab door, and before exiting, put a twenty-dollar bill in the little tray in the plastic partition that separated the driver from the passenger. "Keep the change," I said.

The driver said, "Thank you," and turned toward me.

I recoiled backwards in revulsion. A death's head within the sweatshirt hood gave me a bony smile. I blinked hard and the face became human. It was just a skinny cab driver with dark circles under his eyes. I quickly got out and slammed the door. Cold air caught me in an icy embrace. The brightly lit street looked garish and unwelcoming. I knew vampire hunters were out there somewhere, after me, after Darius, and maybe after my friends. If ever there were omens given in warning of what was about to come, they had surely been given to me.

Even so, I did not expect what awaited me when I pushed through the pub's door into the steamy interior.

CHAPTER 5

A Long Day's Journey into Night

At seven p.m., earlier than most people begin their Saturday nights out, Kevin St. James was nearly empty, and the sound system sounded tinny as scattered lines of Lou Reed's "What's Good" echoed around my ears. I unwound the scarf from my throat, unbuttoned my coat, and took a quick look over at the bar. Fitz wasn't there. *Damn*, I thought.

Then I looked at the chalkboard to check out what group would be performing upstairs later tonight. I wanted to catch Beyond the Pale, the Irish group that had played last night. I hoped they'd be there for the entire weekend. As I read the white-on-black notice, I felt as if I had turned to stone, trying to comprehend what my eyes beheld:

TONIGHT AT KEVIN ST. JAMES
DARIUS D.C. & VAMPIRE PROJECT
SHOWS AT 10, MIDNIGHT, 2 A.M.
SECOND FLOOR LOUNGE. $10 COVER CHARGE.

I had one of those moments when logical thought fails. I was looking at something I found impossible to believe. Was it *my* Darius? If it was, what the hell was he doing? Adrenaline surging through my veins, I went over to the bar and put my butt on a chair.

The face of Jennifer the bartender lit up in a smile when she saw me. "Hey! Daphne, right?" I nodded yes. "I'm glad you came back. Can I get you a Guinness?"

"I think I need something a wee bit stronger," I said. *Oh right*, a part of me said to the part that had just thrown caution to the winds, *lower your inhibitions,* that *will solve everything*. "But you know what," I said, listening to reason, "give me a Pellegrino with a piece of lime, no ice."

Jennifer gave me a questioning look, but retrieved a little green bottle of mineral water from the refrigerator beneath the bar, set up a glass with a slice of lime, and brought them over to me.

"Sounds like man trouble to me," she said, grinning. "I'm an expert in that department."

"Bull's-eye," I laughed. "I'd better not drink or I'll be crying in my beer."

"Hey, that's what bars are for," she said. "If I had a dime for every sad story I hear, I'd be a millionaire. If you change your mind and want something stronger, just let me know. For you, the drinks are on the house."

Since she wasn't busy and seemed inclined to chat, I plunged in. "Fitz not in tonight?"

"No, I haven't seen him. But weekends aren't his thing. He usually comes in after work."

"Yeah, I was just hoping."

"He's a doll, he really is. I wish you luck," she said. "You know, you're the first woman he's paid any attention to, and believe me, girls throw themselves at him. Well, you'd make a gorgeous couple, so go for it, girlfriend," she said, putting clean wine glasses in an overhead rack as she talked to me.

"Jennifer, can I ask you something about the group playing upstairs later?" I ventured.

"Sure, shoot." She leaned a hip against the bar and continued with a smile, "Talk about good lookers. The lead singer in the band is something else." She raised her eyebrows and rolled her eyes. "Sexy, ohmygod."

"Yeah, well, I think I know him. Is his name Darius della Chiesa?"

"Darius D.C.? Could be, but I don't know."

"Well, what does he look like?"

"Hot!" she laughed. "Tight jeans, broad shoulders. Woooeee. He's no kid, though. Now let me think about this," she said, and squinted her eyes. "I guess he's maybe thirty. Longish hair, blond. Nasty scar on his cheek, but I like that. Adds an element of mystery."

"Have you talked to him?" I asked.

Jennifer started cutting up some lemons, keeping busy while she talked to me. "Nah. The keyboard player had a couple of drinks at the bar, though, and he told me they're getting a really great response to the whole vampire idea. He and the bass player tried a werewolf theme with another band, last year I think he said, but they like this approach much better. The vampire stuff was your friend's idea by the way. The band is pretty good too. I heard them practicing. They do covers, nothing original. Mostly Lou Reed, Cowboy Junkies, a few Leonard Cohen songs. No headbanging stuff. This isn't that kind of place. We generally get Celtic groups or girl singers, traditional, you know."

"Maybe I'll stick around for the first show," I said while I violently mashed the slice of lime into the bottom of my glass with a swizzle stick.

"If you know the lead singer, you definitely should. New groups always need support. He's a little Goth, what with the black cape and all, but he rocks," she said, moving off to serve a customer who sat down at the far end of the bar. Over her shoulder she said one more thing to me: "I think he has something going with the girl in the band, though. Just a heads-up."

"Thanks," I said trying to keep my voice steady. I bit into the lime, and the sourness made me wince. *Something going with the girl in the band.* The lime wasn't all that tasted sour. *First I'm going to tell him off, then I'm going to frigging kill him* was my first thought. Then I calmed down and reconsidered the situation. Darius said he was working with this girl on a project. He didn't act guilty. He seemed sort of surprised I asked. That's more like him. I saw how he responded to other women when he was with me: He never even noticed them. I just didn't see him fooling around with this chick. But she clearly acted possessive with him. She was playing something, I'd bet on it. And I had a gut reaction to that little bitch—an instant dislike. She was not what she pretended to be. She was up to something; I had a strong hunch about that. I intended to watch her closely, and I had really bad feelings about her closeness with Darius. That thought made me feel antsy, and I was tempted to call Jennifer back and order a single-malt Scotch neat, no ice, no chaser. I used to have a taste for it. I was trying to ignore the part of my brain saying that I still did. I sat at the bar with my nerves doing a tap dance.

I spent the next few hours at the bar, jumpy as a cat, shredding paper napkins, and watching the room as the bottles of Pellegrino multiplied on the bar in front of me. I kept scanning the place for Green Day and Buddy Holly. They didn't show. I also thought about how I'd approach Darius. I figured I'd wait until after the ten o'clock set since I reasoned he would be preoccupied with the evening performance before that.

With all the mineral water I consumed, I finally had to make my way to the ladies' room. There was a line waiting to get in. I stood there, eavesdropping on conversations, and I hit pay dirt.

A willowy girl was arguing with a friend. She stared down at the floor so that her long straight blond hair fell forward and hid her face. "I told you I don't want to," she whispered urgently to her friend, a freckle-faced imp who looked sixteen despite the false eyelashes and rose tattoo where there would have been cleavage if her breasts had been big enough to create any. "It scares me. I'm not going to do it."

"You are such a wimp," Freckles said peevishly in a louder voice. "I've heard it's better than meth. And you know how hard it was to get it. I mean I had to ask my brother at Yale. Like now I really owe him. And I'm practically broke. Do you have any idea how much it cost?"

"I'm sorry," the blonde said in a voice so low I could hardly hear her. "Emma, I'm really sorry. I just don't want to. My mom's sick. If she found out, it would kill her."

"Oh, you're such a goody-goody," the imp countered. "Thanks a lot. You said you would, you know. You promised! We said we'd both try it. Like I just can't believe you're not going to do it. Just wait until I tell everybody how you chickened out."

"I don't care. Be a bitch and tell them. So what. They didn't want to take it. I'm not doing it. I don't care what you say." Blondie still didn't look up but she wasn't going to change her mind either.

"Oh all right. Now what am I going to do with this shit? I don't dare take it home."

"Emma, just throw it out," the taller girl said. "Please."

"Are you crazy? *Throw it out?* I'm going to sell it. I can't even go to the mall, I'm so broke." Her voice was petulant.

"Excuse me," I said. "I couldn't help but overhear. Do you really have it? That drug that's better than meth? I heard it's better than freebasing even. It would be so cool to try it. I'd be willing to buy it off of you. It's called susto."

The willowy girl looked up for the first time, her eyes wide with fear and her face paper-white. I guess she thought I was a narc or something. "Nooo. We don't have anything."

"Oh, Muffy, shut up," Emma snapped. The eyes that looked at me were shrewd beyond her years. "I might be able to get you some. What's it worth to you?"

"I'll pay whatever it costs. Really," I said.

"It's a grand," Emma said. "And that's for one glass. Take it or leave it."

"Emma!" Muffy protested.

"No, that's okay. It's cool," I said. "I appreciate it."

The bathroom's occupant left and Emma grabbed the door. "Come into the bathroom with me. Muffy, wait right here."

I did, and a minute later I had a vial of susto in my backpack. At least one thing had gone right. I hoped I hadn't used up my good luck for the night.

I went to the pub's upstairs lounge a little after ten. I didn't want any hassle about getting a table as a single, so I sat at a tiny one near the wall. My nerves had unraveled totally as I waited for the set to start. I ordered a pint of Guinness, but I didn't have any intention of drinking it. Well, the road to hell is paved with good intentions. "Tonight, Tonight" by Smashing Pumpkins was playing over the loudspeakers and I was sliding into melancholy. I don't know who was choosing the songs, but I'd have personally strangled him if I could. Right about the time the Pumpkins' Billy Corgan began whining about the world being a vampire, I sucked down the Guinness without thinking about what I was doing.

The selections coming over the speaker system were adding to my feelings of disquiet. I guess the whole idea of the pre-show mix was to set up Darius's group because I sat there listening to Concrete Blonde's "Bloodletting (The Vampire Song)." I thought about Mar-Mar's insistence that we vampires are supposed to be a myth and the general public doesn't believe we are real. My mother definitely doesn't listen to the same music I do. I think a lot of people know we're here.

My reality did some more slipping and sliding between what I wanted to believe and what I could see was true as the room filled up, the lights went down, and a red spotlight hit a platform in the front of the room. The Smashing Pumpkins' song "We Only Come Out at Night" played, and four people looking like shadows took their places on the eerie red-lit platform. They were all dressed in black. My heart was racing. A yellow light replaced the red and I could see that a skinny guy was playing keyboard; a shirtless guy with a shaved head and wearing a cape was at the drums; the girl singer with her eyes heavily made up stood at one microphone; and Darius, swathed in a Zorro-like black cape and dressed in tight black leather pants, was at another mike, an electric guitar in his arms.

A bluish spotlight hit him. A diamond stud winked in his ear. His blond hair was loose, and when he smiled at the crowd, his incisors were long. He looked scary and sexy both at the same time. "Welcome to Vampire Project," he said. "We walk the night. We drink your blood. And we hope to turn you on with our music. Thank you," he said softly, his voice low and sensual as the lights went all red again, and the band slid into Lou Reed's "Sword of Damocles." I sat anonymously at my little table far away from the stage along the wall. I knew Darius couldn't see me beyond the spotlight. I hoped he couldn't sense my presence.

Although they were only doing covers, Vampire Project was good. Too good. I worried that they'd soon be attracting media attention. Darius was hiding in plain sight, but it was a risky and maybe a deadly strategy. It did seem to be working so far, though. I'm sure the other band members would say Darius was no more a vampire than Marilyn Manson. The guy on the drums and the keyboard player looked like pretty typical rock musicians to me. To them the whole vampire idea was just show business. The girl, though, bothered me more than ever. She was thin, but exceptionally muscular. Her face had no innocence in it. To me she seemed hard, even cruel. I didn't like her. Maybe I was just jealous, but I didn't think so.

The Guinness was going to my head and emotions were

flooding through me. Sitting there listening to the love of my life "going public" and potentially initiating what could be a catastrophe for every vampire in Manhattan was beyond my worst nightmare. In my wildest dreams I had never imagined anything like this. And every damned song the band did I felt was directed right at me. What was I supposed to think when Darius was singing Smashing Pumpkin's "Galapagos," with its haunting last line. When Darius sang it, he looked right out into the crowd and straight at me—even though I was sure he really couldn't see me. The set ended with Leonard Cohen's "I'm Your Man," where Cohen promises to please his woman in every way possible. *Yeah, right,* I thought. I was taking everything personally.

The lights went out and I managed to push my way through the darkness to come up behind Darius before he could get off the platform. The red light enveloped both of us. "Darius . . ." I said. "Got a minute?" My voice sounded calm and controlled; my heart was beating crazily; my soul was descending into chaos.

"Daphne? Oh, hi. Look, could we talk later? This isn't exactly a good time." He didn't look thrilled to see me, but he didn't look unhappy about it either.

"No. I need to talk to you right now. It's important." Again I kept my voice unemotional while my insides were doing somersaults.

He drew his brows together and nodded. "Okay," he said. "Cass?" he turned to the keyboard player. "Can you take this?" Darius put the strap over his head and handed the skinny guy his guitar. The girl singer broke in with a whining voice. "D, you and me have some business to take care of, remember." Her red mouth was in a pout and her eyes were glittering.

Darius said to her, "I know, Julie. I'll only be a minute." He turned toward me and didn't see the look of pure malevolence she directed at me as he took my elbow and steered me over to the small bar that's set up on the second floor of the pub.

"Daphne," he said in a low voice filled with concern. "We can't really talk about anything in this crowd. What is it?"

I knew he was right, but what I needed to say couldn't wait. "Darius, I don't know why you're doing this, but you have to stop. And you've got to stop the vigilante stuff too. You can't appear in public as a vampire. You just can't."

"Why not? How can I accept who I am, if I have to deny who I am? I'm Darius the vampire, remember?" His voice had a hard edge.

"Darius, for God's sake," I said in an urgent whisper, "Don't you understand? If you don't hide your identity, you'll be exterminated."

"Exterminated? By whom? Your mother?" He spat out the words. "She's not exactly the Terminator, Daphne. Or do you mean vampire hunters? Daphne, I *was* one. I know what they do. They'll have to catch me first. Now, look, I really have to go." Anger had displaced any tenderness in his voice.

"Darius, please, you really can get yourself killed. You have to listen to me."

"I don't *have* to do anything, Daphne. And I'm not going to hide. Somebody wants to kill me? Just let them fucking try. What's the worst that can happen? They'll put me out of my misery." He started to walk away. I reacted to that by reaching and grabbing his sleeve. When I touched him, he stopped in his tracks. He looked at me through a mask of pain. I rushed the words out. "Darius. Don't you understand. You are not the only one your behavior jeopardizes. I was almost killed! You could bring destruction to us all," I said urgently.

He looked at me then, looked right into my eyes and I could see a well of sadness that was so infinitely deep it threatened to swallow me. "It's not my intention to get anybody killed," he replied without rancor. "But I have things I have to do. And Daphne, I have no doubt *you* can take care of yourself. As far as any other vampire is concerned, I really don't give a damn. I'm going," he said and melted into the crowd of people, leaving me standing there like a woman carved of alabaster.

Once Darius left, I shook off my immobility but I was so emotionally keyed up I moved stiffly like an automaton. I started downstairs. Talking with Darius hadn't worked. It had turned out even worse than I feared. I was chilled by his words, and yet I didn't want to believe that he truly meant them. If I did, I'd have to accept that a hatred of vampires remained in his heart, that he didn't care if he got killed—and worst of all, that I'd better watch my own back, because he wasn't going to stop "going public" even if his behavior endangered me and everyone I cared about. My head was so screwed up by it all that I felt dizzy. I didn't know how to stop the locomotive of disaster speeding down the track toward him and me.

I reached the bottom step, planning to retrieve my coat and hat and get the hell out of the pub to do some thinking. The noise, the heat of other people's bodies, the smell of beer—all of it was starting to make me feel sick. A wave of faintness hit me and I realized that the only blood I had drunk in the last few days had been Darius's, and he had drained a great deal of mine. I should have replenished myself before I left the house. I had been careless. I was making mistakes. If I wanted to stay alive, I'd better think less about sex and more about security. Right now I was thinking I needed fresh air—and fresh blood. I hoped to make an exit as soon as possible. But when I looked toward the bar, there was Fitz. He spotted me and started walking in my direction.

"Are you okay?" were the first words out of his mouth. "You're dead white. Come on, sit down for a minute." He put an arm around my shoulders and led me back to where he had been seated at the bar. There wasn't an unoccupied stool, but he pulled me next to him, keeping an arm around my waist. I suspected he could feel how cold I was. An iciness of flesh and spirit seemed to have consumed me.

"You're freezing! Drink something," he ordered.

"I don't think—" I started to protest.

"Don't argue with me. Listen to someone who knows. Jennifer," he called over to the bartender. "Get Daphne a Jameson. And a glass of water."

Jennifer brought the drink over fast. "You okay?" she asked.

"I'm fine, really. Just got a little dizzy upstairs. I didn't eat—"

I don't know if either of them bought that, but Jennifer said, "I'll get you something from the kitchen," and she went over to a waitress who was walking by.

"So what really happened?" Fitz asked me, not letting go. His touch was comforting, solid, and warm. I let myself lean against him. I liked his support, not just physically, but emotionally. Fitz seemed so normal and steady. Darius's bad-boy sexiness, kickass courage, and aura of danger attracted me, but our conflicts had become exhausting. Constant fighting wasn't fun. Now I felt a wave of relief at being with someone who wasn't turning me inside out.

To answer Fitz, I figured half the truth was better than a complete lie. I looked at him and smiled. "Just the same old same old. I ran into my ex. We had some nasty words. I lost it, I guess. I feel foolish now."

"Why should you feel foolish? I understand. I saw Jessie in the supermarket a couple of weeks ago. I left my cart and ran out the door. Even if somebody mentions her name, it still hurts. I wish it didn't, but you know what they say about wishes. I'm glad I could be here for you. I e-mailed you and said I'd be here tonight. Did you get my message?"

"You did? No, I didn't get it. I didn't go online today. But I admit I was hoping you'd be here. And I am glad you are."

As I said it, I realized I was happy to see him. I felt a little guilty because I intended to spy on him, but I genuinely liked this man.

A wide grin lit up Fitz's easygoing, friendly face. "Well, that's what I like to hear. But I better tell you, I was pretty forward in the e-mail and asked you out. It was easier to do it in writing. Now I have to risk getting shot down in person."

"You asked me out? When? For tonight?" I responded.

"Actually it was a bigger deal than meeting me here tonight, and it would mean you doing me a huge favor. I won't feel bad if you say no. Well, yeah, I will feel bad, but I wouldn't blame you."

"What were you asking, for me to be your date to somebody's wedding? I can't think of anything worse than that, but I still might say yes." I took a sip of Jameson followed by a very big gulp of water. Jennifer brought over a heaping platter of tortilla chips smothered with melted cheese and layered with guacamole. "Enjoy," she said.

Suddenly I did feel like eating, and both Fitz and I dug in. He still had one arm around my waist and he fed me a chip with his free hand. I was trying to lick up the guacamole before it fell off the chip, laughing all the while, when I looked up and saw Darius coming down the stairs from the lounge. His face registered his shock. I deliberately looked away and started talking to Fitz. *Two can play this game,* I thought to myself.

"So about the date. If it's not a wedding, what is it?" I asked.

"Really Daphne, it's almost as bad." He shook his head. "There's a reception at my uncle's place out on the Island tomorrow evening. There'll be a lot of stuffed shirts there. It's mostly an older crowd plus the whole Fitzmaurice clan. That's a good fifty relatives downing drinks, deciding to play touch football at midnight, or getting into arguments that started a generation ago. It can be fun, or a total disaster. I have to put in an appearance, and I was thinking it wouldn't be so bad if you came along. It's a crazy idea. Maybe you don't have a dysfunctional family, and mine will scare you off. All I can promise is that the food will be good, and you'll have me for company."

Just then a customer left and freed up a tall chair at the bar. I gently extracted myself from Fitz's casual embrace, grabbed the seat, and pulled it over next to him. To make up for moving away, I fed Fitz a tortilla chip and laughed. "Really the 'date' sounds great, but I might have to work. I don't know yet. Can I e-mail you tomorrow and let you know? I hate to put you off, but I have to check my messages when I get home."

"Hey, that's more than fair. But I have another idea, too. Will you go out with me tonight? I mean somewhere besides here. We can spend some time getting to know each other. Have some dinner. We can do whatever you'd like," he said and looked at me hopefully.

I hesitated for a moment. I did need to bolster my strength with some blood, but a steak would tide me over. An empty apartment didn't appeal to me at the moment. "Yes," I said, smiling at him. "I'd like that."

"Great!" Fitz said. "I'll drink to that!" He saluted the air and ordered another Jameson. It was his third since we started on the nachos. Nothing in his manner betrayed how much he had had to drink, but his face was flushed and when he wasn't careful, some of his words slurred just the smallest bit. It wasn't any of my business whether or not he got drunk, and it was Saturday night. I was feeling the alcohol myself, and to tell you the truth, the buzz felt good. I guess I was drowning my sorrows, but I was acutely aware how risky it was for me to be even a little tipsy and not in total control of myself.

"What kind of food would you prefer?" Fitz asked as he drained his glass.

"Something bloody," I answered and grinned. "Eaten in a quiet place, if you please," I added.

Fitz tapped his empty glass up and down on the bar. He thought for a minute, then said, "I have just the place. We can leave as soon as I make a few calls." He took out his cell phone.

"I'll grab my coat while you do that," I whispered and slipped away to retrieve my jacket and hat. By the time I got back to the bar, Fitz had settled up with Jennifer. He grabbed his topcoat as we left the bar and we pushed through the door into the cold, damp air of the New York night.

A shroud of gray mist was crawling southward from the Hudson north of the city. There was no moon. A streetlight near us caught the fog and turned it into a garish yellow pool. I shivered. It wasn't a night to be out. I was thinking I should have gone back to my apartment alone and pulled the covers up over my head. Instead I was freezing to death, standing on the sidewalk. Fitz made no move to call a cab.

"Are we going to walk?" I asked him, dismay creeping into my voice.

"Absolutely not," he said. "I see that you're cold and you're probably wondering why we're just standing here. Daphne, I promise you this will be the last uncomfortable moment you will spend this evening." He stood in front of me then and closed the top button of my jacket, turned up my collar, and wrapped the scarf around my neck. "Our ride is on the way," he said as he put his arm around my shoulders. "In fact, here it is."

A black stretch limousine pulled up to the curb. The driver got out and opened the back door. I climbed in with Fitz right behind me. The deep leather interior could have held ten people. There was a fully equipped bar with crystal glasses, the space was illuminated by low lighting, and soft music was being piped in. The limo's interior was also toasty warm. I sank into the seat and looked questioningly at Fitz.

"The limo is a perk of my uncle's business," he said. "It's all ours for the night. But first, dinner is waiting." The limo pulled away from the curb and in a few minutes stopped in front of Ben Benson's Steak House on West Fifty-second Street. A waiter was already out on the sidewalk, anticipating our arrival with a silver tray laden with covered dishes. The limo door opened, and he handed the tray inside. Fitz flipped down a table and set the tray on it. He winked at me. "We're not eating yet. We'll park by the river before we dine."

The limo started moving once more and drove us over to the Hudson River, stopping near an old pier. I could see the water, but the thickening fog obscured the lights of New Jersey beyond. The mist soon surrounded us. With little traffic passing, this spot was quiet for Manhattan. The calming sound of a classical piano concerto played over the limo's music system. I felt as if Fitz and I were in our own little world. "Dinner is only phase one, Daphne," Fitz said as he uncovered dishes and put a plate holding a thick piece of filet mignon and hash browns in front of me. He handed me a napkin, then uncorked a bottle of red wine. A glass soon stood next to my plate.

He was so attentive, I blurted out, "Don't you dare try to cut my meat for me!"

He laughed. "I only will if you ask me to. You are the guest of honor tonight, and I am here to take care of you."

"You're spoiling me," I said as I cut off a piece of the steak and stuffed it in my mouth. It was nearly raw and I relished its bloody taste.

"I think spoiling you is an excellent idea," Fitz replied and started in on his own steak. "I only regret that the luxurious vehicle is borrowed."

"I appreciate it all the same," I said, watching him. "It's a grand gesture. Now tell me something about yourself, St. Julien Fitzmaurice."

"Just the facts, ma'am?" he responded.

"Anything you want to tell me," I said and took a sip of my wine. Fitz watched me taste it.

"Napa Valley," he explained. "A Peju Estate Cabernet Sauvignon, 2001."

"So you are letting me know that you're a wine buff," I said. "I'm not, but let's see—" I sniffed the wine's bouquet and took another sip. "This wine tastes of berries, cherries, currant fruit, and oak. Lots of oak. It has an elegance and harmony throughout. Good structure." I looked at him. "How'd I do?"

"You nailed it." He grinned. "Yes, I like wine. It's a hobby of sorts."

Later, after I had finished off the last of my filet and relaxed back into the seat, I asked, "And what else should I know about you, St. Julien Fitzmaurice?" I felt stronger, warmer, and a lot happier than I had a half hour ago.

"I'm an only child, but I have a lot of cousins. I had a good childhood. I can't complain a bit. I went to Harvard, but don't hold that against me. It was a family thing. I studied law. It took me two tries to pass the New York bar exam, and within a year I quickly found out, much to my father's dismay, that I hated the legal profession. So I quit. I went to work for Habitat for Humanity in Alabama as a volunteer. I did that for a couple of years, then went back home."

"So there's nothing even remotely dangerous about you?" I asked.

"I play a cutthroat game of tennis. That's about as violent as I get," he joked and smiled.

"And you've never killed anybody?" The question slipped out of my mouth before my brain could stop it.

Fitz sputtered and raised his eyebrows. "No! Jesus, God I've never killed anybody." He paused and looked at me. "Do you mean in war? I didn't go into the military, Daphne. Are you disappointed?"

"Not in the least," I sighed. "I'm relieved."

"You certainly threw me with that. You're not like anyone I've ever met before, Daphne." He shook his head. "But I like that. A lot. Are you finished eating? Can I get you something else? Dessert?" he asked.

"I'm done, thank you. The steak was delicious." I squeezed his hand gently, not coming on to him. At least not consciously coming on. "And you were very thoughtful to do this, you know."

Fitz knocked on the partition and in a twinkling the driver opened the door and took away the tray of dirty dishes. Fitz sat next to me and put his arm across the seat behind me, but didn't try anything. I didn't feel the least bit uncomfortable. One thing he didn't have to tell me was that he was a gentleman.

"Do you mind taking a ride?" he said, looking down at me. "You asked about me, so there's something I'd like to show you."

"A ride sounds just perfect," I said as the limo started up and began moving through the foggy streets of Manhattan.

"You are beautiful, Daphne," Fitz said abruptly, then turned his gaze to the window, embarrassed.

"Thank you," I said softly. His hand left the back of the seat and softly stroked my hair.

We ended up at Battery Park, on the tip of lower Manhattan near Castle Clinton, where tourists buy tickets for the Statue of Liberty and Ellis Island ferry rides. The limo came to a stop. The fog hadn't reached this far south, and the air was clear over the water.

"Would you mind if we got out a moment? I want to show you something," Fitz queried. "If you get cold, we can pop right back in."

"I'm warm now. Sure, let's go outside." I had no sooner uttered the words when the driver opened the car door, and I stepped into the night. Fitz was right behind me. I looked over at the limo driver for the first time. He was younger than I had first thought, and I suspected he was wearing a shoulder holster. It made me feel a little safer to know he was armed, although I wasn't feeling any threat here with Fitz.

Fitz took my hand. I squeezed it. We walked as close to the bay as we could get and stood in front of an iron railing. I could hear the waves slapping the seawall below us. "The Statue of Liberty's out there." Fitz pointed toward the west. "You can actually see her a lot better from the Jersey side. She's pretty far out in the bay to spot from here."

"I think I can see her," I said.

"Even when I can't physically see her, I see her," Fitz said, "in here." He tapped his chest above his heart. "You asked me to tell you about myself. That statue has become the guiding light of my life. I've never killed anyone, Daphne, and I hope I never have to, but I know I'm in a desperate fight for liberty. So many of us are these days. Nothing is more important to me than keeping this country free, Daphne, to protect our way of life from threats coming from outside our borders, and worse, from inside. Do you sort of understand what I'm saying?" he said solemnly.

"I think I do, Fitz. Perhaps better than you know." I stared out over the dark water.

"Poverty threatens our country, Daphne. So do drugs. So many things try to dim Lady Liberty's torch. I need to help in any way I can to preserve our freedom. I've discovered there are no simple answers, but I intend to keep trying. I thought I should tell you that." He tucked my hand under his arm. "Does it sound hokey to you? Hopelessly idealistic?"

"Not in the least." I smiled up at him and something shifted inside of me. He pressed me against the railing then. His kiss was open-mouthed and hungry. I was surprised at how much I liked it. We stood there in the night air and just kissed. I opened his coat and slipped my arms inside it, hugging him. Our intimacy went no further than that. The wind off the water blew through my hair. The salt breeze was cold, but I wasn't, not anymore.

Fitz didn't ask anything of me, and I promised nothing to

him. But I felt calm and safe in his arms. We kissed like teenagers. Our eyes were closed, and we slipped into our own private world. The thought occurred to me that perhaps there could be a life without Darius, but even as I pushed the idea away, I shivered.

"I'm getting a little chilled," I said.

We got back into the limo. Fitz leaned over and poured us each a glass of Irish whiskey. He handed it to me. I hesitated, but a chill had penetrated my flesh, and I wanted warmth. I drank it down quickly, feeling the burn spread through my insides. Fitz drank his too. He poured alcohol into the glasses a second time. I hesitated. He leaned toward me then, kissing the remaining whiskey from my lips. My stomach clenched with a stab of desire. I decided I could use that drink. I downed it and turned toward Fitz, my hand beginning to unbutton my coat. He reached out to help me. One by one, the buttons opened.

And just then my cell phone rang. *Damn, I meant to put it on vibrate.* "Sorry," I said to Fitz. "I better get this." I answered and heard Benny's urgent voice.

"Y'all need to get over here, Daphne. I'm at 43 East Thirty-eighth Street."

"Got it."

I hung up and turned to Fitz. "I've got to go. Sorry."

"Nothing wrong, I hope."

I put on a bright smile, phony as could be. "Prior commitment. A colleague from work. I told her I'd meet with her tonight and I confess, after I saw you I just forgot. That's all. But I'll e-mail you tomorrow as early as I can, and Fitz—"

"Yes?"

"About tomorrow, I really want to say *yes*." I leaned over and kissed him lightly on the cheek. "And thanks for tonight. I mean that."

"And I thank you, Daphne Urban, from the bottom of my heart," he said. "Give me the address where you need to go, and I'll drop you off."

* * *

We soon arrived in Murray Hill off Park Avenue South, where the Silverleaf Tavern was an upscale restaurant. I tumbled out of Fitz's limo with less than firm footing. I made an effort to clear my mind and focus on my mission. I had a pretty good idea why Benny had called. I figured susto had claimed another victim.

Plunging forward, I burst through the Silverleaf's door only to be stopped by the maître d', who asked if he could help me. My first thought was *Why is it so dark in here?* Then the room lurched sideways. I felt dizzy and grabbed the edge of the maître d's station. The two glasses of whiskey and the cold air had combined to hit me between the eyes with a sledgehammer. I made a great effort not to sway and spoke, taking care to deliberately form each syllable.

"I'm meeting a friend," I said, trying hard not to let the maître d' catch on that I had just climbed aboard an invisible carousel and was watching the room spin past. "Miss Polycarp."

If the maître d' noticed my impairment, he didn't comment, but said, "Oh yes, right this way," and led me into the posh interior of the Silverleaf. With a decor that combined the baroque with the offbeat, the restaurant pleased my occasionally over-the-top taste. In jewels, furnishings, clothes, and evidently men, moderation is not my middle name.

Benny was sitting with Bubba on a leather-covered banquette. Bubba jumped up and let me scoot in next to Benny. His hair, no longer hidden by his trademark John Deere hat, was the color of wild chestnuts, and he had dressed up for the night with a pin-striped, well tailored suit jacket, fine linen shirt, and expensive silk tie. That was on the top half. He still wore his jeans and Wolverine work boots on the bottom half. As I slid into the seat, I realized I was fixated on his boots.

Oh hell, I'm drunk, I thought. Bubba's boots had triggered a memory and I was rushing back through time. Suddenly I was out in the Hamptons with Mar-Mar back in the early nineteen-seventies. It was summer. A warm wind was flinging my hair in a wild tangle as I tried to still it with my hands. I was riding in the narrow space behind the front seat of an old silver Porsche convertible being driven too fast by Abbie Hoffman. He and Mar-Mar were screaming over the wind, trying to have a strategy meeting about an antiwar protest coming up. Mar-Mar always wanted me to get involved in her "causes," so she had asked me along, but their talk bored me. Abbie careened into a dirt driveway, and we stopped next to a once-elegant, but now ramshackle beach house owned by the pop artist Larry Rivers. I remember climbing out of the car, my legs stiff from the cramped ride and my skin stinging from windburn. The earth was dank and the branches of the trees were low.

A screen door banged and Larry Rivers came out of the house to greet us. My eyes were drawn to his feet. Despite the August heat, the artist was wearing heavy pull-on work boots, only he had painted them silver—and he was pretty much stoned out of his mind.

"Miss Daphne, do y'all need some help?" Bubba was saying. He appeared to be perfectly sober.

And I wasn't—sober, that is. "Uh-uh," I said. "I'm okay." I dragged my eyes away from his boots and pulled myself across the banquette until I bumped into Benny. I felt the softness of her against me, then put my hands on the edge of the white tablecloth and steadied myself upright.

"You're drunk as a skunk," Benny whispered vehemently in my ear. "You don't hardly ever drink. What in blue blazes happened?"

"You wouldn't frigging believe it," I said, trying to focus on the leaves, which were spray painted silver and hung above my head. *More silver, like Larry Rivers' boots,* I thought. I was afraid to move my head because even the smallest motion made the room start whirling. "Bubba, would you please order me some coffee?" I asked, keeping myself immobile. "And do you think they have any steak tartare? I need, uhhh, I might need, you know, something raw . . . and bloody."

Bubba, still standing, said, "Don't you worry none, Miss Daphne. I'll leave Benjamina to fill you in, and I'll get the waiter to rustle up something." He disappeared in the direction of the bar.

I ever-so-slowly turned my head to look at Benny's face, which had four eyes instead of two. "So why'd you call? I figured there was another OD. But nothing seems to have happened here."

"Something did too happen, Miss Smarty Pants, and you need to know about it," she said with urgency.

"Why?" I said as my glance strayed to a pillar that looked as if it were made out of old tires covered with metallic paint. That tiny turn was enough to make the room go around. "Benny, hold up a minute. Okay? Don't tell me anything yet. I need to wait for Bubba to get back."

"I just don't believe this," she said. "Daphne, this is so not you. Was it something with Darius?"

"Oh was it ever something with Darius," I answered, carefully leaning back against the tufted seat. At that moment, Bubba came back with a black coffee, which he put down in front of me. "It's already been saucered and blowed on," he said, meaning I wouldn't burn my tongue on it.

I reached out with slow deliberation and brought the cup to my lips, holding it with both hands. The coffee was only lukewarm. I drank as much as I could without gagging.

By that time a waiter appeared with a plate holding an open-faced London broil sandwich on toasted baguette. The meat had just been passed once lightly over a flame. It was essentially raw. "Excuse me," I said to Benny and Bubba as I delicately picked off purple onion slivers garnishing the top of the sandwich and speared a piece of meat. I picked it up and let it slide down my throat. It wasn't human blood but it would have to do. I polished off the other slices without chewing once and delicately wiped the red juice from my lips with a napkin. The room had stopped spinning, though it still jiggled a bit, and I was happy to note I didn't feel as if I were going to throw up. I was still drunk, but more in control of myself.

"Feel better?" Bubba asked, watching me intently. "It looks like you was rode hard and put away wet."

"Gee, thanks for the compliment," I said and Bubba started to say he didn't mean anything by it. "Never mind," I interrupted. "But you don't know the half of it. I'm doing a little better, though. So what happened here?" I hiccupped. "Excuse me." In the midst of a second hiccup my eyes were drawn to the wineglasses lined up like soldiers on parade in front of Benny.

She saw where I was staring. "Hey, a *Southern* girl can hold her likker," she said and giggled. "This restaurant has this bottomless wineglass deal here. Y'all get to sample seven different wines. I'm up to number five. It's some kind of see-rah." She held the glass of ruby liquid up to the light then took a closer look at me. "Bubba, she's listing to one side. Maybe we'd better get her another cup of coffee?" she asked. He signaled the waiter, and Benny began her report on the events of the night.

"I moseyed in here 'bout seven," she said. "I figured I'd just sit a bit and watch. There was this homely guy wearing heavy black glasses at the bar, and I mean he fell out of an ugly tree and hit every branch on the way down. Pretty soon he got to arguing with two other fellows, real good-looking ones. They were jumping on him like a duck on a June bug. It started to get a tad loud, and I could catch a couple of words, something about a drug deal. Well, butter my butt and call me a biscuit, I heard them mention susto. The maître d' started giving them the old fish eye, and I guess they figured they might get thrown on out of here, so the two good old boys escorted the glasses guy out the front door. I got up and followed them, just to see what was going on."

"So what happened?" I said thinking that the guy with the glasses sounded like Buddy Holly from Kevin St. James last night.

"They was yelling that the ugly guy was supposed to bring more susto and they had an agreement and all. At least that's the gist of it. I couldn't hear everything from where I was hiding in the doorway. Well, they started to beat him up, you know. They skint him good, shoving him around and knocking him down on the cement. It got real nasty. Ugly guy had his arms up trying to protect his glasses, and the two friends just started kicking the begeezus out of him. One kicked him in the face and he got a nosebleed. The other was kicking him in the back."

Bubba broke in to explain to me, "That's what bikers down home do when they want to rough a guy up: If you kick him you won't get no blood on your clothes."

I just nodded at this piece of street wisdom, and Benny went on. "The two guys were swearing and calling the fellow on the ground a no-good lowlife double-crossing scum-sucking motherfucker and stuff like that. I was thinking they was fixin' to kick him to death when all of a sudden a taxi pulled up. The two guys stopped, and they were looking to run off when a tall fellow jumped out of the cab with a gun in his hand. He told them not to move one fuckin' muscle. And they sure didn't.

"The tall guy rushed over and grabbed the ugly guy by one arm, dragged him like he was a sack of potatoes, and shoved him into the cab. I'm telling you it happened so quick it was a blur. Then the big guy held his gun at his side and went over to talk to the two friends who just stood there. I couldn't see everything, but I think they pulled out some cash, and he gave them something."

"Benny, it sounds pretty brutal, but so far it just sounds like a drug deal that got complicated." The second cup of coffee had arrived and I was concentrating on drinking it.

"Well now, sugar, I ain't done yet. I got back to my seat

right quick. The two guys were a few seconds behind me coming in the door, and they went over to their friends at the bar, laughing pretty loud. And oh, maybe a half hour passed with nothing going on except me drinking my wine. Then a waiter came rushing out from the direction of the men's room and whispered to the maître d'. The waiter's face was all pasty and he was shaking like a leaf. I put two and two together—and slipped some money to another waiter to find out what happened. It turns out a guy had died in the bathroom. The whole incident was handled real quiet-like. Most of the other diners didn't even know anything was wrong. The EMS came in the back way, but before they did I snuck over to the men's room. It didn't take too many more twenties to get a look at the body. Wouldn't you know it was one of the fellows who had been out in the street earlier. He was as blue as mold on cream cheese. So then I called Bubba to come on over here, and he said I should call you."

"Well sure, I guess we should call Cormac too."

"No, Daphne, you don't get it. The tall guy who showed up in the cab? It was the cute fellow you were sitting at the bar with the other night."

CHAPTER 6

"The world is as you see it."

—The *Yoga Vasistha*

I didn't ask Benny if she was sure. I believed she had seen accurately. I was the one whose vision reflected my own desires and not the cold hard truth. I had swallowed every word Fitz told me without questioning anything. I was totally taken in. I wanted him to be a good guy, just as I wanted to believe Darius could stop hating vampires. So I didn't question Fitz as closely as I should have. I didn't reserve judgment. I just started making out with him. Now reality had jumped up and bitten me in the ass again. I swear I never learn.

That's what I was feeling. All I said was, "Oh, shit." I put my hand over my eyes.

"No, Daphy, don't be upset. This is a good thing. It's a real lead. If that guy is a dealer, you can find out where he's getting his stuff. You were a genius to spot him in the pub last night."

I was f'ing brilliant all right. But Benny had a point. I needed to take the lemon and make lemonade. I had gotten close to Fitz—and I had almost gotten a lot closer—and without intending to I had found a link to the source of the susto.

At that moment, just when I figured I had fallen in a pile

of shit and come up smelling like roses, we got company—unwelcome company.

"Mind if I join you." It wasn't a request; it was an order. An angry face looked directly at mine. NYPD Detective Johnson stood at the end of the banquette. We all moved over, and he sat down next to Bubba, but not too close. He made very sure he didn't make any physical contact.

"Would you like to introduce me to your friends, Miss Urban?" he asked with a voice devoid of civility.

Not really, I thought. "Benny Polycarp, Bubba Lee, this is Moses Johnson. He says he's with the NYPD."

"And you say you're with the Department of the Interior," he snapped back. "So what are you doing here?"

"Now, just hold on a minute," Bubba said. "I don't want to be rude, but what the hell business is it of yours?"

"A man died here tonight, just like the girl last night. You were there. You're here."

"Just a coincidence," Bubba said.

"I don't believe in coincidence. And I don't believe in bullshit. Besides that, I did some checking, on Miss Urban."

I shrugged. "And . . . ?"

"You *do* work for the U.S. Department of the Interior. Other than that, you're a mystery woman, Miss Urban. You don't even have a parking ticket. Or a credit card."

I just shrugged again. "I don't own a car. I only pay cash. And that's a crime?"

Moses Johnson took a deep breath. "I think we need to lay our cards on the table here. I don't have time to tap-dance."

Bubba's face was blank. He made a good poker player. "So what do you want, Detective Johnson?" he asked.

"I want to tell you something, and I want you to listen."

"We're all ears," Bubba said, his hostility rising to meet Johnson's.

"Look. I don't know who you are. But there's something about you people that I don't like. I've dealt with the Feds before. Their arrogance and outright stupidity got my partner killed. So maybe you're Feds, and that's enough for me not to like you. And maybe you're something else, because just being near you people makes my skin crawl. But listen up, and listen good. This is a NYPD case. You people come in here and you don't know your ass from your elbow. All you're going to do is get in the way. You're not city cops. You don't know these streets. You don't know New York's narcotics trade. Whoever is behind this drug is dangerous. They're not playing. I don't give a shit if you get yourself killed. I do give a shit if you screw up my investigation. Is that clear?"

Bubba, still impassive, said, "Now that's not very neighborly of you, Detective. It surely ain't. Maybe you could use our help, you know, that is if we had anything to do with what you're talking about, which we don't."

Moses Johnson's mouth was a hard line; his brows were drawn together. His whole face was rigid. "I told you I don't have time for bullshit. And not for nothing, *Mr. Bubba Lee,* the day you can help me is the day hell freezes over. I'm going to be watching you. I think there's something rotten about you three. And I'd love to bust your asses." Johnson stood up. He gave a quick nod to Benny and me and walked off.

"Now, what was that for?" Benny said. "We never did nothing to him, now did we, Daphne?"

"Maybe I pissed him off the other night," I said, thinking about Johnson's visceral dislike of me, as if he sensed I was undead.

"Or maybe he just doesn't like white Southerners," Bubba said. "But I think it's something else. He's got something personal at stake in this case."

"How'd you figure that?" I asked.

"He cares too much about our being here. He thinks we're FBI or DEA. We're on his turf, sure. But he's overreacting. Nah, something else is going on. Anyways, enough of Detective Johnson. What's our next move?"

I filled them in on my buying a vial of susto. I didn't say anything about my possible date with Fitz. I had the beginnings of a pounding headache. I was also mentally beating myself up, not for drinking the whiskey and getting drunk, but over my consistent attraction to the most fucked-up men in the world. I mean, was it some kind of self-destructive thing with me? Maybe subconsciously I didn't want to get involved in a relationship that would work out. The guys I went nuts for, from Byron to Darius and now to Fitz, were outlaws and rebels, every single last one of them. They rejected convention. They courted danger. Hell, they liked flirting with death. But maybe that's why they wanted me. *Face it, Daphne, old girl*, I said to myself. *Who's going to love a vampire except somebody who gets a kick out of embracing the forbidden?* But I didn't think Fitz was like that. I was sure he was different. I really truly was.

To chase away that depressing train of thought, I decided to concentrate on being a spy. I figured it was time to talk with J; I had to get him the drug sample anyway. Benny had put in a call to J earlier about the overdose at the Silverleaf, and when I called, J told me to get on down to the office. The other two could go home, or wherever, he said. I relayed the message and told Benny I'd call her later.

"You sure better call me, Miss Daphne," she warned.

I was tempted to walk down to Twenty-third Street to clear my head, but it was too far for my Manolo boots to handle and I had an eerie tingling that was hitting me between the shoulder blades. I really believed I was being followed again. After all, the vampire hunters were out there, and they knew who I was. So I hailed a taxi, my third ride of the night.

Some New York cabbies talk. Most don't, especially if they're foreigners. Native-born Americans seem to be in the minority among New York taxi drivers, but this cabbie was a middle-aged black man with a seen-it-all world-weariness written on his face. He had tuned in to a right-wing "diss-jockey" on an AM talk-radio station. A host with a hysterical edge to his voice had picked up on the same article Mar-Mar had circled in the *New York Post* about the mysterious death of a drug dealer and the sighting of a giant bat in Brooklyn. My head had been pounding before I got into the cab. Now a jackhammer started hitting my temples.

"So, whaddya think?" the cabbie asked me. "You think there are monsters in Brooklyn?"

"I wouldn't doubt it for a minute," I said while I probed my scalp with my fingers, trying to locate an acupressure point to alleviate the dull throbbing in my head. "There are monsters everywhere in the city. But they're all human."

"You got that right, lady," he said, and looked at me in the rearview mirror. There I was with my thumbs grinding into the pressure points on my temples, my eyes looking totally spacey, my mouth open a little. If my behavior surprised him, he didn't show it. He just went on with his conversation.

"We're all animals, you know. And any animal will kill. It's instinct. That's why humans need laws. Right back to the Bible, you know? Kill or be killed, it's human nature. So society has to set down rules. Now the rules say it's okay to kill sometimes. But not okay to kill other times. Where do you draw the line? It's a wonder more people don't pick up a gun to solve their problems. I was reading *Maxine,* you know, the cartoon. She said, 'The original point and click tool was a Smith and Wesson.' When you take away all the nicey-nice, we're nothing but animals."

"So," I said, "in your opinion, these addicts in Brooklyn really didn't see a giant bat?" I was still doing my acupressure, but it didn't seem to be working. I tried massaging my eyelids.

"Hey, I'm not saying they did or they didn't," the cabbie said. "Those dumbass drug dealers were probably too stoned to know what they saw, you know. And if a giant bat killed them, good riddance to bad rubbish. Lowlifes. Nothing but lowlifes. And the way I see it, we all have a bat side, you know. The part of us we don't show to nobody. Except maybe our old lady," he said and laughed.

"So you don't believe in vampires?" I asked as we pulled up at the Flatiron Building.

"Vampires? Never really thought about it, but shit, after driving this cab for twenty years, I sure as hell believe in the devil," he said and laughed again. I paid him the fare, added a big tip, and got out of the cab.

Once I was out on the sidewalk, my legs felt shaky, and a sudden gust of wind gave me a hard shove, almost knocking me off balance. It rushed on, curling around the buildings with a moaning sound. A few yellow cabs raced down Broadway when the light changed but nothing else moved. Loneliness seemed to lie on the city like a pall. I didn't feel like seeing J, but duty called. It's not as if I had a choice. At least I had accomplished something by getting the susto.

J waited for me in the dimly lit conference room. He stood there straight and firm, his shoulders back, and his khaki shirt and pants crisply ironed in true military fashion. I couldn't see his feet, but I knew his shoes were spit-shined. As for me, I looked like a squiggly cartoon character. My hair was blown and tangled. My lipstick had long since disappeared. And when I started to take off my coat, I discovered I had buttoned it up wrong, having skipped a button so that the collar rose crazily on one side and the hem dipped down on the other. Nothing like impressing the boss. I sat down, glad that the lighting was murky and the room filled with shadows.

J raised an eyebrow, and a flicker of a smile touched the corners of his mouth, but he kept his voice flat and businesslike when he asked me, "You have the drug with you, Miss Urban?"

I nodded and dug it out of my backpack. I handed it over. "Did you get the bark analyzed?" I asked.

He nodded. "Yeah, but it didn't tell us much. We don't know if it has anything to do with susto. This sample is critical, thanks." He closed his large hand around the little glass vial.

"What was the bark? Do you know?"

"Some Amazon Basin tree. The lab says if it's ingested it could cause general anxiety, but that's about it. It stimulates adrenaline, epinephrine, and cortisone, but it only induces about the same level of stress as a day at the office or about as much fear as somebody coming up behind you and saying 'boo.' Nothing intoxicating. Nothing addictive. And nothing even remotely toxic."

"So you think it's unrelated to susto?" I asked, thinking it would have been just too easy if the South American Indian had handed us the answers.

J looked at the little vial of fine brown powder I had handed him. "I don't know, Miss Urban. Now what's this Miss Polycarp tells me about you talking to one of the dealers?"

"Benny jumped to a conclusion. I don't know if he's a dealer. His name is St. Julien Fitzmaurice. Maybe you can run a check on him. I'm going out to the Island to some party with him tomorrow evening."

"Good work, Miss Urban. I'm going to bring the whole team in Monday night to see where we stand. So get a report together for the meeting." Again he closed his hand over the vial. "By then I'll have this analyzed. I don't have to tell you time is running out."

"No, you don't have to tell me." I sighed and stood up. "I'd like to get out of here if we're done. I'm pretty beat." I just wanted to drag my sorry ass home and take a shower. The steak and nearly raw London broil had stuck a finger in the dike of the rising tide of my need for fresh blood, but my energy was ebbing fast. I wanted to partake of some of the pouches from the blood bank home in the refrigerator. I didn't need to swoop down on a human in a dark alley, although still half drunk as I was, the idea held some appeal. Sipping cold blood isn't half so satisfying as drinking it fresh and warm from a vein. I chased the thought away with a frown and tried not to stare at J's neck, which was thick, muscular, and very inviting.

J looked as if he were going to say something, but didn't. He was studying me as if I were under a microscope. I couldn't tell what he was thinking. He just nodded an okay at me. I picked up my bag and headed for the door.

"Watch your back, Miss Urban," he said.

I looked at him questioningly.

"Tomorrow," he clarified.

"I can handle myself," I said.

"I know that," he said with a gentle voice that surprised me. "But we don't really know what or who we're dealing with here."

"Right, boss," I answered and gave him a smile as I walked out, leaving him standing alone in the half-lighted room.

I couldn't face climbing in and out of another cab tonight, so despite the risks lurking in the night, I headed for the subway. It was late, and the trains would be few and far between. I didn't care. Descending into the underground tunnels would be comforting, like entering a cave. I went down the stairs on the east side of the Flatiron Building and walked through the tunnel that went under Broadway to the uptown platform of the Twenty-third Street station. I could hear the sound of my own footsteps echoing on the gray cement floor.

It's in my nature to be watchful. I always look around for a potential threat. I am one of the hunted of the world, as my kind have been for millennia. Fear has always been my close companion. Sadly, today—after Nine-eleven—most people are more cautious and wary. And below the surface of modern life a dark current of fear runs like a contagion, harming bodies and souls.

I slid my metrocard in the slot, pushed through the turnstile, and stood waiting for the next train on the platform, having feelings of *deja vu* and fighting a growing sadness. Just a few months ago, at the beginning of my career as a spy, Darius had been in this station too, following me. He had both frightened me and excited me. No one was here tonight but a drunk sprawled out on a bench against the wall, his mouth open catching flies. The N train pulled in and I got on the brightly lit car. I could have used sunglasses to tone down the glare bouncing off the plastic seats and aluminum doors. I sat on the hard gray bench. The doors banged shut. The train pulled out of the station. The car was empty except for a small man sitting to my right. He got up and walked over to me. It was the South American shaman we had seen last night. He took a seat across from me. "I am Don Manuel."

"I remember. What do you want?" I asked as the train swayed and moved along, its wheels going *clack clack clack.*

"To stop the susto," he said. "Like you, but not like you."

"What do you mean? You speak in riddles," I said, watching his bright eyes.

"Not a riddle," he said. "Truth. You want to catch the men who have taken the bark from my jungles. To you, that is stopping the susto, yes? You and your friends can do that. I want to stop the susto by teaching you what it is."

"Well what is it? The bark you gave us isn't susto." The train pulled into the Twenty-eighth Street station. The doors opened. No one got on. The doors closed. The train lurched and moved on into the dark tunnel again.

"No, the bark is not susto. But the bark is what makes the powder the men sell." The outlines of his body shimmered with an aura, and I noticed he appeared to be sitting, but he didn't really touch the seat.

I thought about putting out my hand to see if he were solid. I felt it would be disrespectful, so I didn't. Watching him intently, I said, "I don't understand. If the powder isn't susto, what is susto?"

"What you in America call fear. The people of my country call it a loss of soul." As he said this, the subway lights dimmed momentarily, and the car was plunged into blackness. When they returned, Don Manuel had shifted his shape again. A yellow Sky Bar candy wrapper scurried crazily down the middle of the subway car, as if blown by a maverick wind. The train pulled into Herald Square; the doors opened. The wrapper leaped up through them and continued its manic journey on invisible currents of air. I rushed over and peered through the open doors at the huge, too-bright, chrome-shiny, white-tiled station, with its maze of stairs, corridors, and confusing mezzanines. The Sky Bar wrapper was nowhere to be seen. I stood there for a moment as the doors shut and the N train pulled out, continuing on its journey, the lonely clack clack of its wheels starting once more.

By the time I put the key into the lock of my apartment door it was after three a.m. A deep-throated "woof woof" greeted me. I had never come home to a dog before, and my mood was immediately lifted by Jade's unconditional joy. The rooms no longer seemed so empty, and inside of me a small flame of happiness flickered into existence.

I walked over to her, stooped down and hugged her, laying my head against her thick fur. The solidity, the warmth, and the positive energy of her body flowed into me. "Want some dinner, Jade, girl?" I asked. "Me too. Just give me a minute."

I took off my Manolos, changed into a sweatshirt and yoga pants, left my feet bare, and put Bach's *Goldberg Variations* in my CD player. I needed some soothing music to get me through the rest of the night. Then I turned my attention to feeding myself and my dog. But when I went into the kitchen, a wave of sadness and longing washed over me. Two empty coffee mugs sat on the counter, left there from the day before when Darius and I had sat together on the sofa, our feet touching, and I had felt happy. I picked up the one Darius had used and put it to my lips, touching the rim where his mouth had been. I closed my eyes for a minute, then put it back down.

Afterwards, I fixed Jade's dinner and set her bowl on the kitchen floor. She buried her face in it, snorting cheerfully. I poured my meal of rich red blood into a Waterford crystal glass and sat down at my dining room table. I let the nourishment flow into me. I sat thinking of what the shaman had told me. According to Don Manuel, susto robbed the user of his or her soul. I supposed that was a metaphor for a user's loss of will or helplessness when in the grips of the drug's effect. Don Manuel also said susto was fear. Did he mean susto caused a fearful hallucination, creating a kind of horror film of the mind? Or did the drug cause the body to flood with fight-or-flight hormones as a reaction to a powerful feeling of terror? Or did it do both? Why did some people die? Perhaps once we had J's analysis of the brown powder we could pinpoint what made the drug so appealing, addictive, and deadly. I needed more information to come up with more than idle speculation about susto.

After I finished dining, I checked my e-mail. There were two messages from Fitz. He had sent the first one before I had seen him in the pub. The second was this:

Daphne, fair lady. I will be your knight in shining armor whenever you need me to be. Your lovely face banishes the sorrow that follows me like a shadow. Dare I hope I will see you tomorrow? If you can grace me with your company, I will pick you up by chariot at 6:00. The event is a reception being thrown by my uncle for some visiting politicos. It's not black tie, but cocktail attire. The thought of you in finery thrills me. I can return you by the hour past midnight. I do not know if you have to rise early on Monday, but alas I do.

Seriously, Daphne, I adored seeing you tonight. If you cannot, or would rather not, go to my uncle's with me, it is completely understandable. Perhaps a dinner and movie would be more to your taste at another time.

Fondly,
Fitz

I clicked on REPLY. It was futile to hope that Benny had been mistaken. I had to accept that Fitz might seem like a nice guy, but he was involved in something criminal if not downright evil. I honestly couldn't envision him pushing susto. That role didn't in any way seem to fit the man I had met and talked to, but he wouldn't be the first person to hide a secret identity behind a deceptive face. Look at me. Well, I had a job to do, and I might as well get it done. I wrote:

Dear Fitz,

My schedule is clear. No work, so I can play. I will be waiting at 6:00 (address and phone number below). Late return okay with me, as long as it's before dawn. And thank you for your understanding—and for that very special dinner—earlier this evening. May you always be my white knight.

Lady Daphne

After I clicked on the SEND button, I closed down the machine and headed for the corner of my apartment I use for meditation. Thoughts were ricocheting through my mind like machine-gun fire, and I needed to shut them off. I assumed the lotus position and emptied my mind. No thought. I let go of all.

My only other task before dawn was to walk Jade, and to my surprise, I found the brisk outing to be a pleasure, except for the pooper-scooping part. The streets of the Upper West Side were still, empty, and quiet. Walking in silence, the dog and I had no need of words. I looked over my shoulder. No one was following. Nothing moved. I felt nothing evil around me. No owls called. No shamans appeared. But turning my face toward the sky, I thought I saw the flash of a bat wing reflected in the pane of an upper-story window. Was this vision real or merely what I wanted to see?

Chapter 7

My thoughts, my words, my crimes forgive:
And, since I soon must cease to live,
Instruct me how to die.

—"The Adieu (written under the impression that the author would soon die)" by Lord Byron

I passed the light of day asleep in my satin-lined coffin. I don't remember my dreams, but tears had dried on my cheeks when I arose after the winter night came again to the city a little after five p,m.

I began the evening by taking Jade out for a brisk jog. Next, I checked my e-mail and found a short message from Fitz confirming he'd pick me up at six. My plan—if the vague ideas in my head even deserved that description—was to get information from Fitz without arousing his suspicions. Beyond that obvious tack, I could only remain watchful and inquisitive. I thought I should call Benny and fill her in, after all I had promised to phone her. And it might be smart to tell her where I was going, but what could I really say? I was headed to a cocktail party in the Hamptons. I didn't know the address. I didn't know the name of my host. I mentally kicked myself. How hard would it have been to just ask Fitz? As a spy, I was still an amateur. If I were taking a course in espionage, my grade would be a big fat "F," and not just for "failing." It might be "F" for "good and fucked."

I didn't have time to primp and pamper myself; I needed a dress that would allow me to shed it quickly—not in order to hop into the sack, but in case I had to transform. I chose a classy black sheath by Mandalay, Sharon Stone's favorite designer, and fuchsia satin shoes with a four-inch heel by Italian designer René Caovilla. I had bought the shoes in the nadir of depression after Darius and I broke up; they were a complete indulgence, but I figured they were cheaper than a shrink. I wanted to look sexy enough to be distracting since I was working on comic Robin Williams's assumption that God gave men a penis and a brain, but not enough blood to use both at the same time. I just hoped I didn't have to do any significant walking. I couldn't exactly fit a pair of Nikes into my clutch purse. It barely had room for my cell phone.

Fitz buzzed my apartment at precisely six. He said he was double-parked, so I told him not to bother coming up, I'd just come down to the lobby. A minute later I was stepping off the elevator, and Fitz's face lit up like it was Christmas morning. He kissed me on the cheek, and I faked a smile. When he escorted me outside, I discovered he was driving a white Toyota Prius. I was expecting no less than a Mercedes. As he opened the passenger side door for me, he said proudly, "It gets seventy miles a gallon. And more important than saving money, it's better for the environment. Screw the big oil companies. You might as well know I'm a big supporter of Bobby Kennedy Jr.—it's time we start fighting the enemy within."

As I ducked down into the Prius I looked up into Fitz's open, handsome face. *You could have been the perfect guy,* I thought, *if you weren't a drug dealer . . . and if I weren't hung up on a vampire who's probably gone off his gourd and decided to be a rock star.*

Fitz climbed in the driver's side and our journey began. "I'm really glad you're here," he said. "I've been thinking about you a lot."

"Hmmm, I've been thinking about you too," I said, looking out the window and not at him. "You know, I should have asked you who your uncle is."

Fitz had an unreadable look on his face when he answered. "I'm glad you didn't. It told me that you're going out with me because you really wanted to see me, not him."

"What do you mean?" I asked and turned toward him in the seat.

"My uncle is my mother's brother, Brent Bradley."

"Brent Bradley, the national security advisor to the president?" I said, thinking, *Holy shit.*

"Yep, that's him."

"Oh," I said. "And do you work for him?" I began feeling, like Alice in Wonderland, that this was getting curiouser and curiouser.

"More or less."

"Whatever that means," I said.

"It's nothing mysterious," he added. "I'm just a glorified go-fer. I guess I still haven't figured out what I want to be when I grow up," he said and grinned at me.

"Me too," I said smiling back.

"And what do you do? Law?" he asked.

"Me a lawyer? You've got to be kidding. No, I'm a curator with the National Park Service."

"You didn't buy *that* on a government salary," he said, looking at my mink.

"My father left me the money," I said cryptically.

"Oh, I'm sorry. When did he die?"

September 27, 1590, I thought. "A long time ago," I said. "I don't really remember him."

"My dad's dead too. He had a massive heart attack a few years ago. It's tough, especially on my mother."

About then I noticed we weren't driving east toward any bridge or tunnel to leave Manhattan. "This isn't the way to Long Island. Where are we going?" I asked, puzzled, as the Prius headed down Twelfth Avenue.

"This is one of the perks of having Brent Bradley as an uncle," Fitz said as he pulled into the VIP heliport at Thirtieth Street. "We don't have to fight traffic on the way to the Hamptons. We get to fly."

* * *

We climbed on board a small commuter helicopter. "You ever flown in one of these before?" Fitz yelled over the noise.

I shook my head no.

"Well don't worry so much," he said loudly. "It's a Bell 206 JetRanger, the safest aircraft in the world. And we'll get to the Hamptons in an hour. It's scheduled to bring us back at midnight."

I nodded at him. I had no fear at all of flying, but he couldn't know that. We flew due east through the dark sky and came down on a helipad behind a magnificent mansion lit up by floodlights and surrounded by a high wall. Brent Bradley must have more money than God. Fitz helped me out of the Bell 206. "Welcome to the Palazzo di Bradley. At least that's what we call it when my uncle can't hear us. Huge, huh?"

"Impressive," I replied.

He took my arm and we walked together to a waiting golf cart, which would deliver us to the house without ruining my shoes.

"I have one important thing to ask of you, Daphne," he said.

"What's that?" I asked as I climbed daintily into the golf cart.

"Don't judge me by my relatives."

I gave him a sincere smile this time. "I hope you'll remember that if you ever meet any of mine," I answered.

As we neared the house, I was impressed by Bradley's security measures. There were motion-detecting devices, cameras, and muscle. Security guards with dogs were walking around the perimeter walls and bodyguards stood like sentries at the front door. I was beginning to get inklings that the "politicos" Fitz had mentioned weren't from the local chamber of commerce.

We walked into a great room that was big enough to hold

a hundred people without a crush. A maid took my coat, and Fitz let out a soft whistle when he saw me in my dress.

"My God, you're beautiful," he whispered in my ear. Then he stepped back and looked at me sternly.

"You were lying about working for the Park Service, weren't you?"

My breath caught a little. "What do you mean?" I asked, wondering if I had been busted. Had Fitz's uncle run a security check on me? What would he find out if he did? Our team was a deep black spy operation. But Brent Bradley was the head of the whole shebang. Was he one of the few people who knew the U.S. government had vampires on the payroll? I carefully kept my face from showing any emotion. "Of course I work for the NPS."

"No way," Fitz said. "I have a sixth sense about these things. You are either an international supermodel or a movie star. But you are most definitely not a park ranger."

"Right, I'm not a park ranger. I'm an exhibit specialist working on a theater project," I said, and gave him a playful tap on the arm. "And flattery will get you everywhere."

The room was filling up with people. Middle-aged men in dark suits greatly outnumbered the chiffon-clad women with stiff hair, most of whom appeared several decades older than I. I was intent on observing my surroundings when I realized Fitz was speaking to me. "There's an open bar over in this direction. Let me get you something. It will help ease the boredom of introductions to dozens of old farts you'll never see again."

"Just mineral water with a slice of lemon for me, thanks."

"Are you sure?" Fitz said. "My uncle stocks a great bar, and he has his own private wine cellar."

"I'm very sure," I said with a smile, determined to keep my wits about me tonight.

"You don't mind if I indulge myself, do you? I hate to say it, but I feel like I already need a drink. I see my mother on the other side of the room."

"You go right ahead," I laughed as he melted into the crowd. I took advantage of his absence to look around. Bradley's home was a virtual palace. Crystal chandeliers twinkled overhead; the floor was pink and white Carerra marble, and on the wall hung large paintings by what looked like Matisse, Courbet, Cezanne, and more than one work by Picasso. I believed they were original—and, if so, were worth literally millions. I decided to get a closer look at a Mary Cassatt when a young man brushed past me. I stopped on a dime. It was the guy from Kevin St. James I had dubbed Green Day. Once again he was decked out in Ralph Lauren from his tweed jacket to his tasseled loafers and the pink shirt with requisite polo player on the pocket. He glanced at me—or rather glanced at my cleavage, and kept going. He didn't seem to recognize me from the pub. I intended to ask Fitz about him and turned to see if my date was on his way back from the bar. I didn't see him. Instead I saw my mother.

She turned in my direction and looked right through me as if she had never seen me before in her life. Mar-Mar, for once out of her Birkenstocks and jeans, looked like a young debutante in a silver cocktail dress with a halter neckline. In reality Mar-Mar is an "old soul"—more than a millennium old—but because vampires don't age, she looks even younger than I do. Tonight Mar-Mar was acting all wide-eyed and naive, hanging on every word uttered by a bald-headed septugenarian I recognized as a Supreme Court justice. A much younger man, a popular New England Congressman, showed up at her elbow, bringing her a drink. She gave him a dazzling smile. What an actress. As far as I knew, the only lovers she's ever taken were kings, popes, generals, and maybe a tsar or two. A mere Congressman wouldn't even get to first base.

At first I felt surprise that she was here. Then anger flooded through me. Mar-Mar had known damn well I wasn't going to run into her at some downtown bar. Once again she had played the puppetmaster, pulling the strings of my life. I don't know how she had engineered my meeting Fitz or how she had known he would invite me here, but I had a gut feeling that she had. That poor schnook of a Congressman had no clue how ruthless his date truly was. She didn't have to bite him to destroy him, if she wished it. I knew her. She only had to make a phone call and any deep dark secret the handsome politician thought he had buried in his past would be all over the tabloids. Or his bank accounts would suddenly be frozen, his car would be stolen, and maybe his house would even burn down. With Mar-Mar I never knew how she would crush someone she decided to eliminate, but I knew she could.

I pointedly turned my back on her in time to see Fitz coming up with a drink in one hand and my glass of mineral water in the other. He handed it to me, saying, "My cousins and the rest of the guests under thirty are downstairs. Uncle Brent has a movie theater on the ground floor, as well as a game room. We'll head there later. Right now duty calls. You need to meet our host."

Fitz put his arm lightly around my waist and steered me over to a small group of men in well tailored suits. Brent Bradley was sipping from a martini glass, and each of the yes-men encircling him held one too. He saw us coming, one eyebrow raised with studied charm, and he produced a practiced smile that showed very white teeth.

"St. Julien, my boy," he said. "Who is this lovely lady with you?"

"Daphne Urban, meet my uncle Brent Bradley," Fitz said as I extended my hand. The great man clasped it warmly with his martini-less hand and held it just a second longer than necessary.

"My nephew has excellent taste," he said and began to introduce me to the men around him. Truthfully they all looked alike, and I wasn't paying close attention to their names until he came to the man next to him on the side away from me.

"John Rodriguez, my business partner," Brent Bradley said about the only person near him who didn't behave like an overeager puppy. Rodriguez smiled at me with no warmth. His light brown eyes were small and deep set. His weak chin gave him the look of a rabbit, if a rabbit could possibly have the eyes of a reptile. Warning bells went off in my head. This man was very dangerous, they clamored. I had the immediate feeling that whatever else he was, he was a villain.

With my brightest smile, I responded, "And what business might that be, Mr. Rodriguez? Do you work for the current administration too?"

"No, Miss Urban, I do not. I am merely a private citizen," he said in an smarmy voice that sent chills down my spine.

"John is much too modest," Bradley said. "He makes sure I can afford to live like this"—he raised his glass to the grand room—"indulge in my hobbies, and still devote my time to public service. He is invaluable in every way."

"John runs Bradley Consulting," Fitz said. "It specializes in international security issues."

"My my, that is fascinating," I simpered and hooked my arm through Fitz's. "And Mr. Bradley—"

"Please, call me Brent."

I gave him a smile that would have melted ice cream faster than a microwave. "Why that's so sweet of you, *Brent.* I was going to say your home is extraordinary, and the art you have hanging in it, it's breathtaking. I've never seen pieces like these outside of a museum." I hit him squarely in his vanity. He basked in my adoration. I hoped I hadn't involuntarily rolled my eyes because in truth I thought he was a pompous ass—an arrogant, very wealthy, pompous ass.

As for Mr. Rodriguez, a dark aura hung around him. In my gut I felt instinctively that I had found my susto mastermind. Shiftiness, dishonesty, and cruelty were all clearly present in the microexpressions that fleetingly crossed his face. To what extent the president's top security advisor was involved in the drug scheme, I didn't know, but I guessed he was profiting from it whether he knew it or not. I wondered how much Mar-Mar had already uncovered. She obviously was aware of Brent Bradley's connection to the growing drug epidemic, and it now became clear why the Darkwings had really been brought into the situation. It was a horrific security breach for the president's closest advisor to be engaged in criminal activities. Morality aside, he could easily be blackmailed or pressured into revealing state secrets or doing something far worse. After all, he was in the very heart of the United States government.

At this point, Brent Bradley decided my allotted time in his presence had expired, and he was saying,"Well my dear, I mustn't monopolize you any longer. St. Julien, be sure to bring this beautiful lady out here again and make it soon. Perhaps we can all have dinner together. I'll have my secretary look at my schedule."

"It would be my pleasure," I said, already determined to make sure Fitz followed through on the invitation. Excitement was building in me. All I needed was the chance to find some evidence that would link Rodriguez and Bradley with the susto.

Bradley gave me a kiss on the cheek before Fitz and I walked away. Rodriguez offered not even a goodbye. His contemptuous glance at me showed that he regarded me as if I were insignificant or more likely just another piece of ass that Bradley might try to bed. I looked right back at him with steely eyes, and that was a mistake. He noticed. I could see in his face that he was reevaluating his opinion of me and taking my measure as an enemy.

Fitz, on the other hand, seemed oblivious to the undercurrents swirling around us. He was clearly enjoying having his arm around my waist and pulled me against him. I admit it felt good. He was big, masculine, and very handsome. He put his lips close to my hair and said softly into my ear, "I can't avoid it any longer. I'm getting dirty looks. You have to meet my mother. Let's swing by the bar first, so I can freshen my drink."

"Is she that bad?" I asked.

"Bad? Oh no, Delores is not bad. She is a saint, and I am her only son. Her only son who doesn't visit often enough, call often enough, take her out to dinner enough. Her only son who is, quite simply, not good enough at anything and certainly not the success his father intended him to be. Another Jameson on the rocks, please," he said to the bartender, whose name tag identified him as part of the catering company's staff.

"Right away, sir," the stocky man said. Fitz stuffed a dollar in the tip jar and took the drink. He drained it on the spot. "Fill it again," he said handing it back. The bartender did and returned the glass topped off.

"All right, my lovely Daphne, I think I am ready to face Mommie Dearest."

We walked over to a thin woman of medium height who was standing in front of French doors that led out to a floodlit garden. She wore an austere black silk dress and her hair was white, not dyed. It was, however, exquisitely styled, and her eyes were like shiny green stones in a classically attractive face. But her beauty was brittle, betraying a hardness of character within. Her bejewelled hand held a drink in a short glass, garnished with a maraschino cherry. I guessed she was sipping a Manhattan although I really hadn't seen the bourbon-and-vermouth concoction since the late nineteen-fifties. Fitz lightly kissed her forehead. "Mother," he said, "how do you feel this evening?"

"I feel with my hands, how do you think I feel," she said with ice in her voice. "But if you are inquiring about my emotional state, I am as well as I can be as a woman alone. We're having a game of bridge later. I don't suppose you can be a fourth?"

"Mother, I'm terribly sorry, but I have a date this evening," he said as if she somehow didn't notice me standing there with his arm around my waist. "Daphne, this is my mother, Delores Fitzmaurice."

"And who are you?" she asked. "Another one of those earnest Wellesley girls? No, you're far too fashionable. Most of them are lesbians anyway."

"Mother! No, Daphne works for the government."

"Oh. How very boring," she said. "Where did you go to school?"

"The Sorbonne," I said without missing a beat. "And before that I was at St. George's British International School in Rome."

"Your father was a diplomat?" she asked, beginning to sound interested. Perhaps I was worth paying attention to after all. She took a long hard look at my face.

"He was attached to the Vatican," I answered truthfully.

"Fitz, you have surprised me," she said to her son. "Does this mean you're finally over that silly little golf player you were so keen on marrying?"

I felt embarrassed for Fitz, but his face didn't betray a thing. "Jessica was the U.S. Women's amateur champion, Mother."

"She was also a two-timing little bitch," Fitz's mother said smoothly, shocking the hell out of me.

"Yes, she was that too," Fitz said evenly. "And now Daphne and I had better get back to circulating. She hasn't met the cousins yet."

Delores Fitzmaurice extended her hand. I took it. The bones seemed fragile and her flesh was cold. "I think you might be very good for my son. He needs a woman who knows something about life besides which putter to use. She was a sexless little ninny as well. You are not."

"Well thank you for the compliment, Mrs. Fitzmaurice. It's been a pl— "

"Don't lie, my dear. It has not been a pleasure. I'm sure I have made both you and Fitz very uncomfortable. But I speak my mind. Maybe you can make a man of my son."

"I think he already is a man," I snapped back.

"Then you have made a good start," she said. "Give Mother a kiss, Fitz. Now go ahead and find the cousins. Good night, Daphne," she said, took a long swallow of her Manhattan, and ignored us both.

"I need another Jameson," Fitz said, and we headed back to the bar. His gait was steady, his voice was clear, and his eyes were only slightly puffy. Fitz held his liquor well and obviously had a reason to drink. I understood him better now. Maybe his double life as a drug dealer made some kind of twisted sense after all. That role still didn't fit what I had seen of him, but the evidence against him so far was damning.

The real party was happening downstairs. Maybe fifty young people were playing video games, munching on popcorn in Brent's private movie theater while watching *Kill Bill 2,* shooting pool, or just standing around drinking beer. The music was loud. The lights were low. Cannabis tainted the air despite the presence of the VIPs upstairs.

"Don't yell out *Fitz* in this crowd," Fitz said to me with a smile. "At least a dozen of the Fitzmaurice cousins will answer. To avoid confusion they call me Saint Fitz. And speaking of the devil—Daphne Urban, these yahoos are my cousins Joe Fitz, Mike Fitz, and Tim Fitz."

Three beer-drinking, good-looking guys grabbed Fitz. One cousin gave him a thump on the back, a second cousin who was even bigger than Fitz gave him a fake noogie on the head, and the third gave him a "man hug." Each of the cousins offered me a hand to shake one at a time. "Good to meet you, Daphne," Joe Fitz said. "You got a good guy here. The best." The other two seconded that thought.

While they exchanged sports news, I looked around and spotted Green Day sitting in a chair with a skinny blonde on his lap. He was dropping peanuts down the front of her silk camisole and she was swatting him playfully. After Fitz told the three cousins he'd catch up with them again later, I tugged at his arm and said, "Who's the dark-haired guy in that leather chair over there, holding the girl with the spiky blond hair? Is he a cousin too?"

"Him? That's Jimbo. He's not a relation. He was Brent's second wife's kid. Now he works for Bradley Consulting. Why do you want to know?"

"He looks familiar. I thought I saw him at Kevin St. James on Friday. Was he there?"

"Yeah, he was. Sometimes he tags along when I leave the office. To be honest, he's hard to take. When he was a kid, he used to lie all the time. He'd make up the dumbest stuff just to sound important. When he was twelve, he grew marijuana in his room and got caught. Once he got hold of a pistol and shot it off out in the school playground. That kind of crap. We always felt sorry for him though. His mother didn't have any time for him, and his father didn't want him. Mostly they kept him in boarding school, but he got thrown out of two or three. He always had a scam going and he always got caught. I guess Uncle Brent feels some sort of responsibility for him even though Jimbo isn't his kid."

"Sounds like a charming person," I said, thinking that Jimbo might be the weak link in the chain. I wondered if J could bring him in for questioning somehow. The kid would probably start screaming for a lawyer, but if we could catch him with some susto on him it might work.

"You'll find out for yourself just how charming he is," Fitz whispered and pulled me over to where Jimbo was sitting.

"Hey, Jimbo, this is Daphne. Daphne, this is Jimbo Armbruster."

Jimbo's dark eyes didn't quite focus. "Hi Daphne. And this is Blondi. She's named after Hitler's dog," he said, laughing, and put his hand under her silk cami, deliberately pulling it up and exposing a perfectly formed silicone breast. "Blondi is Euro-trash, aren't you, honey?"

"Jimmee, you are a naughty boy," Blondi protested with a Hungarian accent that made her sound like Eva Gabor on a rerun of *Green Acres.* She pushed his hand away and pulled her silk cami back down, but didn't really seem offended. To us she said, "I am actress, not Euro-trash."

"Yeah, the name of her last movie was *Blood, Sweat, and Rears.* It didn't get an Oscar nomination," he said and started inching his hand along her thigh under her little leather skirt.

"I was very good in that," she sniffed and slapped his hand. Her eyes were so heavily made up with black eyeliner that she looked like a raccoon, and her lips were a very bright red. "And Jimmee says he can get me into movies in America," she said brightly.

"Well we just wanted to say hi," Fitz answered. "See you later, Jimbo."

As we walked away, I whispered fiercely, "Were you giving me some kind of test?"

Fitz looked at me mischievously. "I guess I was. I figured I should show you the worst. And you still haven't met Uncle Hilbert or Auntie Kathleen. One of them's simply a drunk, the other one is certifiable, but nobody's supposed to notice."

"We can't choose our relatives, Fitz. Every family has its skeletons and secrets."

His voice got sadder. "I wish my family would have the decency to keep the skeletons secret. But no, we line 'em all up at the dinner table and pass them the mashed potatoes. And nobody's supposed to notice that Aunt Janice has taken so many pills she's drooling. You know, this music is giving me a headache. Would you mind if we grabbed your coat and just went out and sat on the patio for some fresh air?" His voice was weary.

"I'd really like that," I said. Actually I was worried I'd soon be freezing, but I too wanted to get away from the tensions that were making it hard to breathe in there. I shouldn't have been concerned. Uncle Brent's patio came with an outdoor hearth in which a roaring applewood fire burned. Heat lamps shone down on the benches, and they gave just enough illumination that you might not notice the security guards patrolling the grounds. Another couple was outside too, but on the far side of the patio and completely absorbed in alternately arguing and kissing. "A Fitzmaurice and his fiancée," Fitz whispered to me when we passed them on our way to the fireplace. "Hey Joan, Kevin," he called out without stopping. "Hey back to you Saint Fitz," Kevin said, then forgot we existed.

Fitz and I sank into deep cushions of a wicker sofa in front of the fire. I wondered if he was going to make a move on me, but all he did was take my hand and hold it. "You're a good girl, Daphne," he said.

"You don't even know me, Fitz," I said. "I'm not so good."

"Yes you are. I've seen enough of you to know that. And I appreciate you being here. I hate these evenings. And since Jessica left, I haven't been able to face them. You don't mind me talking about her, do you?"

"No, I really don't. I told you, I'd be glad to listen."

"Would it bore you to just sit here for a while?" he asked and stared into the flames.

"No, it would suit me just fine," I answered. He put his arm around my shoulder and pulled me close to him, and the effect was more companionable than seductive. We sat there in silence with the flames dancing hypnotically before our eyes. Fitz's lids drooped and he fell asleep. I stayed wide awake looking into the fire and soon my memories took me back to another party, the one I had entered in London nearly two centuries ago.

There, on that long-ago winter evening, my face was masked, my form was clad in scarlet satin and stiff white lace, and I was descending into the crush of Almack's at the height of the Season. Heads turned. Whispers began. Lord Byron looked at me. His eyes narrowed, a small smile lit his lips, and it seemed to me that during this first glance he decided I was a delicious ripe fruit he had to pluck. He pushed through the sycophants who encircled him to walk over and stand in front of me. He was stunning in his good looks. His face had a soft, almost luminous beauty, but as he was broad of shoulder, narrow of hip, and self-assured in his manner, he projected a maleness that charged the air around him. I lowered my mask and gazed at him. The naked desire with which he looked back at me made me tremble.

Byron was only twenty years old, and he still had a year before he reached his majority. Already he had provided a feast for the gossipmongers, causing scandal after scandal during this London season. He had gambled without restraint, piled up debts, and become a libertine, taking both men and women into his bed. But beneath his public persona I could glimpse a terrible sadness. Complexies, I thought. What had put that haunted look in his eyes? He was exactly the kind of bad boy with a poet's soul that I couldn't resist. In fact, I had plotted to meet him like this in order to become part of the "abyss of sensuality," as he later described this year of his life, into which he was descending. Yes, I was shameful and amoral. Why not? I was a vampire, and I had never been in love.

"Fair lady, who might you be?" he said taking my hand and bringing it to his lips.

"Daphne Castagna, Lady Webster," I murmured, tingling at the spot where he had lightly kissed my fingers.

"Lady Webster?" he said, amused. "Oh I think not. You are no familiar member of the *ton,* your accent is Continental, not English, and your beauty is so ethereal, you appear not even a creature of this earth. You are an enigma and I love mysteries."

"Then I am hoping you will love me," I said, looking at him coquettishly from under my lashes. The nearness of his body was affecting my reason. This encounter was working out exactly as I had hoped. After several hundred years I had become jaded to living, which was turning out to be both eternal and utterly boring. Obviously Byron had seduction on his mind. He could not know what I had on mine. Seduction? Most certainly, but dare I confess I wanted more? Could this wild, brilliant boy arouse my mind as well as my body? Would he prove so unpredictable, outrageous, and amusing that time would pass easily once more? And as my heart squeezed painfully at the thought, was it possible at last to dream of truly loving and being loved in return?

Byron's words broke into my ponderings. "I have a coach. Shall we go somewhere less crowded?" His language was polite, but his tone was laden with lewd suggestion. My body began to burn with sexual heat. My breathing quickened. A sweet ache suffused my loins, but I had to be careful to hide these signs from Byron. I couldn't be a woman easy to have, for what is won without effort is not prized.

"Do you think I am a whore, sir?" I said, taking mock offense.

"A thousand apologies, dear lady," he said, realizing he had made a miscalculation. "An odalisque perhaps, lately escaped from the seraglio, but not a common whore."

"You are outrageous, sir. I think I shall take my leave," I said and raised my mask, making as if to go.

He reached out then and daringly grabbed my hand, pulling me back. "I apologize again. You have made me mad with desire. I am not in my right mind, you see. Please don't leave me in such torment. I shall behave like a gentleman, but I beg you, *Lady Webster,* let us leave these public apartments and find a place where Eros can be set free."

I lowered my mask again and looked into his eyes, my own full of mischief. "You must prove yourself worthy of me first, my lord," I said sternly. "Fetch me some lemonade, and some for yourself. If you can win me by the time I drink the cup, I shall surrender to you. If you cannot, more's the pity." I gently removed my hand from his grasp. He smiled at me and took my elbow, escorting me to a chair with a seat of white brocade that sat along the wall. Every eye in the room stared at us. I sat straight and regal, filled with arrogance and pride.

Byron brought back two crystal glasses of lemonade, both quite small. He sat on the next chair and handed me the smallest.

"You cheat, sir," I said with a smile. "I shall sip this very slowly in punishment for your tricks."

"I would relish punishment from your dainty hands," he said. "How must I win you?"

"I shall make it easy for you. Recite a verse to me, one you have not spoken to anyone before. They must be beautiful words, and you must promise to dedicate them to me, and me alone. It must not be a trifle you've said a thousand times before to some puling maid. If I approve, I shall leave with you without further ado."

"I have just the one," he said and gave me a foxy grin. "You shall soon be forfeit."

"I am the judge and jury, you the poor petitioner. Please begin," I said imperiously. He looked very young, although not innocent, and commenced his recitation:

So, we'll go no more a roving
So late into the night,
Though the heart be still as loving,
And the moon be still as bright.

For the sword outwears its sheath,
And the soul wears out the breast,
And the heart must pause to breathe,
And Love itself have rest.

Though the night was made for loving,
And the day returns too soon,
Yet we'll go no more a roving,
By the light of the moon.

"Well, that was quite pretty," I said and tapped his jacket with my fan.

"Yes, and I have not yet published it. I only finished penning it this very night. I shall dedicate it to Lady Webster, this I vow. Now, I believe I have won the wager. And before I scandalize all London by taking you right here at Almack's, let us leave. I have a carriage."

"Do you want me that much, my lord?" I said, all wide-eyed.

"I want you desperately, my lady," he said. "I am on fire with longing for you."

"Then we must find your coach," I said.

Within minutes, we were in the back of a swaying landau, bundled in furs. "To my rooms," Byron said to the driver.

"Yes, my lord," the old man called down from his seat.

"Lady," Byron said. "Who are you to drive me so mad so quickly?"

"As you said, I am a mystery woman. Shall you try to solve the puzzle?" I said, lowering my eyes and looking at him from beneath my lashes.

"No, your mystery excites me," he said, "and so little excites me anymore. I am unexcited by drink and even by women. Yet you make me swoon by your very nearness." He pulled me to him then and kissed me. It was as if stars collided, and in the conflagration our souls were melted and merged. In those days I had so little control over my impulses that I wanted to bite him at once, but I did not. I was enjoying the sensation of his lips against mine too much. His tongue forced its way past my teeth and filled my mouth. I pushed away.

"Sir, you frighten me," I lied, knowing that prolonging my surrender would make it all the more sweet. "I do not know you."

"Then I shall let you know me in every way possible," he said. "Will you come up to my rooms?"

"Are you being disingenuous, my lord? That's where you

told the driver to take us. You believed I would." I grasped his jacket with my small pale hands and whispered softly to him, my lips inches from his, my breath touching his face.

"I hoped you would, and in my arrogance I assumed you would. Now I am begging you to, for I cannot live out the night without you in my arms," he said, his eyes closing and his head bowing. "Cupid's arrow has struck me and I am doomed."

"Sir, your reputation precedes you. You have a different lover every night," I scolded. "Why should I believe you love me?"

"Because I do," he said and looked into my eyes. "There is something about you I do not understand. It terrifies me because I cannot resist it. I feel you will cause my death, but without you there can be no life."

The landau deposited us at Byron's London town house, and a servant held the door open for us to enter. Byron handed over our coats and my hat and muff. "Please bring us wine, then the lady and I don't wish to be disturbed," he instructed.

"Very good, sir," the servant replied and disappeared down the hall as we climbed the stairs to his velvet-draped bedroom. I sat primly in a chair before a low fire and Byron stood staring at me, drinking in my features by candlelight. The servant appeared with the wine and quietly withdrew. I was glad he had brought an entire bottle, for I intended to get Byron very drunk so if I bit him, and I thought I might, he would not remember.

"Please drink with me, my lord," I said, "for I am very nervous of a sudden and wary of you. You look at me as if you are the cat and I am the bird upon which you will feast."

"Whatever you wish, shall be done," he said and handed me a glass of wine, draining his own in an instant. He sank to my feet then, sitting upon the Persian carpet, and he put his head on my lap. I stroked his hair. He sighed.

"More wine?" I asked.

"Only if we drink it together," he suggested. "Take a sip and hold the wine in your mouth, then let me take it from your sweet lips. A kiss of wine, what could be more enticing." I did as he instructed and held the tart liquid in my mouth. He covered my lips with his and he sucked the liquid into his mouth. We thus shared the wine, although I swallowed none at all. We continued our intimate quaffing until the bottle was empty, but I had taken nary a drop. The exchange had left us both very aroused. Byron stood and faltered. "The wine has made me dizzy," he said, and pointing to the bulge in his pants, "but not impaired, as you can see."

He took my hand and raised me from the chair, leading me to the bed. He lay down then and pulled me on top of him, unlacing the back of my gown as he bore my weight upon him. He pulled the scarlet fabric down exposing my breasts. He pushed me off him then and I lay flat upon the bed as he used force to pull my gown from me. Then his strong fingers ripped away my undergarments, frantically and almost cruelly, until I lay naked on the velvet covers.

Something changed in his face then. If there had been any innocence, it vanished and a wolf's rapacious hunger came upon him. He stroked my stomach and trailed his hand down between my thighs. "Your flesh is icy cold," he said. "Like death."

"You must heat me up, my lord," I admonished.

He pushed a finger into me. "You are no virgin," he suggested.

"No, my lord, I surely am not," I said and reached my hand to the bulge in his satin breeches. I grabbed him hard, and he groaned, his eyes closing. "And neither are you," I said.

"No," he said. "Not since I was a boy of nine, when my nurse May Gray showed me what a man and woman do."

"And what is that, my lord?" I said, reaching up and pulling his lips to mine. The darkness and the hunger were closing over me now, taking away my reason and leaving me with a great thirst. I was a depraved creature as my vampire self, my dark self, began to surface.

Byron reached down and unbuttoned his breeches, releasing his stiff member. He parted my thighs, brushing his fingers between them and sending arousal through my body. He held my wet nether lips open with his fingers, and put the hardness of him between them. "This," he sighed and pushed into me. "This is what a man and woman do together," he said with a growl.

I moaned as I felt him pierce me and fill me. Soon the rhythm of our joining teased me toward orgasm. Without tenderness his hands found my nipples. He rubbed and pinched the nibs until the sensation was pushing me toward rapture. Suddenly his body was trembling violently. "I cannot wait," he whispered.

He moaned and quivered, spilling his seed inside of me. He spasmed again and made another great moan before he became still, leaving me still not satisfied. He looked at me beneath him, and a beam of moonlight reached its ghostly glow across the bed. He pulled his sword from my warm sheath with a jerk, and I cried out. "I shall make you cry in pleasure, now," he promised, and put his fingers where his shaft had been. Gently pushing into me with his hand and against my sweet spot with his thumb, he coaxed me toward completion. My body twitched and trembled. He held me close against him and pushed his hand more deeply into me, until my legs were splayed wide and his hand pumped mercilessly as I screamed in pain and pleasure both as an orgasm racked my body. When I stilled, he gently pushed the wet hair from my forehead.

"My mystery lady," he said, "are you quite finished now?"

The moonlight fell across his face, and he bent down to kiss me. His neck was white in the cold light.

"No, my lord," I whispered with a breathiness that was almost a hiss. "No, I am not done," and I reached my thin arms up around his neck, and before he knew what was happening, my teeth pierced his flesh. His blood flowed into my mouth as the wine had done, but this special wine of life I swallowed greedily. Warmth spread through my cold flesh.

Not even when my small sharp teeth bit into his vein did Byron attempt to pull away. Instead he moaned a long slow moan and folded his arms around me in a loving embrace. He wanted darkness. He searched for what was feared by others. My vicious kiss of pleasure and pain was nirvana to him. He lay on his back against the covers, me atop him, and he lifted his chin to give me complete access to his flesh. Then the succubus who was I, the vampire, shamelessly rubbed my naked body upon him and drank his blood until he slipped away into unconciousness. But I was careful not to drink too much, so that he would not become a vampire like me.

I slipped away from his quarters before the morning light. All I left behind was a stain of red blood upon the pillow. Cupid's arrow had hit us both, and I was smitten by him. But I knew if I stayed, I would either kill him or turn him into the monster that I was. So I vanished before dawn, and I believed I would disappear forever from his life. I had gotten my poem, my thrill, and my fill of his blood.

But I was wrong, for he would soon come seeking me.

CHAPTER 8

Old age and treachery will overcome youth and skill.

—Anonymous

A man's voice, taut with urgency, roused me from my reveries. Mike Fitz, his face white and serious, had his hand on Fitz's shoulder. "Saint Fitz, get up. Bradley wants you. Hurry."

Fitz pulled himself up on his feet and said sleepily, "Huh? What's going on?"

"There's a problem. Better get inside pronto."

I stood too, and Mike Fitz looked at me. "Sorry, miss. It's family stuff. Maybe you best just rejoin the party."

Fitz turned to me, saying, "Daphne, I apologize for bailing out on you like this. I'll be back as soon as I can, but if I'm not around by midnight, get on the helicopter without me."

"You're kidding me," I said, wide-eyed.

"It's probably nothing. Maybe a bigwig had too much to drink. But I have to go." He gave me a quick kiss on the cheek and walked toward the house in a hurry.

Or maybe it's another OD, I thought to myself. I intended to find out. I also saw this situation as a golden opportunity to snoop.

I slipped back into the house and, except for Bradley's absence, nothing seemed amiss. Rodriguez was gone too. My first impulse was to find the ladies' room and then "get lost" in the other parts of the house. I asked a maid carrying a tray of canapes where to find the "little girls' room." I followed her instructions and went down a hall on the far side of the bar. The wallpaper was green-flocked and the recessed lighting in the ceiling bathed the hallway with a soft rose light. Classical music was piped in through a sound system. I recognized Brahms' Piano Concerto No. 2, Opus 83, a work grander than any of his symphonies. I was reaching for the door to the bathroom when it opened. The light was off inside, and standing in the shadowy interior with her hand on the doorknob was my mother.

"Quick, get in here," she whispered, tugging me inside.

I slid through the door, and she closed it firmly behind me.

"What's going on?" I asked. "Do you know?" I didn't bother asking why she was at the party or what she was doing with the Congressman. She'd tell me as much as she pleased and no more.

"No. Just that there's a problem. That weasely kid with the Ralph Lauren obsession came in and pulled Bradley aside. Then Bradley, Rodriguez, and a few of his underlings went rushing off toward the back of the house. I don't know how much time we have, but we need to use it wisely."

"Doing what?" I asked.

"Looking for evidence of susto—and seeing if we can find out what just happened. I'm going to search the house. You take the grounds."

"Yeah right, how am I supposed to get by the guards with the dogs?"

My mother gave a deep sigh that clearly expressed her disappointment in having to tell me what was obvious. "Daphne, you'll have to transform. Get up above the floodlights and do an aerial search. The guards aren't going to be scanning the skies for a giant bat."

Damn it, I thought. *Not only is it frigging cold out but I would hate anything happening to my dress and shoes.*

As usual, my mother was reading my mind. "There's a door into the garage at the end of this corridor. Leave your clothes there and get outside that way. They've left one garage door open so the chauffeurs can get in and out. There's a line of limos in the driveway. Just keep your eyes open for the drivers. Most of them are in the kitchen area eating, but somebody may be out by his car smoking."

"*May be?* Sounds like the odds are somebody's going to spot me."

"Daphne, I trust you can handle it. You always do," she said sweetly. And just as sweetly she added, "Now get the hell out of here."

I didn't like the situation one little bit. It was risky, but it was my job. And my mother was my boss—and that made my current position more like a nightmare scenario than the career of my dreams. I left the bathroom and found the door leading to the garage, a cavernous place big enough for four cars. One of the bay doors was open, just as Mar-Mar had said. I wouldn't have been surprised if she had already been out there and rigged it that way.

I quickly shed my dress and shoes, stashing them under a tarp that was lying on the floor along one wall. The cold bit into my bare flesh like a piranha. I inhaled deeply and felt a strange energy buzzing through my veins. The harsh winter air whirled around me, and flashes of light within it became strobes in the darkness. I was beyond caring if they attracted any attention. I was beyond anything but becoming my dark side, the animal inside me leaping up to emerge. Wings burst free from my back, my pale human flesh became sleek fur, and my eyes, now golden orbs, saw as clearly into the darkness as if it were broad daylight. I moved to the edge of the garage bay and prepared to leap into the night, when I heard a voice shout in Spanish. "*¡Diablo! ¡Ay Dios mio! ¡Diablo!*"

A liveried chauffeur dropped his cigarette and began running away from me down the aisle between two rows of parked limos. I flew toward him and hit him hard with my feet, knocking him to the ground. He bounced off a fender and fell. I grabbed him with my claws and picked up his limp body. He reeked of beer. *That's a stroke of luck,* I thought. *He's drunk.* I figured he had probably fainted. With a powerful thrust of my bat wings, I flew quickly to a line of hedges and dropped him carefully on the lawn. Hopefully he wouldn't freeze to death before he woke up or someone came looking for him. Whatever, I didn't have time to worry about his health and well-being.

I took to the skies again, climbing high above the Bradley compound. I could see a greenhouse and a number of outbuildings. A semi was parked behind one of the larger buildings far from the main house. A wire mesh fence surrounded the blue prefab metal-sided building. The squat structure looked new and seemed the kind of commercial eyesore that didn't belong in the Hamptons. But you know what they say about an eight-hundred-pound gorilla like Bradley. He can do whatever the hell he wants.

I let myself down in the shadows on one side of the prefab, hoping to get a look inside. There were no exterior windows, and since I was three times human size, with a fifteen-foot wingspan to boot, I wasn't going to get through the front door, which was probably locked in any event. I slithered around the corner of the building to where the big rig was parked in the back. No open garage doors here. The large pull-down doors were shut tight. No way in there. However, I could smell a sweet, chemical odor, and I could hear a murmur of voices inside the structure. Maybe they were manufacturing the susto right here. What safer place? Who was going to search the home of one of the most powerful men in the United States government? Nobody, that's who.

The trailer truck had Florida license plates. Unlike the garage doors, the back of the truck was open a few feet. I pushed the door up enough to shimmy underneath and roll inside. Most of the interior was empty, but a row of cartons lined the back wall. I glided over and pulled one off the top of the stack. I set it on the floor and carefully opened it. Inside were empty glass ampoules. *Bingo.* I closed the box up again, and returned it to its place on the pile. I felt exuberant. I rolled back out from beneath the back door of the truck and landed lightly on the asphalt. I returned the cargo door to the way I found it, and leaped up into the frigid night air. But it was all too easy. I should have known better.

I had started flying back to the house when I saw four men headed for the greenhouse. Two of them were carrying a rolled-up Persian rug that sagged suspiciously in the middle. Bradley wasn't among the troupe, but Rodriguez was. And so was my Fitz. Mike Fitz and Green Day, aka Jimbo, completed my head count. They pushed open the door to the greenhouse and it banged loudly against something. Rodriguez was clearly in charge. I couldn't see through the glass panes, which were fogged over with moisture, so I landed behind the building, hoping to be able to find an opening to peer through.

I saw a sliver of light coming through a cracked pane and put my eye to it. Rodriguez was telling the two Fitzes to unfold a tarp they took out of a cabinet. It was one of those ubiquitous blue ones they sell at every Home Depot. "Line it with rocks," he was saying.

"Where the hell are we going to get rocks?" my Fitz mouthed off. His movements were stiff and his face rigid with anger.

"Over there, stacked by the shelves. Those are bags of river rocks, used around the shrubs. Bring the bags over. Don't open them."

The two Fitzes went over and brought back a bag apiece. "These weigh sixty pounds each," Fitz said flatly. "That should hold her down. Any more might bust through the tarp. Besides it's going to be damned heavy to carry."

"We'll leave her in the rug," Rodriguez said coldly. "Get it."

Fitz gave Jimbo a look thick with disgust. "You pick her up. You did this, you son of a bitch."

"I told you it was an accident," Jimbo whined. "I was just fooling around."

"Fooling around? You sick fuck. You broke her neck." Fitz's words were filled with loathing.

"She was nothing but a whore," Jimbo shot back, his whining gone. "She deserved it. And nobody's gonna even know."

"*I* know. Mike knows. Rodriguez knows. Even Bradley—" Fitz said.

"That's enough." Rodriguez cut him off. "Let's just get this over with. Get her on the tarp. Mike, help him. Saint Fitz, you go get the SUV."

Fitz stomped out and I heard the door slam behind him. Gravel crunched beneath his feet as he walked toward the house. Under his breath I could hear him saying, "Fuck fuck fuck."

I continued to watch what was going on through the crack in a pane of steamed-up glass. Rodriguez was telling Jimbo and Mike to wrap the tarp around the girl in the rug and use bungee cords to hold it. By the time they finished, the sound of a vehicle was getting closer.

Fitz came back in the door. "Now what?" he said.

Rodriguez turned to him. "Take her down to the boat and dump her in the Atlantic. It's not rocket science. I thought you were supposed to be the smart one. Now get her out of here. I'm going back to the house." He exited, leaving the other three to carry the body in the tarp out of the greenhouse. I went airborne again and watched them stuff the girl into the back of a white Cadillac Escalade, then drive off. I followed, staying maybe two hundred feet above the SUV. I didn't know what I could do to stop them. It was too late to help the girl, but the murder, if we could prove there had been one, could give some honest judge a good reason to issue a search warrant for the Bradley compound. I hoped I could find a way to keep them from dumping her.

For now, all I could do was watch as the SUV pulled up to a dock. Saint Fitz climbed out of the driver's side and walked across a gangplank into a forty-two-foot center-cockpit Beneteau sailing yacht. The other two guys climbed out of the passenger side and went around to lift up the back of the SUV and pull out the girl in the tarp. They were struggling up the gangplank with their heavy burden while I heard Fitz trying to start the engine. It sounded to me as if he was flooding it. I guess he was nervous. Whatever was going on, the engine wasn't starting.

He came forward and yelled down to the men before they threw the girl onto the deck. "Don't! Something's wrong. The engine won't start."

"Well I can't hold this thing much longer," Jimbo said and dropped his end.

"You stupid putz," Mike said. "If she falls into the water here, you're screwed. We're screwed. Hang on to her."

Jimbo picked up his end of the rolled-up tarp, his knees nearly buckling under the weight. "Let's put her back in the Escalade," he grunted.

Mike started arguing with him. "And then what? We got to get rid of this."

"I have an idea," Fitz said. "Go ahead, put her back in the SUV."

They did, then all three of them climbed back into the vehicle, turned it around, and took off back the way they had come. I had been out for nearly an hour now, and I was getting worried about the time. I had to get back to Manhattan before dawn, and flying all the way under my own steam wasn't going to work. I can swoop and dive with great speed, but I'm no long-distance flyer and it was over a hundred miles to get home. I needed to catch the ride back on the helicopter. But putting that worry aside, I flew above the white Escalade again. I had to find out what they did with the body.

The SUV went back to the state highway, stayed on it for a short distance, then turned off onto a sandy dirt track. The SUV swayed and bumped along for a few minutes until the road ran into a stand of oaks and scrub pines. The SUV pulled into the grove and disappeared from my line of sight. I heard the engine die. I carefully flew between the tops of some trees, most of which were short and scruffy but full enough to obscure the view below. I found the stout branch of an oak and hung upside down, finally able to see where the men had gone. They were parked next to a large plot of ghostly-white grave stones, some of them poking up from behind old-fashioned black-iron fences. I figured this was some kind of local or family cemetery. Mike Fitz and Jimbo pulled the tarp with the girl inside out of the back of the Escalade and dumped it on the ground.

"Now what?" Mike whispered, looking around the dank and dark cemetery with fear clearly written on his face.

"We bury her," Fitz said. "The ground's just sand, and it's not frozen."

"What'll we dig with? We don't have any shovels," Jimbo said petulantly. "Any other bright ideas, Einstein?"

I could see Fitz clench his fists and heard him say, in a voice that thudded like a stone dropped into mud, "Well I guess you will have to drive back and get some. Mike, go with the little fuck. I don't trust him. I'll wait here. And for fuck's sake, don't tell Rodriguez."

"Don't worry," Mike answered, "we'll be back in ten minutes. You sure you want to stay here?"

"Yeah. I don't suppose anything would happen, but it would be a helluva thing if we came back and she was gone. I'm staying," he said and sat down on the edge of a monument topped by a marble child kneeling in prayer. "Hurry up, though, it's cold out here."

The SUV pulled out fast, spraying sand as it accelerated.

In the dark and silent night Fitz sat on the marble stone, not moving. Time was ticking away. I had seen enough, and I needed to get out of there. I carefully spread my wings and started to fly off, but I crashed through a branch with an audible crack.

"What's that? Who's there!" Fitz called out. I flew on.

I cleared the trees and started back toward the compound. I hoped he hadn't seen me, but even if he had, it wouldn't matter. I was sure he'd doubt his own eyes. And if he told anyone, who would believe him? It would be just another giant-bat story from a man who drank too much. I was excited by what I had witnessed. The body could be retrieved and we'd have probable cause to get a warrant. But I felt horribly sad too. Not only was a girl dead, but Fitz was now more than a drug dealer. He was an accessory to murder.

I swooped low as I approached the house, trying to hide my bulk by blending into the shadowy black line of limousines. I ducked into the garage and with a whoosh changed back to human form. I felt like a rag doll, totally devoid of energy. I slipped my dress and shoes back on and rushed into the house. A few people sat in overstuffed chairs, but almost everyone else was gone. I didn't see my mother. It was almost midnight. I retrieved my mink from the cloakroom and went rushing out of the front door. I could hear the helicopter starting up its rotors. *Damn it!* I had to get there before it lifted off. I jumped into a golf cart and turned it on, careening out onto the lawn, which was now covered with a layer of white frost. I started driving like a maniac toward the copter, beeping the cart's horn.

The pilot must have seen me. He stopped the spinning blades and I skidded to a halt, jumped out, and ran toward the Bell Ranger. The door was flung open. Rodriguez sat inside.

"You nearly missed your ride," he said in an oily voice.

"I was downstairs in the movie theater," I said lamely. "I must have fallen asleep."

I buckled myself into my seat and the copter took off. I found it uncomfortable to sit so close to this man. Negative energy radiated from him as if he were strontium 90.

"Did you enjoy your evening?" he said.

"Yes, at first," I said. "But then my date disappeared. Do you know what happened to St. Julien?" I asked, all innocence.

"No," Rodriguez said. "I have no idea whatsoever." Then he turned his head away and stared into the darkness.

The ride back to Manhattan passed in an uncomfortable silence. The adrenaline drained from my body, and it was all I could do to stay awake. But I wasn't about to fall asleep in the presence of Rodriguez. He was too dangerous to close my eyes on. We landed at the Twelfth Street heliport. Rodriguez got out first and walked to a waiting car. He didn't look back and he didn't offer me a ride.

My cab arrived in front of my apartment house a little after three a.m. I figured I'd write up a report, walk Jade, and get into my coffin by dawn. Preoccupied with my thoughts and tired from the events of the night, I wasn't watching the shadows. As the taxi pulled away from the curb, I took maybe three steps toward the apartment-house door when I saw a blur in my peripheral vision. I turned to see a lithe, dark figure rushing at me, a sharply pointed stake held in her small fist, ready to strike. Yes, *her* fist. Although a ski mask obscured my attacker's face, I got the immediate impression that this was a woman. Nearly upon me, she thrust upward with the stake, and I kicked desperately at her arm, but gave her only a glancing blow with my light slingbacks. It was enough to deflect her aim. The stake penetrated my coat sleeve and I felt a hot, burning pain as it sliced viciously through my upper arm. Another four inches to the right and she would have pierced my heart.

My left arm went numb and useless, but I reached out

and grabbed the front of the ski mask with my right hand, working with her forward momentum to direct her face toward the brick wall of the building. She hit it with a satisfying smack, but immediately whirled around. She shifted her weight and used her long leg to aim a ferocious kick at my kneecap. Her steel-toed boot struck me hard as I dove onto her, using my good hand to take a firm grip of her weapon-holding arm, flipping her backwards, and landing atop her. I got my knee on her chest, but she was fighting like a wildcat, trying to bite me anywhere she could reach and hitting me relentlessly with her free hand.

At one point during the struggle our eyes locked. I could see hers glittering even in the gray tones of the night. Her features were hidden by the mask, but I felt in my gut that the hate-filled glance of those dark eyes belonged to Darius's band singer. "I'll kill you, you bitch," she hissed. "I'll kill you!"

Annoyed by her flailing blows, but hampered by my wounded arm, I jumped backwards off of her, grabbing the neckline of the dark sweater she wore as I did. It tore downward, exposing her breasts. This seemed to both shock and enrage her. She snarled like an animal, and I thought she was about to leap at me. I got into position to do a tae kwon do front kick, the ap chaki. Performed correctly, it's among the most powerful blows a woman can land. I wanted to break my attacker's collarbone, or better yet, her nose. But once my weight left her, my attacker scuttled sideways out of my reach. Then she got to her feet and, still clutching her polished, deadly weapon, she turned and ran down the block. I didn't chase her. My arm was bleeding, and I had snapped the heel of my shoe when I kicked her. I slipped the shoe off and held it in my good hand. I was hurt and angry to my core.

I slipped into my building. The doorman was dozing in a chair in the little lobby, and I didn't wake him before I pushed the button for the elevator. The doors slid open. Darius stood inside the elevator. Our eyes locked.

"What the hell are you doing here?" I spit out, all my anger now directed at him.

"Whoa!" he said, and held his hands up in front of him. "I was just waiting for you. What happened? Your coat's ripped," he added, as I stepped through the open doors into the lift, and he pushed the button for the tenth floor. "Are you all right?" He went to touch my sleeve. I smacked him in the chest with the shoe I was holding in my hand and he stepped back.

"Don't you fucking touch me," I said. The elevator jolted upward. "This is your fault. I was almost killed out in front of the building. What did you do, set it up?"

"What are you talking about?" he said. "Were you attacked?"

"No, I slipped on a banana peel," I said sarcastically as the elevator stopped at my floor. I brushed past him and got off.

Darius hesitated. "Do you want me to leave?"

"Yes! No! Stay. We'd better talk. I've got some things to say to you, Mr. Darius della Chiesa," I practically screamed at him. Shadows crossed his angular face, and his eyes looked pained as he stepped off the elevator, but he didn't say anything.

I opened the door to my apartment, and we went in. Jade greeted us with a joyful bark. She ran over to me and pushed her head against my hand. Then she jumped up and put her front paws on Darius's chest. She was so big she could nearly look him in the eye. He rubbed her head, and she licked his face before getting down.

"You're the one who gave her the steak," I said to Darius. "Obviously her loyalty *can* be bought."

He ignored my comment. "We need to take a look at your arm," he said, his voice subdued.

I was still bristling with anger. "I need to get out of these clothes first. Make yourself useful. Go ahead and give Jade her dinner," I remarked in a nasty tone as I gingerly peeled off my coat. Blood had run down my arm. The stake had torn an ugly four-inch gash down my bicep.

Darius inhaled sharply. "Shit. That's wicked. Do you have a first-aid kit?" he asked.

"Yes. I'll get it. You take care of Jade. Right now I don't even want to look at you," I said tightly, turned away, and walked into my bedroom.

When I got out of his sight, I pressed my eyes closed and breathed deeply. I was in turmoil inside. I was furious with Darius. I blamed him for the attack. But I felt a stab of guilt too, because I had been with Fitz and because I had kissed him and liked kissing him, even if those feelings were stopped cold after I found out he was involved in the susto ring. Yet in kissing Fitz I had gone beyond anything I had to do as a spy. Now, in my mind, I had cheated on Darius. I didn't feel good about him at the moment, but I felt even worse about myself.

I took off my dress and tossed it on the bed. It was ruined. With my good arm I pulled on a pair of old sweatpants. I left my torso bare. I went into the bathroom and washed the blood off my arm. The stab wound was deep and the edges were jagged, but it had missed the bone and artery. It hurt, but I didn't think it was serious. I grabbed the first-aid kit and walked back into the living room. Darius was standing there. He took the kit from me. We didn't really look at each other as he expertly cleaned the wound with antiseptic and bandaged it. His touch was gentle.

"Is that okay?" he asked. "Do you hurt?"

"It's fine, thanks," I answered, my voice tight. I still didn't look at him. "Darius, we need to get some things straight," I said. "Starting with who attacked me."

"Daphne, look at me," he said. He put his fingers under my chin and turned my head around to face him. "I don't know who attacked you. But I'm sorry. I really am."

I looked into his face, trying not to react to his eyes, trying not to look at his mouth, trying not to weaken because he was so close to me. "Darius. My attacker was that girl in your band. She came at me with a stake. What is going on? Level with me. I need you to tell me the truth."

"Daphne, I *am* telling you the truth. I can't believe it was Julie. That's nuts. She's not just a singer. She works for the agency. You know what I mean. She's on assignment with me. The vampire hunters don't have anything to do with her. Maybe they are after me, I give you that. And perhaps I endangered you as well. But I don't know who they are, I swear I don't."

"And I'm telling you, my attacker was your band singer," I said with an icy voice.

"Look, Daphne, I told you, that's impossible. You're just upset. I don't blame you. But it's night. It's dark. Did you see your attacker's face?"

"No," I said. "But I saw her eyes."

Darius stood there holding my arms. He finally said, "I'll find out. I'll make sure it's not her. I'm trying to identify the team of vampire hunters that we fought with the other night. I promise you I'll clear this up."

"Can you keep that promise, Darius?" I asked, my body rigid. "Can you keep it before I get killed?"

"Yes," Darius said. "I swear it." He leaned toward me then. He kissed me. I didn't kiss him back, but my body was beginning to betray me. My nipples contracted and got hard. I felt as if my intellect and my emotions were in total disconnect. How could I want him when I was so angry at him?

"I need to put a shirt on," I said, turning away from him.

"Daphne, I don't want it to be like this," he said and reached out, coming up behind me and wrapping his arms around me. "I don't want to live without you. I don't want to be undead without you." He nuzzled his face into my hair. "I'm asking you to trust me and to wait for me."

I was stiff and unyielding in his arms, but it was only by

a tremendous force of will. His hands found my breasts and held them, softly brushing his fingers over them. It felt good and I was forgetting about being angry with him. Now he was kissing the back of my neck. "No, Darius, don't," I said, gritting my teeth. But I didn't push him away and actions speak louder than words. He pulled my sweatpants down, holding my body against him with one arm. I could have stopped him. I only had to step away. I didn't. My body played the traitor once more. I gave in to my dark side and pushed reason away instead.

"Your skin is so smooth, Daphne," he murmured in my ear. "I love your ass. Did I ever tell you how much I love your ass?" he whispered. He ran his hands over me, still standing behind me where I couldn't see him. The denim of his jeans against my naked thighs was rough and cool. My knees were starting to feel weak. My breath was coming faster. I still could walk away, but I no longer wanted to. He kissed the top of my shoulder. Every nerve in my body was humming from the imprint of his lips. I seemed to melt beneath him. I was beginning to go mad from wanting him.

Then I heard Darius unzip his fly. I tensed waiting and wanting. I was damp and hot for him. Still standing behind me, he entered me from behind with a quick hard thrust. Then with his arms around my waist, he lowered me to my knees, and stood behind me. "Oh. Oh, no," I said as he went into me doggy style. He was hard and stiff inside me, pounding against me and plunging more deeply inside me than he had ever been before. My body was soon covered in sweat as he grew wilder and pushed deeper. His fingers dug into my flesh almost cruelly. He moaned loudly. I looked over my shoulder at him. He eyes were closed. His head was back. My muscles tightened around him as my eyes fell on his white, vulnerable throat. Just then I felt him shudder and come. But he didn't withdraw from me. Instead he pulled me upright against him, my naked back full length against his body. His hand had slipped around to the front of me, his fingers circling in the wetness, rubbing expertly until a tension began to build in me that I couldn't stop, spiraling up into a quick, intense orgasm with him still inside me.

Afterwards we stood there for a few moments. Then he pulled out and turned me to face him, holding me tightly against him, his cheek next to mine. "I can't stay away from you," he said. "I try to, I really do. And I should. I don't care if I am killed, Daphne. I might even welcome it. But I don't want anything to happen to you."

"How can you not care if you die?" I said with hurt in my voice. "If for no other reason, you know what it would do to me to lose you."

He took my face in his hands. "You'd be better off without me, Daphne. I'm always going to walk the edge. I'm never going to play it safe. I want to get as many of those bastards that are out there and I don't care how. If there are terrorist cells in this city, and there are, I'm going to find them and destroy them. My own way. Fear is everywhere. A suicide bombing could happen at any time, anywhere. I need to fight back."

"Getting yourself killed isn't going to protect anyone, Darius. Don't you see that?" I asked and tried to step away from his encircling arms.

He held me still. He kissed my eyelids. "Don't misunderstand me. I'm not trying to get killed, Daphne. All I'm saying is that I'm going to be the aggressor. I'm going to be the hunter. It's what I've always been, and I can't let becoming a vampire change that."

I finally pushed out of his arms and picked up my sweatpants off the floor. I put them on. Then I turned back to Darius, my stance firm, my voice steady. "Okay, I see that. I accept it even if I don't like it. But what about your band, Darius? You need to quit it."

"Why? It is part of my new assignment from my agency. You have your job. I have mine. Why should I blow it off, Daphne?" His voice sounded annoyed.

"I told you, it's too public," I countered. "You can't go around calling yourself a vampire. Some nut is going to believe you really are." I stepped closer to him and in a conciliatory gesture put my arms around his waist.

"But I really am a vampire," he said, almost mockingly. "And this way I don't have to hide it. Like you said, only the nuts will think I'm geniune."

I looked up at him. Our faces were only inches apart. I felt as if he just didn't want to hear me. "Darius, you just don't get it. We vampires have to hide who we are. We have to wear a mask. You're putting us all in jeopardy and besides—"

"Besides what?" His voice was harsher now, and he abruptly stepped away from me.

"If the vampire hunters don't get you, the others will stop you," I said, my arms dangling uselessly by my sides.

"Screw 'the others.' I'm not afraid of them. I told you that," he said and paced back and forth across the living room, his agitated gait betraying his intense emotions.

"Darius, you're a vampire now. You're part of the culture. You can't betray your own. You're scaring me with your attitude," I said.

He stopped and gave me a hard look. "Don't give me that, Daphne. I know you. You have ice water in your veins, same as me. Nothing scares you, not really. You're the most fearless person I ever met. I couldn't love you otherwise."

"Do you really love me?" I asked.

He threw his hands up in the air. "Of course I love you. Isn't it obvious? Why am I here? Why can't I forget you? Why can't I keep my hands off of you?" He reached out for me then and pulled me against him. He kissed me so hard the room started to spin. He tore my sweatpants off me again and picked me up. He carried me into the bedroom and dropped me on the bed. He pulled off his jeans and climbed above me. The muscles on his chest were clearly defined. His arms were sinewy and strong. I relished looking at him.

My stomach grew tight at the thought of touching him. My eyes got smoky with desire. I wanted him hard. I wanted him hot. I wanted him in me.

"I can't stay away from you, Daphne," he said. "I can't get enough of you. I want you when I'm with you. I want you when I'm not with you."

"Then stay with me, Darius," I insisted. "Stay with me."

"I don't know if fate will let me do that, Daphne, but I can do this," he said and pushed into me again with a mighty thrust. I grabbed his shoulders. I was panting, pulling myself up against him. I sought his mouth with mine. He was pounding into me with great hard strokes. It was taking my breath away. It was good. It was what I wanted. I didn't want to give it up. I didn't want to give Darius up. I intended to fight in every way I could to do this again. To keep Darius forever.

Afterward, we lay there together on the bed in the dark room, listening to each other breathe. I drew lazy circles on his bare back with my fingers. He stroked my hair. "I have to go," Darius said at last. "It's almost dawn and I have a lot to do before tonight."

"What's tonight?" I asked.

Darius had gotten up and was dressing, pulling on his tight jeans followed by cowboy boots. I watched him, feeling uneasy.

"What's tonight?" I asked again, more loudly, raising up on my elbows.

"Just another gig. That's all." He said it so quietly I had to strain to hear him.

"You're playing tonight? Where?"

"Downtown. In the Village."

My good feelings drained away like dirty water down the kitchen sink. "Darius, please, stop it. Please don't do this," I said loudly.

He pulled on his other boot, stood up, and faced me, his mouth a tight line again. "Daphne, I have to do this. Don't ask me to stop. This isn't something I can give up. It's who I am and you can't control me."

"I'm not trying to control you, you idiot! I'm trying to protect you," I shot back. They were angry words that slipped out thoughtlessly, and they were a mistake. Darius's face got red. His veins bulged on his temples.

"I don't need or want you to protect me. Can't you understand that?" he said while he grabbed his jacket and I watched his every move.

"No, I don't. I care about you."

"You need to mind your own business and not mine, Daphne. Worry about keeping yourself safe. You're doing your job. I respect that. You don't see me trying to stop you from flying out to the Hamptons in a helicopter. With another guy," he said, his voice taking on a tinge of anger.

"You followed me again? And you have the nerve to tell me to mind *my* own business! And what about you? You're with that girl Julie, who I believe with all my heart is a vampire hunter. Tell me, Darius, if she's just a singer in the band, why does she act so jealous? Why does she look at me with such hatred? Is it that she knows I'm a vampire, or is it that you're screwing her?" I yelled.

"That's none of your business," he yelled back. "But for your information I'm not—not yet."

I grabbed the nearest thing I could reach. It was a ceramic vase on a nightstand. I threw it with all my might at Darius. He ducked, and it smashed against the wall behind him. Jade started barking frantically.

Darius gave me a furious look and walked out of the bedroom, slamming the door behind him. I heard him go out the front door and slam that too.

I was so mad I didn't know what to do with myself. I certainly wasn't going to sit down at the computer and write a report. I wanted to scream. I wanted to cry. I needed to do what any normal woman would do under the circumstances. I needed to call a girlfriend.

I picked up the phone and dialed. Benny answered on the first ring. "Hello?" she said.

"Hello, Benny," I said, my voice breaking like glass.

"Daphne, is that you?" she said.

"Oh Benny," I wailed.

"It's Darius, isn't it," she said. "I'll kill that son of a bitch," she raged. "Come on, sugar, tell me what he did this time!"

Chapter 9

Walking east
rain, light rain
falling . . .
rain, or is it love?

—"Collage in November" by Irving Stettner

I told Benny everything: the makeup sex the other night, the breakup after it, the first makeup sex tonight and then the second makeup sex followed by the fight when Darius left, slamming the door behind him. The telephone receiver was hot from pressing against my ear for a good hour. Benny listened while I rattled on, sometimes repeating myself, trying to convey Darius's every word. Benny kept quiet except to exclaim, "What a jerk!" and, "All men are such pigs," about ninety-nine times. Finally I felt drained. I wasn't mad anymore; I felt as if my heart were breaking. Dawn was coming, I still had to walk Jade, and after that I hoped I'd be able to fall asleep. I was ready to hang up, but to my surprise Benny wasn't.

My best bud had let me talk it out before she finally gave me her two cents. "Daphy, I surely wish I could run right up there with a plate of fried chicken and a bowl of potato salad. It's what my Mama back in Branson always recommended for helping folks in trouble. And if she just heard how low you're a feeling, she'd add a big helping of banana puddin' too. But you know, honey, Darius has a point."

"What are you talking about? How can you say that?"

"Now don't get your knickers in a twist. All I'm saying is he's broken and you want to fix him. But you can't. He has to heal from the inside out. Sugar, it's one of those things you just can't make happen 'cause you want it to. He may come around by and by, but on his time, not yours. Aw, shoot, I'm guessing you didn't want to hear that."

I didn't answer right away. Then I said, "It's hard to hear what you're saying. But you're probably right. I just have a bad feeling that by and by will never come—because something really bad is going to happen first."

And so it was with a heavy step that I took Jade out onto the empty streets. I turned up my collar against the cold and shoved the hand not holding Jade's leash deep into a pocket. It didn't take long for the other hand to be stiff and hurting when the icy temperatures closed a tight fist around mine. Among the dark apartment-house windows, one or two glowed yellow as a few people awoke before the sunrise. I imagined them moving with slippered feet, filling the coffeemaker, and then softly entering the bathroom to turn on the shower. One of the loneliest of times is right before morning, when silence lies like a shroud on the land, muffling everything in grayness. My dog and I walked quietly along the cement sidewalks, stepped off the curbs onto black asphalt, and crossed the deserted street whether the light was green or red. In a little while the noises of the day would start again: honking horns and radios blaring as people burst out of their front doors to face the morning. By then I'd be settling in for my day's sleep. Humans walked by light. I walked by darkness.

Now, solitary and sad, I tugged on Jade's leash and turned her around. I told her we needed to go back home.

She agreeably changed her direction, yet when we started back up the block I heard a little drum tap-tap-tapping. It was a pleasant sound, almost a happy one. Well, the unusual is *de rigueur* in New York City, and I figured some half-stoned musician was practicing at four-thirty a.m. But with every step I took the sound of the little drum seemed to tap louder: rat-a-tat, rat-a-tat, a staccato that I finally decided was coming up from the ground. Suddenly I thought I could feel the earth turning on its axis beneath my feet, the buildings seemed to go cockeyed on their foundations, and the setting moon was spinning crazily in the sky. Jade had stopped in her tracks, lifted up her muzzle and let out a howl that chilled my blood.

That's when I saw the owl sitting in the middle of the sidewalk right in front of me. It was a small thing, and it blinked its yellow eyes slowly. I'm superstitious. Owls are bad omens, and as I watched, it started to twirl around until the spin became a blur and the owl turned into Don Manuel. Jade barked and lunged at him so fast I almost lost hold of the leash. Don Manuel just smiled and raised himself up about eight feet in the air out of her reach and hung there suspended.

"You have found the men who have the susto?" he asked.

"I think so," I said to his face which was now floating above me like the Cheshire cat's smile.

"But you have not found the answer," he said.

"I don't know the question," I replied.

"The question is 'What is killing those people?' " he said, starting to fade away.

"So what *is* the answer?" I yelled upward as he became more and more transparent.

"The sickness of fear," he replied in a voice as thin as the air where he had been. "Susto . . ."

Then all was quiet, and an owl's feather came floating gently earthward. It landed at my feet. Jade came over and sniffed it. I picked it up and put it in my coat pocket before we turned for home.

Back in the apartment, with the sun not far below the horizon, fatigue was beginning to overtake me, but what the shape-shifter had said was wriggling around in my brain and starting to crystallize into an idea. I didn't know exactly how susto and fear were related, but I knew fear itself was both primal and deadly. All the great modern psychologists had written about fear, from the angst and existential dread of Søren Kierkegaard to the theories concerning fear and the formation of personality of Sigmund Freud, Karl Jung, and Ernest Becker. For New Yorkers today, and probably for all Americans, differing degrees of fear, from a low-level anxiety to the outright terror of panic attacks, have become constant if unwelcome companions. Joie de vivre has fled and been replaced by watchful eyes and nervous mannerisms, nightmares and stress disorders. I knew, we all knew, that over the past few years, fear had become the worm at the core of this city.

Thinking about this, it dawned on me that the shaman's voice was not that of a Western philosopher. To understand him I had to look to a different mindset, a different worldview. I walked into my library and reached up to remove a book by Krishnamurti from the shelf. Born in 1895 in Andhra Pradesh, India, Jiddu Krishnamurti had been found as a teenager by members of the Theosophical Society and adopted by a lady named Annie Besant. The Society believed this Indian boy was the new World Teacher, and whether he was or not, the riddle-speak of the shaman reminded me of Krishnamurti's teachings, which sound both profound yet oversimplified. But one thing I remembered vividly was that Jiddu Krishnamurti had identified fear as the enemy of an evolving consciousness. Fear was the iron chain which held people to materialism and tradition.

I found the book I was seeking, Krishnamurti's *Life*

Ahead, and began to read. It required patience, as Krishnamurti's message is not linear. It repeats, loops back, and circles around, and his printed words are not "writing" at all, but a transcription of his lectures and conversations. As I sank into the white satin covers of my coffin, the book in my hand, I fought to keep my eyes from dropping shut as I scanned the pages. I found no information about the lethalness of fear. That doesn't mean my search was fruitless. What I did take away from Krishnamurti's teaching was an invaluable piece of wisdom: the only way to defeat fear is to confront it. But how that could apply to the threat of a drug epidemic I didn't know.

After I awoke from my long winter's nap, I found instructions from J on my answering machine. A meeting of the team was scheduled for six p.m., which is pretty damned early for a vampire. Sometimes I think J just doesn't get it. It was after five when I got up. I barely had time to shower and change, and it takes over ten minutes just to blow-dry my hair. It's a good thirty-minute trip down to Twenty-third Street. Realizing that I had maybe fifteen minutes to get out of my apartment, I felt my pulse speed up and my anxiety level start to rise. I had to feed Jade. I had to walk her. I had to feed Gunther, my pet rat, who had been feeling totally neglected. A six o'clock meeting was nuts.

I was in the midst of frantically pulling clothes out of the closet when I suddenly said to myself, *Whoa! Take a deep cleansing breath. Slow down.* I stopped. I took a slow breath, and I accepted the fact that, you know what? I was going to be late. J and I already had a rocky relationship; this would be just one more friction point.

I didn't dally, but I stopped rushing. I pulled on my jeans, my favorite square-toed Frye boots, and a thick wool turtleneck. I topped this off with a leather bomber jacket, mittens, and a white knit cap that I picked up in Dingle, Ireland a few years back. I was ready to roll. I winced when I realized I hadn't written up my report on the events out in the Hamptons. More black marks against my good name. I was headed for J's shit list for sure. Then I remembered that the best defense is a good offense, so I made a mental note to bring plenty of attitude to the meeting.

And I did, slamming through the door to the conference room in the Flatiron Building at around six forty-five with a lot of noise and a chip on my shoulder. I shouldn't have bothered. Outside of J, who was seated at the head of the table thumbing through a file, I was the first one there. I wasn't really surprised. Vampires are notoriously unreliable when it comes to following rules and regulations. For one thing, we never had to follow any rules except the ones dictated by the needs of our race, like craving blood to live. And for another thing, we aren't joiners or team players. When you live alone in a castle for five hundred years or so, you don't need a day planner, or a night planner either.

Besides a vampire's natural tendency toward tardiness, Cormac, for example, has always been so self-absorbed that the only thing he ever gets to promptly is a Broadway audition. As for the other two, I didn't know Bubba all that well, but he was from Kentucky, Benny was from Missouri, and they just didn't move as fast as New Yorkers. Now don't misunderstand me, I'm not being critical. I think the toe-the-line-arrive-on-the-dot-obey-orders mindset is a load of crap. I mean, even Mar-Mar embraced the counterculture back in the nineteen-sixties. She's still more a rule-breaker than a rule-maker. Of course then there is J, my polar opposite, my nemesis, my almost lover. . . .

"Oh, hi," I said, the wind gone from my sails. I dropped my backpack and plopped down in a chair.

J gave me a broad smile. My guard went up. He was being far too nice. "I hear you made some major breakthroughs yesterday, Miss Urban. Congratulations."

"You heard? I guess you were talking with my mother," I said suspiciously.

"Yes. She said she believed you had information that could bring this mission to a successful conclusion. I knew we could count on you." He sat back in his chair, relaxed, acting like he was trying to be my friend.

"I think it's a possibility, yes. I'd like to run it past the entire team though," I said. Talk about flying by the seat of my pants. I hadn't given the matter any thought whatsoever. I pulled a yellow legal pad out of my backpack and furiously started making notes. To tell the truth, outside of doing some ruminating on the meaning of fear, all I had thought about was Darius. I guess I was never going to be the poster girl for spy of the month. Lives were at stake, the whole U. S. government might be hanging in the balance, and I was moping around and obsessing about my "relationship." *Get a grip, girl*, I mentally yelled at myself.

By the time Bubba, Benny, and Cormac straggled in, I had actually come up with a plan.

J started the meeting off by reporting on the analysis of the powder in the ampoule I'd obtained at Kevin St. James. According to the lab, the powder broke down into several substances, but the main active agent provoked a strong adrenaline rush. The other ingredients were mostly unknown compounds in the tree bark that was the base for making the susto. The lab guys didn't know what these substances were or what they did. It might take months to find out, but their best guess was that these trace materials had a powerful psychotropic effect on the user. In their opinion, susto would provoke the kind of thrill a person feels when he's on a monster roller coaster that's just reached the top of the first hill and begins flying down. Feeling scared can be a tremendous rush, as the mind floods the body with chemicals. Some people say they feel more alive. Others describe it as an incomparable high. Susto maintained that peak experience for as much as fifteen minutes. Most people would feel good and even get addicted to that chemical cascade of fear hormones. Some users wouldn't, however. They would be literally scared to death. They might have a heart attack or stroke, or they would stop breathing for a number of other reasons. To make the action of the drug more understandable, the lab report compared susto to LSD. With the latter hallucinogen, there were good trips and bad trips, but in a few instances, a person became so disoriented or terrified that he jumped out of a window or took some other fatal misstep. With susto, fear could thrill—or kill.

"Why do the users turn blue? Why can we hear their heartbeat?" Bubba asked. "And are they hallucinating or something? 'Cause it sure looked to us like the person was being strangled by hands we couldn't see. Isn't that right, team?"

We all nodded.

J explained, "The analysts feel that effect comes from one of the trace substances. Some people may have a severe allergic reaction to it and succumb to anaphylactic shock. Their throat swells and closes, and they can't breathe."

I felt there was a lot more to susto than the lab had come up with in its analysis. "You know," I broke in, "Don Manuel said susto steals a person's soul. Maybe that's what we witnessed."

J gave me an impatient look, then removed a piece of paper from his file and quickly scanned it. Then he looked at me again. "That information wasn't in Agent Lee's report on your meeting with the South American—what did you call him?" J looked back down at the paper. "The South American shaman and shape-shifter."

"Well, umm, no," I said. "Don Manuel didn't say it then. I saw him again, after I left here Saturday night."

"You didn't report it," J said sternly.

"I haven't had a chance," I countered. "I wasn't sitting around playing video games since then, you know."

"Please fill us in on your meeting with Don Manuel, and then you can move on to what you found out yesterday at the

Brent Bradley compound in the Hamptons." How quickly one can fall from grace. J wasn't smiling at me anymore.

Benny looked at me quizzically. All I had discussed with her was Darius. She was going to be a little miffed I hadn't told her about the party.

"Sure, be glad to," I said. "After I left here, late Saturday night, I decided to take the uptown train home, and when I got on here at Twenty-third Street, Don Manuel was already in the subway car. He came over and sat by me, told me susto was fear, and told me that it stole a person's soul. Then he turned into a Sky Bar wrapper and blew out the door at Thirty-fourth Street. That's Herald Square," I added helpfully.

I heard Benny stiffle a giggle. J's face was turning red and the veins on his temple were throbbing. "Did you just say he turned into a Sky Bar wrapper?" he asked, and it sounded as if he was speaking through gritted teeth.

"Yes. It was yellow and I could see the logo clearly," I said.

"Agent Urban, I wasn't asking you to verify the brand of candy." J was close to losing it. "A person cannot change into a piece of paper. Were you drunk?"

"Well, no," I said. "I did have something to drink earlier that evening after I saw, well, never mind what I saw. It's personal, but I had something to drink, yes, and I was a little tipsy, that's all. But I was sober by the time I saw you."

I heard a snort from Benny's direction. She was close to cracking up and laughing her fool head off. I gave her a dirty look. With that, she started coughing to cover up the peals of laugher she couldn't stop. Bubba was having a helluva time trying not to laugh too. He had the nerve to put his head down on the desk in his arms and his shoulders were shaking with his silent laughter. Cormac just looked pissed off that he wasn't in on the joke. I swear, I hadn't been all that drunk.

"People!" J yelled. "Get hold of yourselves. We have

business to cover." J was obviously trying to keep his anger under control, never an easy task for a man who seemed to spend most of his waking moments getting mad or getting over getting mad. I saw him take a few deep breaths before he answered. Benny and Bubba had managed to stifle themselves. All of us were sitting there staring at him.

"Look, Agent Urban, I'll give you the benefit of the doubt. You thought you were sober, and you thought you talked to a shaman who turned into a candy wrapper. I'm not even going to entertain the possibility that susto can steal a person's soul. A soul is a spiritual concept, not a scientific one. Let's stick to facts. I think it might be more useful at this time if you reported to the team about what you found out yesterday."

I pulled out my legal pad and ran through what had happened from the time I arrived at the party, was introduced to Rodriguez and spotted Jimbo Armbruster—the person I called Green Day, who I was sure was pushing susto—to the murder of the girl, my discovery of the truck containing ampoules, the building where I suspected the susto was being manufactured, and the burial of the girl in the little graveyard. The others listened to me in stunned silence. Even J looked surprised.

"To summarize," I said, and looked straight at J, "I think the agency was already aware of Rodriguez's involvement in the drug scheme and the possibility that one of the most powerful men in the government, Brent Bradley, was implicated. I think there is a clear national-security threat, and you already knew that. You were hoping Team Darkwing could bring in some hard evidence to confirm it.

"We did. First we obtained samples of the drug. Now there is a body that links a member of the Bradley household to a murder. I assume a search warrant can be issued, and the arrest of Jimbo Armbruster can be effected. I suspect he is a major pusher of the drug. Hopefully, the murder charge can be used as a bargaining chip to make him identify others who are also distributing susto so they can be picked up and arrested.

"Then the authorities can raid the susto lab, and arrest Rodriguez and Bradley. Mission accomplished," I said and looked up hopefully.

J didn't seem to be jumping for joy. "That's very interesting, Agent Urban, but a little naive."

"What do you mean? Of course you can get Armbruster to talk. They do it all the time on 'Law and Order'," I said, and I wasn't really trying to be a wiseass. I just knew instinctively he was about to shoot down my whole scenario. "And I know I'm right about this."

"I didn't say you were wrong. I said you were naive. Listen, you did great work. But let me ask you a few things. You said you didn't wait around to actually see them bury the body, is that right?"

"Yes. Two of the men went back to get shovels. I left before they returned."

"So you don't know exactly where the girl is buried, or if she is really buried in that cemetery. They could have ended up taking her somewhere else, or even decided it was safer to dump her in the ocean after all and found access to another boat. Isn't that true?"

"Anything's possible, but I'm sure they buried her where I left them."

"You can't be sure, and that's the point," J said. "We can't risk doing anything until we are positive where we can find the body. And yes, you are right, if we find the body, we can arrest Bradley's stepson. And that is of critical importance in breaking up the chain of susto distribution. But we're dealing with very powerful people here. The chances of us being able to quickly arrest Rodriguez and Bradley, even if they are guilty—"

I started to sputter that of course they were guilty, but J held up his hand and went on.

"—Yes, we know Rodriguez is behind most of this—but

arresting him would be very messy and chances are by the time he came to trial, things would have happened to make sure we didn't have any evidence or a case. Agent Urban, you filled in a lot of the missing pieces of the susto puzzle. You obtained a sample of the drug. You confirmed where it's being manufactured. You identified many people directly involved with the drug, and alerted us to a *possible* national-security breach. I'm not belittling what you accomplished. Far from it. But we need to take care of this outside of legal channels.

"As soon as my superiors and I complete our plan of attack, I'll contact each of you. In the meantime, Agent Urban—"

"Yes?" I asked skeptically.

"I need you to go back to the Hamptons and find that body. I don't want you to move it. I don't want you to touch it. I just want you to verify that it is buried where you suspect it is. I realize you can't do this tonight. It's important that you head out there tomorrow night."

I nodded, already trying to figure out how the hell I was going to get out there, find the girl, and get back before dawn.

"What about the rest of us?" Bubba asked.

"Just sit tight until you get your orders," J commanded.

"You know, I never get to do anything," Cormac whined. "I don't know why I should even bother showing up for these meetings."

"And I want to do something too," Benny joined in. "Daphne's doing everything. I don't even think you need a team. I mean, what good are we?"

It finally seemed to dawn on J that he couldn't just order vampires around and expect them to say "Sir! Yes, sir!" He looked around the room, then stood up and began to speak.

"You are a team. It's a committed relationship. Your first loyalties, your first concerns must be to each other. Are you familiar with the Ranger's Creed? No? I'll get you all copies, but the part you need to hear—no, not hear—the part you need to take to heart is this: *Energetically will I meet the enemies of my country. I shall defeat them on the field of battle for I am better trained and will fight with all my might. Surrender is not a Ranger word. I will never leave a fallen comrade to fall into the hands of the enemy.*

"Did you hear what I said? A Ranger will never leave a comrade behind. The loyalty of Rangers to each other is stronger than blood ties. You aren't Rangers, no. But you are vampires, and you are linked by a heritage as old as recorded time. You have a bond that cannot be broken. And now, this team, Team Darkwing, the first vampire spies ever to be deployed by a government, is vital to the safety of this nation. As a team. One agent acting alone cannot accomplish what needs to be done to stop this threat—and do not underestimate this threat. Unchecked, this drug has the potential to destroy this country. Not only can it take thousands of young lives, but the fact that it is linked to the very highest circles of power makes its elimination of critical importance.

"National-security advisor Brent Bradley is privy to the top secrets of this nation. He is literally the president's right-hand man. If he can be influenced by venal forces or by his own rapacious greed, the president's life is at risk. And that's the bottom line.

"And because of Bradley's position, we cannot chance turning this operation over to any other government agency. Bradley can co-opt it, or simply stop it. As I said before, you are the new Untouchables. And while Agent Urban has an immediate task ahead of her in this mission, you all have a greater one awaiting you."

"And what is that?" Bubba asked.

"I was going to wait until we had the specifics nailed down, but to put it bluntly—you need to destroy the susto lab on the Bradley compound."

"Won't Rodriguez just move it somewhere else?" Cormac chimed in, showing that he's not as silly and shallow as he likes the world to think he is. "How will you stop him?"

"*You* will stop him," J said grimly.

"Oh," Benny said. "I get it. We're not just going to blow up the building. We are going to terminate Rodriquez."

"That's correct," J said.

"Well, what about Bradley?" I said. "He can't be arrested either. So are we going to terminate him too?" I had deep moral reservations about acting as an assassin. I'd kill in the heat of battle, but not like a thief in the night.

"No."

"Why the hell not?" Bubba demanded, evidently not sharing my sentiments.

J looked at me and then at all the others. "First off, we don't know what he knows or how deep he's into this. But even if he's guilty as hell, the facts of life are these. Some people are so rich and so powerful they *can* get away with murder. And far worse. The suspicious death of a top public official would bring national and international attention. Publicizing our connection to susto could cause irreparable harm to the stability of our government. However, we feel—if Team Darkwing is successful—that Bradley will learn his lesson, and he can be controlled. I think he will see that he has made a major error. He's not stupid. We think he can be convinced to change his ways *if* Team Darkwing can accomplish its mission."

"Is the Pope Catholic?" Benny said.

J suggested, but stopped short of ordering, that we could spend the night continuing to monitor New York nightspots to keep an eye on susto use, but he didn't assign us to anyplace specific. Then he dismissed us, saying he'd get us specifics on the plan of action within forty-eight hours. Coming down to the lobby in the extraordinarily slow elevators of the Flatiron Building, Cormac dubbed the coming mission the Big Bang. Benny suggested the Blowout in the

Hamptons. And in high spirits, we vampires quickly agreed to spend the evening together *as a team.* Acknowledging that special relationship seemed to be affecting each one of us; at least it had made an impression on me.

Before we pushed through the glass-and-chrome doors out into the night, intending to find a spot for dinner and conversation, we stood together on the ground floor of the Flatiron Building. Bubba spoke up first. "You know, y'all, we haven't been looking to take care of business, our business. We've waited around for J to give us directions, we've gone our separate ways, and we let each other down."

We all knew what he meant, and we all nodded in agreement.

Benny broke in. "You're right. Daphne and I have spent time together, but this week was the first I had hung out with you. And Cormac, I apologize. I usually don't even give you a thought. It's like you're not even here."

"That's how I feel," he said with a sigh. "Daphne and I have a history, not a friendship exactly, more like a rivalry. But I don't know you two at all."

"It's time to change that," Bubba said, "starting now." I took another look at Bubba then. He had dressed differently tonight. In place of his John Deere cap he wore a brimmed leather hat cocked to one side with a peacock feather dramatically fanning over the crown. It was quite extraordinary. He had replaced his usual red-and-black checked jacket with a gray overcoat in a military cut with a red ribbon love knot in its lapel. He looked less a country boy and more a Southern gentleman. Once again I wondered who he had been before he was Bubba Lee.

Now he spoke again. "When I was recruited out of Belfry, Kentucky, thanks to Benny here, I was told that we were special. We're supposed to be the first and best homeland defense in this nation's war on terror. We're all smart. We're all fighters. And we all know that united we stand, divided we fall. I feel that it's time we became one *Team* Darkwing and not the Four Darkwings."

"I second that," Benny agreed.

"Me too," I said.

Cormac nodded, but he voiced his reservations. "Listen guys, saying we're a team doesn't make it so. We need to learn to work together. When I get a part in a Broadway show, the cast rehearses to make it all come together. There aren't any shortcuts to the process that I know of. Will we have enough time to become a team before the shit hits the fan?"

Bubba answered. "I don't know, Cormac, but we've made the commitment to do it. We've made a commitment to each other. I think we've got a fighting chance."

I did too, but I had a feeling it wasn't going to be easy. And it might not happen without a price.

Chapter 10

"The prime virtue in life is courage, because it makes all the other virtues possible."

—attributed to Winston Churchill

Human blood is our elixir of life. The blood gives us immortality and eternal youth. Vampires cannot exist without it for long. But contrary to popular lore, vampires do like to eat, for pleasure above all else. After all, we are creatures who indulge in the sensual of all kinds. And when human blood is unavailable, we can survive for some time by consuming other warm-blooded beasts. That's why all vampires are carnivores, and Team Darkwing quickly agreed we wanted a restaurant where we could all get a nice juicy steak. Cormac suggested a place called the Garage on Seventh Avenue in the West Village, and we took the subway down to Christopher Street and Seventh Avenue South. We didn't talk much on the way there, but I liked being part of a group. It felt comfortable; I felt as if I belonged. Benny informed me that she wanted every detail of the party in the Hamptons, and that she forgave me for not telling her earlier, but that it better not happen again. I promised, and swore with my pinky up to God.

It was after seven o'clock, and I was famished by the time we all slid into a dark red booth located on the balcony inside the Garage Restaurant and Café.

"This place is cozy," Benny said. "I love the exposed

beams and the fireplace. I'm not so sure about the car parts on the walls, though. What's that all about?"

"This place once was a real automotive garage." Cormac was eager to explain. "Did you see the mosaic sign out front that's still embedded in the front of the building? No? Take a look when we leave. Later the garage was converted into a comedy club called the Nut Club—"

"Sounds like your kind of place, Cormac," I quipped, which earned me a dirty look.

"—Afterwards it became an off-Broadway theater. Now there's live jazz seven nights a week. But I come here for the food."

"Sure you do," I couldn't stop myself from saying. "I also bet they have a cute waiter or gorgeous bartender you like better than the food."

"Daphne Urban," Cormac said, "I have been nothing but nice to you all night. Why do you want to start up with me?"

I sighed. "Sorry, Cormac, it's just habit. I'll try harder."

"Thank you. I appreciate it, especially since we are trying to build camaraderie. Aren't we?" he said haughtily, throwing his head back the way he always does.

Benny reached out and gave his hand a little squeeze. "Cormac, honey, we are. And a little kindness to each other is definitely called for."

I thought I was going to throw up because Cormac is usually as mean as a rattlesnake. His tongue is positively venomous, and he would diss his own mother, but Benny had a point.

The waiter came over. He was short and boyish-looking. He handed each of us a menu and said, "My name is Chris, and I'll be your server tonight. Can I get you something from the bar?"

"You bet you can," Bubba boomed in his resonating bass voice. "Do you have Yuengling on draft? Yes? Okay, that's for me. What about you, Cormac? Ladies?"

Cormac ordered a Captain Morgan and Coke, Benny

asked for the house merlot, and I stuck with mineral water. I had learned my lesson, or so I thought. Then we all buried our heads in the menu.

"What are y'all going to have?" Benny said. "I'm thinking about New York sirloin 'au poivre.' Now what is that?"

"With peppercorn sauce," I said.

"Now thanks, Daphne. I've never been east of Branson before I was recruited for this here team, and you know, in Missouri we serve our steaks barbequed. None of this French stuff."

"Barbeque is serious business, Miss Benny," Bubba said. "Don't know why anybody would want a steak any other way, but I'm game to try this here grilled steak frites. And what the goldurn is a frite?"

"A French fry," I said.

"They could have just said so," he grumped.

"I'm going to have the filet mignon béarnaise," Cormac announced with flawless pronunciation, and I swear I could detect a smirk. Cormac had been knocking around the capitals of Europe before coming to America and was a bit of a snob. I give him credit though, he didn't make even one cutting remark.

My mouth was watering just from reading the menu. And as soon as the waiter returned with the drinks, we all ordered and I opted for the grilled filet mignon.

"And how do you want your steaks?" Chris the waiter asked us, holding his pen over his ordering pad, poised and ready.

"Any way but wooden!" Benny piped up.

"And absolutely no garlic on *anything,*" Cormac put in as Benny broke down in helpless giggles.

"Steaks, medium rare?" Chris the waiter said with a totally straight face. We all yelled, "No, rare! Very very rare!" and tried not to laugh.

"And you said to hold the garlic?" he noted as he rolled his eyes.

"You got it," Bubba said.

The waiter left and I could practically hear him thinking, *This used to be a comedy club and everybody's gotta be a comedian.*

"Now let's get down to business," Bubba said. "It seems to me that we're the ones who have the only viable chance to stop this susto before it becomes an epidemic. We do it in three steps," he said and ticked each one off on his fingers. "First we get the evidence on the dealers; second we blow up their manufacturing lab; third, we take care of the kingpin."

"You know, I asked for training in explosives the first time we met J, didn't I, Daphne?" Benny said.

"Yes you did," I agreed, "and he put you down for asking. Now we're expected to blow up a building. Sometimes I think—maybe I better not say what I think, but I don't have a very high opinion of our intelligence organization. They seem to have a communication and command problem."

"I can handle explosives," Bubba said quietly. "Don't you worry none about it."

Benny gave me a questioning look. It was the perfect opening to find out something about Bubba's past. "Where did you learn about explosives?" I asked.

"I was in the military service for many years," Bubba said. "I worked with black powder mostly, and later on with dynamite. Before I came here to New York, I did some brushing up on newer stuff, plastic. That's what the terrorists use. That there shoe bomber found out how to make explosives on the Internet. But you know, dynamite works just as good."

"No, I don't know," I said. "I don't know a thing about it. None of us do, and it just makes me mad that J didn't bother to send us to basic training like we asked him to. One consequence of that training would have been to make us come together as a team. I'm really not so sure how much J wants us to succeed. He's not one of us, and he never supported the formation of this unit, he said so himself."

"But after our last mission, he said he changed his mind, Daphy," Benny said quietly. "I think he meant it."

"That's water under the bridge now," Bubba said. "It's all on us. We can be as strong a team as we decide to be. Let's come up with our own plan and get this job done. Agreed?"

"Yes," each of us said.

Chris the waiter came back and put a basket of bread on the table. Bubba took a slice and handed the basket around as he went on talking. "I don't think you should be going out to the Hamptons alone. It's not that you can't handle yourself; it's just safer if someone is covering your back. Like J said, we're supposed to be a team, not lone operatives."

"I'll go with Daphne," Benny said. "Together we can come up with a better cover story for both of us if we need one."

"Good idea," I said. "It won't be so boring traveling out there if I don't have to go by myself. And I'm going to need a car. Maybe I can borrow something from Mar-Mar." I pulled out my cell phone and called her at her home in Scarsdale while the others talked. She answered, and said she was busy. "My Save the Trees group is having a meeting," she told me. "You remember them, don't you dear? You met that sweet little girl Sage Thyme at my party."

I did remember. It was the night Benny met Louis, a vampire from New Orleans who was supposed to be my mother's latest choice for me. Instead, he and Benny hit it off, and they had a fling that lasted probably two days at most. It ended badly, with Louis walking out on Benny—and getting himself killed. "Yes, Mar-Mar. I remember. Look, I need a car," and I told her why. She said she'd have one waiting in front of my apartment building at nine the following night.

Meanwhile Cormac and Bubba had put their heads together. They were going to contact J to get an aerial photo of the prefab building and to find out what explosives were available. Bubba promised to teach Cormac about detonators and timing mechanisms. To my surprise, Cormac seemed enthusiastic at the prospect. Since his main interests were cooking, opera, shopping, and Broadway tunes, I thought the truck gene had bypassed him entirely.

The salads arrived, which didn't interest us much, followed by the steaks. They were big and rare enough to light a fire under my appetite. None of us talked much while we ate. As we were taking our final bites, and Bubba was mopping up the blood on his plate with a piece of bread, earning him a disparaging look from Cormac, Benny said, "So what shall we do once we finish up here?"

"Don't know. Go out for some more beers?" Bubba suggested.

"How about a dance club?" Cormac tentatively offered, then said, "Oh, never mind, it's Monday. Not many clubs are open. This is a dead night in Manhattan."

Benny laughed. "Well, now it's an undead night."

I knew what I wanted to do. I wanted to get another look at the girl singer in Darius's band, and damn it, as irrational as it was, I wanted to see Darius. I couldn't figure out if we were together or not together, whether I should just make a clean break, or whether I should try to make our relationship work. One thing I did know for certain: I had powerful, uncontrollable feelings for him. Those feelings troubled me, yes, but I couldn't deny I had them. Tonight, I wanted to know where he was and what was really going on in that band, but I felt reluctant to drag the other three into it. Finally I said, "I'd like to hear Darius, my ex-boyfriend—or maybe he's my boyfriend again, I don't know—play tonight. He's started a band. I told Benny about what he's doing. He's, uhmm, he's recently become a vampire, Bubba. I don't know how much you know about it."

"Benjamina filled me in. Sounds like he's not easy in his mind over the transformation," he said sagely while he pushed his plate back, brushed some bread crumbs to one side with his bread knife, leaned forward a bit, and folded his big, careworn hands together on the table.

"That's an understatement," I said. "I think he's asking for trouble with what he's doing, and I'd rather see it coming than be blindsided."

"About the band. Is it any good?" Cormac asked.

"I think so," I replied. "I wish he stunk, and this all would just go away."

Benny, understanding, nodded sadly. "But it don't work that way, Daphy. My mama always said, 'If wishes were horses beggars would ride, if horse turds were biscuits we'd all eat till we died.' Even if we don't like it, we just have to play the hand we're dealt. That's all."

After picking up the *Village Voice* and making some calls, we found out that Darius was playing at the Bitter End, once the most famous nightclub in Greenwich Village. No longer the hottest or hippest spot, it was still a landmark at 147 Bleecker. Mar-Mar used to spend many nights there during the hell-raisin' nineteen-sixties. Some of her friends hinted that she might have had something going with the then-manager Paul Colby, but I doubted it. She just liked being around people who accepted her and her "eccentricities"—only going out after sundown, driving around in a hearse, and sleeping in a coffin—with no questions asked. There were kids doing a lot weirder things back then. It's been nearly forty years since Bob Dylan, the Mothers of Invention, and Neil Diamond headlined at the Bitter End, but for Darius D.C. and Vampire Project to be appearing there was still a very big deal.

By the time the four of us reached Bleecker at Thompson, sometime after nine thirty, a cold wind had pushed in from the northeast, and a hard rain had started to fall. Caught in the steady downpour, I was glad I wore jeans, a heavy leather jacket, and nothing dainty on my feet. I still felt the cold through the soles of my Frye boots, but it was the cold in my soul that was so troubling. I had an overwhelming feeling of dread such that at one point I slipped my arm through Benny's, just to feel her warmth.

The four of us trudged past the vintage sign for the Village Gate, the 1960's folk singers' hangout, but that's all that's left of the place—the sign. Then we tumbled, wet and dripping, into the Bitter End. It was a Monday night, but the place was crowded. My heart was going like a triphammer. I figured Darius was sure to spot us, and I was getting a different kind of cold feet. I would have preferred a loud, anonymous dance club like Cielo up in the Meatpacking District, but no such luck. We were here and what would be, would be. Not that I didn't recognize the bright side of things. As somebody once said, the crowd at the Bitter End was old enough that you won't get your shoes puked on.

The four of us sat down at one of the wooden tables, and everybody ordered a brew except me. I got a dirty look from the grouchy waitress but I stuck to mineral water, martyr that I am.

"Hey, come on, Daphne, smile," Bubba said. "This could be fun."

"Yeah, as much fun as a funeral," I said morosely, picking up the frosty glass of mineral water, which made my hand even colder than it had been already.

"Well, I'm glad we're here," Benny said. "This place is a landmark. Imagine what these brick walls have seen. I wish I had been in New York during those wild days, instead of in boring old Branson, Missouri. Those rednecks down there ran hippies out of town or tried to tar-and-feather them. I don't care if y'all think I'm nothing but a tourist. I'm excited."

Cormac, for his part, was still behaving well. He didn't whine or complain. He just ran his fingers through his wet hair and then picked up a napkin and dabbed at the drips. My own hair had turned into damp, tangled strands that were starting to frizz, and the leather of my jacket was spotted. I was sure my makeup had also gone with the wind. This drowned-rat look wasn't giving me a lot of confidence to face Darius and that hussy with the band. *She* wouldn't be looking like a cast member of "The Munsters," that was for sure.

We weren't seated more than fifteen minutes when the ten o'clock show got started. Several groups were slated to appear tonight. We sat through three other acts that were pretty experimental, including the Oz Noy Trio, an Israeli group that in the sixties would have been described as "far out." "Alternative" was a more contemporary description of their eclectic, innovative sound, which sometimes resembled a scratchy vinyl recording. They definitely fit the Bitter End's reputation for giving new musicians a chance. My three fellow team members were having a grand old time, but since two of them were newcomers to New York, I wasn't surprised. All of them were on their third beer by the time Darius was introduced. The lights dimmed. I was hyperventilating and kicking myself for not going to the ladies' room earlier and at least reapplying my lipstick.

Finally the house lights went completely out. A red spotlight turned on, illuminating the four performers of Vampire Project. Wrapped from shoulder to floor in black capes, the band members stood there immobile with their heads down. Then they looked up and extended their arms, unfolding the capes, which were cut to look like bat wings. The girl singer wore a sequined T-shirt under her cape, which cropped to show her flat stomach complete with a pierced navel. To me, her face looked bruised and puffy under her stage makeup. I was sure she had been my attacker. The keyboard player, shirtless and covered with tattoos like a member of the Red Hot Chili Peppers, lowered his arms and hit some discordant notes then segued into some very creepy sounds. Darius looked out at the audience. His face was starkly white, his lips were deep red, his teeth—I hoped the audience thought they were fake—were long and sharp when he smiled. He said, "Welcome to Vampire Project. We explore the dark side and we embrace the night. Our music comes from the world you can't see, from the fears you can't escape, from the thoughts that you can't stop, the ones that make shivers run up and down your spine. I am Darius D.C., and this is Vampire Project, and here is my music—"

The spotlight changed to violet, and Vampire Project launched into an original composition, not a cover, that asked

What will you do
Where will you go
How will you die
When fear comes for you? Once you had dreams,
Once you had desires,
Then came the nightmare out of the skies
Who sent it who sent it who sent it
The vampire walks
The vampire talks
The vampire comes for you . . .

That was pretty much the gist of things. I've got to admit the crowd was stomping and cheering when they finished the song, which had a great beat and soaring accompaniment. Cormac was on his feet yelling "Bravo!" and Benny looked starstruck. I just slunk down lower in my seat, misery closing over me. Running through my brain was the fear I did face but couldn't bear: that Darius would soon be killed, staked by a vampire slayer, and he might take some or all of us down with him. I had to do something to stop that eventuality, but I didn't know what. Frustration crashed down on me like an ocean wave.

Then Vampire Project switched to a cover of Smashing Pumpkins' "Take Me Down (to the Underground)" before starting their next original number which, to the best of my recollection, went something like this—

Can you accept the man that I am, when I am no longer human?
Can you love the creature I've become, when I am no longer human?
I can't exist can't exist can't exist with no soul no name no way to see the sun again
I can't exist can't exist can't exist with no soul no name no way to leave the shadowy plain
So how can I love you divided in twain between the man I was and the man I am?
Gone to the darkness gone to the night gone to the end of time gone to hell to see the devil gone down gone down unable to rise
So how can I touch you when I'm dead inside hurt inside bleeding and lost? So how can I find you when I'm lost?
How can I love you when I'm doomed? . . . .

While the audience whistled and stomped, Benny saw my solemn face and reached over to squeeze my fingers. The sound system started playing Pumpkins' "We Only Go Out at Night," which I guess was Vampire Project's theme song, and the house lights went to black again as Darius and his band completed their act.

"Wow!" Cormac said to me when the cheering stopped. "Darius is good, and he's sure got balls to appear in public like that." I gave Cormac the dirtiest look I could in response. "What? What did I say?" he said back at me.

Bubba was clapping too, but without much enthusiasm, and he looked lost in thought. I started to ask him what he was thinking, when some woman started screaming in the back of the room. Then a man's voice yelled out, "Call nine-one-one!" The room started buzzing with talking, then suddenly like an ebbing wave the voices subsided. In their place was the terrible sound of a heart beating, too loud, like a doleful sound of a slowly played drum. Someone was dying, horribly, just like the girl in Kevin St. James on Friday night. I knew that susto's blue death had struck again.

"Let's get out of here," Bubba said.

"Yeah," Benny added. "We don't need to be spotted by the cops at another drug overdose."

I especially wanted to avoid Detective Moses Johnson. Bubba felt the detective had a problem with our being federal agents. He could have been right, but I felt Johnson had a problem with our being vampires. Good cops are always very intuitive. From the first time he laid eyes on me, Johnson had reacted as if I were poison. I suspected he had a visceral response, feeling something was not quite kosher about me. Even if Johnson hadn't pegged me for an undead, nonhuman, bloodsucking monster, I was certain that our running into him again would raise all sorts of red flags. Darius had already given vampires too much public exposure. If Johnson decided to take a closer look at us and asked the right questions of the right people, our being "outed" by the NYPD was a distinct possibility—and who knows? The information could be leaked, and a news story such as "Vampires in New York" could turn into a media feeding frenzy.

With this concern running through my mind, the four of us squeezed past the crowd and burst through the red exit door out into the night. As soon as we got outside, we were nearly blinded by the flashing yellow lights of emergency vehicles parked at the ends of the block in either direction. Dozens of sirens wailed to our left, to our right, everywhere it seemed, so that it sounded as if they surrounded us. As far as we could see up and down the block, EMTs were rushing in and out of bars and clubs with stretchers.

"Holy shit," Cormac said. "Are you thinking what I'm thinking?"

"Probably," Bubba said grimly. "It's started. Susto is available and on the streets—and this is our first taste of what's going to happen again and again, across America."

I wondered if it was going to be possible to keep susto a secret after this. Team Darkwing had done a lot since Friday, but it wasn't enough. We didn't have much time to quash this epidemic. In fact, we might not have any time left at all. Death had descended on Greenwich Village, and susto had brought it here.

From that point on, the cold dark night became emotional as well as physical for me, wrapping itself around me so intensely I felt as if I had stepped into a refrigerator. I zipped up my jacket and hugged myself, putting my hands under my armpits and hunching my shoulders against the night air. The rain had slowed down to an icy drizzle. Flashes from the pulsing emergency lights bounced off of the puddles and wet sidewalks, off the plate-glass windows and metal street signposts while a cacophony of sirens became a deafening howl through the streets. I felt a tension running through me like an electric current. I realized that my hair was standing on end. My head snapped up. My nostrils flared. My animal instincts were coming awake. I could feel death all around me, yes, but I sensed danger coming closer. I reached out to tug on Bubba's gray coat to warn him of something, someone, I didn't know what. Before my fingers could clutch his sleeve, Bubba had let out a rebel yell and was racing down the block. None of the team hesitated; we ran with him toward an unseen enemy, but what or who I didn't know.

Then I saw them—two huge dark figures lurking next to the buildings on Bleecker Street. One of them had a bandolier of wooden stakes across his chest. The men were bearded, dressed in leather, draped in chains. And on the other side of the street from them, just emerging from a side entrance of the Bitter End, was Darius. Before he could spot the vampire hunters, the girl singer came rushing through the door behind him, grabbed his arm and turned him away from the street. I could see her begin speaking urgently to him, distracting him. *That bitch!* I thought.

A blast of adrenaline surged through my veins. I wanted to transform, but to do so on this public street would be foolish and perhaps fatal. The others shared my thoughts I knew. This was a fight we'd have to make in human form. I leaped ahead of Bubba, who was heavier and slower. Without slowing my momentum I hit one of the vampire hunters against the side of his head with my left elbow, grabbed him around the neck with my right hand, and dragged him down to the ground. He was big, outweighing me by a good hundred pounds. He threw me off as if I were a rag doll, and I went sailing backward, slamming into a parked car. As the vampire hunter got to his feet, Bubba came in like a Sherman tank and rolled over him. Bubba was yelling with an ungodly sound, and the two men were wrestling around on the asphalt street. Meanwhile Benny and Cormac came buzzing down on the other leather-clad hunter like two fighter jets, hitting him with their fists and feet, but the guy was big and powerful. He fought back with superhuman strength and started lashing out with a chain, which he whipped around him like a lariat. My friends danced back out of the way.

By this time Darius was fully aware of what was going on. I was vaguely aware of him pushing the girl singer back toward the club entrance, screaming at her to get inside. I had already regained my feet and could see him running toward us. Meanwhile Bubba was lost in the blind rage of battle. He ripped the stakes from the hunter's bandolier. They hit the ground with the sound of bowling pins tipping over. But the hunter had a huge wooden stake in his hand, its point aimed at Bubba's chest. Bubba closed his big fist over the guy's wrist, and I could hear the bones crunch, but the hunter didn't drop the stake. I jumped on the guy's back, putting my forearm across his neck, trying to choke him while he was attempting to shake me off like a dog shedding water. I don't know what would have happened if an NYPD cruiser hadn't come screaming down the block, but somebody would have died. The blue-and-white screeched to a halt, and two cops came barreling out with guns drawn.

The vampire hunters saw them and pulled free of us, taking off down the street the way we had come, and ignored the cops' order to halt. We four vampires stood there unmoving. Darius stopped too, a dozen feet away. I couldn't read the expression on his face. But I sure could read the angry one on Moses Johnson, who came running around the corner from Thompson Street with his badge held high in one hand, as he called out his identity to the uniformed cops. He exchanged some terse words with them next to the squad car. They put their guns away, got into their squad car, and went careening down the block after the two vampire hunters.

Then the NYPD detective came over to us, his face dark and grim as death. "What the hell is going on here?" he screamed.

Bubba, his breath heaving, stooped down to pick his hat up from the ground and slapped it against his leg to get the water off. Benny pushed her hair back out of her face, then she pulled a tissue out of her pocket to wrap around her hand, where her knuckles were bloody. Cormac was inspecting his coat, which had ripped under the armpit. Then, taking his sweet time about it, Bubba, as solid as a brick shithouse, as the saying goes, looked Johnson in the eye and answered with a voice hard as rocks. "A couple of creeps tried to mug our friend over there," he said, nodding at Darius.

"And you just happened to be walking by?" Moses said, his mouth looking like he'd bitten into a lemon.

"Yes sir, you about hit the nail on the head, excepting that we had just been in that there club listening to him sing. When we came out those two fellers were laying for him. We did what we could in the situation."

"You! Come over here," Johnson yelled at Darius.

Darius walked toward us, calm and easy, almost arrogant.

"What's your name?" Johnson snapped, taking in Darius's long blond hair, scarred face, and black cape with a look of derision. You could almost hear him thinking *druggie.*

"Darius della Chiesa," Darius answered, looking Johnson in the eye.

"You know those two men who were waiting for you?" Johnson barked.

"No, I never saw them before."

"And you're a musician? Can you show me some ID?" Johnson was brusque, his anger barely in check.

Darius took out his wallet and pulled out some folded papers, which he handed over to Johnson saying, "Yeah, I have a band, but that's not my full-time job."

Johnson scrutinized what Darius had handed him. He took his time with the information, his eyebrows raising in surprise. He took out his notebook and copied down something. When he spoke to Darius again, his voice was absent of any hostility. "Okay, Commander," he said, handing back the ID. "I'll check this out. You were lucky your friends were here." Johnson then turned to Bubba and the rest of us. "I don't know what the hell is really going on here, or what *this* is all about," he said as he kicked one of the wooden stakes that had fallen out of the bandolier and was now lying in the street. It rolled over and over until it struck the curb. "But maybe we better take some time in the next few days to discuss it. Right now, I have my hands full. Miss Urban?"

"Yes, Detective?" I said.

"Walk over here with me for a minute," he ordered and started moving away from the others.

I shrugged my shoulders and went over to where Johnson was standing. The flashing yellow lights of the emergency vehicles reflected like strobe lights across his damp face. He watched me intently. His eyes held no friendliness, and from his sour expression I'd say he still didn't like me, and that if anything his aversion to me was even stronger than before.

When I stopped in front of him, he stepped back to put more distance between us, as if I were a wild animal that he didn't want to get too close to. *In case I bite*, I thought with irony.

"Listen, Miss Urban," he said flatly. "I know there's something going on here with you and your buddies. Okay, you're Feds. Probably spooks. I've found out that much. And you, in particular, seem to have friends in high places. But I know you have information about this drug, and I want it. So don't play games with me. I'll be in touch with you soon. Expect it. And Miss Urban—"

"Yes?" I said.

"The NYPD doesn't have time to waste holding your hand or saving your ass." He turned his back on me then, put his hands in his pockets, and hurried off in the direction of Thompson Street.

I walked back to my friends and overheard Darius talking to Bubba, saying, "I appreciate what you did. What unit were you in?"

"Cavalry Corps," Bubba answered, his voice low.

"Don't know it. Army?"

Bubba nodded in reply.

"Thought so. You are one helluva fighter. You too," Darius said, looking over at Benny and Cormac. "Thanks." Then he gave me what I can only describe as a haunted look. "I'll call you," he said to me, and before I could answer he walked off toward the club.

I stood there, my left pant leg all wet and dirty from sliding across the asphalt, the side of my jacket the same way, my palms scraped from the fall, and my hair in wild tangles. My injured arm throbbed like a toothache. I felt like crap, and I was sure of one immutable fact: What just happened was not a good thing, not a good thing at all.

Chapter 11

A flash of lightning
Gives an eerie glint in the evening sky
Where dark clouds have risen.
The night heron crosses the sky
In the opposite direction
Which is total darkness.
His uncanny voice fills the air
But I see no sight of him.

—Bashō, poem written a month before his death,
translation by Mihoko Cato Stettner

We four Darkwings left Greenwich Village in silence. We had to walk a number of blocks to get past the emergency vehicles and hail a cab. Nobody said a word blaming Darius for the appearance of the vampire hunters. They didn't have to. Why state the obvious? Before we went our separate ways, I reminded Benny I'd pick her up a little after nine tomorrow night to head to the Island. I arrived back at my apartment emotionally drained. No message from Darius awaited me on my answering machine. He hadn't called yet, and I wondered when he would.

Gunther squeaked frantically in his cage when I opened my front door, and Jade barked, not joyfully, but purposefully, as if asking where I had been. I walked over to her and fell on my knees, putting my arms around her neck and burying my face in her thick coat. She smelled faintly like dog; she felt solid under my hands. I liked having her waiting for me. Our relationship didn't need words. It was direct, simple, and comforting. *Who needs men?* I thought, only half-sarcastically. *I'm happier with a dog.*

And speaking of my relationship with men, I noticed that, unlike Darius, Fitz had called and left a message. His voice sounded a little sad and completely sincere. It went like this: *Daphne, I am so very sorry. I wrote you a long e-mail yesterday. You didn't answer. I hope you're still speaking to me. There was an emergency, and I couldn't get back to you before you left the party. I can't imagine what you thought. If you're mad, I don't blame you. I found out from Rodriguez you were able to get back to Manhattan on the copter, and I'm grateful for that. Please let me know you got home okay. And there's something I need to tell you. Something you should know about me. Please call me and tell me when I can see you again.*

Damn, but the guy sounded straight and honest. I had a hard time fitting his criminal activities with the way he behaved with me and with my emotional reaction to him. In truth, I didn't expect I would ever see him again. Within the next two days, the susto lab would be destroyed, the principals behind the drug would be dead or—like Fitz, I believed—arrested, and the mission would be over. At least that's the way it was supposed to go down—if nothing went wrong.

I decided to walk Jade early tonight and get into my coffin before dawn for a good day's rest. I felt anxious and worn out. It was around three a.m. when we descended from my tenth-floor apartment to the streets below, my dog and I. A chilly drizzle continued to fall, bathing my face in a fine mist. Halos of fog wrapped around street lights. Tiny water droplets clung to Jade's fur. While I shivered from the cold and damp, she—a doggy grin on her face—relished the weather. Born of the Arctic, able to survive subzero cold, Jade was a dog built for snow and sleds.

I had read up on the breed, and my mind could hardly

credit what I had learned, a history of tragedy and man's treachery that is nearly unthinkable toward a dog whose courage and loyalty are immeasurable. Jade's kind, originally bred by the group of Eskimos called Mahlemiuts, could effortlessly survive killing temperatures in excess of seventy-five degrees below zero Fahrenheit, and individually pull loads as heavy as a pickup truck—that is, over two thousand pounds. Trained to carry machine guns in packs on their backs during World War II, malamutes accompanied GIs in France, they pulled the sleds of the doomed DeLong expedition of 1881 to find the North Pole, where they were butchered for food, and they were the unsung heroes of the two Admiral Byrd expeditions to reach the South Pole in the Antarctic, where the weakened dogs were shot or abandoned. Malamutes went where mechanical equipment, horses, and airplanes could not. If the breed had a fault, it was that they loved to fight.

I hadn't tried to track down Jade's original owner through the info on her rabies tag. I couldn't get past the fact that she had been abandoned to die. I would never surrender her to anyone who would have done such a thing. In truth, I didn't think I could give her up under any circumstances. She was my dog now. If I had to pay a fortune to keep her, I would.

These were the pathways my thoughts followed as Jade and I walked down the quiet Manhattan streets. As I had for centuries, I roamed the night world. I didn't fear what hid in the dark shadows, for what usually hid there was me. I was the demon that humans worried about meeting. I felt no threat from those who hunted me, for I believed I could, if I kept my wits about me, outrun them, outfight them, or outsmart them. I thought again about my recent encounters with the hunters. I got the idea that the only times I had been attacked, Darius had been nearby. Chances were, I thought, that he was their target, not me. Even when the girl had come at me, maybe it wasn't because I was a vampire, but because I was a threat to whatever scheme she had going regarding Darius. Was it really a stake in her hand? I thought it was. Could it have been a knife? If you asked me to swear about it now, I couldn't. My perception had been formed by what I assumed she held. It was sharp and it was pointed. That's all I knew for sure.

I was being watchful, but Jade caught the scent of something before I did. She stopped short and lifted her head to give a long, mournful howl, then she refused to budge. Alerted by her behavior, I looked toward the shadows near a stairwell. Something moved. *Crap,* I thought. *There goes my nice relaxing walk.* My heart started beating faster. I tensed and got ready to fight. I saw another movement and a small man stepped from the darkness. It was the shaman. I felt relief and some annoyance. My quiet stroll was over.

"Don Manuel," I said, "what do you want?"

"To tell you to hurry," Don Manuel said, coming closer and stepping under a streetlight. I could see him clearly there, a nut-brown Indian in a poncho and black round-brimmed hat. The encounter felt like a dream.

"You mean hurry to stop the drug?"

"Yes. Time is running out. Susto will kill, quickly, as you have seen, or slowly over time. It is a contagion. It must be stopped."

"How do I stop it?" I asked, noticing that Jade had put herself between me and the shaman and was watching him intently.

"There are many methods to combat fear," he said. "You must find your way."

I was feeling impatient. I wanted the shaman to tell me to give victims an injection of atropine or some other medication. I didn't want mystic double-talk. "Can you tell me exactly what I can do to save people?" I said. "What's in the drug? Many are dying," I added all the while thinking how weird this meeting was. I was just standing there in the cold, talking to an Indian, my dog like a guard before me.

"The antidote is love. That feeling you so struggle with.

Love. The energy of love is more powerful than the energy of fear. The two cannot exist together. One must die. Love is stronger. Simply love."

"Don Manuel, meaning no disrespect, but the drug that is killing people, susto, cannot be stopped by love."

Don Manuel started to walk away from me then. Jade stood up and barked. The shaman's head was down, and he looked very small. He halted and turned, saying to me in a weary voice, "You must stop the distribution of the drug. But be warned, another will soon take its place. You really want to save this country? The antidote *is* love."

"Don Manuel, that's not scientific," I said.

"Why do you prize science without mystery? Life is filled with mystery. Death is filled with mystery. Do not put chains on your mind," Don Manuel said before he hurried off down the street.

"Shaman! I don't understand you," I called out to him.

"Shift your consciousness," his voice said as he walked into the gathering darkness at the end of the block and I could see him no more.

I awoke at dusk on Tuesday and retrieved the newspapers from the mat in front of my apartment door. I cringed when I read the headlines of the *Daily News:* ODS KO DOZENS. A picture of emergency vehicles in Greenwich Village was printed below the headlines. The story on page three blamed the deaths on a contaminated batch of methamphetamine and said nothing about the victims turning blue. But it was only a matter of time before the sensational aspects of a susto death were picked up by some smart reporter, and then the newspaper report would read like something written by Stephen King. Stonewalling the truth if a second night of rampant ODs occurred might be impossible. The quicker we got the susto lab destroyed and the sooner the cops could arrest the major dealers the better. The plan, as I envisioned it, was for Green Day Jimbo Armbruster to be picked up as soon as I could verify the location of the girl's body. I figured that Benny and I would get out to the Hamptons by twelve and could phone J by one. Then he could obtain both a search warrant and an arrest before morning.

That was the plan. And like the best-laid ones, it was about to run into trouble.

Choosing the proper attire to go snooping in a boneyard presented me with a problem. How casual? How sporty? It wasn't as if we were going to have to dig up anything, at least I hoped not. We were just looking for a fresh grave. If we were stopped by guards or ran into someone, we needed to have a plausible explanation, like that we were invited to a party and had taken a wrong turn. I hoped Benny had some ideas—and wore something low-cut as a diversionary measure.

As for me, I decided I was going to the Hamptons, so I needed to dress up instead of down, which in retrospect might have been a mistake. I put on Cole Haan boots, a washable suede skirt, a cashmere sweater, and from the back of my closet I retrieved a short fur jacket with matching hat. No one would mistake me for a grave robber, that's for sure. I was well dressed for a night of cemetery snooping. I felt good—until the doorman rang up from downstairs to tell me my car was here. He was snickering. I wondered why.

I didn't wonder long. When I walked out of the double glass front doors of my building, there parked in all its stubby splendor was a Smart car. The doorman was stifling giggles. Here I was dressed for a Mercedes, a BMW, or at the very least a Mini Cooper, and my mother sent down this vehicle that looked like somebody sliced a Prius in half and just used the front part. The whole car was eight feet long and only seated two people. And just to make sure this one would really stand out in the crowd for people to point at and laugh, Mar-Mar's Smart had bright red door panels. I would look as if I were driving a gumball down the highway. I think the woman stayed up nights thinking of ways to humiliate me, I really do. She even had a personalized license plate put on the Smart that said 60MPG. I bet all the members of her Save the Trees group had bought one. They probably purchased them at fleet rates.

I had no other option for getting to the Hamptons. I climbed in, feeling as if I were sitting in an amusement-park bumper car, and drove off.

I phoned Benny from my cell, told her to meet me in front of her building, and pulled up there a few minutes later. Her reaction was about the same as mine. "Does it use gas or do we have to pedal it?" she asked as she got in. "It's a good thing I didn't bring a big purse. We'd have to strap it on the roof."

"I feel exactly the same way," I said miserably. "Worse than the size, this damned car is so rarely seen in America, it's going to attract a lot of attention, which we don't need or want. I hope some state trooper doesn't pull us over just to look at the damned thing. You're looking nice by the way." Benny had dressed straight from the Gorsuch catalog, which features upscale ski attire. She would be warm and definitely trendy in a quilted down jacket with a fox-fur hood. Her boots, which were shearling-lined, looked cozy and comfortable.

"Why thank you, girlfriend," she said. "I finally got me some good winter clothes. Since we are going to where the rich and famous live, I wanted to look like I was arm candy for some bijillionaire."

"Spies with clothes to die for, that's us," I said, smiling. "But I hope we don't see a living soul, and we're in and out in a few minutes."

"I hope we don't see a dead soul either, Daphy. Walking around in an old graveyard isn't my idea of a good time."

"You're not afraid of ghosts, are you, Benny?" I teased. "After all, you're a vampire."

"There's a whole passel of things I'm afraid of, starting

with spiders," she said with a shiver. "And maybe I am an undead vampire, but I'm a creature of flesh and blood. I don't know what a ghost is, where it comes from, or what it's going to do to me, and I sure don't want to find out."

"You have a point, Benny. But Mar-Mar used to tell me that the dead weren't anything to fear. It was the living you had to watch out for," I said, as we went from the Cross Bronx Expressway onto the Throgs Neck Bridge. I was looking for I-495 according to my driving directions from Yahoo. The Hamptons were 109 miles from the Upper West Side of Manhattan, and the ride should take about two and a half hours as long as we didn't hit traffic. I was thinking positive.

Benny fiddled with the radio until she found an oldies station. "Oldies" in our case was strictly relative. Benny got turned into a vampire in the 1930s, so she was several centuries younger than I was. Even though she looked as if she were in her early twenties, at one hundred years old she was no spring chicken. We both knew a lot of oldies, that's for sure. My memory of tunes went back to the Elizabethan madrigals.

As we drove, we had some prime girlfriend talk time. I filled her in on the party at the Hamptons on Sunday night. Then I asked her point-blank if she had anything going with Bubba Lee. She just laughed and said, "Oh Lord, no. I just love him to death, he's such a sweetie, but he's too old for me. Why he must have been nearly forty when he was turned. I never liked older men. 'Course, the young ones do bore me half to death sometimes. And after getting dumped by Louis, and he surely had his nerve, I am taking it slow before getting involved again."

As I mentioned earlier, Benny didn't know that Louis was dead, and it was entirely possible Darius, then a vampire hunter, had been Louis's killer. At the windup of our last spy mission, I found the remains of the lanky, green-eyed vampire—a pile of dust—in the posh Fifth Avenue apartment of the gun dealer I had been sent to spy on. Louis had gone to the apartment to rip off the place, and he happened to be in the wrong place at the wrong time. I also found my favorite ring in his dust, and so I discovered that Louis had stolen that too. While I wouldn't say Louis deserved his fate, he was no Mr. Nice Guy. That was one vampire who wasn't worth Benny's tears, so I let her think he was just a jerk. There are some things girlfriends should never tell.

"Well what happened to Larry D. Lee, that adorable soldier you were seeing? You never did give me the whole story," I asked as I found the highway we needed. People in the vehicles who passed us—and just about every other car on the road was passing us—were swiveling their heads and staring. I was trying to ignore them.

"Oh, sugar, there was no story. We had a couple of fun dates and some all-night romps in the sack, I do admit, but then he got transferred down South. I never bit him or anything, you know."

"But you did tell your young man that you were a vampire spy. Next thing we know, his cousin Bubba was recruited for Team Darkwing. I mean how did that little nugget of information about you being a spy and a vampire come up in casual conversation, Benny?"

"Now Daphne, I know I slipped up. But Larry D. was just so innocent and trusting I couldn't stand it. He could get really hurt by some unscrupulous woman, and I was trying to make a point. The fact that we was both a little tipsy and playing strip poker at the time didn't have nothing to do with it," she insisted. "And bless his heart, he was falling for me, and I was telling him why he shouldn't, that's all."

Any man could fall for Benjamina Polycarp, and I hated to tell her, but chances were that Bubba Lee was already half in love with her. I glanced over, and she was totally absorbed with singing along with the oldies, appearing to be happy to be alive, or undead, if you wanted to get technical about it. When the Everly Brothers started singing "Dream," we both jumped in and harmonized. We had a pretty good trip even if the Smart car didn't do much over fifty-five miles per hour safely, and I thought a stiff breeze might blow us off the road.

Right on schedule I drove into the Hamptons and hoped I could find the dirt road leading to the little cemetery just beyond the Bradley compound. I wasn't scared, of course, but I was tense as a taut rubber band. If this damned Smart car got bogged down in the sand, I guess Benny and I could just get out and lift it up, but I mentally kicked myself for not asking Mar-Mar for a vehicle with four-wheel drive. If I have any flaws, it's that I really am bad at nailing down details. I disappoint myself a lot. I hoped there wasn't any other point I was overlooking.

I found the turnoff from the state road and started driving slowly down the dark, unlit track. There were no lights to the left of us and no lights to the right of us. It was black as pitch everywhere I looked. Benny turned the radio off and stared with wide, wild eyes out the front window at the headlights' glare. She looked truly terrified. "Get your cell phone out, will you?" I said to distract her.

She fumbled around in her purse and found her phone. She flipped it open. "Judas priest!" she swore. "We don't have no service. Lord knows how far we're going to have to drive back to call J."

"It's probably just a bad spot," I said, trying to reassure her. "I'm sure I had service the other night when I was out here at the party. Don't get all nervous. It's going to be okay. We should only be here a minute, honest."

"If you say so," she said. "But it's inky black out here. Last time I was on a road like this I was in Branson looking for a place to neck with my boyfriend. I never could relax enough to enjoy myself. All I could think of was that stupid story they told all the kids to scare them so they wouldn't go out parking."

"I never heard it," I said. Since I hadn't been a teenager

since the sixteenth century and had never gone parking with any boy, it figured I wouldn't have.

"Oh, it's old as the hills. It goes something like this: These two teenagers have driven down a dark country road to find a spot to make out when they hear over the car radio that there's an escaped maniac in the area. The psychopath has a hook instead of a hand, and he slashes his victims to death. The girl freaks out and begs her boyfriend to take her home right away, she's just about scared out of her skin. He wants to keep fooling around, but she pleads and cries, so he gives in. When they get home, and the boy goes around the car to open the door for her, there's a bloody hook hanging from the door handle.

"Damn it, Daphne, now I'm going to be thinking about some killer out there with a hook for a hand all night. I was already as jumpy as spit on a hot skillet. Now I'm as scared as a sinner in a cyclone."

It was just midnight when I pulled the Smart car under the boughs of the pine trees. Its headlights lit up dozens of white gravestones. Time and weather had eroded them so badly that the names were barely visible anymore. I looked over at Benny. "Ready?"

"I'm never going to be ready for this, but I'll get out anyway," she said and opened her door. It creaked on its hinges, and she squealed. We both climbed out of the Smart car onto the sandy soil. I turned the headlights off, which left us standing in the darkness until I could find the flashlight I had brought in my old but treasured Vuitton backpack and turned it on.

It was quiet as a tomb out there. I shone the beam of my flashlight around and spotted a rabbit that limped trembling through the sparse strands of frozen grass. The cold was running icy fingers up and down my spine. Our breaths were as white as if we were exhaling smoke. Benny stood right next to me clutching my arm. I could feel her shaking through the sleeve of my jacket.

"Let's circle around the whole perimeter," I whispered, though why I was whispering I couldn't say.

"Good idea," she agreed, "but let's stay together, okay?"

"Sure," I answered. The way she was holding my arm, we couldn't have done anything else. We turned left and walked along the front of the graveyard, then made a right turn and started walking toward the back. I shone the light ahead of me, and Benny gasped. It lit up a stone angel standing atop a small mausoleum, its granite hands clasped, its eyes turned heavenward, and its wings billowing out behind it. "It's only a monument on top of a crypt. Take it easy, Benny. There's nobody here."

"So you say," she whispered back. "I don't like this. It's giving me the creeps. I hope we find that grave fast and get out of here."

The cemetery wasn't more than three hundred feet on a side, so we quickly walked up the side, icy pine needles crunching beneath our feet. Except for that, the place was eerily silent. A ship's horn sounded mournfully in the distance. It made the quiet even more intense when it stopped. I turned my light toward the interior of the graveyard and nothing looked disturbed. We started down the back side of the graveyard and I thought I saw something light and shimmering on a sandy mound ahead of us.

"Oh shee-it!" Benny said, stopping suddenly. "I think we found where they put that dead girl cause right there she is."

I froze. My flashlight was illuminating something weird. Maybe it was mist or a shadow but it seemed to be floating in the air above the small hill of freshly dug earth. Just then the wind started to blow and a moaning sound rang in my ears. It started out low then got louder and louder. My scalp began to crawl and my skin was covered in goosebumps.

"Daphy, we need to get outta here!" Benny squealed and started dragging me straight across the middle of the graveyard to get back to the car the fastest way we could. She let go of me and we both started running. I tried to stay ahead of her to light up the way, but I could feel her breath on my neck. I tripped over a gravestone and nearly fell flat on my face. We were almost to the Smart car when I saw that there was a figure standing right next to it.

"What's that?" Benny said excitedly, grabbing my jacket from behind and and pulling me to a halt.

I swung the beam of my flashlight toward the figure and said, "It's not a ghost," as I started moving forward again, walking, not running. "It's Fitz."

When we reached him, I could see that Fitz's face was pale and worried. He said urgently, "Daphne, I don't know what you're doing here, but you've got to get in your car and leave. And fast, before the others get here."

"What are you talking about—" I started to say when suddenly a heavy object hit me from behind, I staggered forward when it hit me again behind my ear, and the world exploded into sparkling lights before I slid wordlessly down a long slippery slope into a great black void.

CHAPTER 12

There is no such thing as darkness; only a failure to see.

—Malcolm Muggeridge

"Daphy, wake up." Benny was shaking me.

"What happened?" I said, sitting up slowly. My head hurt, and wherever we were, it was completely without light and felt like the inside of a freezer. I opened my eyes but saw no better than when they were shut. Blindness enveloped me and anxiety crept in with the biting cold. Even bats can't see in absolute darkness.

"Somebody came up behind us and hit us with something. They must have put us in here. I think we're in the back of a tractor trailer," Benny said. I couldn't see her, but I could hear her breathing and feel the warmth of her hand on my shoulder.

"It must be the truck by the susto lab," I said. "Shit, my head hurts. Are you okay?"

"I've got a bump the size of a goose egg behind my ear, and I don't remember nothing about getting put in here. But you know what, I'm fine. My big hair protected my little old head better than a crash helmet," she said. "How about you? Are you bleeding?"

I felt my hair with my hands. "No blood. I just have a headache as big as Texas," I said, rubbing a sore spot on the back of my skull and standing up on wobbly legs. "Have you searched around in here yet?"

"I felt my way around some," she answered. "It's just a big old tractor trailer and it's awful cold. I sure would like to get out."

"Me too. There should be a row of cartons toward the front of the trailer. Did you find them?" I asked.

"Yeah. There are boxes stacked up to the ceiling, I think. And I stumbled over a hand truck," she said. "I whacked my shin pretty bad on it. And I tried to lift up the back door. It wouldn't budge. Maybe they padlocked it. Do you have any ideas about how we can out of here?"

"I think we're going to have to push out the side of the truck or the roof. It's only sheet metal between the ribs. You find anything we can use besides the hand truck?" I asked.

"There's a crowbar. That should help," she said.

"You know, if we make a lot of noise getting out of here, somebody's going to come to see what's going on," I said.

"I don't know of any quiet way of ripping through metal," Benny said. "Shit, I just thought of something. We never called J. Do you still have your cell phone?"

"No. It's probably back in the cemetery in the Smart car with my backpack. Once we get out, we'll have to go back there and get it. Do you know what time it is?" I asked.

"No clue, but I don't think we were unconscious very long. I hope not, or we're going to have a problem getting back to the city before dawn," she said nervously. "What do you think we should do? Transform? Go ahead and bust out?"

"No, not yet. Maybe as a last resort. First let's try to do it quietly. We'll blow everything if anybody spots a couple of giant bats flying out of here. I bet they'd pack up that lab and head for the border faster than we could get anybody arrested. Let's see what the story is with the walls. Grab my hand, and let's stay together."

We made our way to the side of the truck. The metal

didn't seem too rigid. It had some give to it, but I didn't think it could be bent enough if we started prying from the floor. I told Benny I thought we should try the roof.

"You know, Daphy," she said, "I've seen these trucks when they try to go through an underpass without enough clearance. Sometimes the top of the roof smashes down, but other times it just peels away like the top of a sardine can. Let's try to pry apart that front top corner. We can use those cartons to stand on."

"Good thinking, Benny. They might not notice the hole up there right away, and it will buy us some time. Can you find that crowbar?" I felt my way over the boxes and pulled a few down to create makeshift steps. I crawled up onto them. It reminded me of being in a barn long ago and climbing up on the bales of hay. The boxes were wobbly, and I didn't know if I could get any leverage.

"I got the crowbar. Can you reach the top seam?" she called up to me from down below.

"Yeah. Hand me the crowbar. Ouch. That was my knee you hit!" I squealed.

"Sorry, but it's as dark as the inside of a well in here," she apologized.

"Now, you know, Benny, my Japanese sensei once said, 'Man stands in his own shadow and wonders why it's dark.'"

"Daphy, don't go all deep and intellectual on me. All we got to do is bash a piece of iron through a piece of steel, and that takes brute force, not brains. I'm about ready to say the hell with this, turn into a bat, and claw the shee-it out of the side of the trailer," she said testily.

"I was just trying to make a joke. I think I feel a spot where the roof is rusted." I poked the end of the crowbar into the rusty place. It took a few jabs, but it went through. It made a banging noise, but nothing much louder than a tablespoon hitting a fifty-five-gallon drum. "Got it!" I said. A tiny square of moonlight peeked into the absolute blackness of the trailer's interior.

"I'm right proud of you, but we're going to need something a tad bit bigger than two or three inches," Benny said.

I pried the bar around as much as I could until I actually had a line of light about two inches wide and a foot long where I bent and bashed through the metal. But it was too little, and it was getting too late. "Benny, it's not going to work," I said, disappointed. I put the crowbar down. Then I had an idea. I slipped off my red silk panties from under my skirt and fastened them as best I could around the jagged metal of the opening I had made, letting them dangle outside the trailer. I had a fleeting notion that they'd be a fast way to identify the trailer if it started rolling toward Manhattan before the lab was destroyed. It was just a thought. I didn't know if it would work, but I figured it couldn't hurt. Then I carefully climbed off the boxes.

"Benny, I don't like the idea of busting out of here but I think we're out of options," I said. "Maybe we can claw through the front of the trailer near the cab and cover it up with the boxes."

"We can try. All I know is that we've got to get out of here, Daphy. We've got to call J or this whole night's been for nothing," Benny said. "Well, I guess we'd better strip down. I'm sure going to hate losing these fancy clothes," she said sadly.

"Hold up on that . . . I think I hear somebody coming," I whispered. The sound of footsteps got louder as someone approached the trailer, then metal hit metal. Somebody was definitely unlatching the trailer door. I reached up and grabbed the crowbar. From what I could hear, I figured out Benny had the hand truck. We stood unmoving, waiting, ready to fight our way out.

The door opened a few feet and some dim light filtered in. A dark figure stood there. "Daphne? Are you okay?" Fitz's voice whispered.

"Yes," I answered, and put down the crowbar.

"Keep your voice low," he whispered. "Don't make any noise. I'm going to try to get you and your girlfriend out of here. Is she conscious?"

"Yes," I called back softly.

"Okay, come on. Quickly, both of you," he said.

Benny and I moved to the back door, stooped down, and scooted under the opening. Fitz guided each of us out. He held a finger up to his lips, then began leading the way around the building. The Cadillac SUV was parked on the asphalt driveway, white against the black. "Get in the back and get down," he said softly. We did, scunching down on the floor of the back seat. Fitz was opening the driver's door when another man's voice said, "St. Julien, where are you going?" Fitz shut the front door, and we could see his back as he blocked our window with his body.

"I was going to take a run up to the house," he said.

"Do it later," the voice ordered. "We've got to get this shipment packed into the trailer. It's supposed to leave here in the morning. Come on, let's get those girls out of there."

Oh shit, I thought. *They're going to find out we're gone and figure out that Fitz let us go.*

"Okay," he said. "Be with you in a minute." Fitz opened the driver's side door again and leaned over as if he were getting something out of the glove compartment. He flipped the car keys into the back. Benny reached out and grabbed them. "Get the hell out of here, now!" he whispered, then pulled back out of the Escalade, shut the door, and started after the other man in the direction of the tractor trailer.

"Benny," I whispered. "Get back to the cemetery and get the cell phone. Call J as soon as you can pick up a signal. I'll meet you where the dirt road intersects with the state road."

"What if you're not there?" she asked.

"Wait a couple of minutes, then get the hell out of here. I'm going to watch what happens. There's going to be trouble. Now move it," I said fiercely. I opened the back door quietly, bailed out, barely shut it, and ran as silently as I could to the back of the building. I pressed myself flat against the metal wall, trying to stay in the shadows.

From where I stood I couldn't see what was going on, but I could hear the back of the trailer being unlatched and raised up. The man with Fitz suddenly yelled, "What the fuck? Where are they?" Just then the Escalade's motor started up, and Benny went tearing like a bat out of hell down the driveway. "Hey! Hey! What's that noise?" the man was yelling. "That's the SUV? Fitz, you son of a bitch, you let them go! Didn't you?"

"Look, Rodriguez," Fitz was saying in a calm voice. "It was just my girl and her friend. I wasn't going to let you hurt them. They didn't know anything."

"You dirty double-crossing bastard. What if they go to the cops? We've got a warehouse full of drugs."

"Rodriguez, put the gun down. They're not going for the cops. I told them to just go home." Fitz's voice was low and calm, as if he were still trying to soothe the agitated man.

"You can't be that dumb. You can't. Something's not right here. No, something's not right. Take off your shirt."

"What? Why?" I could hear Fitz's voice change to a protest tinged with something like fear. I didn't dare put my head around the corner to watch. I could only listen.

"Just take it the fuck off, now! Before I blow your fucking head off," Rodriguez screamed. He sounded out of control. I didn't know what was going on, but I knew that Fitz was in deep trouble.

Then I heard Rodriguez screaming again. "You're wired. You son of a bitch, you're wired." Then the gun went off, and I heard an agonized groan. I could barely keep myself from transforming, but I was overriding my instincts with every bit of my willpower. I got down low to the ground where I was less likely to be seen and took the chance of looking around the corner. Fitz was curled up on the ground in a fetal position; dark blood was pouring from between his fingers as he pressed them over the wound.

Rodriguez was standing over Fitz with the pistol aimed at his head. "Who are you working for?" he screamed at Fitz. Fitz didn't answer, he just moaned. Rodriguez put the gun to his temple. "I don't give a shit if you're DEA or FBI, you're going to die you dirty double-crossing bastard," Rodriguez said. He pulled the trigger—and nothing. Just a click. The gun didn't fire. He tried again. The gun just clicked. "Fuck this," Rodriguez said and threw it into the dirt.

My heart felt as if it had stopped and sourness came up into my throat. I heard Rodriguez's footsteps walking away and a door opening. Then it slammed shut.

I looked around the corner again. Rodriguez was gone. I ran over to Fitz. Blood was everywhere. "Fitz! Fitz!" I said softly. "Can you hear me? I've got to get you out of here."

"Daphne," he said in a voice so weak it was barely audible. "No. Get out of here. Before Rodriguez gets back."

"No! I won't leave you. I'll get you out of here."

"Daphne. Listen to me." He stopped and struggled for a breath. "Get my cell phone. In my jacket. Call the first number. They'll know I'm down. Tell them where I am." His voice faded away, but he was still breathing. I stooped down and frantically searched through his jacket. His wallet, along with the cell phone, was stashed in the inside pocket. I pulled them both out in wild haste. The wallet flipped open as I did. Right there in laminated plastic was a government ID: ST. JULIEN FITZMAURICE. SPECIAL AGENT, UNITED STATES SECRET SERVICE.

Hot tears came up behind my eyes. My instincts had been right about him all along. But my attention now was on the cell phone. I hit the speed dial, and as soon as it was answered, I whispered urgently, "Man down. Man down. Get a medic! Stat!"

"Your position," a calm voice said.

"Next to the Bradley drug lab. Hurry."

"We're already moving." The connection was severed.

"Fitz! Can you hear me?" I said, putting my lips close to his ear.

He just groaned. I felt the pulse in his neck. It was strong. I didn't want to leave him, but I had to get out of there. I figured he had a chance. I didn't know how good a chance, but he was still alive. I grabbed his jacket and wadded it up, pressing it against the wound. Just then I saw some dark figures crouched down and running crablike toward the building. I figured it was the cavalry. I decided to take off. I scrambled back around the building and trotted down the long asphalt drive, past the greenhouses, and headed toward the state road. It was another quarter-mile down that two-lane highway before I got to the dirt track leading to the graveyard. I was out of breath and panting when I saw the Escalade come flying down the dirt road. Benny caught me in the headlights and came to a stop. I rushed over to the passenger side and jumped in.

"What happened?" Benny said.

"Rodriguez shot Fitz—"

"Oh no," Benny said.

"Yeah, Rodriguez found out Fitz was wired. Turns out Fitz was working for the Secret Service." The thought flashed through my mind that once again the right hand didn't know what the left hand was doing when it came to U.S. intelligence agencies. Fitz was working the same case we were. For all I knew, maybe Darius was too. And nobody was communicating. Nobody was coordinating. I remembered how dangerous the duplication of effort had been on our last assignment. Now this time nobody from our agency knew the Secret Service was investigating Bradley and Rodriguez. Then from the back of my mind an idea started to emerge. It was black and ugly and hurtful. The thought was, *Unless somebody did know. Unless Mar-Mar knew all along and set up the whole meeting between Fitz and me at Kevin St. James.* That possibility that she had manipulated me again did a number on my head and I couldn't bear to think about it.

"Daphy?" Benny said, calling me back from that dark place. "We have to get out of here. Where should we go?" she said urgently.

"Do we have time to get to the city before the sun comes up?" I asked as I looked around until I spotted the LED clock above the dash. It was after five a.m. "Oh shit. No way. We're going to have to find someplace dark to get through the day. Let's go back to the cemetery."

"Ohmygod! I was scared out of my skin just to go get the cell phone. I have your backpack. What good is it going to do to go back there? Do you want to retrieve the Smart car?"

"No. That's not it."

"What do you mean?" she said skeptically.

"You're not going to like it. And we're going to have a lot to do first."

"I swear to God you'd go ahead and charge hell with a bucket of ice water. What are you planning?"

"To have us spend the day in that mausoleum we spotted in the graveyard," I said, bracing myself for Benny's reaction.

"*No way!* That place is haunted. And that crypt probably is just loaded with spiders, snakes, and other creepy-crawly things. I'm not doing it!" she said, turning so white she reflected the moonlight coming through the SUV window.

"Benny, it's winter. There are no bugs and no snakes," I said, trying to calm her down.

"Yeah, well!!! There sure are ghosts, now aren't there? How do we take care of that?" she asked.

"An African witch doctor told me that what you have to do with any kind of ghost or evil spirit to get rid of them is laugh at them," I said, feeling it sounded pretty lame.

"Oh that's rich," Benny said as she jerked the steering wheel around to do a K-turn across the dirt track and started driving at an unsafe speed back to the graveyard. "Laugh at them. Are you out of your mind?"

"Seriously. I heard it works," I said. I figured I'd try reasoning with her. "Look, Benny. How can ghosts hurt us? We are undead, and all. And we don't have any other options."

"I told you I don't know what they can do. I just know I don't want to find out, so will you do me a favor?" she said in a tight voice.

"What?"

"Shut up about them!"

I did stop talking for maybe a minute, but I had to tell Benny the rest of the plan. "Benny? What we have to do is this—I'll get the Smart car and follow while you drive this SUV down to the water's edge. If we can, we'll push the SUV off a dock. If we can't, we'll just abandon it. Then we'll both drive back to the cemetery."

"Why don't we just drive to a motel or something? We don't have to go through all that," she pleaded as she pulled in under the trees.

"Benny, what motel? We don't have time to go looking for one, and if we do find one at six in the morning, we'd better hope it's open in the off season. We can't chance it. Look at the sky back there. I swear I see it getting light at the horizon. If we can't get in that crypt, we're both going to be dust."

"Oh damn damn damn. Just hurry. And I still didn't call J. There's no reception in the graveyard, remember?"

"Shit! Okay, put it on the to-do list," I quipped with a lightness I really didn't feel as I got out of the SUV.

"Now drive like a maniac back to the main road," I explained while leaning back into the vehicle. "Make a right. Make your first left and don't make any turns. It goes straight back to the boat dock. And once you leave the main road, kill your headlights. They might be able to see you from the warehouse." Then I stood up, slammed my door, and watched her back out.

I got into the Smart car as swiftly I as I could. I made a U-turn so fast sand splattered the pine trees, then raced off after Benny. The sky was definitely lighter. I guessed we had less than half an hour before the sun came up. One ray of morning light would cut through my flesh like a laser. A dose of full sun and I would fry like a fresh donut at Krispy Kreme. This was definitely not my idea of a good time.

By the time I pulled up next to the bay, Benny had already pulled onto a long dock and driven to the end. She climbed out of the SUV and turned around, looking for me, her movements stiff with tension. I left the Smart car idling and ran out onto the dock. I could smell the pungent tang of the salt water and hear the soft rhythm of the waves hitting the aluminum pilings. I came up breathless next to Benny.

"I put the transmission in neutral," she said. She had also left the windows down, and we both got behind the Escalade and pushed. The SUV rolled off the end of the dock, floated for a minute, then slowly started to sink. We didn't wait around to watch it disappear beneath the black water, but went running back to the Smart car. It was close to daybreak, and we had to get into the dark of the mausoleum fast. I put the Smart in drive but suddenly hit the brake and said to Benny, "Grab my cell phone. Do we have service?"

"Yes," she said with an edge of panic in her voice.

I didn't move the car an inch, unwilling to take the chance of losing the signal. I put the transmission back in park while Benny handed me the phone. I speed-dialed J. He answered on the first ring, and before he could ask me anything, I blurted out, "J, don't talk, just listen. First off, the girl's body is in the cemetery. Toward the back. Get the warrants. Second, a truckload of susto is scheduled to leave the Bradley compound this morning. Stop it. The top left front corner of the trailer has a hole in it, and you'll see a piece of red fabric in the hole. It might help you spot the right truck. Third, Rodriguez shot St. Julien, who was wired and working for the Secret Service. Rodriguez is probably going to run. And J, get somebody over to my apartment to walk and feed my dog, okay?"

"Consider it done," J responded.

"And one more thing, Benny and I have to get into cover. We'll be in the cemetery. Whatever you do, don't open the door of the mausoleum with the angel on it. Got that?"

"Roger," J said, his voice betraying nothing of what he was thinking.

"I've got to go. We'll contact you at sundown." I flipped the phone shut, cutting him off, shifted into drive, and pushed the gas pedal of the Smart car down to the floor. It jerked forward, and we tore hellbent for leather down the asphalt drive, got onto the main road, and finally skidded onto the dirt track. I could feel the Grim Reaper breathing down my neck. I was closer to death than I had ever been in my undead existence. I give Benny credit, she wasn't saying a word. She had my backpack clutched tightly in her hands and was ready to roll the minute I stopped the car. I pulled in under the trees, trying to park the Smart car as close to where we had originally left it as possible.

Rosy streaks were starting to light the morning sky. We threw ourselves out of the Smart and dashed over to the mausoleum. Its weathered bronze door was only about three feet high and it was shut tight. I grabbed the door handle, turned it, and pushed as hard as I could. It opened about an inch and then just stopped. It was jammed. Benny squeezed next to me and around. We pushed together. It started opening with excruciating slowness. Finally there was just enough space for us to squeeze inside.

"Get in!" I yelled at Benny. She gave me a questioning look. "Go!" I insisted. She bent down and worked her body through the narrow opening. I looked around for something to jam the door shut from inside, worried that Rodriguez or his men could still come looking for us. The mausoleum was an obvious place for someone to hide, but we didn't have a choice. I saw an old iron cross tilting at a forty-five-degree angle where it marked one of the graves. I went over to grab it even though I knew what would happen when I did. I was about to prove that one piece of vampire lore was all too true.

Oh shit, I thought, *This is going to hurt.* Sure enough, as my hands closed around the cross, the metal burned my flesh as if it were red-hot. I gritted my teeth, ignoring the pain, and pulled it out of the ground. I carried the heavy cross into the mausoleum and got inside. Benny helped push the door shut behind me. My hands hurt so badly that tears ran involuntarily down my face. In the enveloping darkness I used the cross as a brace, wedging it between the door and the floor. Then I let go of the rusty iron with a moan. I hurt, but I felt a tremendous relief. Without demolishing the marble crypt, nobody could get in. The space inside was small and cramped, but it was dark, and that's all that mattered. We were safe. And we were back in the dark, only this time coffins, not cardboard boxes, lined the walls.

Chapter 13

Between two worlds life hovers like a star,
'Twixt night and morn, upon the horizon's
verge,
How little do we know that which we are!

—*Don Juan,* Canto XV, Stanza 49, by Lord Byron

Darkness. Safety. A tomb. A womb. We were safe. I exhaled with a deep sigh. "How you doing, Benny?" I asked.

"Hanging in there. Cold, cramped, and damp. No biggie. I've felt about the same in some cheap motels in Branson. Those rockabilly guys don't spring for the big bucks." She laughed. "Some of those dumps had cockroaches bigger than cats. Of course, the owners called 'em waterbugs. This ain't so bad."

"Yeah, it could be worse. The main thing is we're still undead and not *dead* dead. We'll make it through the day. Hopefully we'll get some sleep," I said.

Benny laughed again, this time with no mirth. "Sleep? That's a good one. I keep waiting for one of these damn coffins to open up and something disgusting to come sliding out."

I sat with my spine against the wall, hugging my knees. The floor was cold marble. The space was only about thirty inches wide and maybe seven feet long. Crammed close together, Benny and I could share whatever warmth passed through my fur coat and her down one. Besides the likelihood that our legs would be stiff by nightfall and our bellies growling with hunger, I figured we'd be okay.

After a few minutes of silence, Benny asked me, "What are you thinking about?"

I snorted. "That if I'm just sitting here for the next nine hours, there's stuff I don't want to think about and I'm afraid I will."

"You mean like Darius?"

"Yeah, mostly. I mean what do I really want from him? If it's to have a guy who's going to be there for me, I'm not going to get it from him. So is that what I want? Or do I want a physical thing with him and for my life to go on pretty much as it always has, with me on my own? When it comes down to it, I don't know what I want."

"I know what you mean. Sex isn't love, but I sure get them mixed up all the time. And I haven't found Mr. Right in all these years. I don't think vampires can be in couples. But everytime I meet a cute guy, I get my hopes up." She sighed.

"I don't think there's anything wrong with getting your hopes up. Hell, it may be crazy, but I still hope Darius and I have a chance."

"So where does Fitz fit in to that, if you don't mind me asking?" Benny said. I felt her shift her weight next to me.

I thought for a moment. My attraction to Fitz had been a surprise to me. Finally I answered, "I think he's another road I could take in my life. I don't know if I ever will. I don't know where it will lead. To be honest, I like knowing that I could, that I have that option. Of course, with Fitz I'm back to the problem that he's not a vampire. He doesn't know I am. If I don't tell him soon, he'll feel I lied to him. But can I trust him enough to reveal myself? I don't know if I can go through that again. Look what happened with Darius."

"Well, hell, Darius was a vampire hunter. What did you expect? It doesn't mean every guy is going to freak out on you. I keep hoping that if a guy loves me, it won't matter."

"Benny, I hate to tell you, but it will matter. When it comes to men, face it: We're fucked," I said.

"Or not fucked!" Benny laughed. "It's the same old story. The hell with it! Let's just have the best time we can and not worry about men. Who needs them anyway? Look at all I've got without a guy. I'm living in New York where I'm no longer the 'weirdo witch from back in the holler' as some folks called me in Branson, and I've been having fun. Sometimes I think that if things get any better, I may have to hire someone to help me enjoy it. Let's get an attitude adjustment, girlfriend, we've got it good."

I started thinking about that, and my mind wandered. "Yeah, we do have it good. And after the Darkwings end, and I guess they will at some point, I could try to make the world better, safer. I have enough money, so I could set up a foundation for animals on a farm somewhere. Or go to those ravaged places of the globe, like Afghanistan, and start a school or a medical clinic. And maybe, even, I could be with Darius. I don't know. He and I could find a life where he could write his poetry and I could paint. I used to paint, you know. But those are only dreams."

"You know," Benny said in a voice that was getting sleepy, "people who don't have dreams don't have much."

Pretty soon I could hear her breathing get even, and she began snoring a little, in a very ladylike, Benny sort of way. I tightened my arms around my legs and rested my head on my knees. I had often tried to analyze why I had cared so deeply about Darius so fast. He wasn't just Darius; he was the type of man I was always attracted to. I suspected my feelings for him were all entangled with my memories of George Gordon, Lord Byron. They were a lot alike, those two. They were both smart young men with a lot of charisma, but they were haunted by inner demons. They were emotionally suffering, and I wanted to save them. They were idealists, drawn to social causes, and heroic. I could admire them. And the icing on the cake for me was they were physically, well, *gifted.* They made love with abandon and they pushed the edge of what a man and a woman did together. I found that exciting, I confess. I liked sensation, danger, and pleasure as much as they did. Each of them had been like a magnet for whatever needs were hidden deep inside me.

Sitting there in the dark, thinking of Darius, then thinking of Byron, my mind started to drift down the corridors of time, back to a castle in Kent, which I had named Castle Indolence, and where I had been living in 1808, the year Byron had come to London determined to be bad.

And he had been bad, losing vast sums in gambling dens, sleeping with both fine ladies and bawdy whores, and consuming great quantities of food, drink, and opiates with reckless abandon. He sought out the forbidden and the dangerous. I suppose that is why, after our night of libertine pleasures and my drinking of his blood, he came searching for me a few weeks later.

Around my castle, deep in the countryside of Kent, the night was drear and stormy. I was wearing a delicate white nightgown of Egyptian cotton so fine it was transparent, and I had modestly covered it with a black velvet robe trimmed in white fox. My bare feet were on an embroidered cushion and my back was toward the fire as I concentrated on a piece of needlepoint in the frame before me. The design was supposed to depict a flying fox hanging upside down from a tree branch laden with cherries. I was playing with the colors, the brown of the bat next to the rich red of the cherries and the bright green leaves, but what color should I make the background? I was sitting there pondering my choices when Jerome, my butler, tapped softly at my chamber door.

"Lady Webster," he said stiffly. "You have a gentleman caller."

Since the hour was late, nearly striking eleven, and I had few acquaintances in Britain, I was surprised. "Who is it?" I said as my eyebrows lifted higher.

"Lord Byron, my lady," he said in a voice that told me

that even Jerome had heard of the most notorious nobleman of the *ton.*

I was stunned, and my pulse began to race as I said, "Please show him into the drawing room and offer him some wine. Put some logs on the fire as well. I don't wish to be cold, and it's quite drafty in there. I'll be down shortly."

"Very good, my lady," Jerome said and withdrew.

Of course I had been thinking of Byron ever since our night together, but I had never intended to see him again. It would be far too dangerous for him, and it would entail too much public exposure for me. But I had a far greater reason to avoid him—he had attracted me far more than I wanted to admit. There was an appealing vulnerability and youth behind his arrogance. And he was extraordinarily handsome. The poet Coleridge had later written, "So beautiful a countenance I scarcely ever saw . . . his eyes the open portals of the sun—things of light, and for light." I was a creature who ran from the light, and I should have known to run from Byron.

Instead, I put on a pair of velvet slippers, brushed my hair, and sprayed on some scent before descending the castle stairs and entering the drawing room.

"Lady Webster—or whoever you really are," Byron said as I entered, getting up from his chair by the fire, "I hope you don't think me presumptuous."

"I do think you are presumptuous, Lord Byron. You have not been invited," I countered. He crossed the space between us and shocked me by falling to his knees before me.

"I beg you not to send me away," he said. "I am a supplicant at the altar of your beauty."

"Lord Byron! Do get up," I said, alarmed.

And with that he laughed and stood. "My lady, you are not very observant if you cannot see that I am already up."

Indeed his trousers bulged with an obvious erection. "My lord, you are outrageous as well as presumptuous," I said. "Did you come here in hopes of satisfying your basest needs? Go find yourself a London whore," I said, and turned to leave.

He grabbed my hand. "Nay, lady. Forgive my crudeness. I jest to keep from crying, to keep from begging you not to turn me out. I have been searching for days to find you."

I stopped and looked at him. He shone with an inner fire so intense its brightness hurt my eyes. "Why have you been searching? I am nothing to you," I said.

"Nothing? Is the great void where all the stars hang in the ether nothing? Or is it everything?" He drew me close to him. "You are everything, my lady, not nothing."

I pulled away from him, walked to the fire, and stared into the flames. "And *you* are a romantic, my lord. You don't know me, nor I you. We don't suit. I am not anything like you may imagine." I turned around and smiled then, hoping to shock him to prove my point. I showed my sharp teeth, the ones with which I had bitten him.

He gasped, but did not move to go.

"You see," I said continuing to stare at him. "I am not to be trifled with. I could be your death."

"Then I crave my death. I hunger for it. I dream of it. For I wish to be in your arms," he responded, coming over to me and taking my hands in his.

"Do you understand what I am, my lord?" I asked.

"No. A creature of some mythic realm perhaps. A succubus, a demon lover, I think. The villagers are afraid of you," he answered, and stood so close that I could peer deeply into his eyes, which I could see held desire but no fear.

"As well they should be," I said. "I am no succubus. I am a vampire. And I do think, before it is too late, you should leave." His eyes looked sad now, but still not afraid.

"I do not wish to leave, my lady. I don't care if you are called a vampire, a demon, or a devil. To me, you are an angel and a kindred spirit to my own," he said, and leaned down and brushed my forehead with his lips.

I pulled back but couldn't move farther away since my hands were held firmly in his. I looked at him and said, "You are very young, not yet one and twenty. You have talent and great courage. Your life should not be made forfeit to your lusts for me, for that is what you feel. There is no kindred spirit here. I am a lost soul, undead, doomed to wander endlessly about the earth, driven by my own thirst to drink the blood of humans. Again I say you need to leave me, before it is too late. I can only be your doom."

Byron closed his eyes for a moment and heaved a deep sigh. He sat down in a chair then, pulling me onto his lap. His muscles were firm beneath me. The smell of him intoxicated me. "Listen to me, my lady. You cannot doom me, fate has already done that. My life has been a tale of horrors as grim as any you could have known. My early years have wounded me so deeply that I try to drown the pain in every pleasure I can find. I, like you, am a lost soul. I see no future but my own end, run through by a rapier in some foolish duel with an enraged husband whose wife I was pleasuring in his absence." He wrapped his arms tightly around me. "And speaking of pleasure," he said, his voice changing and becoming heavy with carnal thoughts, "let me give you what I can."

I was tempted. I was torn between my sense of decency telling me not to destroy this talented man and my base desires. I took his hands from around my waist and stood up. "My lord, I cannot be taken at *your* will for your pleasure or used to sate your passions. If you want me for your kindred spirit, you must woo me, as you would any woman. If you want me for your whore, I'm afraid you will be disappointed. I have no need of a whoremaster," I said and turned to leave the room.

He looked crestfallen. "I can only beg your forgiveness, my lady. I did not mean to offend you. I don't want you as a whore. I want you as my soulmate."

That surprised me. Was he sincere? I decided to play this

out and see what would happen. "Then you shall have to earn my respect and win my affections," I said. "Now I wish to retire. Alone. You may return tomorrow evening if you wish. For dinner. At eight." I pulled the servants' bell. Jerome appeared at the door. "Please show Lord Byron out," I said.

It was all a game, you see. And one could not win it, if one surrendered too easily.

Those were the memories that trailed through my mind like wisps of smoke as I sat waiting for the day to pass, sealed in this hard, cold crypt. Benny was snoring gently and eventually I was beginning to be sleepy. I thought I heard muffled voices outside, and hoped they belonged to police coming to look for that poor girl's body and not Rodriguez and his men. There was nothing I could do in any event, so I let myself drift off into a troubled slumber.

My sleep was troubled because my dreams immediately returned to England, to Castle Indolence, and to Byron. Or was he Darius? Byron now had Darius's face, his eyes. My mind was confusing the two men in my dreams. I supposed I confused them in my heart as well.

As I once again followed my memories into the past, gray mists gathered and parted. A winter moon shone down, and the turrets of Castle Indolence gleamed in the pale light. Some days, nay some weeks, had passed since Byron had first shown up at my castle. He had come back to dinner the next night, and many thereafter. I spent no time alone with him, carefully arranging for my maid and Jerome to hover, often intrusively, no matter how long the evening stretched. Byron and I talked of politics and the revolutions in America and France. We argued over the talents of Percy Shelley and John Keats versus the merits of Alexander Pope and Samuel Coleridge. Surprisingly, we had much in common. He also wrote me poetry, often casting the paper in the fire after he read the verse to me, causing me much distress. He just laughed and called them trifles.

Finally the time came when he was to leave on a tour through Portugal, Spain and Malta, then east to Albania and Asia Minor. I had been planning to travel too, leaving behind the damp of England to go south. He suggested we should journey together. I said it would not be possible. I traveled only at night, accompanied by my faithful servants and a great deal of luggage.

I did agree to correspond with him, and suggested I might return to England too when he was done with his tour. In truth, I never intended to come back in his lifetime. So it was on the very last night before he returned to London to depart for the continent that the unthinkable happened. It was entirely my fault. I had dismissed the servants after dinner, and Byron and I were completely alone in the great cold rooms of Castle Indolence.

He heard me tell them to go. He looked at me curiously, and said, "Lady, are you teasing me? Are you tempting me only to leave me in torment? Or do you at last believe me when I say I love you? I have been both chaste and true these many weeks. Can you believe me now when I say I wish to possess you only as a lover who vows to honor and cherish you for all your days?"

I patted the cushions of the settee where I sat and told him to come over to me. I put my hands alongside his cheeks, cradling his face. "Dear George," I said, and kissed his forehead. "You cannot possess a vampire, but a vampire can possess you. And my days will outnumber yours by so many that they cannot be counted." His breath came heavier now, and his eyes looked glazed and heavy-lidded with desire. I wonder if he were listening to me at all.

I went on, saying, "Wisely, you will be sailing for the Continent within the next few days. But I confess, you have won my heart and now you will break it. And because I love you, I must let you go. Only not yet," I whispered, and brought my lips to his. It was as if I had unleashed a tiger. He encircled me with arms as strong as steel bands, kissing me back with a ferocity that was nearly brutal. He reached up and pulled down the front of my gown, freeing my breasts. His lips sought my nipples, sucking hard and sending a wild yearning racing though my veins.

"Daphne," he said. "Will you give me this night? All this night to be with you?"

"Yes," I sighed.

"Will you let me take you as many times as I am able?" he said, his voice hoarse and hungry.

"As many times as you wish," I said, desire making my own voice low and breathy.

I felt his teeth nip my breasts, teasing them. Then he lifted me into his arms, and set me gently down on the deep red of the Oriental carpet at our feet. His hand reached under my skirts and found my curls, and the sweet cleft within them. His fingers plunged into me, and I was slippery with desire. He withdrew then, and undid his trousers, pulling them down to release his stiff throbbing member. With no other foreplay, and no further kisses, he ravaged me then, pushing into me with a rapacious force, rocking against me as I was rising toward release, my moans matching his as we soared toward completion. He came before me, and I whimpered, unsatisfied. But I should not have fretted. His hand replaced his member and he teased me with such expert skill, I knew he had been taught by a skilled courtesan about what would satisfy a woman. I peaked and screamed with pleasure.

And that was just the first of many couplings of that long night. It should have been a memorable bout of sweet lovemaking, had I not agreed to join him during the wee hours in refreshing ourselves with a bottle of wine.

Naked we lay before the fire. We drank from the same glass, and I did not know how much I was consuming. When the bottle was empty, Bryon stood up and pulled me to my feet. I was a bit dizzy, I realized, but I felt so fuzzy and warm that I ignored what should have been a warning. He leaned me against the warm stones of the chimney and dropped to his knees, as he had done that first night. But this time, I was not alarmed. I looked down at him lazily, wondering what he was about to do.

Byron buried his face in my curls and with his tongue licked the hooded part between the cleft, where the darkness is primal and hot and animal in its taste. I buried my hands in his hair and widened my stance to give him access. He roused me to heights I had never been to. I lost my senses. I lost my reason. I said to him, "My lord, you say you seek out the forbidden. I think I should like to show you something."

He looked up at me, his eyes shining. He was a libertine and very bad, even if his heart was good. "Show me, my lady. I am your obedient servant."

Naked, I took him by the hand and led the way to a great door. I opened it and a wide staircase led down into a yawning blackness. "Are you afraid, my lord?" I asked.

"I am trembling with desire," he said as we descended stair by stair, his nakedness now covered with darkness. A single candle had been left burning in the dimness ahead. I went to it and used its flame to ignite a low-hanging candlelabra, so that the small stone room was bathed in a golden light. Byron's breath caught, and he froze.

I had taken him to the vampire's lair.

My coffin stood open on a bier. Nearby a bloodstained satin coverlet hung like a shroud over what looked like a table, but in fact was an altar beneath. Here I drank the blood of my "volunteers." They were all healthy, sturdy young men who wanted gold to start their fortunes. I took no one by force, but paid them well for both their vital elixir and their silence. Once I had finished with them, they, by arrangement, were taken away in my carriage to catch a ship sailing to the New World or Africa or the Orient, wherever they desired. I felt no guilt, though sometimes I felt remorse when they begged me to stay and let me bite them again.

As I have said, no human can resist the lure of the vampire.

"Lie down upon the altar, my lord," I ordered. Knowing Byron as I did, and how he sought out both the forbidden and his own destruction, I realized that my words would prove intoxicating and irresistible.

He did as I asked, his breath coming raggedly now. His member was stiff and trembling, as indeed his entire body trembled. I bound his hands then to the straps set there for that purpose. I knew he would not struggle to escape, but I also knew he would enjoy the binding. He had his perversions, and for this night and only for this night, I would indulge them. I restrained his ankles in the same way. His eyes were smoky, hungry, and he strained against his bonds to try to reach me, pleading with me to kiss him.

I did, leaning down so my breasts brushed tantalizingly against his chest. He was breathing even harder now, and chanting, "Take me, take me, my mistress, my master, take me." I was overwrought with excitement. I was nearly out of control. I climbed over him and straddled his hips, lowering myself upon his stiffened rod and arching my back. I rode him hard and fast. His head went frantically from side to side. I did not let him come, however. Instead I slowed, and reached down with my hand to turn his head to the side, so his neck caught the golden candlelight.

And then I leaned forward, him still inside me, and lay full length upon him. "Now, now," he screamed at me. "Don't keep me in this torment. Have me now!" With that, I lost control completely. I lost my humanity. I became a beast. And as on that first wild night together, I sought his flesh with my lips and his vein with my sharp teeth. I bit him. I bit him hard and drank from him deeply. He exploded within me and his body was racked with spasms of pleasure as long as I sucked. He was in ecstasy and would have died happily if I had drained him dry. But instead I simply sucked until I felt sated, drunk with both wine and blood. I fell asleep atop him and had no dreams.

I awoke shortly afterward, suffused with shame and horror. I had sworn to myself that I would never bite this man again. I didn't want to turn him into a monster like myself. I certainly didn't want to kill him. I searched for his pulse. It was thready and weak. He was not dead, but he was unconscious. I untied him, then ran upstairs for my clothes. I dressed and frantically summoned Jerome. I instructed him to take Byron in my carriage to London, to accompany him safely to his rooms, and to summon a doctor if he felt it necessary. With quiet efficiency Jerome did as I asked. A dank ground fog curled around the castle walls as I watched him carry Byron out and put him in my carriage. I stood there until they disappeared down the long drive as it wound through rows of dark cypresses. I sagged against the doorframe. I was a monster. I was a demon lover. I vowed never to see George Gordon again.

He did write me, of course. I read his letters, then consigned them to the flames. I never answered. I left England and went to the south of France. As I said, I loved Byron too much to destroy him, so I kept my distance. At least I did so for another twenty years. Then I was compelled to go find him, and more was the pity, for it didn't turn out well.

As for the many poems he sent me, I read them all. But I kept only this, now one of his best-known. The history books will not tell you, but I shall, that he wrote it for me—

When we two parted
In silence and tears,
Half broken-hearted
To sever for years,
Pale grew thy cheek and cold,
Colder thy kiss;
Truly that hour foretold
Sorrow to this.

The dew of the morning
Sunk chill in my brow—
It felt like the warning
Of what I feel now.
Thy vows are all broken,
And light is thy fame:
I hear thy name spoken,
And share in its shame.

They name thee before me,
A knell to mine ear;
A shudder comes o'er me—
Why wert thou so dear?
They know not I knew thee,
Who knew thee too well:
Long, long shall I rue thee,
Too deeply to tell.

In secret we met—
In silence I grieve,
That thy heart could forget,
Thy spirit deceive.
If I should meet thee
After long years,
How should I greet thee?
With silence and tears.
George Gordon, Lord Byron, 1816

I awoke surrounded by the darkness, my legs aching from their cramped position. I fumbled around in my backpack and found my cell phone. I flipped it open to get the time. It was after five thirty, the hour when the sun dips below the horizon during this week in February. It should be dusk, and we could safely open the door.

"Benny," I called. "Wake up."

"I am awake," she answered. "And I have to use the facilities, if you know what I mean. Can we get out of here?"

"I'll get the door open in a minute." I found a pair of leather gloves in my backpack and put them on before dislodging the iron cross. It gave way, and I pulled the old metal door open to see the gloomy dusk. I stooped through the opening and felt pain shoot through my back and legs as I stood up.

J was sitting on a gravestone watching me. Nobody else was around. The cemetery's quiet was broken only by the soft whisper of the winter wind through the pines.

"You two okay?" he asked.

"Just a little stiff, thanks. I'm glad to see you here, but can we wait on the debriefing? Benny and I need a bathroom, coffee, and then something to eat," I said as I grabbed Benny's hand and helped her out of the crypt.

"Hot damn, that was worse than a night in a Georgia jail," she said, arching her back and stretching. "And howdy to you," she called to J.

"Come on, ladies," he said. "I will take you out to the nearest Mickey D's and you can freshen up."

"You are a real gentleman, J," I said and followed him to his vehicle. He was driving a Hummer. I looked at it. I looked back at my Smart car.

J grinned and said, "Rank has its privileges."

It felt as if we had to drive halfway back to Manhattan before we found a McDonald's. Benny didn't complain, but she ran in to find the ladies' room almost before the Hummer stopped moving. A few minutes later, she and I sat down with cups of coffee. J took a seat on the other side of the table with a quarter pounder and a large order of fries. He told us that Cormac and Bubba were driving out from Manhattan and should get there around nine. When we hadn't called in the night before, they had wanted to come out, but J gave them a direct order not to. It was too close to dawn, and besides, J said, he had faith that we could get out of whatever we had gotten ourselves into.

"Any word on Fitz?" I asked at that point.

"His people picked him up. More than that, I don't know. I'm not in that particular loop," he said tersely. "You know, his wearing a wire may blow the whole operation. Give Bradley and Rodriguez time to cover their asses. But the lab's still running, as of this afternoon anyway. Maybe Bradley's greed has trumped reason."

"What about the warrants? Did you make any arrests?" Benny asked as she dumped three packets of sugar into her coffee cup. I wrinkled up my nose at that. I drank my java black, no sugar.

Between bites, J explained, "We found the body, and arrest warrants are ready, but we don't want to tip anybody off until after we destroy the lab. Armbruster and the Fitzmaurice cousins don't seem to be hanging around, though."

"What about Rodriguez?" I put in.

"He's in the city somewhere, we think. We're trying to find him. Sooner or later we will," he said, still munching.

I didn't share his optimism. Rodriguez could have chartered a plane and gotten to the Bahamas by that afternoon. "He shot St. Julien Fitzmaurice, a federal agent," I said, crushing my empty styrofoam cup in my hand. "Isn't that enough to start a major manhunt?"

"It's not the way it's got to be handled," J said, shaking his head. "Look, don't worry about him. After tonight, the susto operation will be history. You did your job, and you did it well. Somebody else will take care of Rodriguez."

I wasn't so sure about that, but I didn't say anything.

Benny and I finally convinced J to find a decent restaurant so we could have a nearly raw steak and rebuild some of our waning strength. We ended up at the Purple Cow in East Hampton. J sat there with a Coke and watched Benny and me dive into a prime porterhouse. A man of few words and no poetry, he revealed nothing of what thoughts were running through his head. He just kept checking his watch and staring off into space. Finally, we finished up and returned to the Hummer in the restaurant parking lot. J turned on the engine and cranked up the heater, but didn't move the vehicle. Turning to us, he said, "I already went over the demolition plan with Agent O'Reilly and Agent Lee. Let me run through it with you."

"I'm all ears, boss," Benny responded. I didn't say anything but tried to stop my thoughts of the last time I had been at that prefab storage building in the back of the Bradley compound, of Fitz's terrible moans, and of the sound of the chilling click, click when Rodriguez's gun didn't fire.

"You four will have to fly in. The compound is still guarded by armed men with dogs. I'll create a diversion out by the state road. If there is anyone in the building, and we don't think there is, just show yourself. That will clear the premises, fast. Agent Lee will instruct you about where to place the explosives, and he will attach the detonators. You'll have two minutes to fly out of there after he sets the timer. Come back to the graveyard. That will be our rendezvous point. That's it. In and out. Short and sweet."

What could go wrong?

Chapter 14

Don't pee down my back and tell me it's raining.

—Southern saying

Cormac's and Bubba's Hummer careened into the cemetery right at nine p.m. sharp, the tires spitting sand. The license plate said BIODIESEL. Leave it to Mar-Mar to make sure a Hummer burned corn oil instead of gas. With the second Hummer's arrival the graveyard was starting to look like a deployment in Iraq—that is, it would have except for the Smart car sitting there like a redheaded stepchild. Bubba barreled out of the Hummer and grabbed Benny and me in a bear hug, lifting us off the ground.

"Glad to see you two are still undead and kicking," he bellowed, nearly cracking our ribs in his embrace.

Cormac climbed carefully out of the passenger side of the Hummer carrying a blue Coleman ice chest. He came over and gave us a genuine smile as he flipped open the top. Four bags of blood fresh from a blood bank sat there, along with four white damask napkins and four Waterford crystal goblets. "We thought we might share a drink before the mission," he said.

I leaned over and brushed the air next to his cheek with a kiss.

Benny planted a big smacker right on his lips, which

made Cormac's eyes go wide with surprise. "You're really an old softie, aren't you," she said.

"No, he's really not," I said, and Cormac gave me a dirty look. "He's narcissistic, sneaky, and hasn't a sentimental bone in his body. But he is a damned good friend," I said, my words shocking Cormac even more than Benny's kiss. A blush started creeping up from the neckline of his black sweater.

J broke in. "You've got five minutes to get moving. I'm leaving to set up a fake car accident. It will happen at exactly nine fifteen. Detonation is planned for nine thirty. That gives you fifteen minutes to get the explosives set up and get the hell out of there. Any questions? No? Good luck, men," he said and got into his Hummer, backed up, K-turned, and headed down the driveway.

The four of us vampires stood alone in the quiet graveyard. As we had decided between us at some point during dinner on Monday night, we began a simple pre-battle ritual. Quietly we formed a circle and together repeated a few sentences adapted from the Ranger creed that J had given us, vowing that we'd never leave one of us behind. We reached out and stacked up our hands, and then, when the top of the pile was reached, we broke apart and high-fived each other. The next part was impromptu, not planned. Benny poured out the blood and passed out the glasses. We touched them together in a toast, then we all drank, sharing a silent communion, quickly draining the goblets.

Benny and I collected the empty glasses while Cormac and Bubba went to the back of the Hummer to transform. The energy released by their changing briefly lit up the trees with flashes of light. A wind picked up and swirled around us, lifting my hair into a wild halo around my head, and suddenly, hopping up on top of the Hummer, were two giant bats, black, huge, and terrifying. The bigger and blacker of the two, undoubtedly Bubba, had another Coleman cooler in his hands. This one I assumed contained the explosives. He hissed at us, showing his jagged teeth, saying "Hurry" as he leaped up into the sky and headed with Cormac toward the storage building at the back of the Bradley compound.

Benny and I stripped down quickly, neatly folded up our clothes, and stashed them in the Smart car. I swung my backpack around my neck, then checked to make sure I had my cell phone. The air near me turned into a whirling funnel as Benny transformed. Then bright sparkling lights were spinning in a mesmerizing swirl of flashing colors, as I too was taking animal form, my reason abating, my instincts leaping forth, my hungers and strengths multiplying until my humanity receded and my vampire nature burst forth into a wild, laughing beast who relished the freedom of flight and the ability to fight.

We flexed our knees, then soared upward into the night sky, spreading out great bat wings to fly effortlessly toward the storage building. Within a minute we were landing in the empty spot where the tractor trailer had been parked—and I silently hoped it hadn't made it to the city with its deadly cargo. I saw that Bubba had smashed through the side door and entered the interior. Just about then, high-pitched screams erupted from inside, and the garage door by Benny and me flew open, revealing the bays inside where a dozen terrified women in white lab coats stood. They stared at us, their eyes crazy with fear, wondering which way to run. Benny and I went around the side of the building to give them a chance to escape. We heard them running down the driveway, still screaming.

Benny looked at me and shrugged her shoulders.

"Nobody in here, right? I wonder what else J's people got wrong," I said as we squeezed our bulk through the side door into the building.

Bubba was stooped down by the open cooler. He saw us coming and handed us something that looked like clear plastic storage bags filled with Play-Doh and some rolls of duct tape. "You," he said to Benny, "take these over on that support beam," pointing to one side. "You," he said and turned to me. "Follow Cormac around with these." Cormac was using what looked like big twist-ties to attach his bags to various spots around the perimeter. As I carried the explosives for Cormac, Bubba circled the room, attaching the timers and detonators to the plastic explosives already in place. He was kneeling down working when the first armed guard came bursting through the side door not far from me.

The guard's eyes went wide with shock when he saw us four giant bats lurking about the warehouse. He stared firing his pistol wildly and the *ping ping ping* of bullets hitting the side of the warehouse rang out. I flew into him, knocking him down with my feet. Meanwhile two more men came running through the door, spraying the interior of the warehouse with bullets, but they were shaking so hard that unless we got hit with a ricochet there wasn't a snowball's chance in hell they were going to shoot us. Benny swooped down on those two guys, bowling them over. Then she leaped on top of one and pummeled him into unconsiousness. I rabbit-punched the other in the back of the head and he went down.

Bubba and Cormac were working as fast as they could wiring up the explosives. Bubba yelled to me, "You two drag those guys out of here. Get them at least five hundred feet from the building and behind something if you can. Then try to make sure we're not interrupted."

"Can do," Benny sang out, and we each grabbed a man in our claws. We dragged them out the door, then flew with them to a relatively safe place in a drainage ditch. That left one man still lying on the cement floor of the storage building. I rushed back to get him, but when I came back through the door, he had come to, gotten to his feet, and was carefully pointing his gun toward Cormac.

"No way!" I yelled and gave him a hard punch to the side of the head. He went down like a sandbag. I threw him over to Benny, who was behind me, and she carried him out. I went running toward the open bay doors through which the women had escaped. I could see the headlights of a van come speeding up the drive. *Oh crap,* I thought, *Benny and I are going to have our hands full. And time is ticking away.* I stole a look at my cell phone. We had four minutes to get the hell out of there. I looked back over my shoulder. Bubba and Cormac were busy finishing up the last side of the building.

"You done yet?" I yelled back at them.

"Another two minutes," Bubba said, not looking up.

My adrenaline was pumping as Benny came back. I pointed to the roof of the building and we flew up there. I figured we'd swoop down on the men as they exited the van. Even so, we were going to have our hands full, and my heart was racing as I tensed up to spring.

Just then another dark bat shape came plummeting out of the sky and landed on the driveway in front of the oncoming van. Its pelt was silver and its wingspan was huge. It was Darius.

What the hell is he doing here? I thought. *I bet he's been working this assignment all along.* Anger ran through my blood like a hot flame. *Lies. Always lies,* I thought.

The van's brakes squealed as the driver cut to the right and careened into the sandy field. The van shuddered, then fell on its side. The side door slid open and six men with rifles started to climb out. They saw Darius and started firing. With a movement so fast he was almost a blur, Darius grabbed two men in his claws, carried them off, and dropped them on the field about two hundred feet from the van. Meanwhile the other four men exited the van and started running. Benny and I didn't wait. We weren't as big as Darius, but we could each lift one, so we did. While the men screamed and squirmed in our claws, we carried them over to where the other two had been dropped and let them go. The fall wasn't enough to badly injure any of them, but it should sprain a few ankles or break an arm if they landed wrong. One man dropped by Darius was standing and ready to fire his gun. Benny flew in and kneecapped him with the tip of her wing. He screamed as he crumbled to the ground. He wouldn't be walking anywhere for a long time. Meanwhile Darius had caught the remaining two, flown over, and dropped them hard. All six men were out of action.

And we were out of time. I saw Bubba and Cormac come running out of the warehouse and leap into the air. "Darius!" I yelled. "The building's gonna blow. Get behind the van!"

The three of us dove for the overturned van and crouched behind it in the sand, covering our sensitive ears with our hands. Suddenly the night lit up as bright as day, and with a tremendous noise the building exploded. The van in front of us rocked and the ground beneath us shook. Sand rained down on us like hailstones, covering us in a layer of grime. Darius put his wings over me. I felt his body press close to mine. "Are you okay?" he whispered in my ear.

"I'm fine," I said. "Benny! How are you doing?"

"Okay," she answered.

I turned to Darius. "We need to get out of here before the emergency vehicles show up. We are supposed to rendezvous with the others back at the graveyard. Come on back with us, I'd like to talk to you. Okay?"

His expression was puzzled, but he said, "Okay, let's go," and we took to the skies. It only took us a minute to get back to the cemetery. Bubba and Cormac were already back in human form. While Benny headed for the Smart car to change, I pulled Darius to the side. Now, back in a relatively safe place, I wanted to talk to him. My emotions were churning.

"What were you doing back there?" I asked him, looking into his bat eyes. We both folded up our wings, which enveloped each of us from shoulder to feet, making us look like sinister and strange upright figures in the muted light.

"Looking for you," he said. "When you didn't come home all night, I knew something was wrong. You didn't answer your cell phone either. I headed over to your apartment building, and your doorman said somebody from 'your office' had shown up to take care of your dog. So I went looking for you."

The cold wind rustled the needles on the pines above our heads. The tombstones gleamed white in the moonlight. "Is that really the truth?" I said. "You came here to find me? To help me? I can't buy it, Darius."

"Why not? Look, I've dropped a load of trouble on you. I wanted to watch your back."

"So how did you find out where I was?"

"I used my contacts. There's been a lot of buzz about J and his secrets. It wasn't that hard."

"Didn't you think I could handle this on my own? You know I can take care of myself." My voice held an edge.

"Look Daphne, I wanted to be here for you. I thought you might need my help. Why can't you accept that?"

"I just can't. I wish I could. I think your being here didn't have anything to do with me. I think you were acting like a vigilante again. You were after somebody. Rodriguez. Bradley. I don't know who. I just happened to be here. I'm right, aren't I?" My heart felt cold and numb.

Darius sighed a deep sigh. Energy seemed to drain out of him. His shoulders sagged and his voice sounded heavy and depressed when he answered me. "Can we talk about this? I've made mistakes, not just with you, in my life. I'm trying to get straight with it all. Why don't you get your clothes and we'll go back to my car. You can drive back to the city with me. I've got a lot to say to you."

I felt as if I were at a crossroads. The pain in his voice touched me. His anguished psyche moved me to want to put my arms around him and comfort him. But his half-truths and lies made me want to walk away. I didn't know if we had a chance to fix our relationship, but I was sure that if I refused to go with him now, it would be over with us. I wasn't ready to end it. My desire for him hadn't lessened in intensity. I might be conflicted, confused, and even pissed off, but I still wanted him. He wasn't out of my system by a long shot.

"All right," I said, and as I did, a ray of hope flickered in my heart. I did want to give Darius and myself one more shot at a relationship. Maybe we could find a way to make it work. "I'll go back with you. Let me grab my things." We walked back over to where the Darkwings were waiting in the graveyard. J stood with the rest of the team. He glowered at Darius. They had never liked each other. They had worked for different intelligence agencies in the past, and their antagonism had started before I ever came into the picture. I had made things worse, even though J and I had never actually gotten together. J was a man who didn't like to lose. He was also possessive about his territory. I knew that soon as he could, he'd be trying to find out exactly why Darius had shown up here, crashing J's mission.

"I'm going to ride back to the city with Darius," I explained to all of them. To J, I said, "I'll call in tomorrow night. I'm done here for now. I'm just going to get my clothes." J's face looked dark and angry. I mentally shrugged. He probably didn't like me sounding as if I were giving him orders. I didn't care. Defiantly, I moved closer to Darius and we moved away together, heading toward the Smart car.

"Wait a minute," J said, his voice cutting and sharp.

I felt Darius tense beside me. We both turned back to look at J. He reached into his jacket and pulled out something. He balled it up and threw it at Darius. "She'll need those," J said as Darius reached out and caught my red silk panties.

Darius gave me a stunned look, his face a mask of hurt.

"It's not what you think!" I tried to explain, reaching for him, but he had already thrown the panties to the ground and taken off before I could stop him.

I turned to J. "You bastard," I said.

Chapter 15

Character determines a man's fate.

—Heraclitus, *On the Universe*

I let Benny drive the Smart back into the city, although allowing Benny behind the wheel at any time was a hair-raising experience. She drove way over the speed limit and was inclined to apply mascara using the vanity mirror while she was going ninety miles an hour. Right now I didn't care how reckless she was. I was feeling too emotionally overwrought to pay attention to traffic. Everytime I thought I could make a decision and settle things between Darius and me, something came along to derail it. I was disappointed and frustrated. But mostly I was so mad at J that my first impulse was to resign from the team. I don't know what his motives were, but I had some ideas. It didn't really matter. He was out of line. What he had done was a low blow, and I didn't know if I could get over it.

Benny didn't even try to talk to me for a good fifty miles. She just let me sit there with a wall up around me that I wasn't about to lower. Finally, she took a deep breath and said, "Now, don't y'all snap my head off, but I want to say something."

I was slumped down in the seat with my collar up around my ears. I didn't look at her but said, in a voice muffled by my coat, "Go ahead and say it. I'm not mad at you."

"I know that, darlin'. And I want you to know I'm so

angry at J I could spit nails. But what's more important, I think you need to find Darius and clear the air. Don't you?"

"Yeah. I had the same thought. I think when he calms down he'll realize that J just set me up. There's bad blood between them. Has been for a long time, according to Darius. I think he'll listen to reason. I hope he will."

"Well, there! Now we got a plan," she said, slapping the steering wheel with one hand and making the car swerve into the other lane. It's lucky we weren't killed.

"We?" I said, peeking at her over the top of the fur collar.

"No offense, Daphy, but do you know where Darius is living?" she asked.

I looked straight ahead again, feeling very out of sorts. "No. No I don't. I don't know what kind of car he drives either. Shit, I never even knew he had a car. There's too damned much I don't know about him."

"So do you know how are we going to find out—" she said, her voice raising in a way that said she was about to give me the answer.

"How?" I answered, feeling this was sort of like a bad knock-knock joke.

"We're going to ask your mother!" she said and slapped the steering wheel once more, sending the Smart car into an S-curve on a straight road.

I groaned. But Benny was right. If anybody knew where I could find Darius, it was Mar-Mar. She probably had a whole dossier worked up on him. No, not probably. She definitely did. I don't know why I'm still so naive when it comes to my mother. You'd think that after nearly five hundred years with her, I would have learned by now that nothing, but nothing about my life goes unnoticed by that woman. "We're going to Scarsdale?" I said.

"Do frogs bump their butts when they bounce?" Benny laughed. "We sure as hell are."

*   *   *

We pulled into Mar-Mar's driveway around two in the morning. Before we got to the front door, she was already opening it. In bell-bottom jeans and a Grateful Dead T-shirt, she hardly looked like one of the most powerful women in the world. The toe rings on her bare feet were a nice touch.

"Ohhh, you brought back my car! That was so sweet of you girls," she said, clapping her hands. Then she got a good look at my face and said, "Daphne, what's wrong? I already heard from J that your mission was a success and everybody's safe and accounted for. What's the matter? You look like you're going to cry."

And that's how I felt all of a sudden. I hung back, turning my head away, afraid I was going to burst into tears. Benny grabbed Mar-Mar's arm and started whispering to her fiercely as they walked ahead of me into the house. Mar-Mar was nodding, her face turning grim. Then she said, "Daphne, go in and sit right down on the couch. I'll get you a nice hot cup of chamomile tea and fetch my files. Benny, you go right along with her. I'll only be a minute."

After about ten minutes without Mar-Mar coming back, I was starting to get upset and wanted to go storming into the kitchen, yelling my head off. This whole situation wasn't her fault, but I was irrationally angry at her. I wanted to yell, I wanted to cry, I wanted somehow to get this terrible empty feeling inside me to go away. Benny saw me getting agitated and put her hand on my shoulder. "Take a deep breath. I know you're in a hurry, but don't get all riled up. Yet," she said and winked.

I nodded at her, but my emotions felt as if they were getting thrown around in the spin cycle of a washing machine. Just then Mar-Mar came into the living room carrying a tray laden with my favorite digestive biscuits, the British kind with the chocolate on top, and two big mugs of steaming tea. Under her arm she had a manila file. The tab on it bore a red label simply marked HIM.

"Here you go, sweetie," she said, and set the tray down

on the coffee table in front of me. "You'll feel much better with something hot in your stomach."

"I'll feel much better when I get a look at Darius's address," I said brusquely and went to take the folder from her hands.

"Uh-uh," she said, stepped backwards, and opened it out of my reach. I could see she had some photos in there as well as sheets of paper.

"Mar-Mar," I snapped. "Let me see the damned file."

"Oh, all right," she said, and handed it over. "But don't say I didn't warn you."

Yeah right, I thought. *If there was anything in this file she didn't want me to see, she would have removed it before she brought it into the living room, and I'm quite sure she did.* I took a couple of deep breaths before I started leafing through the papers. There were pictures of Darius with his band, of Darius walking into my apartment building, of Darius and the girl singer in conversation, their heads close together, nearly touching. I felt a stab of jealousy.

Next I picked up a digital snapshot of the girl singer looking at Darius while they were performing on stage, and her face was turned toward him. I studied it for a minute. Her expression was difficult to read. She was smiling at Darius with her mouth, but her eyes were hard and unfriendly. In another photo the girl was putting a lit cigarette in Darius's mouth while he played his guitar. She was looking at the camera, leaning toward him, her hand lightly on his shoulder, but there was something off about her body language. She wanted to give the appearance that she and he were a couple, but if I had to guess I'd say she didn't really want to touch him, that, in fact, she despised him. Darius appeared to be totally into his music, oblivious to her. I thumbed through the photos again. The more I looked at the girl singer, the more I felt she was up to something. One thing I knew for sure, Darius was definitely not screwing her. If he was, I know damn well Mar-Mar would have made sure I saw *that* picture.

I quickly found the sheet giving his home address. He lived over in Weehawken, the town on the Palisades overlooking the Hudson River on the Jersey side, where Aaron Burr shot Alexander Hamilton in a famous duel. I folded up the paper and put it in my backpack. My mind was already racing ahead. It was going to take us about fifty minutes to get to Weehawken. The hours were already winding down toward morning. I didn't want to run out of time, and we'd have to take the Smart car. Mar-Mar was looking at me as if she could read my thoughts.

"I'll put these cookies in a bag to take with you," she said.

I glanced over at her. I could see the concern in her eyes. "How am I supposed to be mad at you if you're feeding me cookies?" I asked her.

She smiled at me. "I'll put some vitamin C and zinc lozenges in the bag, too," she said, walking toward the kitchen. "Stress can bring on a cold." She was back in seconds, handing me the plastic bag by the time Benny and I got to the front door. We were about to leave when my mother put her hand on my arm and stopped me.

"Daphne," she said, "Two things I want to tell you."

I figured she was going to tell me she loved me, as she usually did.

"What?" I sighed, anxious to be going.

"When you get to Darius's, keep your eyes open. Promise?" she said with a worried voice.

"Sure, okay. That's one thing. What's the other."

"I'm going to rip J a new asshole when I see him," she said, and closed the door behind us.

"Here, you drive," Benny said, laughing her fool head off when she handed me the keys to the car. "You know the area better than I do." Then she hooted. "Your mother is something else."

"She's 'something else' all right," I said, then I started laughing too. Mar-Mar may scheme ruthlessly her every waking moment and meddle in my life, but nobody else better mess with me. I almost felt sorry for J. Almost. Actually he deserved whatever he had coming to him. She was his boss, after all. Suddenly I was in a much better mood. I felt sure I could talk sense into Darius and we could take it from there. Start over. Build a relationship. Yes, I was looking at the glass as half full. I drove as fast as I dared at two thirty in the morning toward Manhattan. The roads were empty, and the weather was crisp and clear. I imagined there was even a hint of spring in the air. I figured I'd drop Benny off, then zoom over the George Washington Bridge to Weehawken. I had time to get to Darius's well before dawn.

We left Mar-Mar's and got on the Bronx River Parkway heading south. We had been on the road about a half hour, and I was making good time. We were just entering Manhattan when a feeling of dread passed over me so powerfully that I shivered.

"What's wrong?" Benny asked, alarmed.

I held my hand up for her to wait a minute. I steered the car over onto the shoulder. My chest was tight. I had this premonition of impending death. I had no rational explanation for the urgency I felt, but I said, "I think I should call Darius. I have a bad feeling." I got my phone out of my bag and speed dialed Darius's cellphone. It rang once. It rang twice. *Answer, damn it!* I thought. Suddenly he picked up.

"Daphne?" he said.

"Darius, I had this feeling . . . well, never mind that. Are you in your apartment?"

"Yes."

"Look, is everything all right there? I mean, are you in trouble?"

There was a long pause before he said calmly, "Actually,

I might have a problem. I was going to try to get out of here, but I think it's too late. I've got some visitors downstairs watching the building."

"Vampire hunters?" I said my breath stopping.

"Yeah."

"How many?" I asked quickly. Benny was listening with her eyes wide.

"Let me take another look out the window." I heard his footsteps as he walked on a wooden floor. "I see six men. From two cars."

"Shit. Look, we're on our way."

"How long?"

"Twenty minutes tops."

"Daphne, it's too late. You won't get here in time. Look, I want to say I'm sorry—"

I cut him off. "We'll get there." I ended the call and stomped on the gas, sending the Smart car screeching back onto the road, making it fishtail until the tires caught the asphalt and we went roaring ahead. "Benny," I said urgently. "Grab that paper I got from Mar-Mar, then take my cell. Call Bubba and Cormac. Their numbers are programmed into my phone book. Tell them vampire hunters are after Darius. Give them his address and tell them to get over there. Fast. If we're lucky, they're still together in the Hummer."

With nervous fingers, Benny flipped open my phone and called Bubba. She asked him where he was, and he told her that he and Cormac were in Manhattan on Hudson Street, near Bleecker, heading uptown.

"Bubba, listen. Vampire slayers, six of them, are after Darius. He doesn't have a chance. He needs our help, fast." She read them his address.

"Give me a second to check the location on the GPS," I could hear Bubba say, then he burst out with: "It's just five miles from here. We're on our way!"

Knowing that Bubba would drive as fast as he could, I

figured he and Cormac should be at Darius's in minutes. Benny and I were twice as far away, and I hoped we got there in time. If we were too late Darius would be gone, and maybe Cormac and Bubba too.

By the time we pulled up in front of Darius's address, an old gray stone apartment house on a residential street in Weehawken, Bubba's Hummer was parked at an angle, jutting out half across the street. Its doors were wide open. I pulled next to the curb, braked the Smart car, and turned off the engine, but left the keys in the ignition as Benny and I jumped out. We looked around, trying to find out where our comrades and the vampire slayers were. We heard muffled noises from above. It sounded as if they were coming from the flat roof of the four-story building. Benny and I exchanged a quick glance. Despite the risk that the fighting might soon have people waking up and calling the cops, we were going to transform.

Once again we stripped down, this time practically tearing our clothes off and carelessly throwing them into the Smart car. We quickly ascended, flying above the rooftop to witness a raging battle, two slayers to every man. Actually it broke down differently, with four slayers surrounding Bubba, the biggest and strongest of them all, and hand-to-hand combat going on between Cormac, Darius, and the two remaining slayers. Bubba was fighting without giving quarter, but he was outnumbered and even from above we could see blood staining his side. Before we could descend, we saw him go down. A slayer pounced on him, a gruesome pointed stake raised high in the killer's hand. Even as I saw this, Benny was already in a dive, crashing headlong into the slayer, knocking him off of Bubba. I came in right behind her and raked another vampire hunter across the scalp with my claws, causing blood to cascade into the man's eyes, blinding him as he staggered away clutching his head.

Benny grabbed a second man with her hind claws and

was dragging him toward the edge of the roof, but he had hold of her legs with a death grip. I rushed over to pull him off of her, when I saw Bubba on his knees, trying to shield himself from the blows of the remaining slayer whose stake had already pierced his forearm. The next strike might hit his heart, and he would be dust.

Benny screamed at me that she could handle her attacker and to go help Bubba. I released my grip on the man, but before I could move, Bubba was bellowing at me: "Go back! Go back! And do your duty, as I have done mine, and our country will be safe. Go back! Go back! I had rather die than be whipped!" For a moment I felt confused, then I recognized those famous lines. With a flash of understanding, I knew who had uttered those words a hundred and fifty years ago during a terrible battle, and what the tragic outcome had been.

"Die? Not this time!" I yelled, and with a bloodcurdling scream threw my entire huge bat body into Bubba's opponent. I clamped my teeth over his wrist, biting him so hard that I shattered the bones, and the stake fell harmlessly to the rooftop. Blind with rage, I lifted the wildly struggling slayer into the air and flew upwards, turning to head out past the cliffs of Weehawken. Above the river I let the slayer go. The man screamed as he fell, silenced only when he hit the black waters of the Hudson.

I returned to the skies above the apartment-house roof to see Benny kneeling by Bubba, while Cormac and Darius pursued three of the slayers as they ran for their lives, hopping over the edge of the parapet onto the old iron fire escape that led downward. I landed next to Benny. Bubba lay bleeding on the roof. "How is he?" I asked, waves of fear cascading through my body.

"He's hurt." Her voice was grim as she tried to evaluate how badly Bubba had been injured. As she examined him, she reported to me, "I think his arm is broken as well as gashed. He's got a nasty wound in his side. His face has some abrasions and deep bruises, but I don't feel a skull fracture. You know, I think he's going to be okay," she said and let out a deep breath. Bubba started to get up, and we couldn't stop him. He got shakily to his feet and shook his head slowly, powerfully like a dazed bull who had just gored the matador trying to kill him.

"Take it easy, Jeb," I said and he gazed at me with solemn eyes. "This time your soldiers did you proud."

"They were good, brave men," he said, ready to defend them. Then he gave me a small sad smile. "But maybe they should have been women."

Benny turned her face toward me and mouthed silently. "Jeb?"

"Tell her, Bubba. Tell her your real name," I said as Benny looked expectantly at him.

"It's James Ewell Brown Stuart, Major General, Cavalry Corps, Army of Northern Virginia," the most famous cavalryman in the Civil War told her in a soft Southern drawl.

Stunned, Benny rocked back on her heels. "Well butter my butt and call me a biscuit," she said. Just then I heard sirens in the distance.

"Your butt's going to be something else, if we don't get out of here, Miss Benjamina," I said. "The police are coming, and we don't exactly look like law-abiding citizens. Bubba, can we help you down to the Hummer?"

"Don't you dare wait on me," he said with a growl. "And this time follow orders. Just get out of here. I'll get downstairs all right."

At that moment Darius came running back onto the roof with Cormac right behind him. "Help Bubba!" I yelled to him. "Then get the Smart car out of here. Meet me back at my place. Benny and I are going to fly back."

"Bossy, isn't she?" I heard Cormac say to Darius as Benny and I got airborne. When I looked down at the rooftop, Darius was grinning, and he threw me a kiss as Benny and I climbed higher into the night.

* * *

The drafts above the cliffs took us upward as if we were raptors, spiraling high to gain altitude while they hunt. Yet we were bats, and soon instead of lazy circles our wings whirred in fluttery beats as we dipped crazily toward the whitecaps of the moving river and bounced back upward toward the moon. In this herky-jerky manner we rode a roller coaster of wind east across the shiny black surface of the Hudson toward the pointed spires of Manhattan. In Japan, all mountains are venerated. In America, perhaps the tallest buildings are the most sacred.

In these few precious minutes of flight, so rarely experienced and so often wished for, I felt as if I could shed my body and mind, my self. I was on the great way that has no gate, taking one of Buddha's eighty-four thousand paths to realization. But what could I, a vampire, realize besides the sorrowful certainty that at the end, I would probably traverse the universe alone?

Benny separated from me as she headed toward her own apartment, farther uptown than my West End building. I landed softly on a ledge by the window I always leave unlocked and partially open for times such as this one. Jade was wildly barking inside. To calm her I changed back to human form while standing on the ledge. Her eyes became puzzled when I called her name and climbed naked over the windowsill. I stroked her head and told her that she was a good dog, then slipped into my bedroom to dress. I put on an old black sweater and a pair of Levis. I wore my favorite square-toed Frye boots. I waited for Darius.

He buzzed from downstairs a few minutes later. He walked in and took me in his arms, holding me tight.

"I'm sorry," he said.

"The panties were just a dirty trick," I said.

"I realize that. I should have known better," he said with his face next to my hair, still holding me against him.

I pulled back a little so I could see him. "Darius," I said. "We have passion, but we're missing so many other things."

"Like what?" he asked.

"Trust," I said. I pulled away and led him over to the sofa. We both sat, me snuggled under his arm, holding onto one of his strong, weather-roughened hands. "That has to change," I added.

"You're right," he said. "We started our relationship with lies, and those lies are like poison pills, coming back to contaminate our relationship."

"Both of us lied, Darius. Now we have to work hard to tell the truth."

"We're spies, Daphne," he said thoughtfully. "I don't know if we can be truthful, even to each other."

"The truth I'm talking about, Darius, isn't about revealing professional secrets. It's about not betraying each other, or using each other," I said. "It's about emotional truth. And it's about making choices, even when they're hard, that consider our relationship. Our commitment to each other has to be a priority. Otherwise we're going to go separate ways."

"Daphne, a spy's loyalty is to his country. A soldier's loyalty is to his brothers," Darius said.

"And a lover's loyalty is to his beloved," I countered. I turned so I could look at him, and I traced his lips with my fingertips.

He stroked the hair back from my face with his hands. "That's hard for me, Daphne. It won't be easy to join our lives when we may be on such different roads."

"Are you afraid to try, Darius?" I asked him.

"I'm not afraid to try. But my feelings for you make me afraid. I can't breathe without wanting you," he said, and kissed me again. He laid me down then against the cushions and sweetly, gently, removed my clothes. Our bodies had become familiar to each other, not less exciting, but infinitely more dear. His skin was scarred, his muscles hard, his stomach rippled, and just the sight of him took my breath away. Our joining was long and lazy and completely satisfying, as he took slow strokes and long kisses as we loved. And during it all I was flying again, spiraling upward like the hawk, toward the white, bright moon.

Chapter 16

No problem can be solved from the same level of consciousness that created it.

—Albert Einstein

Afterward, in the short time remaining before dawn, we took Jade down to the streets for a quick walk before we retired for the day. We headed for the river, walking briskly. We figured we had fifteen minutes tops to give her some exercise. No one followed us, nothing moved in the shadows. Yet I felt uneasy, imagining more vampire hunters coming out of nowhere. I wondered how we could ever feel safe in the city again.

Darius, who had been silent for most of the outing, suddenly urged, "I think we'd better get inside."

We went quickly back to my building and noticed that the lobby was empty. I thought nothing of that since the doorman is often absent at this early hour. We took the elevator to the tenth floor, and I unlocked my door. When we walked inside, Jade lunged forward, tearing her leash from my hand. Like a snarling wolf, she leaped with her white fangs gleaming and closed her great jaws around the gun hand of Jimbo Armbruster. He screamed as the furred fury of Jade furiously bit and tore his flesh. Her red mouth and sharp teeth were only inches from Armbruster's throat when a shot rang out. Jade whimpered and fell to the floor, tried to rise and collapsed. Jimbo sank to his knees moaning, holding his ravaged arm.

Darius and I were already in motion when Rodriguez said, "One more step and I'll shoot her again." I froze. So did Darius. All I could think of was saving my dog.

"What do you want?" I shrieked at him.

"To kill you," he said coldly. "You and your friends ruined everything. But I'm willing to negotiate. Jimbo and I need cash. A lot of it. You left me a bit short."

"Just tell me how much you want and get out of here!" I was still frantically shrieking, my reason short-circuited by emotion. Darius, unmoving by my side, said nothing. He just watched. Had I been thinking clearly, I would have understood that once I gave him the money, Rodriguez would shoot us all. He might have needed the cash, but he had come here for vengeance. Shooting me or Darius with a regular bullet would not be fatal since we were undead, but Jade would die, was already dying, and I was crazy with grief.

"Get me whatever you have on hand," he said.

"It's in the bedroom," I said.

"Get it," he ordered, giving me a venomous look. "Jimbo. Follow her," he said, and the wounded man followed me out of the room. I wanted nothing more than to rip Jimbo Armbruster limb from limb. I grabbed wads of cash from my dresser drawer. The money meant nothing to me, but even as I picked them up, a shot rang out in the other room. The last of my reason left me. I drove one fist into Armbruster's face and the other into his stomach, sending him to his knees. I kicked him hard under the chin and he fell backwards, knocked cold. I rushed into the living room to see Darius, neatly, horribly, holding Rodriguez's gun hand immobilized in one of his while, with his other hand, he calmly slit the man's throat with a commando knife. Rodriguez's eyes looked at me, still filled with hate as the light died in them. Dark red blood poured down his chest with a deadly finality.

Even before Darius let Rodriguez fall to the floor, I ran to Jade and picked her up. She was limp and unmoving in my arms, but she was breathing. I was hurrying toward the door when Darius called urgently to me. “Stop! You can’t leave. The sun is coming up.”

“Nooooo,” I screamed. “Noooo.”

Just then a pounding came on my apartment door. “Police, open up!”

I stood still holding my dog as Darius grabbed the door and flung it open. With that, Detective Moses Johnson appeared in the doorway. His gun was drawn. “What’s going on here? I was a block away when we got reports of shots fired,” he said to Darius. Then he saw Rodriguez’s body on the floor behind me.

Darius took Johnson by the arm and pulled him aside. I could hear Darius talking fast, telling him that Rodriguez had been masterminding the drug epidemic. Darius’s voice got low then and he said something else I couldn’t hear. The two men talked together for a minute and, to my astonishment, Moses Johnson didn’t seem to be arguing. Then he looked right at me. Jade’s blood was streaking down my jeans. Johnson didn’t talk about jurisdiction. He didn’t accuse me of murder. He didn’t react as if I were a pariah. He did none of those things. He walked over to me and gently took Jade from my arms, nearly staggering under her great weight.

“Get her to a vet,” I pleaded urgently. “Save her, please save her.” Johnson didn’t talk to me. He just nodded to Darius and hurried out. A complete feeling of helplessness came down upon me with a lowering darkness.

“Daphne!” Darius’s voice snapped me out of my stupor. “Give me your cell phone. Quick.”

I grabbed my backpack and pulled the phone out as fast as I could. Darius took it from my hand. In a minute, he was saying, “J? Darius. I’m at Daphne’s. Rodriguez is dead. Armbruster is unconscious but alive in the bedroom. What? Right. It’s nearly dawn. Get them out of here. You’ll need a cleanup squad. Another thing. Daphne’s dog was shot. A New York cop named Moses Johnson has her. He’s trying to get her to a vet. And J—” Darius said with a voice that sent chills through me. "That dog better live, you hear me?" With that Darius flipped the phone shut and gave it back to me. Anguish at the thought of losing Jade wracked me to my very soul.

Although I had blackout curtains on my apartment, and sunlight was not a problem, Darius and I decided to go into my hidden room before J or whomever he was sending arrived. I was physically and emotionally exhausted, and I wasn't up to talking to strangers or answering any questions. Darius, I concluded, did not want anyone from an intelligence agency to see him here. I worked a mechanism hidden behind my books, and a large bookcase swung away from the wall, revealing my lair behind it. I climbed into my coffin and Darius stretched out on the floor. I started to protest that he should get a blanket. He silenced me by saying he'd slept on harder, colder ground. And I knew he had. I fell asleep, tumbling into a grieving darkness where there was no light.

When I awoke, Darius was no longer on the floor next to my coffin. I padded on bare feet toward the kitchen. Rodriguez's body was gone; only a wet area remained on the carpet where someone had scrubbed out the blood. I barely noticed. My only thought was to discover where Johnson had taken Jade and to find out if she was alive. Darius had made coffee and was sitting at the breakfast counter with the paper. He got up and poured me a cup, handed it to me, and answered my unasked question.

"J left a message. Jade is with the police department's vet, the one who takes care of their dogs. She's still alive but to tell the truth, she's hanging on by a thread. It doesn't look good. They said you could see her around seven tonight."

I felt a lightening of the sadness weighing me down. She was still alive. It wasn't time to cry. There was still hope.

"Here, read this article," he said, pushing this morning's edition of the *New York Times* toward me. A headline on the front page read:

Fire, Murder at L.I. Estate

U.S. Security Chief Brent Bradley Dead

BY ROBERTSON CHAN AND STEVEN ALTMAN

EAST HAMPTON, Feb. 26 — After an explosion and fire rocked a storage building on the grounds of the estate of U.S. Security Chief Brent Bradley, investigating officers made a grisly discovery inside the Bradley mansion. Dead from a single bullet wound was Bradley, who maintained this summer home and a town house in Virginia. The shooter, sitting in a nearby chair, was apparently his sister, Delores Bradley Fitzmaurice, widow of former Democratic Party Chairman Michael Fitzmaurice.

Mrs. Fitzmaurice told police she had killed her brother because "he was a villain" and that he had shot her only son, St. Julien Fitzmaurice, who was employed by Bradley's consulting firm. According to an unnamed source, Fitzmaurice was wounded Tuesday evening during an altercation at the Bradley compound. The source connected the shooting to a recent influx of illicit drugs into the metropolitan area. Area hospitals have no record of his admission. Fitzmaurice's condition and whereabouts are unknown. No arrests have been made, but police confirm that Brent Bradley was never a suspect in his nephew's shooting.

Police have taken Mrs. Fitzmaurice into custody but as of press time, she had not been charged. A spokesperson for the East Hampton police department said that they are waiting for the results of forensic tests. There is no apparent link between the explosion, caused by a gas leak, and Bradley's shooting.

In a brief statement, the president expressed his shock and grief at Bradley's death. He sent his condolences to the Bradley and Fitzmaurice families, calling the incident a tragedy. Bradley was appointed to his White House position nearly two years ago and was considered by most Washington analysts to be a key advisor to the administration. Speculation has already begun about Bradley's replacement.

---

continued on Page 3

I stopped reading at that point. *I wonder where Fitz is. I hope he's okay,* I thought. But I said to Darius, "That's a surprise. So much for J's plans to leave Bradley in power. He didn't count on a mother's wrath."

"J and his people often ignore the human factor when they dream up their schemes," Darius said flatly. I didn't have a comeback for that. I didn't think Darius's assertion was true, but it wasn't worth arguing about.

"How's Bubba?" I asked. "Have you heard anything?"

Darius grinned. "I called Benny. Eventually the old warhorse had his arm set and refused further medical treatment. Benny says he's fine. She's babysitting him for a few days—or less. She said he's already trying to throw her out of his apartment. And something else I did while you were still sleeping—"

"What's that?" I said.

"I did some research online and I came up with information about Jade's previous owner from tracking down the number on her rabies tag."

"I don't really care any more," I said, finishing off the last of my coffee.

"I think you will when you hear this," he said.

"Why?"

"Jade's owner was a Manny Manuel. He gave an address up in the Bronx. It's phony. All buildings on that block were razed last year for a highway project."

I nearly dropped the coffee cup. I set it down carefully and said, "Do you think Manny Manuel could be Don Manuel? How did Jade get in that shed? I don't understand this at all."

At seven, Darius and I showed up at the NYPD K-9 units' vet. With a feeling of dread I entered a bland white hospital-like waiting room containing cheap plastic seats in a glaring orange and a few old magazines on a beat-up coffee table. When I asked a receptionist about Jade, she sent for a veterinary technician and told me to take a seat. My heart fell. To tell the truth I was waiting to hear Jade was dead.

A young girl in a pink smock walked into the room. She smiled at me. "Daphne Urban? Jade's doing fine, and it's the strangest thing," she said, shaking her head. "We were losing her earlier this evening. The vet was trying everything he could. He had gotten the bullet out okay, and he had already given her a blood transfusion, but nothing seemed to be helping. She was close to death when the front desk called back to the hospital to tell us that Jade's original owner was out front and was demanding to see her. This guy had his receipts for her tags and rabies shots, and nobody could stop him from coming right into the examining room where the vet was working on her.

"The man, he was small and looked Indian, you know, went over to Jade and pushed the vet away from her. The vet grabbed the phone and called security, but meanwhile the little man started chanting and crumbling up some leaves over your dog's wound. Suddenly Jade opened her eyes and lifted up her head. Right in front of our eyes, we could see her start to look better. The man leaned down and whispered to her. He ran his hands over her body and chanted some more. By the time security arrived, the vet told them to go away.

"The man kept this up for about five minutes, and we all could see the dog improving minute by minute. Her tail started wagging and then she started barking. The little man motioned for the vet to come over and look at her. The vet started to examine Jade and while he did that, the little man left. Well, we didn't see him leave, but he must have, because by the time we thought to look for him he was gone. But come on back and see for yourself. Your dog is doing great."

The vet tech led us to a room where Jade was standing in a large cage. Her side was bandaged and one of her front legs was shaved and had white tape on it. When she saw me she began a joyful barking and started pawing at the bars, trying to get out. I went over to her and stooped down, reaching through the bars to stroke her head. "When can I take her home?" I asked.

"Probably tomorrow. Give us a call early in the evening. The vet wants to watch her overnight, but all her vital signs are normal, and her wound is healing at an astonishing rate. It's a miracle, I guess. There's no scientific explanation for it."

Maybe it was a miracle. I don't know about that, but I do know it was definitely Don Manuel working his magic. I had seen similar recoveries in seriously ill patients in Africa after a shaman performed his rituals. I had never seen a shaman work on a dog though. I always figured the shaman's power to manipulate the sick person's mind caused the healing. But that certainly wouldn't work for an animal, so I don't know why it worked. I was just grateful it had.

* * *

It was still early, so Darius suggested we stop somewhere for a drink. Besides, he said, he wanted to talk with me. I gave him a puzzled look. "About what?" I asked.

"Us. The future. I have some things to run by you," he said and took my hand.

We found a little neighborhood place. It was virtually empty, so we grabbed a booth in the back. The light was dingy, the walls could have used some fresh paint, and the fortysomething waitress had bags under her eyes and wore orthopedic shoes. I wasn't hungry, so Darius ordered himself a burger and a beer. I stuck with mineral water. I didn't drink it. I sat there and watched it go flat. I knew halfway through his burger that Darius was leaving.

"Look, I have to go away for a while," he said.

"What?" I said. "Why?"

"For one thing, I've got to get away from the vampire slayers. The last attack nearly finished me. I don't know how many more have been sent to kill me. You were right that I've endangered all of us. I'm sorry. Until I get that sorted out, it's better if I'm traveling."

"Where are you going?" I said, trying to figure out what I felt and what I should do.

"That's the thing. I'm not sure yet, but my manager has set up a tour. A European tour. For the band. He thinks it will be good exposure and really take us out of being just a New York group."

"Wait a minute," I said, getting confused. "First you say you're leaving because the vampire slayers know about you. Then you tell me you're going on tour with the band, appearing in public. What makes you think the vampire slayers aren't going to be following you? This doesn't make a lot of sense, Darius," I said starting to feel angry. "I have a feeling you're leaving something out. Hiding something. What happened to *honesty,* Darius? What happened to making our relationship a priority?"

"Daphne, please. Don't get upset. I want you to come with me."

That threw me. Of all the things he could have said, that wasn't one of them. Finally I said, "I don't know that I can do that Darius. I have responsibilities here. To the Darkwings. Let me think about it."

"You told me to make our relationship a priority, so resign, Daphne. Quit." His voice was excited now. He reached across the table and squeezed my hand. "Listen. We can be a team. I'm serious about the band, but it's basically just a great cover for my intelligence work. Listen, Daphne, I'm not asking you to give up spying. My agency would take you on. I already talked to my handler. They figure if J can run vampires, they can too. Come with me, Daphne. I'm tracking down an al Qaeda terrorist cell in Germany. Some of its members may be operating in Italy. We could go back to your villa, Daphne. Come with me. We can do it all."

I should be happy, I told myself. Wasn't it what I had dreamed about? Part of me wanted to grab the gold ring he was offering. But a small dark part of me whispered that I was being manipulated. And a little voice in my head added that maybe Darius still wanted to get back at J. Destroying the Darkwings, or even just stealing me away, would be a huge win for Darius and a big loss for J. I could be replaced on the team eventually, I guessed, but meanwhile it would be crippled. "I don't know," I said. "I do want to be with you, but you've just sprung this on me with no advance notice. I need to think out how this could work. When do I have to let you know?"

"In forty-eight hours. This whole operation is moving quickly. I'm going to get my gear together and meet with my handler tomorrow. I'll be able to nail down some of the details. I think we're flying out of the States on Sunday night, probably heading to Hamburg. And Daphne, you can't tell anybody about this. You understand that, don't you?"

"You mean if I quit the Darkwings I can't tell them why?"

"Pretty much. Tell them part of the truth. You're coming with me. On tour, because we want to be together. If J hears you're switching to a different agency, there's going to be hell to pay. And he doesn't need to know, Daphne. At least not yet. And neither does your mother," he added, giving me a meaningful look. He got up then and came over to my side of the booth. He slid in beside me and turned my head with his hand. He kissed me there in that dingy light in that crummy old bar. My body responded as it always did to his touch. But even his kiss couldn't stop the doubts racing through my brain.

I wanted to think. I needed to think. I needed time to think. Darius said he had to get going. He had a lot to do yet that night. He finished up his beer and paid the bill. We left the bar and stood outside on the dark sidewalk. We were only a couple of blocks from my apartment.

"I'll walk you back," he said.

"No, don't bother, really." I wanted time to myself. The walk might clear my head. "It's early."

"I don't like you out here alone," he said stubbornly.

"Look, it's not even ten o'clock. There are lots of people on the streets. I'll be fine," I said firmly.

He saw I wasn't going to change my mind. "All right. I'll get a cab and head downtown. How about if I come back to your place before dawn? Is that cool?"

"Sure," I said without much enthusiasm. "Sure. We'll talk more then."

He came close to me and put his arms around me, pulling me to him. "Daphne? I thought this would be what you wanted. It's a chance for us. Maybe our only chance."

"I know, Darius. It's just happening so fast."

Then he put his lips close to my ear and told me when he came back to my apartment before dawn we'd make love, and he told me what he wanted to do when he did. He said all that in a hoarse whisper, kissing my eyes, my hair, my lips as he said it. My knees turned to water. I groaned and sank into him. "That's not helping," I said breathlessly.

"I wasn't trying to help," he whispered. "I was trying to convince you." He took his hands away then and I felt cold when they were gone. He kissed me once more, walked over to the curb, and hailed a cab. He waved at me through the window when it pulled into traffic, and I had an irrational feeling that things might never be the same between us again.

I walked slowly in the direction of my building, arguing with myself. I was bitterly aware of the irony of my indecision. I was the one who had lectured Darius on making our relationship important and our commitment to each other a priority. But when I had to make the hard choices, I hesitated. Maybe I was just too old to give up everything and go running off with a man. Darius was only in his early thirties. I was over five hundred years old. I had seen many relationships between all sorts of men and women in those centuries, and few of them had lasted. Many of them had ended in betrayal. True love was a rarity. Yet I would be miserable without Darius, and I couldn't discount our passion. The level of our physical intensity was also rare, and the vampire in me, the dark side of my being, was drawn to the sybaritic, the sensational, the forbidden. It was drawn to Darius.

But the human cost of being with him would be high. I would have to abandon my friends. I couldn't take my dog with me. And if my mother believed I was quitting the Darkwings for love, she would be sure to let me know how disappointed she was in me *again*. Yet the idea of losing Darius and relinquishing all my dreams of our being together brought with it a blinding pain. I would be alone again.

Suddenly resentment at my fate welled up with me. As a vampire, I had given up any man I cared about because I feared destroying him. The one time I didn't—with

Byron—I had ultimately caused his death. For centuries I had wandered with no permanent home, always alone. What vampire ever had a lasting relationship? It was nearly impossible. This was a once-in-a-lifetime opportunity. Darius was right, it might be our only chance. Why shouldn't I take it? Didn't I deserve to be happy? My heart wanted me to choose Darius.

But that little voice in my head kept whispering doubts. It reminded me that Darius was still secretive. Would that change? I didn't know that it would. Look how different he was from Fitz. On my second date with Fitz, I had met his family. He had willingly told me about his past, and I believed he had told me the truth. I knew nothing about Darius's background. I didn't even know where his family lived, who they were, or if what he had told me about them was a pack of lies. I had never met his friends. He had never told me where he lived. Should I trust him now—or would it be a terrible mistake? The decision was mine. I truly believed that whatever future lay before me would be the result of my choices.

But sometimes shit just happens.

I crossed noisy, traffic-clogged Broadway and was headed up a side street when I realized I was being followed. The block was quiet and relatively dark. No one was about. It was a good place for a mugging, only I never for an instant believed it was a mugger behind me. I increased my stride, stopping short of breaking into a run. I reached the corner, turned to my right, and flattened myself against the wall of an apartment building, waiting for my pursuer to catch up with me. I soon heard footsteps. A figure wearing a ski mask rushed around the corner, and I kicked out with all my strength. The person flew backwards and landed hard against a tall city refuse can painted with the saying I ❤ NEW YORK. I reached out and grabbed the ski mask, ripping it free. Dark hair cascaded down, and Darius's band singer looked at me with fury and hatred.

She leaped at me, and I deftly moved aside. She landed on the sidewalk without harm, rolled, and got into a fighting stance. I did the same. From a quiver on her back, she pulled a long wooden stake polished and sharpened like a knife. "Now you're going to die," she said and began to circle me.

"One of us is," I replied, not taking my eyes from her. "But it's not going to be me." I lashed out then with blinding speed, viciously landing my booted foot on her collarbone, which cracked with a sickening sound. Her left arm went limp. I was on her in a flash, pinning her to the pavement, holding her wrist and immobilizing the stake in her hand. I slammed her hand down again and again on the cement walk until she dropped it. All the while her eyes bored into mine. Spit flecked her red lips. My other hand closed over her throat. She was beaten. She knew it.

"Who sent you?" I said, squeezing my hand tighter around her throat, then letting up. She didn't answer. She just glared at me. I squeezed harder. Her eyes bulged. "Who sent you?" I asked again, then let up on her neck.

Her lips twisted into a cruel smile then. "Darius, you fool," she hissed.

The words hit me like the blows of a hammer. I jumped off of her. She slowly got to her feet. "You're lying," I screamed at her.

"Am I?" she said. "So kill me. What are you waiting for?"

Why didn't I kill her? Her arm was useless. She was no longer a threat. The fight had gone out of me but mostly I didn't want her blood on my hands, or her body to deal with. The street was no longer empty. I saw people across the avenue, watching. Nobody intervened but I could bet somebody had called 911. I didn't want to talk with the cops right now.

"Get out of here," I said, "before I do kill you." She grabbed her ski mask off the ground and ran. And I ran too. I could hear sirens in the distance. I didn't look back.

* * *

The rest of the night passed with excruciating slowness as I waited for Darius's return to my apartment. I paced back and forth. I didn't know what to think, but I needed to confront him. I had no explanation for the girl's accusation, but it disturbed me. And despite everything, it rang true.

Darius rang from downstairs shortly before five a.m. I buzzed him into the lobby, and he came through my front door a minute later. I was sitting on the couch when he walked in. He took one look at my sober face and said, "What's the matter?"

"You tell me," I said in a voice devoid of warmth.

"What are you talking about? Did something happen?" He sounded genuinely puzzled.

"I was attacked on the way home"—I said and kept talking before he could say anything—"by your singer."

"What? That's crazy!" he said.

"No, Darius, it isn't crazy. She tried to kill me. And this time I pulled off her mask. It was her."

"Daphne, I don't understand this. It makes no sense."

"Well, here's something else that doesn't make sense. She told me you sent her to kill me." I stood up and walked over to the window, turning my back on him.

"What! Of course I didn't. How could you believe that?" He came up behind me and started to put his arms around me. I stepped away.

"I'm not saying I believe it. But I do believe you are keeping something from me, and it's time you came clean. Who is she? Why did she want me dead? And tell me the truth, Darius, or get the hell out of here."

"All right, Daphne. I'll tell you. Maybe you better sit down."

"I'll stand, thanks," I said. My voice didn't reveal the emotions churning in me. I didn't know how deeply I had been betrayed but I was about to find out.

"Okay. This situation looks worse than it is, Daphne. I

swear to you I didn't know she attacked you. I had nothing to do with that."

"Talk, Darius. So far you haven't said anything." I felt like a block of ice inside.

"Julie works for the same covert agency I do. She has for years. A long time ago, and Daphne, I mean a good six years ago when I first was recruited to intelligence work, she and I had a relationship. It didn't last; it ended amicably. So when I got this new assignment—"

"And what was that assignment, Darius?" I interrupted.

"To see where that drug, susto, was coming from. Same as you. Our agency knew the DEA had been co-opted, and we knew somebody in a security position was involved. A rock band was perfect cover, you see."

"Yeah, I see," I said, once more pissed off at the way intelligence in this country was handled.

Darius started talking fast then, as if he just wanted to finish. His eyes had taken on a haunted look, his voice was anguished, and he was squeezing his hands together nervously. "Anyway, Julie seemed a good fit. She was told I had become a vampire. She seemed okay with it. In fact, I was worried that she wanted a physical relationship again. I didn't, you know that. When you first told me you thought she had attacked you, I started watching her. I ran a check on her. I asked questions. She seemed clean. Now, I have to face that she was double-crossing me the whole time."

"How?" I said.

"Look, when I was a vampire hunter, Julie knew about it. She went with me a few times when we were together. I figured she was just watching my back. I didn't suspect she was a hunter herself, not really. Maybe I was naive, but I thought she was just doing it for me. So I didn't think it mattered to her that I had been transformed."

"Did she know I was the one who bit you?" I asked.

"No, not that I know of. I never told her you were a vampire, just that I was seeing you. I wouldn't have told her anything more."

"Didn't it occur to you that she might have led the vampire hunters to you? That she might have followed you to find other vampires? I mean you're supposed to be smart, Darius. Why didn't you figure it out?" I sounded skeptical and I was.

"I don't know," he said. "I was wrapped up in my own problems. That's not a good excuse, but it's the truth."

"So what now? What are you going to do about her?"

"I'll report it. I'll make sure she's no longer a threat to you, or anybody."

I was very worked up by now. "Is that it, Darius? You'll report it?"

"Listen, Daphne, I need to get to the bottom of this. Who else is Julie working for? Who's behind the influx of vampire hunters? What went wrong here? She was always a top agent. Look, don't worry about it. I'll take care of it, I promise." He came to me then. "I promise. I screwed up, but I'll straighten it out." He put his arms around me. I was rigid in his embrace.

"I don't know, Darius. This changes things," I said.

"How does it change anything? Daphne, don't do this."

"Do what? Doubt you? I do, Darius. I can't help it. Your actions nearly got me killed. You were nearly exterminated, and you brought danger to everyone I know. Maybe that's what you wanted. Maybe you still hate vampires, Darius. How do I know you don't?"

He stood in front of me but he didn't try to touch me any more. There was so much pain in his voice when he spoke, I could barely hear him. "Daphne, listen to me, please. I can't say I don't hate vampires. That would be a lie because I feel so screwed up about it. I have even hated myself. But I don't hate you. I love you. I would never have stopped blaming myself if you had been killed. I'll try to make this right. Please. Don't let this come between us."

I didn't want to let it come between us, I really didn't. I believed him, or maybe I mostly believed him. But I still had reservations. I couldn't be sure he was telling me the truth, or all of the truth. I looked into his eyes then. His lips were close to mine. He was bad, he was dangerous. It was foolish to trust him. But as angry as I was, and in conflict inside, I was a vampire to the core. I wanted what I wanted. And right now my vampire nature was calling to me. What did it matter if he had led the hunters to me? I didn't die. I wouldn't die. I was being offered him here, now. The passion inside me grew.

And Darius couldn't leave. It was nearly dawn. The long day stretched in front of us, and we had to spend it together. Maybe it would be the last day we ever had, I just didn't know. I stopped thinking about it at that point. And Darius didn't ask me anything. He simply pulled me into his embrace. I knew where this was heading. I wanted the pleasure. I wanted to be sated. He picked me up in his strong arms. He carried me into the bedroom and laid me down upon the covers. I let him do what he wanted with me, and I let him do it again and again.

CHAPTER 17

If at first you don't succeed, try, try again.
Then quit. No use being a damn fool about it.
—W. C. Fields

Awakening that evening around six o'clock, I discovered Darius had already gone. He left me a note that he'd call me. He signed it with a heart. I also found a message on my answering machine from J, telling me a meeting was scheduled for seven thirty tonight. All my reluctance about quitting the Darkwings and joining Darius in Europe came flooding back. Asking me to just overlook that he had a vampire hunter as a partner was nuts. I thought he probably didn't think of it that way. As the old joke goes, "What's the insensitive bit at the base of a penis called? A man."

Taking a good hard look at myself I acknowledged again that if I did go away with Darius, I would have to give up huge chunks of my life and people who mattered deeply to me. Was I willing to do that? And what was he giving up? Nothing, nothing at all. As I began to throw clothes out of my closet to find something to wear tonight, I had an epiphany—or maybe just saw the obvious. When it came to Darius, I didn't think straight. I could list all the qualities I loved about him, the ones I felt made us a good couple with more going for us than chemistry. But if I were totally honest with myself, it was the powerful sexual chemistry that was driving my willingness to still go with him. Talk about smart women and foolish choices—I was a prime example.

So what had happened to my pretty speech about trust? Could Darius trust me? I thought he could. Could I trust him? Maybe, someday. But the unavoidable reality was—and it killed me to admit it—I still didn't. Yet when I was with him, all that rationality flew out the window. It didn't matter what I thought. I obeyed what I felt. I thoroughly understood why intelligent, accomplished women ended up with total losers. And I don't judge them—women are fools for love.

But the *coup de grace* came when I finally checked my e-mail. It had been days since I turned on my computer, and I had forgotten that Fitz mentioned on the phone days before that he had sent me a message after he abandoned me at the party. It had been written before he let Benny and me out of the trailer, before he had been shot. I had never seen it, and when his name popped up in my mailbox, I experienced a terrible pang of sorrow. I opened the e-mail and read—

Daphne, fair lady. I know I have disappointed you, and I hope you will let me explain. I made a decision a few years ago that I needed to make my life count, that my existence on this planet should be spent in a more important way than just trying to accumulate as much money as I can. My family has been enormously successful at getting rich, but it hasn't made any of them happy. So I made a commitment and took a position that demanded my absolute loyalty and a great deal of courage, perhaps more than I possess. I hope, when the time comes that I am tested, I don't fail myself or my country.

I know this all sounds very vague. There's a great deal I can't write, but that I'd like to explain to you in person. I have been told you are someone I can trust absolutely. Who told me? Let's just say a little bird. Yet my instincts tell me the same thing.

Can we meet again as soon as possible? I would hate for you to go on thinking I am someone I'm not and that I'd just abandon you as I did, if there wasn't an overwhelming reason for my behavior. I did mean it when I said I would like to be your knight in shining armor. But at the very least, I hope to be a true and faithful friend.

Fondly,
St. Julien Fitzmaurice

The message left me close to tears. He had faced his own death with absolute courage, and he had not failed me. He was a thoroughly good man, not a "bad boy" with dozens of emotional issues. And he had left a road open for me if I wished to take it.

When in emotional turmoil, what is my usual modus operandi? Put on new clothes and look as damned good as I possibly can. Tonight I went for a funky appearance with an outfit I got from Anthropologie. Catalogs and online shopping have been a godsend for me, a woman who loves to shop but can only do it after dark. I put on a cami in caramel-colored silk topped by a wildly romantic teal velvet wrap. I wore chocolate-brown seamed corduroy pants and donned a pair of Anthropologie's Hyde Park Oxfords, which were nearly as comfortable as sneakers. For outerwear I chose a vanilla velveteen calf-length coat. My hair was clean and silky as dark mountain water running over rocks. I slipped on my favorite ring, a Renaissance gold depiction of panther heads made of pavé diamonds, the very ring that Benny's vampire boyfriend Louis had stolen a few months before. Tonight, from what I could see as I stood in front of the mirror, I liked what I saw.

My confidence was bolstered and my strength renewed by a tall glass of blood. I had a "blood high," if you want to know the truth. I was hyped up and immensely powerful. I felt better about myself. I felt better about Darius. *No man is perfect,* I reminded myself, and I wasn't immaculate in either my behavior or my character. What was I being so moral for? I was a vampire. We're supposed to be degenerate beasts.

I headed for the subway and the meeting with J. My heart was beating a little too fast and my hands betrayed the slightest of tremors. Was I going to quit the team tonight? I could use a series of deep cleansing breaths, but taking them in the rank, stale air of the New York subway system was not advisable.

I came up out of the subway exit at Twenty-third Street and went into the Flatiron Building. I entered the conference room to find my team members already sitting around the table. Everyone seemed to be waiting for me. Okay, I was late. Vampires always are. I was just surprised I was the last one to get here.

Giving me a wink, Benny was her usual upbeat self. Cormac seemed a little different, improved I might say. He greeted me with a smile—a smile. From Cormac. I was taken aback. Nodding hello, Bubba on the other hand seemed subdued, his energy tamped down, and his aura—and yes, we all have them—was dark. Maybe he had been injured a lot more seriously than he had let on. And then there was J. Starched, staid, a flint-hard rock of a man, J greeted me with a curt nod and a snide, "Good evening, Agent Urban. I'm glad you finally decided to join us."

I hadn't forgotten the shit he'd pulled on me by throwing my underwear at Darius. If I did quit the team, believe me, that would be a major factor. I gave him some attitude by taking my seat with a great deal more noise than was necessary. Benny, who was sitting next to me, reached over and gave me a surreptitious pinch while she stifled a giggle.

J began talking. "Once again, I want to congratulate the team on a successful mission. You prevented a dangerous drug from killing thousands of young people, helped us apprehend and eliminate the criminals behind the operation, and destroyed the facility where the drug was being manufactured. I commend you all.

"However, not everything went as planned. We did lose Bradley, whom we would have been able to both use and control. The consequences of that have yet to be faced. But of greater concern to me, and to my superiors, is the influx of vampire slayers into the city. We almost lost Agent Lee the other evening. These slayers are thugs. They may not even be human; we have some sources that say they are not. And, unfortunately, Agent Urban, they are here because of your boyfriend, Darius della Chiesa."

It was all too true; I just didn't like hearing J say it. I broke in, "Look, Darius is leaving the city. The vampire-slayer problem will be solved."

J raised his eyebrows, unprepared for my outburst. "I'm glad to hear that, Miss Urban. It keeps us from having to take more radical measures to remove the problem."

"Or do you mean to remove Darius?" I said heatedly.

"It's a moot point, it seems," he said flatly. "Let me get back to the meeting's agenda. The team's outstanding performance has not gone unnoticed. Your next mission will be, shall we say, challenging. We're nailing down the details and getting things in place. I would like us to meet back here in one week. Meanwhile, I'm happy to tell you, you'll be on leave—as soon as each of you turns in a written debriefing. You can access the form on your office computer. Please complete the information within the next twenty-four hours. Then our hope is that you get some R & R. Agent Lee, especially, needs some time to recover, and we need you all in peak condition. Any questions? No? Then may I say again, your performance was superlative. I'm proud of you all. Now, you are dismissed."

He stood, saluted us, and without a personal word to me, or any one of us, he gathered up some papers lying in front of him and went into his office. The door slammed behind him. I surmised, with a small glimmer of satisfaction, that he had been royally reamed out by Mar-Mar and faced some sort of reprimand. No doubt in his heart he blamed me and Darius for his own stupid move. Well, screw him. He'd get over it—or not, especially if I left.

The four of us vampires got up and headed for elevators to go down to the lobby. Once on the ground floor, we pushed through the glass doors onto Fifth Avenue. After business hours, the avenue was nearly empty. A few yellow cabs went speeding past, but only a handful of pedestrians were in sight. In fact, the hint of spring I had felt the other day was back, and while I wouldn't have called the weather balmy, the iron grip of winter had definitely loosened.

Bubba broke our silence by saying, "I need to say something to y'all before we go another step."

The three of us looked at him. His voice lacked its usual vitality, and we had never seen him so down.

"I want you to know, I thank you for what you did the other night. You fought like tigers, with a courage that made me proud to know you." We all started to protest, but he silenced us. "Hear me out now. I've been a soldier for a long time. I've fought in many battles, and sometimes I didn't know why I wasn't killed. Men all around me were. It just wasn't my time, I guess. When I finally was mortally wounded and a vampire pulled me out of the valley of the shadow of death to make me one of you, I cheated fate. But soldiers sometimes know when their time is up. They'll tell you before the battle starts to say good-bye to their wives and families, cause they know they're not coming back. It's not that they're scared. They just know."

I didn't want to hear what Bubba was about to say next.

"I have that feeling, darlin's. Maybe I was supposed to die on that rooftop the other night, and you cheated Death out of his due once again. But I want you to understand, that if it's my time, if anything happens and I'm killed, you must not blame yourself. You can't stop it. I can't stop it. What will be, will be. It's how it's writ. None of us can escape our fate. Oh, darlin's, don't look like that. J. E. B. Stuart doesn't mean to make you sad. Remember, I've had it all. I've lived more than my fourscore years and ten and done just wonderful things. Don't y'all be sad. Now, come on, let's find a place to get a beer!" he finished with some of the old energy back in his voice.

Benny looked sad. So did Cormac. I felt like shit. We walked without talking down the block.

"Where do you want to go for the beer?" Benny finally asked.

Bubba put his arm, the one not in a cast, around her shoulders, pulling her to him. "Now give me a smile, sweetheart. We'll just go into the first place we see. A beer's a beer. How about that place right across the street?"

We all nodded and started to cross the avenue. We had just reached the other side when a black Lincoln Town Car drove up fast and a rifle barrel extended from the window. We heard *bang bang bang.* Suddenly Bubba said in a whisper, "I am shot," as he crumbled to the ground. Benny fell on her knees beside him. I turned, on the alert, ready to fight, only to see the Lincoln speeding off.

A silver bullet from a slayer's gun must have pierced Bubba's heart. By the time I turned back to see how he was, Bubba was already fading away into dust. Benny was beside herself, crying hysterically. I pulled her up, away from all that remained of the gallant soldier. She buried her face in my coat. As I held her, I looked up at the tavern we were about to enter. With a squeeze of my heart I saw its name: YELLOW TAVERN, ESTABLISHED 1864.

Cormac picked up Bubba's leather hat with its peacock feather from where it lay on the pavement in the dust, and the gray military-like coat with its red love knot in the lapel. "Do you mind if I keep these?" Cormac asked, his voice so tight he could barely make a sound.

"I think he'd want you to have them," I said, my own voice breaking with emotion. I saw something else in the dust. I let go of Benny long enough to stoop down and pick it up. It was a West Point ring. Inscribed inside was J. E. B. STUART, 1854. I pressed it into Benny's hand. "Keep this."

She closed her fingers around it, then wiped her eyes. Tearstains streaked her cheeks. "I'm glad I knew him," she said. "I'm glad we all knew him."

Cormac came over and embraced us both. "We lost his body," he said. "But we have his spirit. And we have each other. We have to fight on."

My heart felt like a stone in my chest. I knew what I had to do, and what decision I had to make. When Darius's plane left on Sunday, I wouldn't be on it. It was the right choice. In fact it would be a test. If Darius loved me, truly loved me and wasn't just using me, he'd come back to me when his tour was done. It was the solution I had been looking for. It was a risk I'd take to finally know the truth. And then there was Fitz. Maybe he was the new beginning I needed, the one that would shut the door on my past. Only time would tell.

The wind had turned cold again, and was howling down Fifth Avenue like an angry wolf. It picked up Bubba's dust and scattered it so finely and so far that nothing remained. He was gone as if he had never existed.

But I was still there. And I knew with certainty what my existence was and what it meant. I was a vampire—and I was a spy. I was a Darkwing, and that was my fate.

Author's Note

Jeb (James Ewell Brown) Stuart (1833–1864), the quintessential poster boy for the Old South, rode hard, fought hard, and died surrounded by mystery and legend. Virginia born and West Point educated, Jeb pledged his loyalty to Virginia—as did General Robert E. Lee—soon after the formation of the Confederate States of America, and became a captain in the cavalry.[1]

Big and bold, his chestnut-colored hair covered by his trademark plumed hat, his gray coat always sporting a red ribbon or flower in its lapel, Jeb was so flamboyant that his fellow officers called him "Beauty."[2] The wild, daring horseman became a household word in the Confederacy and a hero for adoring women. Southern diarist Mary Boykin Chesnut reported in her journal that one matron complained about Jeb's habit of kissing the girls who bedecked his horse with garlands of flowers. After that, Stuart "was forbidden to kiss one unless he could kiss *all*."[3] Often appearing to flirt with death as well as with women by riding recklessly into the thick of battle, Jeb countered critics by saying, "I go where [bullets] are because it is my duty."[4] Perhaps Jeb's most famous escapade was taking 1800 men and completely encircling George McClellan's Union Army, stealing their horses, sniping at soldiers, and taunting the Federal troops to try to catch them. Contemporary reports said that McClellan was left feeling foolish and his men humiliated.[5]

Jeb kept the hopes of the South alive even as their armies lost battle after battle. But that was all to end on the afternoon of May 11, 1864, at a deserted inn called Yellow Tavern outside Richmond, Virginia.[6] Here the North, under the command of General Philip Sheridan and General George Armstrong Custer, and the South fought a desperate campaign, with the Confederates outnumbered but holding their ground. Finally the Union forces were given the order to fall back. As they did, a Union soldier on foot, Private John A. Huff, haphazardly fired his pistol at a group of Confederates on horseback about thirty feet away from him.[7]

According to some accounts, Jeb Stuart clutched his side while whispering, "I am shot." His famous hat slipped from his head to rest on the dusty ground. He was taken to the rear by some of his men, and others quickly gave up the fight after they discovered that their leader had fallen. Seeing this, Stuart called out to his retreating troops, "Go back! Go back! Do your duty as I've done mine. I would rather die than be whipped."[8]

Die he did—or perhaps not, as I suggest. Certainly his spirit has lived on.

For those of you who wish to see for yourself, the battlefield at Yellow Tavern is located outside Richmond, Virginia, near Exit 82 (Route 301) off I-95. It is a National Park Service historic site. A monument marking the exact spot where Jeb Stuart was shot is maintained by the Daughters of the Confederacy.[9]

1. James Truslow Adams. *The Epic of America* (Boston: Little, Brown, and Co., 1931), 262.

2. John S. Bowman, ed. *The Cambridge Dictionary of American Biography* (Cambridge, England: Cambridge University Press, 1995), 708.

3. Mary Boykin Chesnut. *Mary Chesnut's Civil War* (New York: Book-of-the-Month Club edition, 1994), 495.

4. Willard E. Rosenfelt, ed., *The Spirit of '76* (Minneapolis: T. S. Denison & Company, 1976), 531.

5. Stephen W. Sears. *Landscape Turned Red* (New York: Book-of-the-Month Club edition, 1994), 327–28.

6. U.S. Government, National Park Service information. Website for Fredericksburg and Spotsylvania National Military Park. http://www.nps.gov/frsp/yellow.htm.

7. Ibid.

8. Ibid.

9. Ibid.

APPENDIX

THE RANGER CREED

Recognizing that I volunteered as a Ranger, fully knowing the hazards of my chosen profession, I will always endeavor to uphold the prestige, honor, and high esprit de corps of the Rangers.

Acknowledging the fact that a Ranger is a more elite soldier, who arrives at the cutting edge of battle by land, sea, or air, I accept the fact that as a Ranger my country expects me to move further, faster, and fight harder than any other soldier.

Never shall I fail my comrades. I will always keep myself mentally alert, physically strong, and morally straight, and I will shoulder more than my share of the task, whatever it may be, 100 percent and then some.

Gallantly will I show the world that I am a specially selected and well trained soldier. My courtesy to superior officers, neatness of dress, and care of equipment shall set the example for others to follow.

Energetically will I meet the enemies of my country. I shall defeat them on the field of battle, for I am better trained and will fight with all my might. Surrender is not a Ranger word. I will never leave a fallen comrade to fall into the hands of the enemy, and under no circumstances will I ever embarrass my country.

R**eadily** will I display the intestinal fortitude required to fight on to the Ranger objective and complete the mission, though I be the lone survivor.

Acknowledgments

Above all others, the person I would most like to thank for her help, her invaluable insights, and her tremendous support is my editor at Signet Books, Martha Bushko. I am so fortunate to have an editor of her caliber. Martha has an exceptional instinct for what works in a story, and she has the patience to pore over every word of a manuscript. But beyond that, she has given her caring and passion to my books. In so many ways, creating a book is a collaborative process, and I have been truly blessed that Martha has been my collaborator. Even more important, she has personally made sure that everything from cover lines to marketing has been done right and done exceedingly well. She is a treasure.

Right up there on the top of my list, too, is my agent, John Talbot of Talbot Fortune Agency, Inc. John has always been there for me—and been there with ideas! A supernice guy and a professional's professional, John Talbot has also been a friend, not just for a little while, but over many years. Thank you, John, or as I like to say, *mille grazie* for everything.

I would also like to thank Allen Davis, Det. (Ret.), NYPD, for his time and real-life accounts of drug trafficking in New York City and undercover police work. He also helped me understand the challenges facing the New York Police Department as well as giving me a look at their operations and procedures.

For Priscilla Adams, of the Haddonfield Society of Friends, who nourishes my spirit and helps me keep my faith, my thanks for her willingness to read my work in manuscript and for her steadfast emotional support.

Regarding malamutes, much of what I know comes from having owned one. Possessed of beauty and strength, they are nevertheless tough dogs to handle and not for the timid. If you are considering owning one, keep in mind that they need cold weather, rigorous training, and work to do. Also it is essential to obtain a puppy from a reputable breeder because some unregistered malamutes have been crossbred with wolves. But all that being said, malamutes are dogs who can steal your heart with a look and will reward your faith in them beyond all expectations. Fascinating information on the malamute breed can be found in *The Complete Alaskan Malamute* by Maxwell Riddle and Eva B. Seeley (New York, Howell Book House, Inc., 1986), and *Mush!: A Beginner's Manual of Sled Dog Training* edited by Bella Levorsen for the Sierra Nevada Dog Drivers, Inc. (Westmoreland, NY, Arner Publications, Inc., 1976).

On the other hand, if a reader wishes to learn about the real-life concept of susto, or the nature of fear, as well as the physical ailments it causes, please consult *The Energy Prescription* by Connie Grauds and Doug Childers (New York: Bantam Books, 2005).

Krishnamurti's teachings on fear can be found in *Life Ahead* by Jiddhu Krishnamurti (San Francisco, New World Library, 2005). He is one of the world's great spiritual guides.

For more information on gut instincts and the science of understanding microexpressions, I would recommend *Blink* by Malcolm Gladwell (Boston: Little, Brown, 2004).

To find out more about the designer Charlotte Tarantola, you can go to her Web site, charlottetarantola.com. Cynthia Steffe's and Mandalay's clothes are available at Neiman Marcus and other fine stores. To see or order catalogs from Anthropologie and Gorsuch, you might wish to visit anthropologie.com or gorsuchltd.com.

And, finally, I once again wish to acknowledge Bat Conservation International, and encourage everyone to visit their Web site at www.batcon.org.

UNDEAD ACTION AND SIZZING ROMANCE FROM

SAVANNAH RUSSE

Beyond the Pale

Book One of the Darkwing Chronicles

The government knows that Daphne Urban is a vampire, and they have an ultimatum: spy for them, or be killed. For Daphne, the choice is easy.

She can speak 13 languages, has a genius IQ, and has escaped detection for nearly five hundred years—making her perfect for Team Darkwing. Her first mission: get close to a shady arms dealer with terrorist connections. But while she's chasing him, someone else is chasing her—the darkly sexy vampire slayer Darius della Chiesa. Daphne must choose between desire and duty—or risk her own destruction.

"Superior supernatural suspense."
—*Best Reviews*

0-451-21564-8

Available wherever books are sold or at penguin.com